The CROSS and the Mask

How the Spanish 'discovered' Florida
—and a proud native nation

AN HISTORICAL NOVEL BY

JAMES D. SNYDER

Snyder, James D.
   The cross and the mask: when Spain 'discovered'
South Florida and two proud cultures collided : an
historical novel / by James D. Snyder.
   p. cm.
   Includes bibliographical references.
   LCCN 2012922327
   ISBN-13: 978-0-9675200-9-4
   ISBN-10: 0-9675200-9-6

1. Florida--History--Spanish colony--1565-1763--Fiction.
2. Indians of North America--First contact with
         Europeans--Fiction.
3. Indians of North America--Florida--Fiction.
4. Explorers--Spain--Fiction.
5. Historical fiction.
   I. Title.
   PS3569.N8915C76 2012
                   813'.54
            QBI12-600230

Cover Illustrations by Theodore Morris.
Graphic design by Rebecca Barbier.

First Printing. Printed in the United States of America

Table of Contents

✳

Acknowledgments

When creating a storyline consistent with Spanish history, the biggest challenge is the abundance of raw material. Spain's well-organized military and meticulous legal-financial recordkeeping system have left scholars to sort among thousands of archives in places like Havana and Seville.

It's quite the opposite with Florida's true founders. Because no Florida Indians of that day left even a scrap of writing, anyone trying to capture their mindset must acknowledge a huge debt to the many archeologists and anthropologists who labor quietly and efficiently seeking clues among rocks, bones and shells.

After using many of their writings as the foundation for this novel, I went hat in hand to three of Florida's preeminent archeologists—only one of whom I'd ever met—and asked if they wouldn't mind too much if I dumped a 400-page manuscript in their laps. And could I have their comments by such and such date?

It was a cheeky thing to do. William H. Marquardt, curator of archeology at the (University of) Florida Museum of Natural History, was in the throes of finishing a 900-page manuscript on the Calusa at Pine Island. Robert S. Carr, executive director of the Archeological and Historical Conservancy, was about to unveil his new book, *Digging Miami.* Dr. Robin Brown, author of *Florida's First People,* and renowned for personally re-creating their foods, implements and weapons, was summering on his farm in Virginia and probably not thinking much about Indians or South Florida.

Still, I wanted to know from their academic perspectives: Were my sixteenth century geographical features realistic? Were the fictional characters plausible? Was canoe-building described accurately? Arrow-making? Weaving? And so forth.

What I got back were three individual critiques, but what seemed in the aggregate to be a team effort. Although each was careful not to intrude on a writer's phraseology or a character s persona, each applied his special expertise as would surgeons in a delicate operation. And so, dozens of inaccuracies were scrubbed from the manuscript: armadillos meandering about Florida before their time, Indians eating mangoes that had yet to be imported, a Spanish priest's name misspelled, gold coins with mottos that weren't struck until a century later. And many more.

These critics gave me confidence about this book and I give them my profound thanks.

Another "expert" was an inspiration and guidance. I was midway into researching this book when I happened onto *Florida's Lost Tribes,* a book featuring the unmatched paintings of early Native Americans in Florida. In artist Theodore Morris' depiction of a powerful-but-melancholy King Calus, I found the essence of the Calusa cacique that had been in my head all along. Other Indians pictured in its pages became mental models for several characters in this book. I thank Ted Morris for permission to show a few of them on the cover—and I acknowledge his copyrights herewith.

Finally, I subjected the supposedly final manuscript to a "focus group" representing "average" readers. Okay, one of them is my sister, Christine Moats, and the other is my beloved Ilse Wolff. They scrubbed hard on some rough spots and boiled off some excess verbiage.

All of the above reviewers made this a better book, and I give them all my profound thanks.

Preface

In the year 1547 Ivan IV crowned himself the first tsar of Moscow and would soon be known as "Ivan the Terrible." In France, another new monarch, Henry II, set out to conquer every Italian city-state in his warpath. In England, nine-year-old Edward VI succeeded Henry VIII and was soon betrothed to Mary, Queen of Scots. She was five.

Nearly everything else, from the Netherlands south through the Iberian Peninsula, paid allegiance to Charles V, emperor of the Holy Roman Empire. But keeping the balky confederation intact meant maintaining a military colossus to combat the spread of the "Protestant Heresy" in northern Europe and of Islam on his southern shores.

In fact, Charles' patchwork empire would quickly tatter and fray were it not for the regular convoys of ships arriving with gold and silver from the mines of Mexico and South America. Hernando Cortés, the soldier of fortune who made it all possible thirty years beforehand by subduing the mighty Aztecs of Mexico, had just paid a king's ransom for his success. Having been deemed so rich and powerful that he might pose a threat to the monarchy, Cortés was nudged into retirement on his estate near Seville, where he finally sulked to death on September 2, 1547.

Meanwhile, the treasure fleet continued to bring Spain and Charles the precious metals that would be forged into the currencies that bought everything from shields and swords to goblets and tapestries. But crossing the Atlantic in a ship a hundred or so feet in length was neither routine nor predictable. August through October was hurricane season, and when the ungainly cargo ships emerged north of Cuba and into the narrow Bahamas Channel, they faced high winds, angry waves and the menace of smaller, swifter French corsairs and English privateers that preyed like leopards on a herd of zebra. All too many men and treasures were washed up on the reefs and sandy shores of Florida or the Bahamas, never to be seen again.

At that time, the term "Florida" applied to everything from Key West to Newfoundland.

Might some outposts be established along this coast to rescue Spanish sailors and salvage their ships? Might this mysterious Florida also contain precious metals? Along this narrow peninsula, might there be an inside waterway to the Gulf of Mexico that would shorten the long trip around the Florida Straits on the way to South America? Might the naked savages who shook their spears at passing ships actually have souls that might be saved for Jesus Christ and the Roman Catholic Church? And/or....might these natives also be potential labor for the silver mines of Mexico or haciendas of Cuba?

The first attempts to answer these questions were in vain. In 1513, Juan Ponce de León, then governor of Puerto Rico, probed the east coast of Florida. He dispatched a landing party in what is Jupiter Inlet today. The foragers had begun collecting fresh water and firewood on shore when two of the men were hit by arrows "tipped with sharpened bones and fish spines." They barely escaped out the inlet.

But Ponce was undaunted. In 1521 he sailed into southwestern Florida waters, only this time with 200 men, priests, horses, cows, sheep, goats and all the tools needed to begin a farming settlement. While still dropping anchor in what is now Charlotte Harbor, the Spaniards were driven off by hundreds of warriors in catamaran canoes firing arrows that could pierce metal armor. Ponce de León himself took an arrow in the thigh that would produce enough gangrene to end his life back in Cuba a few weeks later.

During the next thirty or so years, other bold Spanish adventurers would meet the same fate. Sometimes they would land and be lured inland with promises of trade, only to vanish from the crews waiting on ship for their return. Father Luis Cáncer de Barbastro, a Dominican priest, was even braver. Convinced that the sight of Spanish weapons had ignited the natives' furor, he asked to be put ashore unarmed. There on the beach he knelt with his crucifix raised in prayer so that any Indians who watched from behind the nearby dunes could witness and understand his godly intent.

As he prayed, Indians rushed out and bludgeoned Father Cáncer to death with whelk hammers.

Wild and naked as they appeared to Spanish eyes, the Indians who first greeted Ponce and others in South Florida were part of a strong tribal network generally controlled by and named for the Calusa. In 1547, when Moscow was just coalescing into Russia, when the term *France* as nation had barely been a concept for a thousand years, when Spain was still a confederation of small kingdoms, indigenous Indians could claim to have occupied South Florida for 12,000 years. They had been a cohesive people called the Calusa for at least 1,000 years before the first Spanish ship appeared on the horizon.

The stronghold of the Calusa lay on the southwest coast, ranging southward from today's Big Pine Island to Charlotte Harbor to the Ten Thousand Islands in the Florida Straits. At its core, and home to the royal family, was Mound Key, today a seldom-visited Florida State Park off the south end of Fort Myers Beach.

In the outer Calusa orbit were vassal chiefdoms whose loyalties waxd and waned over the centuries. These were the Mayaimi around Lake Okeechobee, the Ais of the Indian River and Hutchinson Island to the east, and below them the Jeaga, clustered mainly around Jupiter Inlet. A hundred miles further south were the Tequesta of Key Biscayne and today's Miami.

Altogether, archeologists more or less agree that the population of the Calusa realm in South Florida at this time may have been roughly 25,000 to 50,000. Immediately to the north of the Calusa were their eternal enemies, the Tocobaga. Clustered around Tampa Bay, they probably spoke the same language as the Timucuans who inhabited the middle of Florida from coast to coast.

Despite the fact that it is a 130-mile trek between South Florida's two coasts, people could move between them by canoe through a labyrinth of natural waterways and ancient canals. Because they did not tend any large-scale crops, the Calusa fished and foraged according to the seasons and available food supply. For example, the villagers around Lake Okeechobee (then called Mayaimi) would probably have come to the eastern seaside in summer when their homeland could be inundated by summer floods and infested with mosquitoes. But in winter the coastal-based people might come to the warmer interior to hunt game and dig for roots that could be ground into flour. As part of all this intermingling, villages traded and chiefs—called *caciques*—arranged marriages to strengthen political ties just as did the aristocratic families of sixteenth century Europe.

Although you will find this book in the fiction shelves of libraries, it is important to note that it adheres to actual people, events and dates that are well documented in the archives of Spain. However, anyone attempting to present the Indian perspective must resort to the fiction genre simply because the Indians of Florida, despite living there for thirty times longer than the United States has been a nation, left no written records. With great help from the spadework of dedicated archeologists, I have attempted to cast some light into that void.

I also offer three observations before you plunge into the sixteenth century.

First, because we know only a few Calusa names for lakes, rivers and other sites, I have used modern ones wherever possible to make it easier for you to recognize places that may be familiar today.

Second, be aware that the geographical makeup of South Florida was markedly different than today's engineered version. For example, there was no dike to hold back the water spilling over Lake Okeechobee (then called Mayaimi Lake) and flowing south. In the rainy summer season, this "river of grass"—along with narrow canals carved out over thousands of years—made canoe travel possible between the east and west coasts. By the same token, the estuary that flowed between the mainland and barrier islands of Florida's east coast (named the "Long River" in this book) was shallow, full of mangrove islands, and bore little relation to the Intracoastal Waterway scoured out by government contractors at the turn of the twentieth century.

Finally, do not confuse the Calusa with the Seminoles. The latter, an amalgam of South Atlantic Indians and runaway slaves from southern plantations, began appearing in Florida at the dawn of the nineteenth century. This was at least fifty years after the last remnants of the once-mighty Calusa had all but vanished from Florida.

But in 1547 the Calusa were still venerable and vibrant, with a new king. His name was Calus, and at age nineteen he was taller and more powerfully built than any European noble.

CHAPTER ONE

The Great Gathering

November, 1547

Red Hawk crouched at the opening to the smoking oven, wiped the sweat from his brow, and pushed in another rack of half-grilled manatee. It was early afternoon on this clear November day on the River of Turtles. Ordinarily Red Hawk would be smoking the catch from the spectacular fall mullet run upriver. Today he was mid-way through slicing, grilling and smoking the 700-pound manatee he had killed with his atlatl-propelled darts in the river that flowed past Jeaga Town. All around, villagers were grinding, pounding, peeling or primping as preparations for the Great Gathering of Calusa-aligned tribes neared their final hours.

Across from the huts of Jeaga Town that lined the river, Red Hawk could make out young men on ladders laying in sabal palm leaves to finish the new thatched roof of the Great House. Beneath it women were stacking clay bowls and carrying in jugs of water. Unseen, the old shaman and his acolytes were no doubt busy wiping down the old and sacred masks that had been in storage since the last Gathering at Jeaga Town five years before.

All around him Red Hawk heard the voices of women—some in the midst of boiling palmetto berry tea, shucking oysters or comparing the jewelry they would wear at tonight's opening ceremonies. The most excitement came from within his own hut, where his wife and married daughter chirped and fussed over a young girl who sat in silence, biting her lip. He understood. His youngest daughter, Morning Dove, would soon be married. To a man she'd never seen.

Red Hawk smirked to himself as he realized that carving and smoking meat wasn't what the thirty-six-year-old head of the Mako Shark Clan ought to be seen doing, but it was wise that he had "stayed quiet," as his wife had counseled. Anhinga, who now came outside to scoop up more saw palmetto berries, also saw the need to feed Red Hawk's male ego. "Your finding that manatee in the river was a sign of favor from Taku," she soothed, "just when we were all wondering if there would be enough to feed three hundred or so visitors. No three women could skin, carve and cook that giant. Besides, King Calus should find it a delightful surprise; they don't have that many manatees over on the other coast."

Red Hawk grunted. "And if the king should ask who wrestled such a big prize to shore, wouldn't it make his eyes bulge if I stood up?"

They laughed, but it was strained and nervous, for many reasons. First, even though a Gathering brought games, songs, dances and marriages, preparing for one as the host tribe always brought anxiety. Oh there was always a pompous pronouncement by whoever was king about the need to celebrate "the peace and unity that exists among us," but the bonds of unity were in fact more like a fish trap woven by Calusa conquest and sustained over centuries by a web of intertwined obligations. The Jeaga people, for example, were expected first to watch for and plunder Spanish ships that wrecked on the beach or tried to send rowed boats into their inlet seeking fresh water and game.

But even before there were Spanish ships the Jeaga performed a valuable service for their Calusa masters. Each winter pods of right whales would head south from their feeding grounds in icy northern waters and some would glide into Jeaga Inlet to bear calves or make new ones. Jeaga warriors could earn new tattoos by heaving their spears into a forty-foot-long whale's back and then leaping on to stab vital organs. Once the meat was sliced up and the blubber boiled into oil, one-half of the processed catch would be taken across the Florida peninsula to the Calusa king to parcel among the noble families. Still, the remainder from a catch of just one or two whales would be enough to sustain the vassal tribes of Jeaga, Mayaimi, Ais and Tequesta with enough to stave off a lean winter.

And what did the Jeaga get in return? They got the right not to be extinguished by the much larger force from the southwest. And they had a punishing protector in case the Ais, Tequesta, or Mayaimi should ever become too large or quarrelsome.

Even the Gathering itself embodied the balance of power. The Calusa had long made it a "tradition" that no vassal tribe could send a delegation of more than fifty. The Calusa, however, might arrive with 150 or 250, and always weighted heavily with warriors.

Red Hawk stiffened up as the wind shifted and surrounded him with smoke from the racks of steaming cutlets. "I wonder if this king will be trying the old game of trading us things we don't want," he said absentmindedly. Anhinga sat silently over her pile of palmetto berries. It was an old lament and she didn't want to encourage any more of it.

"We produce shark skin that they need," he muttered. "We get sore backs digging coontie root that they hardly have over there. We produce oysters that make theirs look like coquinas. So in turn they 'trade' us fish nets and forbid us from making our own when we could make them just as well. And they send us chert arrowheads that they get from up north and yet deny us the right to trade with those same tribes!"

Red Hawk was beginning to generate more steam than his smoke house and Anhinga already had too much of it. "All this is putting you in no proper mood for this evening," she scolded. "Take a rest, get your pipe and smoke something better than that manatee."

Both knew they'd gotten to the core of his distemper.

"How strange, "he said, stretching his back, sore from bending over the low smoke house. "For all the reasons I just mentioned—and for his own selfish reasons—Eagle Feather starts talking rebellion. I walk and paddle a canoe for three days to tell King Calus about it, and he rewards me with insult to me and my clan. Now we have *less* independence."

Anhinga stirred her pot in silence lest her husband's own cauldron boil over.

The "core of his distemper" was first ignited some two years before at Mound Key, the seat of the Calusa kingdom on the peninsula's west coast. At that time, the aging Great Cacique had been unable to produce a son despite the exhaustive efforts of three wives and all the shaman's special roots, herbs, talismans and incantations. After the god Taku appeared to him in a dream to say that his time on earth was running out, he adopted Escampaba, the son of his chief warrior, and betrothed him to his own daughter.

When the old king died, Escampaba was not yet old enough to assume the throne, so the head shaman, Senquene, agreed to serve as regent until the lad came of age. But when the patient Escampaba reached the agreed-upon age, the regent stunned the Calusa by installing his own son, Calus, as king.

It is likely that the lesser Calusa chiefs and vassal tribes would have risen up against Calus—had they sufficient time to organize. Calus and his inner circle knew it, too. When word reached the new Great Cacique on Mound Key that three village chiefs to the north were about to strike an alliance with the hated Tocobaga of Tampa Bay, Calus immediately dispatched fifty warriors in a dozen war canoes and beheaded all three within a single day. The message was not lost on the outlying Mayaimi, Ais, Jeaga and Tequesta. Soon, all four sent delegations to Mound Key with supplications to the man whose very name meant "cruel" or "fierce."

Later that same year, 130 miles to the east of the Calusa center, a Spanish galleon with a crew of forty toppled in a hurricane and broke apart on the beach a mile south of Jeaga Inlet. As drowned bodies began to wash in with the tide, the Jeaga rounded up eleven survivors, killed three to demonstrate their ferocity, and set off with the others towards Mound Key as they were supposed to do. They were to learn later that eight other exhausted survivors had dragged themselves above the dune line and staggered up the beach that night, only to be captured by the Ais as dawn broke over St. Lucie Inlet.

When the tide receded, Jeaga youths had scoured the broken hull and forecastle. They dragged out a wooden chest and filled it with gold and silver bars from the hull until even four men couldn't lift it. Beside it they heaped up piles of cups, forks, mirrors, jugs, clothing and other remnants of life aboard ship.

When the Jeaga council met to discuss the matter, it was already a formality, as Red Hawk and the others soon found. Old, rotund Eagle Feather was patriarch of the Gray Panther clan and cacique of the Jeaga. He ruled the council sternly with his arrogant son, Coral Snake. Eagle Feather surveyed the sacks of gold and silver that had been brought before the council and said with a crooked smile: "I think it's simply too heavy to carry all the way to Mound Key." The old cacique was already wearing a dead Spaniard's blue cotton shirt, gathered at the waist with a thick black belt, and seemed even fuller of himself than usual.

"With so many survivors, the 'Hairy Faces' may send another ship to save them and all these metal pieces they prize so much," he said. "If so, we can trade them for things of real worth and *then* give some of that to the Great Cacique.

Eagle Feather spoke with a bemused smirk. "Besides," he said, "let us just keep it here for now until we see how long this *boy* Calus will really be our king."

Red Hawk held his tongue because he knew that neither he nor anyone in Mako Shark clan ever delivered an opinion that counted with Eagle Feather. But the old Jeaga cacique was playing with fire and Red Hawk decided that this time he would get burned. From everything Red Hawk had heard, the new Great Cacique was no timid boy. He just might be the bow to shoot the arrow that would rid the Mako Shark clan and the rest of Jeaga Town from the insufferable old codger and his overbearing son.

A week later Red Hawk packed his atlatl, bow and arrows and shoved off in his canoe before dawn, telling his wife to say he'd gone off deer hunting if anyone asked.

In two days Red Hawk had reached the town of Guacata, the largest town on Lake Mayaimi and the gateway to a chain of ponds and streams that linked the big lake to the Calusahatchee River and Florida's west coast. In another day he had canoed into Estero Bay and on the late afternoon of the fourth was raising his hand in a peace greeting to the three men in a war canoe who patrolled the small beach at Mound Key. Even the head of a loyal clan could not escape the scowls and suspicious stares of the Great Cacique's protective circle. As they climbed uphill to the Great House that he'd come to know from attending previous Gatherings, Red Hawk wondered, "Why is it that everyone here seems a head taller than our own people? The "pure" or aristocratic Calusa at the center of power exceeded six feet in height and were more muscular—and that alone was enough to convey a menacing air of superiority.

Heaped on that was the suffocating air of pomposity, mixed with a malevolent miasma that hung about the place—one conveying a cruelty that might be unleashed on anyone at any time.

As he climbed the steep hill, Red Hawk felt the sea breeze grow cooler. Across from this mound he could see the adjoining hilltop where the Great Cacique's family lived, and through its shield of sea grapes and gumbo limbo trees he could glimpse forms of women and servants moving about in their daily chores. When he looked back, he could share briefly the cacique's commanding view of the mangrove islands in Estero Bay and, beyond that, the glistening Gulf of Mexico.

Red Hawk already knew that Calus would not be at the top to greet him. It was part of a Great Cacique's mystique never to be seen with any subject on what might be taken as equal footing. No, Calus would be seated on a dais at the far end of the tall-roofed Great House that dominated this particular mound. Red Hawk could see the backs of men standing as they waited their turn to see the king.

At the end of their climb, he was motioned to wait while one of the Mound Key guardsmen disappeared into the long thatched building that contained a huge, soot-stained feasting hall with small rooms for guests along its perimeter. He soon emerged with two servants—no doubt slaves—who ushered the visitor into one of the small guest rooms. It was now evident that Red Hawk would not see Calus that afternoon and that his bare "guest" room was more a detention cell. But the Jeaga's fatigue outweighed the insult. After being brought a meal of grilled fish, root cakes and papayas, he spread out his deerskin blanket on the floor and fell dead asleep.

Late the next morning Red Hawk found himself before the Great Cacique in the Great House and immediately sensed that his gamble against Eagle Feather had been a smart one. Calus stood something like six foot three, with a pile of bobbed hair on top that added six more inches. With a massive chest and thick biceps covered with heavy black and red body paint, he resembled more an ageless, powerful god of war than a youth of nineteen summers. This was clearly a king who would not yield his throne without slicing the hearts from a gaggle of village caciques like the blustery, bluffing Eagle Feather.

A somber, older councilor stood on each side of Calus as Red Hawk knelt. When he had finished relating his story of the shipwreck and Eagle Feather's greed, the king stood to his full height and glared down at the Jeaga for the longest five seconds of his life. Then he smiled as if a plate of succulent oysters had been placed before him. "Ah, then," he said, "we will soon dance with his head."

Just as quickly, one of the advisers stepped from the wings, whispered something to the Great Cacique, and said to Red Hawk evenly, "You will return to our guest quarters. We will discuss this and inform you of our decision"

For a long day and night the visitor from Jeaga Town agonized in silence under the watchful gaze of his two slave-servants—one a gaunt leathery Spaniard and one a short Indian no doubt captured from some hostile northern tribe. As a "guest," Red Hawk could roam within the ceremonial house, but his status was too unclear to risk venturing beyond it. So, alone with his thoughts, he re-lived the audience. There had been no thanks, no hint of making him cacique of the Jeaga after they danced with Eagle Feather's head. Had he insulted Calus? Had his clan somehow offended the Calusa at some previous meeting? Might the Calusa decide simply to obliterate the Jeaga and re-settle the inlet with their own people?

On the morning of the next day the same adviser who whispered in the king's ear appeared at the opening of Red Hawk's sleeping room as the "guest" sat on a low stool drinking palmetto tea.

"Do you have daughters?" he asked.

Startled, Red Hawk stammered, "Yes, two."

"And married?"

"Uh...one."

"How old is the other one?"

"Seventeen...next summer."

"And she is, ah...." The man searched awkwardly.

"Yes, comely. Beautiful. Very healthy. Good teeth, too."

The councilor nodded and walked away without another word.

"Good teeth? Why did I say *that?*" Red Hawk scolded himself in angry silence. Then the man re-appeared suddenly in his doorway.

"Her name?" he asked.

"Er, Morning Dove."

Then he was gone again. Red Hawk's eyes followed him as he strode evenly from the ceremonial hall, across the broad courtyard and into the Great House where Calus no doubt waited.

The morning of the next day Red Hawk, by now uncertain that his own life was safe, again found himself before the stiff and august Calus. With no flicker of emotion, the Great Cacique said "Yesterday we sent warriors to Jeaga Town. They will remove the three you told us about and come back to Mound Key with the tribute from the ship. You will stay until they return to Mound Key with the treasures you told us about. If your story is true, you should have no trouble."

Have no trouble? Replacing Eagle Feather or just being allowed to live?

Red Hawk was on one knee with his eyes lowered as were all supplicants to the Great Cacique. He *had* to learn more before he left. "You said *removed?*" he asked.

"Removed," echoed Calus, "As in removing their heads." And with that he let out a half-roar, half-laugh.

"Who will replace them? Will the Jeaga Council..."

"No," interrupted the same adviser from the wings. "The king will replace the chief. The new cacique can choose his advisers." And as if to anticipate the next question, the elder said, "It cannot be you. While your, ah, efforts are proper and appreciated, it is not wise to name as cacique one who has conspired or sworn against the former one. It makes for bad blood. Under the circumstances, we will appoint a new chief from another Calusa clan. But in recognition of your loyalty and service, we will arrange a marriage between that chief and your daughter."

"Morning Dove?"

"Morning Dove."

Red Hawk could feel his time before the king elapsing. But he also knew that if his life could be prolonged here, it could also be cut short by a revengeful Gray Panther clan back in Jeaga Town.

"Great Cacique, will the Jeaga know who it is who has come to you?"

Calus was silent until he could feel that fear had seeped into every pore of Red Hawk's body. "No," he said at last. "As long as you and your daughter are loyal to your new chief, no one need know who *informed* me. I told my warriors that Taku told me about all this in a dream, and that is what they will tell your people."

Now, more than a year of unease had gone by in Jeaga Town with no new chief and no recrimination against himself and Mako Clan. Even though Red Hawk had brought back a dressed deer, displayed it prominently along the riverside and feigned outrage at the surprise attack by the Calusa, he could feel the eyes of Gray Panthers burning holes inside him. They were stopped from doing anything more, he reasoned, by the fact that Red Hawk himself had been doomed to spend the rest of *his* life in homage to a young cacique from "outside." "If I had told this to Calus," he was prepared to argue with anyone who accused him, "why didn't he make me chief of the Jeaga as a reward?"

And now all of Red Hawk's anxieties would soon converge. At the Great Gathering of tribes today, the Calusa king was coming to Jeaga Town to demonstrate his complete control of the kingdom, bringing with him an outsider cacique to marry a girl who had no idea of what he even looked like.

Cruel, scheming scoundrel, this Calus! Or am I just a small scoundrel who got swallowed by a bigger one?

The sun was about to set on this late afternoon as Red Hawk looked up from the last of his meat cutting and saw two young boys shouting as they ran breathlessly up the row of huts overlooking the river. In a few seconds women were poking their heads out and passing on the news faster than the boys could run. "His party is coming. They just crossed the Southwest Fork. They'll be here soon!"

But Red Hawk knew they *wouldn't*—not just yet. Although Calus' entourage was only two miles west, the Mako Shark elder knew the king's scouts would bring his catamaran to a halt in the water until the vassal tribes appeared first. Across the river in the Great House, the last of the ladders had been removed and celebrants could look forward to the smell of clean palm thatch and no bugs to fall into one's bowl in the middle of a meal. Inside his own hut, Morning

Dove's mother licked her finger to wipe away a smudge on her daughter's cheek and placed on her bare neck the same polished shell necklace she had worn as a bride.

Just then an excited shout went up as the delegation from the Ais appeared to the north where Long River met the River of Turtles. Within minutes lookouts from Jeaga Inlet reported excitedly that ten canoes had appeared in the ocean carrying the Tequesta from the south. Red Hawk instinctively looked to the east, recalling the stories of how even the Lucayans once would cross the fifty-mile-wide Bahamas Channel in their outrigger canoes to pay homage to the Calusa. But their numbers had been depleted by a mysterious plague in recent decades and no Lucayan canoes had appeared during Red Hawk's lifetime.

So where were the Mayaimi? Once the Tequesta had entered the inlet and made their way across the river to the Gathering Place, Red Hawk heard the sound of conch horns to the west. Then, emerging from the setting sun above the riverside trail came a great canoe convoy of warriors, bearers and important personages.

So many Calusa? No, wait. They were Mayaimi as well, mixed together. At the center he could easily pick out the red-black painted figure of King Calus. In another sedan chair in the catamaran behind him was a smaller, stockier young warrior of maybe twenty-five years, seated next to a woman. *I know him, but where from? Where? Where? Ah, from the Mayaimi town of Guacata, the gateway to the Calusahatchee River.*

His mind raced on.

Ah ha! He would have to be the Guacata cacique's youngest son. A strategic town to Calus. Guardian of the waterways that led from Lake Mayaimi to the Calusahatchee. The first defense against any Spaniards who might try to sneak up on Mound Key from inland. Inspectors and customs collectors of northern trading missions to the Calusa. *Youngest son can't become cacique, so send him to Jeaga Town as Calus' surrogate! Then marry him into Mako Shark clan, which must support him or have its hearts cut out by the Gray Panther clan. Brilliant! That scheming slimy son of a salamander!*

One thing didn't add up. *Who is the handsome woman in that other catamaran behind Calus? Not a wife. Not a mother. Older than the usual bride. Adorned with bracelets and pendants. But who....and why?*

The retinue of King Calus had begun at Mound Key and was joined at the mouth of the Calusahatchee by delegations from Sanibel Island, Pine Island, Cayo Costa and other major towns. Together they had canoed eastward for seventy miles through the Calusahatchee and the waterways that led to Guacata at the entrance to Lake Mayaimi. There they camped and reconnoitered with the chiefs of the lakeside towns known collectively as The Mayaimi, the remnants of a people who had existed perhaps even longer than the Calusa.

On the trip upriver King Calus had sat upon a wide woven seat that sprawled across two war canoes lashed together and paddled by four warriors.

Directly behind the Great Cacique's catamaran canoe came the leading family of Guacata. They included the cacique, Alligator Teeth, his wife Night Heron, Deerstalker, the youngest of two sons, and eldest daughter Bright Moon. All in the entourage knew by now that Deerstalker would be installed as chief of the Jeaga. Few knew that the king had "selected" Bright Moon to accompany her older brother to Jeaga Town and that the king himself would marry her there. As her anxious father had explained, "Trying to install an outsider as cacique there would be too precarious unless the king also placed a member of the royal family to strengthen the alliance." After all, great caciques traditionally married the sisters of leading vassal chiefs—sometimes two or three at once at the Calusa Gathering.

Bright Moon, who learned of all this only a week before, said little and thought much. When she had first married Black Crow at age fifteen, she had assumed that her destiny was to mother a large family on Mayaimi Lake. But then her young husband left for the north with a trading party and just simply vanished. No word, no hint. Only shrugs from other traders who came to Guacata.

Now, just having passed her twentieth summer, Bright Moon was restless. Her father had hotly discouraged any suitors because it was still "assumed" that Black Crow would re-appear one day. Now Calus had put an end to that fiction. Should she be grateful?

As the Calusa canoe caravan wound its way over the ancient trail that cut through the saw palmetto and pine forest, Calus swayed back and forth in front of her on his platform, the sunlight playing off the golden clasp that bound his topknot. A bracelet taken from a Spanish ship? How it glittered as the sun moved in and out of the clouds! And wrapped around his neck were three strands of a gold chain that must be very long when stretched out. Bright Moon fingered her polished shell necklace and earrings. All the jewelry she owned was of stone or shell and kept in one small box. Yes, she wanted to wear jewelry like his, wanted to wear the red ocher that signified royal blood, wanted servants to fetch her water.

Above all, her body yearned to bear children before she was consigned to delivering other babies and helping the old women of Guacata sew and weave. She did not yet know if Calus had other wives and her father simply shrugged when she asked. If she were the first, might she give birth to the next king?

More torment. Would the royal family accept her? The women of Mound Key were taller and more graceful than the shorter, stouter Mayaimi. Calus himself stood more than a head taller than she. He was bound to be large between the legs and she hadn't been with a man for four years. "Oh Mother of Taku, what am I getting into?" she agonized to herself. "I am afraid of this person, even though he is a year younger. He has a fearsome demeanor and gives off a scent of contempt. They say he personally kills servants who displease him. He has not so much smiled at me or uttered a kind word."

Deerstalker sat beside her lost in his own thoughts. "Has he talked to you much, brother?" she whispered behind the swaying hulk.

"Not much," he said without a glance. "He said I have to show strength as cacique. I asked how. He said 'I don't know. Kill someone and eat his heart.' I don't know if he was joking, but I didn't ask any more."

Actually, Deerstalker was not in the same distress as his sister. To be installed as a cacique at age twenty two by the king was an intriguing prospect for a young warrior who would have always languished in the shadows of his older brother back home. Now he would have his own "kingdom," one even larger than his father's town of Guacata.

Besides, he had pleasant memories of Jeaga Town. In many summer months heavy rains would turn everything alongside Lake Mayaimi into steamy marshes. When all Guacata became too soggy to find bread root and one couldn't take a breath without inhaling a mosquito, her father would lead his people to the seashore near Jeaga Town. There they'd swim, fish in the ocean and luxuriate in the cool night breezes.

"You should like Jeaga Town," Deerstalker said absentmindedly. "Remember the summers? The constant breezes that kept the bugs from us?"

"I do, but I don't know how I'll like it in winter when those breezes become biting winds," she said. "If you try to warm yourself by a fire, the wind changes and suddenly your skirt goes up in flames and your hair gets singed."

Both laughed, then lapsed into their own thoughts again. Going to a place for a month or so is different than trying to live there all the time, mused Bright Moon. But could she do this for months on end? The Mayaimi were used to their bread root, fruits, deer, turtle, alligator, and large luscious eels from the rivers. The Jeaga lived mostly on oysters, fish, and dried whale meat. They liked sea grapes and prickly pear. They chewed sassafras root and swore that it cured all sorts of ailments. But it was the saw palmetto berries that made her nose wrinkle to think about. Some of the Jeaga were so addicted to chewing them that they had permanent purple stains around their mouths.

And what awaited *her* in Jeaga Town? How long must she support her brother as chief before she was called by the king to Mound Key? How strong and friendly was the Mako Shark clan? Would she be accepted as this new bride of the king?

Amidst her inner disquiet, the only thing Bright Moon clung to for self-confidence was her unmatched skill as a weaver of cloth and basketry. In the large deerskin sack in the supply canoe behind her was a basket made from split palmetto stems, a second basket tightly wound with sabal palm roots, and a lovely small one artistically woven from grapevine. Also in the sack was her dismantled loom along with several wooden spools, each wound with fibers such as mulberry bark, cypress bark, and sabal palm trunk.

"Yes, they have baskets and fiber in Jeaga Town," Bright Moon said out loud, "but when the women see mine they will know at once that their new cacique doesn't have an idle ignoramus for a sister."

Deerstalker didn't comprehend, but didn't bother. He smiled and patted his younger sister on the knee.

The strange woman that Red Hawk spotted from his riverfront mound was seated in the middle of a strung-out convoy now crossing the river to the Great Gathering Place. In the lead canoes were the hunter-scouts, followed by warriors, the large catamaran with the raised figure of Calus, the honored guests from Guacata, the royal householders and personal servants, bearers with ceremonial gifts, and more bearers with camping supplies.

The Mayaimi chiefs and families came last. Half-way across the river they veered off towards a shore a half-mile from where the Calusa delegation landed. There they would set up their camp, the last night Bright Moon would spend with her mother and family. The large Calusa force made its camp surrounding the Great House and the base of the nearby mound topped by The Place of Sun and Moon. Upon this fifty-foot high natural dune, the Great Cacique and his shamans would greet the sun each day and summon its power to flow into the spirit that dwelt within the king's heart. When he had received the strength to sustain his superiority for the day, the other caciques would be invited into the sun's presence—but only if they faced away from it lest they receive more power than the king.

On the final night of the Great Gathering the Place of Sun and Moon would be the site of an altogether different ceremony.

"See, the moon is full tonight," said Night Heron to her daughter as their canoe nosed into the landing across the river. "A good omen for someone named Bright Moon." Now the Council House loomed large above the waterfront, its far wall of warrior masks and animal carvings casting eerie shadows in the light of many torches. Hungry travelers from all over South Florida ware inhaling the smoke and addictive aroma of sizzling meats and fish.

The Gathering would not officially begin until the caciques paid tribute to their king, but the grassy plaza in front of them was crowded with men, some in earnest discussion, some hawking trade offers.

"Arrowheads! Finest from the land of stone," shouted a young Ais warrior, showing a basket full of sharpened chert pieces.

"Best hammers you can have!" said a Tequesta holding up a conch mallet fastened to a wood handle.

One Mayaimi joined in as soon as feet had touched the shore. "Deerskins. Deerskins. Big ones for your hut, medium ones for cloaks. Little ones for the baby. Winter's coming. Don't be cold."

For the men there, the Gathering offered a chance to trade for things that could make their lives a little easier. But for caciques and their families, it was a rare time in which to negotiate marriages and forge agreements. Some of the latter centered on rights to fishing spots or oyster beds or groves of rare trees.

Not discussed on this informal evening were clan blood feuds, unpunished murders, charges of adultery and the like. They would arise the next day. Resolving disputes was a big reason why Gatherings were held and why a Great Cacique was needed to settle them.

But tonight was for tired travelers to feast and rejuvenate. Calus sat at the far end on a raised seat covered with deerskin and rimmed with polished shells, the tall shadow behind him dancing in the torchlight each time he moved. He hadn't changed dress; but his face was now painted in streaks of red, white and black. And now Bright Moon could see the long yellow chain more fully as it hung across his bare chest. It had a cross at the end that shone in the sunlight like the gold clasp around his topknot.

Along the walls sat caciques. Their families sprawled into the middle, leaving only a small dancing space in front of the king. Outside along the partially open walls stood warriors and servants looking on and eating quietly. Bright Moon and her mother nudged each other when someone pointed out that among the Jeagas seating themselves along the opposite wall was the family of Red Hawk.

Deerstalker on her other side strained to get the first look of his intended bride. Bright Moon saw a seated girl beside Red Hawk and a woman who had to be their mother. She looked like a child. "Ah, that must be your Morning Dove," she said with another poke in his side. Deerstalker gawked and said nothing. Neither wedding couple nor their families were permitted to converse until the next night

15

at the wedding feast, but Bright Moon thought she saw the mother give her a demur nod of welcome. She nodded back, thankful for any sign that the Jeaga weren't waiting to murder her in her sleep.

Food! Platters of it! A giant grilled grouper sprawled and sliced on a single pallet. Stacks of smoked manatee cakes. Mullet filets. Oysters of all sizes and ways of preparation. Delicious root bread, papayas, sliced prickly pears, hog plums, muscadine grapes and, wherever one looked, large baskets of purplish black palmetto berries. By the time King Calus stood to speak the room was so smoky from the torches and pipes being lit that some in the back could hardly see him. They could only hear snippets of speech, which seemed to be all about Calusa family unity and Taku's blessing. But what they cheered most was his call to music and dance.

With that two flute players began piping. Another man kept time by beating conch hammers on a loggerhead tortoise shell. Another pounded a deerskin drum. Calus had also brought some of the women singers and dancers who attended him on Mound Key. For another hour the cream of the Calusa sang the songs that made them a united people. But only the young danced, and since the delegations were made up mostly of older caciques, many heads were already nodding around midnight when Calus stood up and left the building with his guards.

The next afternoon, as the caciques and their captains convened in the same smoky Great House, Bright Moon's mother tried her best at making her bride beautiful in the midst of their open lean-to at the Mayaimi camp. Night Heron poked a stray dog with a stick from her cook fire and contemplated her last day before her daughter became part of another family. "I remember the day you were born," she said telling an oft-heard story. "Your eyes were as bright as little stars, and I wanted to call you *Bright Stars. But* your father said 'Oh the moon is also bright tonight, and the moon spirit will embrace her if we call her *Bright Moon.'* So that was that. Men always win."

"Mother, do you know that more people today call me 'the Weaver Widow' than they do Bright Moon?"

Night Heron knew, but she hated repeating a name that could well be her own one day. "Well, they won't any longer," she said. "They'll be calling you queen of the Calusa."

"I really don't know what will become of me," Bright Moon said softly, her eyes lowered.

Her mother didn't either. "The same could be said for all of us," she replied.

Seeing no need to wallow in worry, Night Heron changed the subject. She scraped a piece of black wood from the fire and began to make the charcoal paste that would decorate her daughter's face that night.

"By now they have installed Deerstalker as Jeaga cacique," she said with a glance across the river. "This day is important for him and your father. Everything must go just right. Your brother must be seen to win the dispute over fishing and the Mayaimi must lose—especially because your father is there."

"Men fight and argue over every little thing,"

"Oh, it's not so small," her mother said. And it certainly was complicated. Originally when the Mayaimi villagers had come to the Jeaga coast in summer, they had been content to catch fish in the river and ocean one at a time. But they had envied how much easier it was for the Jeaga, who lined the inlet with large weirs and stockades for storing their catch. When some of the bolder Mayaimi began placing their own traps in the inlet, fights broke out. The lake people let the matter simmer but vowed that the king would hear about it at the next Great Gathering.

"You'll see," said Night Heron. "The Jeaga clans that don't like the Mako Sharks will be daring their new cacique from Lake Mayaimi to decide in favor of his own people. But Deerstalker will surprise them and tell the Mayaimi they can't build traps in the inlet. Your father will put on a show of grumbling in front of our people, but he will accept it.

"Then if your brother can survive the whaling dispute, I think you two will have the foundation of support you will need to keep the Jeaga mollified."

Bright Moon nodded, although the fuss over whales seemed more about the pride of hot-blooded males than about food supplies. A big reason why the Jeaga had straddled their inlet to the sea for centuries was that the right whales came down most winters from their northern feeding grounds. Just inside the inlet they would languish in the calm waters and deliver their calves. There, unguarded and preoccupied, they were easy trophies for young would-be Jeaga warriors who would stun them with arrows and then leap on their backs for a spear kill. In fact, it had become so routine that the boldest lads would now wait outside the inlet and leap on passing whales, producing the combined thrill of surfing and killing. Ocean whale kills earned tattoo marks almost as prized as the stripes for killing a man in battle.

The Jeaga were never stingy with their bounty of whale meat—the Great Cacique made sure of it. Generous portions were brought to Mound Key and made available to the other vassal tribes if they showed up in Jeaga Town and traded something suitable. But now the other caciques, no doubt pressured by their young hot bloods, were saying that because the whales came from the great sea of all men, they should have the right to slaughter their fair number of whales and do their own processing.

"I guess King Calus is here to rule on the whale matter as much as he is for me." Bright Moon mused.

"Well, it's all part of keeping the balance of things," answered Night Heron, now arranging a cluster of eagle feathers and alamanda blossoms in her daughter's long black hair. "He can't run over here and kill caciques every time they have an argument. So, your father told me last night it has been arranged that Calus will rule against any change, thereby showing that he smiles on the Jeaga once again and supports Deerstalker, the new cacique.

"But don't think that's the end of all the word trading over there in the Great House. Calus never does a favor for nothing. Your father says he will ask the Jeaga to make an excursion across the ocean to investigate what's become of the Lucayans. Do you remember when we came to the Great Gathering when you were a small child?"

"I still remember," said Bright Moon wistfully. "We walked to the beach on a clear morning, and we were playing in the sand when suddenly we saw all these huge canoes with something like wings on each side. I had never seen an outrigger before. How fast the boats went! And the men all singing and rowing as they disappeared into the inlet. When you told me they had come from across the sea, I couldn't believe it. How could there be anything across so great a sea? I thought they might have been dropped from the clouds."

"They came to pay tribute to the Great Cacique," said Night Heron. "Now they come no more."

The Jeaga, the fish traps and whales were only some of the issues that would keep King Calus upright on his bearskin-covered judgment seat in the Council Hall until even his young back ached. Over this and the next day he would be asked to decide between a disputed hunting ground, judge an accused murderer and rule on whether a shaman's magic had caused a Tequesta family to wither and die.

He had his own agenda as well. Calus had brought the biggest gifts to the Ais because he wanted to enlist them in his never-ending war against the Tocobaga of Tampa Bay. But Oathcaqua, chief of the Ais, wanted permission instead to attack the Jororo, his rivals to the north. And for good measure he would argue for the right to trade directly with peaceful tribes who sent missions from the far north. Young Calus had scant experience to judge any of this, but as long as he had his father's elderly advisers to whisper in his ear and kept an imperial sneer behind his fierce mask of ocher and charcoal, all the others seemed satisfied to be lesser men. All the Great Cacique knew was that it was wise to get in and out of Jeaga Town as soon as possible. Who knew what plots might be brewing back on Mound Key?

The sun was setting when the Mayaimi visitors canoed downriver from their camp and landed on the shore of the Gathering Place. Most of the Mayaimi caciques were in no mood for weddings and feasts: they had been pressured to yield both on their quests for fish trapping and whaling in the inlet. But Alligator Teeth could barely keep from bursting with pride. His son was now chief of the Jeaga and soon the family secret would be shared: his daughter would be wed to the king of the Calusa! It meant stronger ties between Mound Key and all the people of Guacata. Perhaps even more Mayaimi marriages to the Calusa nobility lay ahead!

Night Heron helped her daughter from the canoe, careful not to smear the elaborate, colorful artwork on her face. On Bright Moon's forehead were three images, a large black and white eye in the middle with a blue three-pointed star on the left side and a round bluish purple circle on the other. One side of her face was painted white and the other black.

When all the visiting tribes had arrived, conch trumpets began to blow—a few at first, then increasing gradually so that it seemed that a hundred trumpets were blaring the call to celebrate. Then on the hillside before the Great House a shaman with a shark's head mask and large raccoon tail behind his breech cloth began motioning for attention. Five pairs of young men and women came forward and stood before King Calus and his seated entourage. All were lesser members of their delegations who had been waiting for weeks for the privilege of being wed before the king. All wore identical white and black paint on each side of their faces to symbolize the mating of man and woman.

The shaman walked among them holding a large staff topped with a gourd on which was painted the Eye of Taku. He touched it to the eye on the forehead of each candidate and shouted incantations that the eye of the god would deliver protection from evil spirits. To each couple he gave a large gourd with a painted eye to be placed outside the door of their hut.

Next, the holy man brought forth a large papaya that had been cut in half. Holding the two parts up in each hand, he implored Taku to provide them with as many children as there were seeds in the papaya. The conch horns brayed in approval.

Thirdly, he repeatedly tapped the three-pointed star on each girl's forehead with his staff, rocking back and forth in rhythm as he swore that it's healing powers would protect them and their families as long as they were faithful and obedient.

It was then the turn of Morning Dove and Deerstalker, who deserved a separate ceremony owing to his status as tribal cacique. When they were standing in place, the shaman bowed to King Calus and handed him his staff. When the Great Cacique had finished the rites, there was no mistaking the favored status of this couple.

But there was to be something more. The women had already begun whispering at the odd sight of a single woman—Bright Moon—standing among the spectators in wedding attire. Now the Great Cacique beckoned her to come forth and touched the eye on her forehead with the staff. Then raising it on high, he shouted for all to hear: "In tribute to my people, the Jeaga, and as a symbol of my protection of them, I will now take as my bride the sister of the Jeaga cacique. From now on I am not only your father but your brother. Just as the eye of Taku protects your spirit, the strength of the Calusa protects you against all enemies."

When the wedding feast began, Calus remained in his bearskin-covered seat and motioned Bright Moon to sit at his feet. There she would remain, unable to gaze upon her groom. At first the king's troupe of girls sang sweetly and twirling their feathery skirts in unison to the peal of flutes. As the evening wore on, the flutes gave way to the quickening beat of drums and dances became more seductive. The sand floor became a field of animal bones, fruit pits, peeled skins, squashed berries, ants and hungry dogs. The air was again heavy with the smoke of pipe and grill fat.

At one point the Great Cacique, who never seemed to cease eating, pointed across the room and said something to one of his bodyguards. Eyes were on one of the Spanish captives who had been brought by the Ais to wait on them. "*My* slaves can dance for me," he said to the gaunt, shirtless older man who stood puzzled before him. "They make me laugh. So dance!"

The crowd quieted and Calus motioned to a drummer with a roll of his hand.

"Dance!"

The man strained as if hard of hearing. The beat intensified.

"You must dance and sing for us!" said the king, showing frustration.

The man shrugged and spread his hands out in supplication. "No comprendo," he kept repeating while glancing for help that never arrived.

Just then one of Calus' guards appeared behind the man with an ax made from a deer's shoulder blade. He had been heating the blade in a nearby brazier and now he swung the flat side into the man's back.

"Yowwww!" the slave cried and began to hop up and down to roars of laughter. Now he could expect a hot slap or a heavy blow to his backside every time his feet stopped. People began to lose interest just about the time that the man crumpled to the floor, half conscious and bleating from his burns and bruises.

"Well, at least he had a chance to be useful on his last night," Calus said to the crowd with a smirk. "Tomorrow he will dance with the moon."

With that king shuffled off his dais and motioned for Bright Moon to follow. They had neither talked nor even exchanged glances all night. Now she had fallen from the height of adulation at the ceremony to the depths of fear and loneliness.

With two spear-carrying guards following them, Calus passed through the doorway of a thatched hut behind the ceremonial hall and beckoned her to follow. A fire pit glowed in the center and in the dim light she could make out spears standing along the wall and a single totem of carved animal faces. On the walls were hides of all kinds: bear, deer, shark, alligator, and some she could not make out.

More skins lined the floor and Calus sprawled on one raising himself up on an elbow. "Come lie down here," he said softly. She could hear one of the guards cough outside.

"You are pretty behind all that paint," he said with the first kind smile she had experienced. He seemed very tired.

"And I think you would be very handsome without yours," she said boldly.

His hand reached out and cupped one of her breasts. He might have been selecting a melon for breakfast.

Hoping to create any kind of affectionate bond, she reached out and ran her fingers over the topknot she had stared at for so long during the voyage. "Do you ever take *that* off? She asked, grasping the golden clasp that held his hair upright. "What is it?"

"It is a woman's bracelet. It has been the best thing I have found for holding up a topknot. It was brought to me from a Spanish wreck."

"Will you take it off for me?" she asked playfully.

Calus changed the subject. "You are not a virgin, right?"

"No, I was married."

"Good," he said. With that he removed his breech cloth and quickly rolled her over on her stomach. Before she could react he was hard and lifting her to her knees. With a searing pain he was inside her like a spear and thrusting away like a dog on a bitch in heat.

In a few minutes The Great Cacique was asleep on his pile of skins. He had more Council business the next morning and Bright Moon had been the last item on a busy day's agenda.

When Bright Moon awoke the next morning, Calus was gone. When she poked her head out, she was startled to find two Calusa warriors again standing guard. They eyed her nervously as she stretched and tried to get her bearings. It had turned cold and an icy breeze was carrying smoke from the nearby Council House. The wind brought the sound of male voices inside. A short walk from the Great House was the base of the great dune mound that led up to the Place of the Sun and Moon. In the other direction she saw three tall, thin women chatting as they walked with baskets, no doubt Mound Key nobles. They glanced over at Bright Moon and kept walking, obviously not eager to greet the new wife of their king. Suddenly she missed her mother terribly, but her mother was across the river with the Mayaimi.

Apparently not welcome among men or women, Bright Moon ventured no further from the king's quarters than the women's latrine. The only break in the most boring, useless day of her life came when a guard stooped inside the doorway and placed on the floor a whelk of ripe persimmon, a plate of root bread and a bowl of nuts. As she sat on her bed skins nibbling at the food, she could see that some of the skins were exquisite: otter pelts, gray wolf, beaver—all no doubt brought down by traders from the north.

Bright Moon's eyes went to the farthest corner where sat a large wooden box covered with leather and bearing strange carvings. She knew it was closed for a reason, but her interminable boredom eventually got the better of her. She opened the lid and jumped back gasping. It was as if she had invoked all the earthly weapons of Taku at once. Staring at her with their open mouths and empty sockets were the masks of hideous men and animals—the very ones that had given her nightmares as a girl when they were paraded in torchlight rituals. She could barely summon the courage to reach over them and slam the lid shut lest they leap out and snatch her souls!

She had scarcely noticed that a much smaller box stood at the base of the big one. Convinced that it was too small to hold masks, she opened the lid and found enough to amuse her for the afternoon. Everything inside was either gold or silver: goblets, bracelets, earrings, necklaces. Draped on top was the long gold chain Calus had worn during their trip from Guacata. How these treasures glittered in the light that streamed inside the doorway!

Bright Moon played with them as a child does with sea shells. Her favorite was a chain with a gold cross and a glass oval where the cross intersected. Inside the oval was the face of a yellow-haired woman about her age. She held a plump infant with pink skin. She had the same melancholy look that Bright Moon felt that day.

Calus did not return. As the afternoon shadows lengthened and the sounds of men no longer came from the Great House, two warriors abruptly appeared inside and carried off the large leather chest. Bright moon followed them into the doorway and stood between the erect guards peering outside. Activity now centered on the tall mound a short walk away on which stood the Place of the Sun and Moon. Men were lugging pine logs, drums and instruments up the steep hillside. From the top the stiff November breeze was already carrying off sparks from what must have been a bonfire. She knew that the Great Gathering always ended with a sacrifice to the god Taku, but she had never been near such a site.

She turned to one of the silent guards, a tall Calusa. "Where is Calus, my Lord and husband?" she asked.

"He is with the Great Shaman preparing," was the only answer.

At darkness another servant arrived with a plate of fish, fruit and nuts, but Bright Moon left it standing. By then the base of the mound was swarming with painted men wearing the contents of the hated box: hideous masks of fish, animals, fanciful spirits and human skulls. Her father and brother would be among them.

The cacophony of voices soon gave way to a chant that became ever louder until suddenly at the top of the mound the figure of Calus appeared. He was wearing a green mask of something like a barracuda— Taku could take any form he wished—and when the king lifted up his arms to the sky the chanting became a roar. Then the masked figures began to howl like wild animals as they climbed the hill single file.

Bright Moon gave a shudder. Marching among them she counted five slaves—one a warrior from the hated Mayaca tribe, one a short, stooped man with black skin, the rest of them Spanish prisoners who had no doubt been captured from wrecked ships and kept at Mound Key for an occasion such as this. She recognized the slave who wouldn't dance being half carried, his legs bowed like buttonwood limbs, his hands tied behind him. Well, they all deserved it! They had come scheming to capture Calusa as their own slaves, her father had said.

Calus remained motionless with arms outstretched, appearing even taller and more awesome as the clouds above him passed swiftly through the moonlight. When the last of the party had climbed to the Place of the Sun and Moon the drums began to beat more furiously and the glow from the fire grew brighter.

Suddenly, silence. Then the voice of Calus, his loud intonations carried beyond her ears by the wind. Then the cacophony of clubs striking and spears thrusting and men howling and shrieking and moaning.

Again, the drums would resume, then the raised voice of Calus, the silence, then the din signifying another violent death.

And so it had been for centuries. Taku had provided his bounty for the feast of his people. He had provided the newly married his protection from evil and had assured them many children. Now he was tired and hungry from his labors. He needed nourishment to assure him the strength to ward off the devil Catalobe and his army of evil spirits.

Bright Moon was back at play with her treasures when she heard the guards speak and shuffle. Inside ducked Calus followed by a girl she recognized as one of his singer-dancers. He seemed startled to see the Mayaimi woman sitting on his skins fondling his favorite gold chain. She in turn was jolted at his appearance. His arms were stained to the elbows with blood and the paint around his face was smeared and pink. Soon another girl arrived with a large bowl of water and the two began to cleanse the Great Cacique.

Bright Moon remained silent until the women had gone away and Calus faced her for the first time with no painted face. He was still the same tall, muscular man, but he was now only a man a year younger than she. And his eyes were so heavy with fatigue she felt the urge to cradle his head in her lap.

"My husband, I have waited for you faithfully all day," she said.

"I had my duties," was all he said. "I am glad that you did not go off with any of *these,*" he said, nodding toward the open box of jewelry.

"No, but I had all day here with nothing else to do."

When he simply grunted, Bright Moon became bolder, holding up some gold chains. "Would none of these do for a wife?"

She assumed a seductive look and leaned into him. "How long will it be before you come to take me back to Mound Key?" she cooed. Her breasts were touching his shoulder and he reached out idly to stroke her thigh.

"That is up to you," he said, his eyes now on her full swaying breasts. "It can only be when we are sure your brother can rule the Jeaga. And deliver the tribute."

She knew she could not press the matter. "My lord, if I am to succeed, it would be very helpful to wear something special that would remind the Jeaga every day that I am your faithful soldier in this endeavor. She reached for the long heavy gold chain he had worn on the first day.

"No, not that one," he said with a flash of irritation.

She fumbled through the jewel case again and came up with the smaller chain that held the cross with the lady's face.

"All right, *that* one," he said. Then he was upon her again. This time she knew what to expect and made all the right sounds to let him know what a great joy it was to be his.

All night Bright Moon slept with the chain of her new golden cross wrapped around her hand. When she opened her eyes in the morning, she looked at the yellow-haired lady in the oval and hoped she would soon hold a pink baby as well.

Chapter Two

Jeaga Child

Like all mothers in the Calusa realm, Bright Moon would simply call her son "little one" or "baby boy" until some deed or trait evoked a specific name that would endure for the rest of his childhood. The son of Calus got his first name at age four after watching older boys trying to spear mullet and snook on the sandy shore where the River of Turtles met the Jeaga Inlet. He begged his mother to give him a spear like the big boys. After he had resorted to sulking and whining he was soon surprised when his uncle Deerstalker handed him a large sharpened stick about as tall as the boy's height. "Now go fish," he said turning on his heel. "And don't put your eye out."

Minutes later Deerstalker was walking the shoreline on his way to another chore when something made him stop. The son of Bright Moon had separated himself from the other boys and stood motionless with his child's spear perched above his shoulder. "How long can an inpatient, wiggly, child stay quiet and concentrated like that?" Deerstalker wondered to himself.

After two or three minutes he saw the boy throw his stick into the water and squeal. He'd speared a fish, but lacked the strength to gaff it. Now spear and fish wobbled away in the water with the tearful lad wading after them.

Deerstalker followed quickly and scooped his nephew in his arms before he got in over his head. "Don't worry, I'll make you another spear," he exclaimed. "But tell me, how did you catch the fish?"

"The boys said to look for the vee in the water and throw ahead of it. So I did."

"You did exactly right," said Deerstalker. "But even a heron doesn't catch a fish every time he hunts. You did it on the first try! So from now on I am going to call you Little Heron."

His mother was only too happy to hear about the episode and would repeat it often. She also accepted the clan leader's choice of a name, if only because she was tired of calling him "my little one."

And Little Heron himself could tell that something had changed. He felt a sense of pride, that he had suddenly grown—enough so that he now began to pester his mother about going into the woods with her on her frequent gatherings. He had already had a taste of it when Bright Moon would bundle him on her back for short walks. The wonder of things in all directions! Big trees. Shrubby trees. Bright flowers. Birds chirping and flying. Things that wiggled on the ground! His mother had names for all of them—more than he could ever remember. With all his might he wanted to jump down, touch and smell all of them. But all of his wiggling had only produced threats to leave him in the hut unless he stopped.

Well now, Bright Moon thought to herself, perhaps the time has come to begin the education of Little Heron and at the same time train a helper to ease her burdens. Lurking in the back of her head was another reason: having the boy along in her walks afforded a symbol of protection against the idle hunter in the woods who might have ideas of taking his pleasure with a woman alone. Her chief protector, however, remained the long gold chain she carried around her neck at all times. She had often opened the oval that hung from the chain and gazed at the face of the yellow-haired lady with the bright round circle above her head. It never failed to give her a sense of comfort and strength. So, too, did the gold chain's reminder to any intruder that she was the wife of Calus, the Great Cacique.

Since Little Heron's "coming of age" happened to be in May, his education would rightfully begin with the picking of saw palmetto berries. Nothing was more important to Bright Moon's survival. As a woman living without a husband, she found it necessary to gather more edibles, sew more garments and weave more baskets than other women because she had to trade them for fish and game. Saw palmetto berries ranked at the top of her "gatherings" because everyone either chewed the pulpy fruits or boiled them into tea. Besides, she had kept on the side of Hawkman, the old shaman, bringing him enough berries for his medical needs. Some he prescribed as aphrodisiacs, some for making balms for aching joints and others for warding off evil spirits.

The month of May was important because it was the secret to Bright Moon's success as a gatherer and trader of saw palmetto berries. Traditionally, most of the women went in search of the berries in August or September, after the summer heat had turned them from yellow-orange to a juicy, succulent black. But the summer berries also tended to drop off on the ground, leaving fewer per plant. They also attracted ravenous bears and deer, which could eat thirty pounds in a single feast. Equally voracious insects bored into the sun-softened berries, making every human bite an adventure.

But Bright Moon discovered that when she went out alone in May when the berries were still hard and green, she could find up to a thousand per saw palmetto plant. She would bring them home to her small compound, putting some out into the sun to ripen each day. Thus, by the time summer rolled around, people could be assured that Bright Moon berries were juicy and bug-free. When winter approached and the saw palmettos became bare, neighbors marveled that Bright Moon would always have supplies on hand—and worth more in trade.

Much later, the son of Bright Moon would laugh at the first thing he could clearly recall in his life—his first "hunt." Before they headed west up the trail, his mother said "Now that you have become my hunter and warrior, you'll want to wear this." From the grapevine basket she would use for berries she produced a deerskin loin cloth with a raccoon tail hanging from the back. "Now you're just like the big warriors," she said.

At the same time, he could remember even more clearly the cuts on his hands. The stinging feet! His mother scolding him. Then holding him close.

It had happened in the first hour of that first day on the trail together. "Stay close behind me," Bright Moon ordered. "When we stop, your task will be to pick the berries that hang below my waist." Since he couldn't lift a large grapevine basket, she gave him a light sack she had woven from sweet grass.

After that Bright Moon said little. Her task was not only to gather berries, which were everywhere, but to scout for any number of plants, vines, and grasses that could be used in her weaving and sewing. The coontie plant, for roots that were ground for starch. Long fibers from century plants for twisting into strong twine. Sabal palmetto, cypress bark and cabbage palm leaf for two-ply cord. To scout for these and more, Bright Moon led her new apprentice off the trodden path, zig-zagging around the spiky saw palmettos. Her concentration was so intense that she didn't notice when Little Heron whimpered after cutting his hand sliding it along a spiny palmetto stalk. Nor did she see when he saw a large gopher tortoise crawling away from a saw palmetto plant so slowly that he surely could catch it. When the tortoise lumbered down a hole in the sand, Little Heron crawled in after it. He looked about in silence for a moment, and then:

"Yow! Yoweeee! Ow! Ow! Ow!"

When Bright Moon lifted him up, his soft little feet were covered with red ants. A spider may have taken his revenge as well, because suddenly the hunt was over. Little Heron's mother shook him in anger, then transported him on her hip back to the well-beaten trail and to their hut by the river. Only then, when she was lathering his feet with mud did she see the extent of the bright red welts and burst into tears. He would always remember those tears of the only one who cared for him, and the warmth of her caress.

A few days later, Little Heron was back on the trail with his first pair of buckskin sandals, and he would come to know the plants and animals of the tropical forest even more than his mother. But as a young boy, he was also happy to stay home. He could stay fascinated and busy with all the many things to do around his home. The Mako Shark clan lived in a cluster of thatched huts overlooking the River of Turtles and the Great Calusa Gathering Place that lay on the other side. Long, long before, individual huts had been built there, each raised above the river level. But over time, families had taken in new brides and huts had filled in the empty spaces. Homes had been burned or replaced—each one atop the other so that the Jeaga dwellings now constituted a con-tinuum along a ridge a dozen or more feet above sea level. It meant that the occupants lived comfortably amidst invigorating breezes, except perhaps on summer afternoons or when the hurricanes blew.

The home of Bright Moon was oval-shaped, built of thin saplings bent at the top into a frame supporting a thick covering of sabal palm fronds except for an opening in the center. Directly below the opening in the roof was a fire pit surrounded with a clutter of wooden bowls with nuts, a clay jar of coontie flour, a basket of sea grapes, a jar of water, a basket of hog plums and various-sized whelks for dipping and drinking.

At one end of the dusky room was the bed of deerskins on which Bright Moon slept curled up with Little Heron snuggled inside her curves. Beside it was a large basket made from sabal palm roots that contained her wedding jewelry. Sometimes when Little Heron awoke before his mother, he would reach into the basket and play with its treasures: bright blue beads, shell necklaces, a shark tooth pendant, a pearl ankle band, feathers for hair decorations and fish bladder ornaments of all sizes and colors. Sometimes when she opened her eyes to the first light, Little Heron would be smiling beside her, festooned with jewelry from head to toe.

At the other end of any other Jeaga home would have been a stash of spears, fish nets, atlatls, bows and arrows. But in a home with no husband Bright Moon had taken up the space with baskets of ripening palmetto berries along the wall and the loom she had brought from her home at Lake Mayaimi. Surrounding the loom in a semi-circle were some baskets of raw bark or fiber. Others held spindles of the finished products—two-ply twine, four-ply yarn, and rope twisted from cypress bark. Some spindles held fibers so strong—such as the leaf of the century plant and inner bark of mulberry tree—that Bright Moon could simply cut them into strips as long as five feet and wind them around the spindle without any splicing or twining.

Twisting and splicing, however, remained awkward for Bright Moon to achieve, and that is how Little Heron came about his first domestic job. Morning Dove, her neighbor and brother's wife, always had to be coaxd into helping Bright Moon with her weaving. Now she had a three-year-old, a new baby, and no appetite for weaving beyond her family's barest essentials. "Get Little Heron to help," she said.

And so, months went by with the boy slicing pieces of soft bark or twisting a spindle while his mother spliced yarn. Every now and then his uncle Deerstalker would stand by the doorway and mutter complaints about a man doing woman's work. Invariably the reply would be "Well, then go tell my husband to raise him like one!"

There had been but one Great Calusa Gathering since Little

Heron's birth and Cacique Calus had not made the trek from Mound Key. Bright Moon's heart had sunk, but she never said so to her son. "We will have another Great Gathering next year," she would say, "and then the king will come to claim his prince. You will see!"

She said as much to anyone within earshot, but what had once been an aloof respect was turning to murmurs of derision behind her back. Some said the king had already taken a new, younger bride on Mound Key. Others said he hadn't come because his position was too shaky to leave his stronghold. Her brother Deerstalker mused that it meant approval of his job as Jeaga cacique. Or maybe that the king was sending someone to remove him⬛and his head.

Meanwhile, Little Heron gained new jobs at home with each growth in years. He picked sea grapes from the trees at the back of his hut and tended the little garden of gourds that grew in front of them. He learned how to burn mangrove twigs in the outdoor fire pit so that the smoke would chase away mosquitoes on calm hot nights without blowing inside. Each day he put enough saw palmetto berries out in the sun to ripen and then trade it for a tray of oysters or fish. As he gained muscle, he took over the hard work grinding and pulverizing the root of the fern-like coontie plant with mortar and pestle into yellowish-white flour produced by straining out toxins and baking it into starch patties. He learned to collect muscadine grapes in a basket and spread them out in the sun until they became tasty raisins.

Little Heron's help at the loom increased to the point where his mother trusted him to assist with the most intricate, important task of all: extracting every last use from a slain deer or bear once the hunters had pared the meat off the bone. In the fall, when deer and bear fattened up on acorns in the forest, hunters would return with their quarry and Bright Moon, who was now becoming known, with a pinch of derision, as "The Weaver Queen," was beseeched to make the most of it. Weaver Queen and son used deer brain oil to make hides more pliable. In turn, hides became clothing, bowstrings, bindings and wrist guards. Deer tendon and ligaments were used for bows and bindings. Bone was made into fishhooks, beads and tools of all kinds. Deer leg bones were used mainly for projectile points.

A black bear carcass was especially welcome. While the fur usually went for some noble's rug or cloak, Bright Moon always managed to sequester an extra amount of bear fat. That way she and Little Heron never went without cooking oil or insect repellant when they gathered fibers and berries in the forest.

One morning just after Little Heron entered his tenth year, he and his mother were softening a deer pelt over a board of in-lain shark teeth when Deerstalker appeared at the opening of their hut. Usually he waited politely outside until invited, but this time he burst right in.

"I see you know how to skin a deer," he said glowering at Little Heron. "But you do not know how to *kill* one. You have never shot an arrow. You don't even have a bow, as far as I know. You have done so much woman's work that you are going to *become* a woman. The time has come for you to learn the ways of a man! Besides you don't look like a 'Little Heron' any more. You're taller and probably stronger than the other boys, but you wouldn't know it because you're never *with* them."

The abruptness of her usually deferential, decorous brother left Bright Moon agape. "But what will I do?" she stammered. "My husband is not here."

"Little Heron, please go outside," he motioned with a thumb-jerk. "Go out back and tend your gourds. And get ready to bid them good-bye."

When the lad exited, the Jeaga cacique looked around him nervously and said with clenched teeth, "Maybe you need a *new* husband." he said. Then in a near whisper: "Maybe this one is never coming back for you. Maybe you need an ordinary Jeaga warrior. Or someone from back home."

"No!" she exclaimed. "King Calus has given me his word. He has sealed his promise with *this,*" she cried, holding out the golden chain from around her neck.

"And maybe no one believes it but you," answered her brother. "Maybe he got that gold chain from some dead Spaniard. In any case, I have made up my mind. Starting today Little Heron will spend some time with the other boys his age, learning how to become a Jeaga or Calusa or whatever isn't a woman. I will find you a woman to help you who knows something about weaving."

"But I *need* him."

Deerstalker drew up close to her face and spat his words with the hiss of a viper. "You need to understand," he said. "I—and you—are supposed to be the leaders of this tribe. Despite what I believe inside, we need to appear as though we have the support of King Calus and his people at Mound Key. This means treating his son—*your* son—like the son of a king. And this means teaching him the ways of a man before it is too late."

"Too late?"

"Yes. I have heard that there will probably be another Calusa Gathering soon. No one seems to know exactly when, but when it happens and the Great Cacique asks to see his son shoot a bow or jump a whale, I don't want to be the one to tell him that his son is in training to be a twirler of twine. And I don't want to lose *my* head, even if you are so willing to risk losing yours."

Deerstalker's hard glare remained with her even after he'd ducked out of the hut and left.

Two days later White Ibis, which this old, fat woman may have resembled all too long ago, appeared in the doorway of Bright Moon and announced that she had been sent to help with the weaving in the afternoons. A few minutes later she was surprised to see a gnarled old hunter she knew only slightly standing awkwardly at the entrance. His name was Cougar Claw and behind him were five boys, all stooping and peering inside curiously. "I have come for your son, Little Heron," he said. "The cacique says I will be their teacher," he added with the sweep of the hand toward the lads behind him.

Bright Moon needed no further explanation. "Go," she said dismissively to Little Heron, who had been winding a strand of mulberry bark around a bone spindle. Inside he felt bone-cold fear, but he stood quickly and managed an outward display of indifference.

Soon Little Heron was tagging along behind the other five, who, judging from their playful poking and jabbering were already friends or maybe even related. The teacher led them down the ridge and south, away from the river. The short, stooped hunter would soon reach old age, but he still managed a quick, light pace as the wide, well-worn trail gave way to a narrow footpath underlain by roots and overgrown with wire grass. Cougar Claw had two long scars beside his flat nose that could have actually been etched by a cougar's claws. His many other tattoos signified many triumphs on the hunt. His black hair was gathered into a short topknot from which dangled a raccoon tail. He wore white paint from ear to nose to ear and it was matched by a necklace and earrings of white shells. Cougar Claw had taken the trouble to impress his young charges with his persona and also convey that that they had begun an important new chapter in their lives.

In a mile or so they saw black smoke rising from the treetops. The boys' banter had already ceased when they reached a large clearing in the forest and saw the source of the smoke. A large longleaf pine trunk had been hacked into three parts of about eighteen feet each. Two fires of small logs cut from the pine branches were burning and two Jeagas were hunched over one of them.

Cougar Claw spoke for the first time since they'd left the village. "You will now learn what it takes to become a Jeaga man. So far you have been riding around in canoes like infants on your mothers' backs. Now you will find that canoes do not just drop from the sky. Each winter we build new canoes and replace old worn out ones. It is now March and we are making canoes. Do you know why we do so in March?"

Silence. Foot shuffling. Finally one boy asked "When will you teach us how to shoot the deer and ride the whale?" The others echoed him in a chorus. "And hunting bears and fighting sharks!"

"Shut up, fools," answered the teacher with a stare that sliced through the babble. "Before you achieve that right, you will learn how to collect and build the tools that are used in hunting. Only then will you be ready to hunt and fish.

"I asked you why we build canoes in March. The answer, you puppies, is that the bark and wood of trees becomes dry in the winter months and we are nearing the end of that time. Fires are easier to build and the wood gives way to the fire more quickly. And do you coquinas know why we walk all this way to build our canoes?"

Cowed silence.

"Because we don't want to drag those heavy tree trunks all the way to Jeaga Town. And because we don't want a wind coming up and burning down huts with babies like you inside!"

"Now then," added Cougar Claw, "you are going to learn how

to soften the inside of these logs for carving without burning a hole through the bottom. We had a boy who did that once....." he let the rest of the remark dangle invitingly.

"What happened to him?" asked a boy on cue.

"We had to cut his balls off to plug the hole up. But they were so little we then had to chop off his *parrata* as well and stuff that in, too." The old man let out a howl that almost doubled him up, and the two canoe builders joined in.

The boys had no time for horseplay the rest of the day—and scarcely even for talking. With three boys assigned to each of the canoe builders, they were told to cut small strips of wood into burnable kindling and put just enough of it on the log for the fire to leave ash or charred wood an inch or so deep and six or eight inches around. Because the pine log contained resin, the fire would spread all too quickly if not kept in check. A pile of wet clay stood beside the log, and when the fire became too aggressive it was the first boy's s' job to slap a handful of the clay in its path to keep it in check.

The second boy would probe the burning trunk for softness with a sharpened deer bone. The third would use a shell ax fashioned from the wall of a lightning whelk to scrape away the removable portion and toss it in a large ceramic pot so that a gust of wind wouldn't carry off sparks into the brittle forest.

They took turns so that only two at a time had to hover their faces over the searing wood and stinging smoke. The only sounds the rest of the morning and afternoon were painful gasps when one of the sweating, sooty boys would inhale too close to the fire. Most of the time Cougar Claw sat several yards away on a fallen cypress trunk, smoking a pipe and humming to himself. From time to time one of the two canoe builders would join him for a muffled conversation, punctuated with guffaws or knee slapping. It always seemed about then when one of them would feel compelled to yell over at his young crew, "easy on that fire! No holes in the bottom!"

It soon became apparent that while educating the young was an important Jeaga ritual, equally hallowed was the tradition of getting boys to do tiresome, dirty, repetitive chores before they grew strong enough to rise up in rebellion.

When Cougar Claw finally led his apprentices back up the trail it was dusk and Little Heron could see his mother standing on the ridge behind their hut scanning the horizon with her arm shielding the setting sun. Her ten-year-old son was returning from his first day as a Jeaga "man," black with soot from the waist up, glistening with sweat, long black hair full of gray ash.

He realized that he hadn't uttered a word to anyone all day.

The next day Little Heron was almost exhilarated when Cougar Claw led his troop of six—not to the "smoke pit," as they'd begun calling it—but down to the cool, clean blue-green waters of the ocean. A gentle wind was blowing from the northwest, which meant that the waves were reduced to a gentle lap. Beneath the water was a kaleidoscope of glitters. Had the water been magically rolled back, it would have revealed a landscape of mottled brown slipper shells, pink fighting conch, black and white zebras, red-spotted cowries, bright red turkey scallops, yellow-orange cones and a hundred other kinds of shells.

The teacher had been carrying a large woven sack around his shoulder. Now he ordered the boys to sit in a circle in the sand while he took several shallow baskets from his sack and handed them around. "Today," he said, "I don't want to hear about teaching you how to wrestle sharks and ride whales and harpoon giant fish," he said. "In your lifetime you will eat many more oysters, whelks, clams and other shellfish than you ever will giant groupers. And the fish you eat will mostly be small ones that you can catch or trap. If you waited around to spear some fish you could brag about, you would probably starve. Why? Because most of the big ones swim in schools and pass this way only a few times a year. So, today and other days until you learn this lesson you are going to walk a couple of miles along the beach and then be ready to tell me what you see."

"Why do we have to walk?" asked the same boy who spoke up the day before. "Beach is beach."

"No, oyster brain," said the teacher. "Where we are now lies too near your houses. Lazy people like you have been scouring the beach for so many Jeaga lifetimes that not much remains in this spot."

They might have waded and swam across the Jeaga inlet at low tide, but Cougar Claw found it more convenient to put the boys in three of the several tribal canoes that were turned over on the shore. Once on the south side of the inlet they walked, crouched and scooped their way until they were within distant sight of the old Spanish ship that had wrecked ashore the year before Little Heron was born. There Cougar Claw stopped and said, "The first thing you will do is use your baskets to scoop up coquinas."

Bending down where the ocean lapped at the shore, he buried his hand in the sand, felt around, and came up with a handful of thumb-nail-sized mollusks. "These, in case your mothers haven't shown you, are coquinas," he said. "Now I want you to use your baskets as scoops. We'll have a contest to see who can bring in the most coquinas before I clap my hands twice. Remember, you can't scoop with your hands."

The leathered old teacher squatted over the sand passively as the boys raced about yelling and elbowing each other as if the spot he had discovered was the only coquina habitat on the beach. After five or so minutes Cougar Claw clapped his hands and the boys came running up with their baskets.

"Well, look here, this one is nearly empty," he said. "So is this and this. This one has a little more. Ah, but *this* one and *that* one are nearly full," he said when Little Heron and another boy produced their baskets.

"There s a lesson here for you. When I took these baskets out of the sack, no one asked me what they were made of or how you were sup-posed to use them. So you simply ran off like the boys you are. These two baskets—the ones that yielded practically nothing—are made of sabal palm. They are woven so tightly that the effort to scoop the coqui-nas is so great that all the shells fall into the water before you can bring them up. This one here is woven from saw palmetto leaves. It is so loose that all the coquinas escape with the water as you are trying to draw them up. The third basket is woven from grapevine. It has just enough space between the weave so as to let water out, yet trap all the coquinas. At the same time, enough water stays on top so that the coquinas are still fresh when you bring them home to Mother."

The boys looked puzzled.

Cougar Claw knew they would be and was ready with a scowl. "The story of the coquina, little minnows, is that you cannot simply grab your bow and arrow and go off in the forest to hunt. You must first know what you are hunting, the weight of the bow required, and the length of the arrows and the nature of the arrow tip that is going to kill your prey. If you do not, you could wind up in the forest being killed by a bear you tried to hunt with a rabbit bow. The lesson applies to coquinas and bears alike. And you must never forget it."

"But coquinas are gathered by girls and women," said the boy who talked too much.

"'Not always," said the teacher solemnly. He paused as if in deep reflection. "Once when we fought the Potanos, I was separated from my fellow Jeaga warriors. We were in their land, so I would have been seen and killed if I had tried to walk home by the inland paths. My only chance was to swim down the shoreline by night and hide myself in the dunes by day. When I was starving, what do you think I did—rush into the forest and kill a bear? No, I would swim in the shallow water like a giant turtle and ease myself into the surf. There I would scoop up any shellfish I could find and crack them open. I was grateful for every coquina or sand flea that provided me with the smallest taste of something to eat. Maybe some day you will be too."

The boys paid more attention as the teacher led them, wading and walking, down the beach. He showed them how to spot a lightning whelk and determine whether it would make a good dipper or a better awl. He held up a queen conch and told them how to tell if its lip would make a hatchet blade or whether the shell would be best used as a hammer. He stood knee deep over a sting ray buried in the sand and showed the boys how to lift it without encountering the crippling whipsaw cut of its tail. He explained how the tail spine made for an arrow or a fish spear.

When it became late afternoon and the sun began to fade beyond the dune line, Cougar Claw led his students along the west side of the inlet instead of returning across it by canoe. It was now low tide, and the boys waded along the inlet, sloshing through the turtle grass as Gray Cougar showed them how to find clams and conch and quahog clams with their feet—conch on top, clams just an inch or two below, and the bulky quahogs a foot or so below wherever one sees a string of bubbles rising to the surface.

"The small fish come here to feed instead of being attacked at sea," he said, "and this is where you will find most of the dinners you will eat once you come to appreciate them. And when August comes, the scallops will come, too, and you will be picking them up by the basketful.

In October the bluefish will be splashing about and in November so many mullet will be jumping in the inlet that all you'll have to do is hold your baskets up and for one to jump in."

"And what happens in January?" he bellowed. .

"The whales!" they all chorused.

"The whales if Taku decides that we are worthy of them."

By the time the boys had emerged from wading along the edge of the inlet they could see the ridge they had left that morning and the long row of huts overlooking the River of Turtles. Little Heron was the oldest and tallest among them, but he was dazed with exhaustion. Another boy named Sandpiper had fallen in with his shuffling feet and Little Heron uttered his first words of the whole two days. "I just can't keep all these things in my head," he said aloud.

The teacher had overheard, and laughed. "You will learn it all, co-quina," he said gently. "We will make these trips over and over until you know it as well as going to the latrine. Your survival depends on it. And so does mine and the Jeaga tribe."

Little Heron quickly realized what those words had meant. On the third day the boys canoed up river and spent the day learning where to find oyster beds and how to harvest them.

On the fourth they were back wading in the inlet learning how to select the right fish nets, how to set a fish trap, and how to direct trapped fish to an enclosed pool where they could be kept until needed for cooking.

On the fifth day they learned that until then Cougar Claw had spoken of things outside his day-to-day experience. As a hunter, his field of special knowledge was the crafting of darts, arrows, knives and spears for literally every occasion. For the first time, the boys could see his enthusiasm for sharing his life-long knowledge. Their heads swam as he described the use of horseshoe crab tails, catfish spine, deer antler, garfish scale and so many more materials that the drying or tanning or sharpening process became lost in a blur. "You may not understand now," he would say, "but you will in time."

Before dispersing the boys to their homes that evening, Cougar Claw told them to meet him at a midway point atop the riverfront ridge of huts where most of them lived. Little Heron stood silently to one side while the others jabbered enthusiastically. They talked of actually making arrows and spears, but when Cougar Claw appeared he had a surprise that made them look back in disbelief.

"You are now going to learn something important about building houses and council houses and great temples," he declared. "At the same time you will learn how important it is to keep mosquitoes and various scavengers away from your home—if you live long enough to build one.

"See this trash pile?" He pointed behind the boys to an indentation in the sand and wire grass a space that lay between two huts. It was piled about two feet above the ridge line with an assortment of discarded oyster shells, conchs, whelks, a broken ax handle, skins of fruit and the husks of a thousand nuts. Cougar Claw jostled the pile with the end of his spear and an army of roaches and land crabs scurried to regain cover. Overhead flies swarmed, seeking crannies in which to lay their eggs.

"You are going to collect this trash today," the teacher announced solemnly to a chorus of groans. "And when you are done with this garbage pit, there are others waiting for you. In case you hadn't noticed, most of this stuff just doesn't melt away. If it was not carried off, it would keep growing and grow so high it would topple over on your hut one night when you are sleeping and bury you in shells and crabs and roaches."

"Where do we take it?" one of the boys wondered aloud.

"I am coming to that," answered the teacher. "So far you are dejected because you must do the work of slaves. But it is all in your mind. What if I told you that you are taking part in building a great work that will still be here for many years after you leave this earth? What if I told you that what you do will help the Jeaga acquire gold, silver, and slaves?"

Mouths came open again and heads cocked to hear more.

"By the time you are grown we are going to have a new council house," he said. "The one you see below you behind this ridge has been there since before my grandfather. It was built on a platform of shells just like these in that pit. Only it has been gradually worn down over the years and one day will no longer be high enough to stay dry in times of heavy rains and floods. The Council has laid out the dimensions of a new meeting house on top of the dune line facing the ocean just beyond where you can see. It will be much higher—and for another reason than avoiding floods. It will serve as a lookout for Spanish ships that may be carrying gold. And it will give more time to assemble our warriors should those ships contain warriors who want to attack us.

"So you see, you are being a part of a great cause. In fact, the Great Cacique has ordered it," he added. As he said it he gave a quick awkward glance at Little Heron, the first evidence the boy had that the teacher was aware of his special importance. What Cougar Claw did *not* say was that another Great Calusa Gathering would be taking place soon and that the king would not be pleased to see the new ship lookout still a mere foundation.

The nobility of the project was soon dissipated among a buzz of sullen muttering as the boys labored all day. Each boy had a large shallow grapevine basket big enough to sit in. Fastened to each basket was a strong cord of mulberry bark. Each would fill his basket with shells and husks and pull it over the sand for a quarter mile to one of two old canoes pulled up in the sand at the inlet. When a canoe filled up, one boy would push and another pull it towards the mouth of the inlet until he reached the spot where they could see the edge of the new platform on the dune line above. The baskets were then loaded again, pulled up the sand and dumped onto the already-leveled sand platform.

At the end of the day, the boys had emptied two of the family trash pits. Little Heron reckoned the six had hauled and emptied thirty or so of the large baskets. When spread out evenly, the combined contents covered just the end of the thirty-foot-wide platform. He calculated that it would take forty more days like this one to cover the whole base of the new council house. And then it would take many more baskets of beach sand to fill in around the garbage in order to raise the whole platform just a foot or so.

"How high is it supposed to go?" he asked Cougar Claw, who was leaning on his spear and staring at the ocean.

"I don't really know," he said, "Not my business." He thought some more. "High enough, I guess, so that we have plenty of time to assemble warriors in case of attack or if we see a gold ship sinking."

Little Heron was still calculating as the six and their teacher trudged back toward the river ridge at day's end. "It could take us sixty days of hauling for each foot we raise that platform," he said morosely. "Ten feet high could mean 600 days."

"We are indeed slaves," groaned Sandpiper.

The teacher had been listening in and decided to have a little fun with his weary workers. "Ten feet? This is nothing. On the other coast the Calusa build things like this almost every day. They say the Great Cacique's house sits more than fifty feet above the water. They must have better boys than you, huh?"

He laughed again. "So you puppies think you are going to do this one all by yourselves! Maybe others will help, too."

Just then they heard the voices of other boys. Cougar Claw swiveled his head long enough to wave quickly at another old Jeaga walking on a parallel path several yards away. He was leading six other youths of about the same age. All were covered with soot.

The next day when Little Heron found himself back burning out canoe trunks at the smoke pit, the whole picture came to him at once. There were probably six groups of ten or eleven year-old boys, each with a teacher. There were basically six "educational" tasks, although some would vary according to the season. Teachers would come and go, depending who had the most skill at his subject.

And so it would go, for almost two years until, as Cougar Claw had put it, they knew how to make canoes, fish traps, bows, arrows and a hundred other things as naturally as going to the latrine.

Their survival would depend on it.

CHAPTER THREE

Charles V

1555

Martin de Guztelo was seething and sulking at the same time. He had been about to pull open the heavy oaken door and leave his lord's private study when something made him turn about and contemplate the sad scene before him. Unaware or unconcerned that his secretary for correspondence was studying him, Charles V, Emperor of the Holy Roman Empire, King of Castile-León and Aragon, Duke of Burgundy, Archduke of Austria, Hungary and Bohemia, King of the Low Countries, and Emperor of New Spain (the entire Western Hemisphere), was tinkering aimlessly with one of the hundred or so clocks that ticked and tocked from every shelf and table in his vacuous study.

The heat of summer in Brussels had barely yielded to the cool of September, but already the stooped, gaunt monarch was wrapped in a plain gray woolen shawl. During the equally chilly conversation with his aide, the emperor had constantly blown a reddened nose into a wet yellowed handkerchief, a sure sign that he would soon regain the cough and raw throat that plagued him through the past two winters. These and the gout—above all, the stabbing throbs in every extremity—would keep him in bed for the majority of each winter day.

The emperor was fifty-three years old, exhausted from the travels and battles and political scheming required to become and remain the most powerful man in the world.

De Guztelo had just turned the iron handle on the study door when it pushed against him to reveal the royal chaplain, Fray Francisco de Vargas.

"You look as if you could use an uplifting word," the friar whispered brightly to the dour secretary.

"This is becoming serious," muttered De Guztelo waving a packet of parchment toward the bent little man winding the hands of a walnut clock engraved with a deer's head. "Just now I tried to get him to read an urgent request from his brother Ferdinand in Italy. And here is a communiqué from the Holy See. He just waved me off. No, he actually *pushed* me away."

"Well, he *is* the Emperor," replied the rotund, red-faced Franciscan with a condescending smile.

"Yes, but how long can an empire go ungoverned? His doctors say his piles are now as painful as his gout. No wonder he is no longer the same man we knew. He has turned into a melancholic who refuses to see even emissaries who have crossed continents and oceans to seek decisions. I tell you this cannot go on, for the sake of all of us."

The royal chaplain knew only that he was there to attempt the emperor's daily communion. "Kings rule for life," he intoned as he waddled toward the preoccupied tinkerer.

Once in the corridor outside the king's study, De Guztelo fumed again in silence. *Am I the only one who isn't oblivious to what's happening? No, they all know, but everyone from physicians to cooks to footmen has a reason to cling to the status quo because change could endanger his livelihood and his prestige a member of the royal household.*

No, this cannot be done by a staff member, he concluded. It must come from the royal family.

De Guztelo had just begun to steel himself for the task when he saw the king's petite sister Lenor approaching her chambers from the far end of the tapestry-lined corridor. Well, if he had to begin somewhere, it might as well be with the most pleasant and beloved member of the royal family. Lenor, born the archduchess of Austria and now the queen consort of Portugal, had the gift of appearing gracious and sagacious in good times and bad. Though just three years younger than Charles, her smooth pink face and ready smile made the contrast in ages seem like decades.

"My lady, might I have an informal word with you?" asked De Guztelo with a slight bow.

Rather than greet him or invite him into her sitting room, she simply stood like one of the Roman statues in the corridor and cocked her head.

"Yes?"

Fumbling for diplomatic words to replace the abrasive ones in his head, De Guztelo began with a litany of papers unread and decisions ignored.

At last Lenor interrupted. "Yes, yes, I see your point. However, a king's advisers—and his secretary for correspondence—exist to serve him when incapacitated," she said softly, as if anything louder might be treasonable. "Can you not just prepare a decree for him—a decision or whatever—and ask him to put the royal signet to it?"

"No, my lady, he has refused the seal more than once."

"You're suggesting abdication?"

After a pause for dramatic effect, he nodded solemnly.

Lenor lowered herself to a settee in the hallway as De Guztelo remained awkwardly leaning over her. "I can't recall an emperor ever abdicating except perhaps when Diocletian did so in A.D. 300 or so."

"Ah, yes your majesty, but he did so because his health was failing."

"But I also recall another Roman emperor before him. Tiberius fled to Rhodes when Caesar Augustus tried to name him as his successor. And even when he was coaxd to return and assume the throne, he soon moved his whole household to the Isle of Capri thinking he could leave Rome to its fate. But the crown and the papers and unmade decisions followed him there for the rest of his life."

Sooner or later the discussion had to turn to Philip, Charles' twenty seven-year-old son and heir. No one could argue that a lifetime of training had not equipped Philip to rule. The fact that he was reared in Spain and hardly knew the Flemish language of his family seat had all but made him a stranger to the people of the Low Countries, but that could be cured in time.

The point was that Philip was at this time in London just across the English Channel. The year before he and seventy ships had landed on the Isle of Wight as one of history's most impressive wedding parties. There the son of Charles V had exchanged vows with Mary, the thirty-seven-year-old daughter of King Henry VIII. Since Mary had been reared in Spain's House of Aragon, Charles had deemed it a politically perfect marriage to the daughter of an old ally. And to make it a match of equals, Charles had allowed Philip to marry as a king by giving him one of his lesser possessions, the Kingdom of Naples. The fact that Mary was round, plain, coarse and "has no eyebrows," as more than one letter writer had described her, demonstrated what Philip would endure to honor his father and serve the empire.

The marriage festivities had consumed over a year beginning with jousts and games on the Isle of Wight and Philip's entourage reveling its way through Sussex and onto Westminster Abbey for the ceremony itself. Afterwards, Philip and his bride had languished for months in Hampton Court and presided over Parliament in November 1554.

So De Guztelo changed the subject. "I suggest that Prince Philip be appraised of the situation and be urged to sail for Brussels as soon as possible," he said addressing the seated lady in a half bow that was beginning to make his back stiff.

"I believe this would put the prince in a difficult situation," she replied. "From his letters I deduce that he has enough challenge accommodating himself to English culture."

"But could it be that he is *too* accommodating?" De Guztelo replied with a mercurial smile. "The reports I receive lack, of course, are not from the perspective of your lordships, coming from ship captains, artillery commanders and the like, but they paint a picture of men weary of drizzle and fog after months of trudging about the English countryside. One such opinion I received just yesterday from Pedro Menéndez, the captain general of Philip's fleet, whom I know your majesties hold in high esteem. He complains of the English as 'white skinned, red cheeked and full of beer to the point of bursting.'"

Lenor was silent and then sighed. "Well, I do know that Philip also enjoys his beer," she said absently.

De Guztelo had spent all of his ammunition save one. "My lady, I will consume no more of your precious time," he said. "I merely wish you to consider this: winter will come soon enough to the English harbors and I know that Menéndez will be urging Philip to sail for Spain before then. Right now Philip is but two or three days from this palace. Should he be in faraway Castile when winter comes and the emperor is incapacitated beyond what you and I now witness, what then? What then for the empire and all that Charles has built over the past nearly forty years?"

On October 25, 1555 all of Brussels was bedecked with banners streaming from balconies and garlands swinging from doorways. The square before the Royal Palace, known to locals simply as The Coudenberg, was filled with people from all stations, but less distinguishable by rank on this day because mayors and knights were dressed as resplendently as dukes and barons. More color was added by the placards of the great guilds that were hoisted above the crowd. In just one corner of the square one could see the banners of the famous Guild of the Tapestry Makers, whose masterpieces filled European palaces. Over there was the Guild of Gardeners, whose floral artistry was evident everywhere despite the chilly fall air. Beside them, the Guild of the Armorers, whose suits of mail were sought by knights everywhere for their resistance to musket balls.

Officially, it was a sad occasion. Emperor Charles V was to announce his abdication. But he had served notice that the event should be as grand a spectacle as a coronation. And why not? the people responded. For most, Charles had reigned throughout their lifetimes, or at least longer than they could remember.

The ceremony would take place in the Aula Magna, or throne room of the Royal Palace, built in the fifteenth century for Charles' grandfather, Philip the Good of Burgundy. From three high walls hung the world's richest tapestries, most of them commemorating the emperor's many conquests. At the farthest end of the Aula Magna a large platform had been erected with a throne and canopy above it. On each side of the throne was a gilded chair—one for Prince Philip, newly arrived from England, and the other for his younger sister Mary, who ruled as regent queen of Austria-Hungary and governess of the Netherlands.

Ringing the royal platform were richly covered seats for nobility and knights. Behind these were plain wooden benches built for ordinary citizens, but on this occasion by the cream of the realm—officers of state, ambassadors, magistrates and provincial officers, most of them heavily weighted with large medallions hanging from their necks to proclaim their importance. Behind the rows of benches were other festively festooned citizens who had managed to bribe or elbow their way inside and who felt fortunate to accept standing room only. Ringing the walls behind them was a phalanx of royal archers and halberdiers in the unlikely need to keep the peace.

As the crowd filed into the Aula Magna, Charles V had already signed the papers of abdication in an adjoining chapel and was concluding a brief mass with his royal retinue. But now the attendees ceased their buzzing as the chapel door opened to reveal Charles, leaning heavily on the arm of the twenty-two year-old William, Duke of Orange.

The crowd reacted almost as one with a soft groan that sounded like a dying man's last expiration. Collectively they had recognized the once handsome Burgundian face with the familiar blue eyes and pointed nose. Some in the crowd had been with the brave, gallant soldier who had taken bold—almost reckless—actions in battle in the course of forging his empire. But this gloomy, gaunt figure was dressed all in black and word would quickly circulate that he had done so to show his humility before God.

After the abdication document was read—a dry recitation of kingships, dukedoms and grand masterships of various knightly orders relinquished—Charles rose to a breathless silence, one arm leaning on a crutch, the other on the young Duke of Orange. He cleared his throat and said weakly that he would reflect on his "achievements." What followed was a rambling recollection of the many trips he made to Germany, Italy, Spain, Portugal, England, Austria, France and The Netherlands. Mixed in were hazy sketches: meeting Martin Luther in Worms in 1520. An audience with Cortés and Pizarro, the conquerors of New Spain. Listening to the tales of the explorer Magellan. A visit with Pope Adrian IV. His verbal jousts with the irascible but entertaining Henry III in England.

Where were the battles? The triumphs? Pedro Menéndez de Avilés was in the rear standing-room-only crowd that strained to hear what could have been an elderly bard or troubadour musing over his wanderings to some travelers seated around a campfire. Then it struck him: this emperor had set out from the beginning to distinguish his rule from all those who had gone before him. Rather than establish a seat of power and compel others to come to him, this emperor decided early that he would rule wherever he happened to be needed the most. Yes, Alexander the Great was also peripatetic, but he stayed only long enough to conquer. Charles had also come to stay and learn the language and customs of his subjects. And his charisma had won them over because he would drink with soldiers, hone a crossbow with their tradesmen and joust with the best of them.

A spark of that charisma remained in the Aula Magna, because women were crying into their fans and men were wiping imaginary specks from their eyes. Perhaps few realized it like Pedro Menéndez de Avilés, but by recounting his wanderings as a humble pilgrim, the emperor had evoked powerful images that encompassed a remarkable life. Just mentioning France, for example, was enough to evoke the capture and imprisonment of his nemesis, King Henry II. Mere mention of the names Cortés and Pizarro conjured up the conquests of Mexico and Peru and the galleons of precious metals that now flowed to the empire. The very name of Luther inflamed all Catholics with their emperor's passion against the Protestant Heresy that threatened the Holy Roman Empire as much as did the Ottoman Turks and their menacing Islam. They could even forget in their tearful emotion the fact that the same Charles V had nearly bankrupted his subject governments to finance his wars, or that his Inquisition had killed thousands including, perhaps, even their own family members.

But more weeping was to follow. The stooped man in black evoked a gasp from the crowd when he said he thought of his life as largely a "failure." He had failed to purge the world from Protestantism in the north, had not repulsed the Turks from the doorstep of Venice, had not stopped French corsairs from plundering Spanish settlements in the New World and raiding the ships that tried to supply them. Perhaps also recalling wives and mistresses discarded or neglected in the name of kingly obligations, he said "I know well that in my long reign I have fallen into many errors and committed some wrongs, but it was only from ignorance. And if there are any here whom I have wronged, they will believe it was not intended and grant me their forgiveness."

Did Philip himself belong among the "failures" of his father? By raising the prince in Spanish Castile-León, he had deprived his son of exposure to northern Europe and its languages, often leaving the impression of an austere and haughty ruler. But now, as the emperor, near fainting, sank back into his throne, Philip was so moved that he dropped to his knees before his father, seized his hand and kissed it. With labored effort, Charles placed his trembling hands on his son's head and, making the sign of the cross, blessed him in the name of the Holy Trinity.

"No, no, he was not a failure," whispered Pedro Menéndez de Avilés to the man next to him. "Only in his own mind. He still has New Spain. And his son will have *us*."

"What is *that* supposed to mean?" Bartolomé Menéndez shot back to his brother from the side of his mouth.

"Later," said Pedro Menéndez. "We will talk."

The emperor's back was now to the crowd as he was being helped back into the chapel—the last time all but fifty or so escorts would ever see him. By then it was widely known that the former emperor and a small retinue would retire to the monastery of St. Jerome in the craggy Spanish mountains of Extramadura. As the pensive attendees were shuffling outside into the sunny palace square, many still wiping their eyes, Bartolomé observed that his older brother seemed almost jaunty. "All right, what is it you want to talk about?" he asked in a challenging tone.

"Not here," said Pedro, enjoying his brother's ignorance. "Let's walk a bit." They left the square and were soon bouncing down a narrow cobblestone alleyway named Herb Market Street. "Few people will be buying herbs today," said Pedro. "All the Low Landers will be in the big beer gardens shouting toasts to the new king."

He steered Bartolomé into a small quiet tavern and ordered two ales. "Besides, we can speak Castilian in here and not worry about being overheard." He leaned back, took a long quaff and propped his boots on an adjacent bench. The low-timbered room was almost dark in mid-afternoon and a lone barmaid was wiping plates with a towel. Neither Menéndez brother had eaten since breakfast and they wasted no time in ordering the sausage and boiled onion special that was already simmering in a large crock beside the open fireplace.

Yes, Pedro Menéndez de Avilés was feeling cheerfully confident because he could sense being in the right place at the right time. Pedro and Bartolomé had been born in the middle of a family with twenty one children in the rugged hills of Austuria on the northernmost coast of Spain, salt-sprayed by the windy Bay of Biscay. Families tended to cluster together in trades for self-protection, and those that failed to entrench themselves in commerce would send their sons off to sea in the king's fleet or work in the shipyards that lined the long harbor that led from the blustery Bay.

The Menéndez clan could at best be described as the offspring of minor Austrian nobles. But they had begun to cobble together a seafaring reputation by investing in shipbuilding, leasing their galleons to the king's agents and/or furnishing the captains and crews to pilot them to the New World. Four Menéndez brothers had already captained vessels to New Spain, but none so conspicuously as Pedro. He had incurred sizeable loans to build two ships, and then recouped his investment by boldly seizing French corsairs in the Caribbean. Menéndez was at last captured by the French and kept in gentlemanly incarceration while his captors cast about for ransom money. After hearing of French plans to launch a massive raid on the Indies, he finagled a loan to ransom himself, and then showed up in Mexico City to report the plot to the Spanish viceroy.

What could be done about the vile threat? The decision, prodded by Menéndez himself, was to appoint him Captain-General of the Indies in charge of forming a powerful armed fleet to withstand any corsair attacks and then escort an especially valuable shipment of gold and silver back to Spain. Until then, Spanish treasure ships had sailed unescorted or in twos and threes. From then on, taking the lead of young Menéndez, nearly all shipments from New Spain traveled to Europe as an armed "treasure fleet."

Reports of his daring and seamanship soon reached Prince Philip, who selected Menéndez for the high honor of commanding his seventy vessels on their wedding journey to England. Now, at age thirty-seven and already with a son in the family seafaring service, he could hardly wait for the next chapter in his life to begin.

Bartolomé tilted his mug, took a long swallow to clear the street dust from his throat and concluded with a well-practiced belch that he knew would make his brother's eyes roll. "So, why did you want to argue with the emperor when he declared his life a failure?" he asked.

"Well, I meant that while he may be a failure in his own eyes, he would not be in ours," answered the older brother. "He is a failure to himself because he is obsessed with the Protestant Heresy. I think the lowest point for him came three years ago when he entered Innsbruck thinking everyone in the Alps would welcome their emperor. It wasn't so much that Henry of France and the Protestant princes ganged up on him, it was having to escape scrambling down the Brenner Pass and into Italy with all that cold rain pelting them and his people tossing their baggage behind them.

"Being down in that valley with Frenchmen still shooting at him might have seemed like the low point of his life at the time. But I think the lowest point was this month when he finally realized he had to sign the Peace of Augsburg. That's what's killing him—especially the section that guarantees every state in the empire the right to decide its own religion.

"But that's not *our* perspective, is it?" Pedro added with mischievous eyes that looked down from his tilted tankard. "Did you hear him say that if it weren't for New Spain he would have lost Europe? Well, New Spain, thanks to his vision years ago, is still there and it's more important than ever to the crown. And the emperor can congratulate himself for raising a son who appreciates it. And we in turn can rejoice because his seat of power is Castile-León, which receives all the money from the Indies."

Pedro Menéndez loved dumping new challenges in his brother's lap. Seven years younger, Bartolomé had been sent to a Jesuit school in Asturia as part of a family strategy to lift at least one of their ilk above the station of seaman and tradesmen. There, Bartolomé would learn Latin, polished Castilian, and a way with words that could charm bankers and barmaids alike. And Pedro felt a twinge of jealousy because, at thirty, the carefree Bartolomé could still eat and drink all he wanted and keep a flat stomach. The older Menéndez had grown thicker in all directions, which he blamed on too many days at sea living on a cramped deck.

"Brother," he added, looking straight into the inquiring eyes of Bartolomé, "the time has come for you to return to Avilés and form a syndicate to build at least two more ships—galleons if you raise enough money, bergantines if you must. I would go with you except for the need to assemble this fleet at Cadiz."

"And what if our investors actually ask for what purpose their money will be used?" asked Bartolomé with an arched eyebrow.

"Yes, I know. For now you'll have to say we expect it to be leased in the king's service, but you can hint at something grander in the offing."

"Such as?"

"Between brothers?" Pedro Menéndez raised his pewter stein and clanked it against Bartolomé's to seal his confidence. "I think all the things I've just mentioned—the pressing need for more money from New Spain plus my increased access to the new emperor, can result in my being named an *adelantado*."

The term made the blood rush in every Asturian boy. Usually it was not a noble, but a hungry, young entrepreneur who was willing to sign a contract with the king granting him almost unlimited authority over an unexplored territory if he financed the expedition himself and gave twenty or so percent of his as-yet-undiscovered riches to the crown. But the adelantado's wealth had to come swiftly because the title was usually granted for only three or four years. If an adelantado succeeded in establishing a profitable settlement, he would in time be replaced by a viceroy or lesser employee of the crown. If he failed, his ship logs and maps might be studied by future explorers who hoped to avoid his mistakes.

"Ah, from captain-general to adelantado," said Bartolomé, this time with both eyebrows raised. "All right, but adelantado of what? We once had adelantados in Mexico, Peru and Guatemala, but now that we have supposedly created civilization there, we have a viceroy. But let me guess. You want to lead another expedition into New Mexico the way Coronado did a few years ago?"

"No, of course not," said Pedro. "The royal family still gets indigestion at the mention of that sad undertaking."

"Well, the only time a king appoints an all-powerful adelantado is when a place is so unexplored or savage that he has nothing to lose. Where, then?"

"You've forgotten to mention Florida," said Pedro sternly, knowing he was being toyed with.

"Florida? All I know is what I've seen from a ship's gunwale. It's all flat, sand and apparently full of cannibals from some of the stories we hear. No mountains. No gold. Oh, Madre de Dios, the bankers of Austuria will surely be eager to hear my story."

"Clot!" said Pedro in his elder brother tone. "It isn't all about gold and silver. Now listen to me! In the 1520s when we began unlocking the mother lode from the new world, the annual return quickly rose to one million pesos a year, with the crown's share at about twenty five percent. But it's taken all of the next twenty five years to inch that return up to around two million pesos a year and it's never enough to support the demands of the empire in Europe. I've been to Mexico City and I've heard the mine operators in their cups complaining that the richest veins of ore are played out and the Indians are wearing out. The king expects what they cannot deliver.

"Now, dear brother, think beyond mining and gold. I would wager that Florida from bow to stern is larger than Mexico. Think of vast estates planted with Valencia oranges and supplying all of Europe at twice today's profit. Think herds of cattle and ships supplying the armies of Europe directly to their port cities. Right now they have begun growing sugar cane on Cuba and Hispaniola and the first harvests are expected to produce one hundred thousand pesos of profit. This is the future for New Spain! Think of what might be grown on the flat sandy fields of Florida. Sugar, bananas, pineapples! I can't say which will prove the best choices, but you have to go there to find out. If all I'm going to do is haul casks of wine and pens of sheep to Mexico, I'd be better off delivering goats from an oxcart in Avilés. At least I could go home every night and see my wife and children."

The food and ale were putting Pedro Menéndez de Avilés in an expansive mood. At least Bartolomé was listening. "Once the enterprise is launched, all sorts of good things can happen," he continued. "Some say that one of the inlets on the Florida coast leads to a great inland sea and from there to a shorter passage to Mexico. Or maybe we can find the Fountain of Youth that Ponce de León believed in so devoutly."

"Before the savages killed him," said Bartolomé with a smirk.

"There's one thing more that you can at least imply to people in the syndicate. You know how I've warned about the French outfitting more—not fewer—Corsairs. Well, I think they're also building a fort somewhere on the eastern shore of Florida. Do you not think that will drive King Philip crazy if I tell him? Do you not see that more corsairs equal more capture and more French goods sold in the harbor of Avilés?"

The beer was making Bartolomé as enthusiastic as it made Pedro expansive, but he liked to tease his brother. "Are you sure you just aren't in love with the *adelantado* title?"

"Dolt!" fumed Pedro Menéndez de Avilés, swinging his feet under the table and facing the younger man four-square. "You may be 'educated,' but you never think on a grand enough scale. This isn't about me. This is about persuading a new king to share our view that the merchants of Seville and the south have acquired a suffocating control of the New Spain trade. This is about the people of Asturia claiming a fairer share of trade and wealth instead of simply sending boys from poor households to sail and die at sea. And if the Menéndez family emerges as the most powerful family all of Biscay because of it, then my glory will be yours as well. If I am to be an adelantado, it means that even a sheep turd like you will at least be an alcaide with entire towns under your command."

Because Bartolomé had remained silent, Pedro added, "Of course you can't tell an investor he's doing this to make the Menéndez family wealthy. You have to be sure to portray the wealth and glory that will come to *him*."

"What about the religious factor?" asked Bartolomé, chewing on the last of his sausage and onions. "There are always some who would invest only if they could be sure they were helping to spread the Holy Gospel to heathens."

"Yes, I know," said Pedro slumping back in his seat and stroking his gray-flecked beard. "This is the most difficult piece in the puzzle. I know for certain that Philip would not approve of the enterprise unless it included some provision for pacifying the natives and converting them peacefully, but it has to involve fresh thinking—some new approach that would capture the king's imagination. I need time to think about it."

"Well, the Dominicans, Franciscans and Augustinians all seem to have mucked things up in Mexico," said Bartolomé crooking his finger at the barmaid for another ale. How about recruiting the Jesuits to our cause?"

"Egad!" declared Pedro with a thump of his tankard on the table. "You've actually come up with a constructive suggestion! You know, it's not a bad idea. They're a sort of new order—what, maybe twenty years old? They're full of young eager priests. Maybe they *would* have a new perspective. At least they wouldn't be arriving in Florida with blood already on their hands. Let me think about it. All I know is that I can't make a presentation to King Philip unless it includes a religious component. In the meantime, when your prospects in Asturia ask about religion, just tell them that we intend to comply in every way with the king's decrees on treatment of Indians."

Pedro and Bartolomé Menéndez went on to finish their late luncheon talking of more immediate matters—letters to be delivered to relatives, a gift of lace from Antwerp for their mother, reports that some of the fresh water casks for the voyage to Spain had been fouled. But always in one corner of Pedro's mind he chewed on that most difficult of all questions: how to pacify and convert native populations. It went beyond Christianity per se. Happy natives were the key to efficient and profitable mining, crop raising, animal herding—even the very survival of settlers whose support system lay in Spain across three thousand miles of unruly ocean.

At the core of the economic conundrum was an institution known by then simply as the *ecomienda*. When the first adelantados left for uncharted explorations, they did so according to a term that embodied royal protection and patronage. That is, an adelantado was granted dominion over a certain expanse of land, along with the right to make claims on Indian labor and other services to assure the prosperity of the community. In turn, he was responsible for protecting native peoples and nurturing them in the Christian faith.

After five years of the first expeditions to Mexico and the Caribbean, forced labor in the silver and gold mines had decimated Indian villages. Conscription and disease had stripped entire islands in the Caribbean of their populations. Scandalous reports of greed and ruthlessness had traveled across the ocean and finally caught up to the Emperor Charles in one of his brocaded European drawing rooms. His alarm was genuine but naïvely idealistic. In 1526 he issued an imperial *Requiremento* stating that upon entering a new territory or recruiting a work force, the appropriate Spanish official was to read aloud to the Indians a long list of their rights against all forms of oppression. Moreover, from that point forward, no Spanish official could enter any war against Indians without the prior approval of the proper religious authorities in that jurisdiction.

Three thousand miles away, the reality was that the proclamation typically would be mumbled by a low-ranking soldier in a language that the blinking Indian chieftain could not understand. In short, it was not only a joke among Spanish settlers, but demonstrated to them the remoteness of Charles from real life in New Spain. Did he not realize, they fumed, that the emperor's fine wine and raiment depended on their ability to mine gold, raise sheep and grow Brazil wood with Indian labor? Did he grasp the struggle they faced in trying to make it happen with a shiftless people who lied, smelled bad, ran off at the touch of a switch and had no understanding of the legal system?

Yet more royal proclamations followed, and by 1542 the cauldron was at a near boil. In that year, Bartolomé de las Casas, the bold reformist bishop of Guatemala, returned to Spain and soon inflamed all Europe with a book claiming that insatiably greedy Spanish colonists had killed from fifteen to twenty million Indians. He won the ear of Charles with his charismatic persona, and in the same year the emperor issued another decree forbidding any Spaniard to buy or sell *any* slaves. Later Charles issued a "personal statement" freeing all slaves and directing his supreme court to "enquire continually into excesses and ill treatment which are or shall be done to natives." As for the *ecomiendas,* "those who hold them without proper titles shall forfeit them." All Indians, it concluded, "shall be under protection of the crown and well treated."

Several Indians in New Spain, had been taught to read by the friars, and it hadn't taken long before the whole native population seized upon the emperor's "personal statement" as emancipation from chiseling ore or picking corn or hauling building blocks. Within three months the fields were bare of workers. The price of wheat and corn had risen tenfold. Spanish families prepared to abandon their homes and signed up en masse for the treasure fleet's next return trip.

Back in Seville, the all-powerful Council of the Indies had already been alarmed by reports of "a law that cannot be obeyed" and made plans to call a conclave of the highest nobles to debate the next course. Meanwhile, it declared the "danger so great that no new expeditions are to be licensed without the (emperor's) express permission and that of the Council."

Jacobo de Testera, head of the Franciscans in Mexico, had been in Spain when the new decrees were issued and had become caught in the wave of magnanimity that had surged through Christendom. Once back in Mexico City, when de Testera announced a mass to proclaim the new laws, a large crowd of cheering Indians greeted him like a viceroy. As he approached the cathedral on foot, they swept the street before him as they had once done for Montezuma.

Then an event in the Yucatán made the cauldron boil over. It's not clear: perhaps colonial landowners had attempted to force their workers back to the plantations, but in 1546 an angry, vicious Indian revolt swept through the peninsula faster than molten lava. It had begun when some marauding Mayans had kidnapped a bishop and cut off his arms and legs. Carrying their bloody trophies, they ran to various villages to give the people courage to join them. In the ensuing rampage Spanish settlers breathed their last by seeing their hearts cut from their chests. Others were put on spits and smoked like meat. Many more were shot through with arrows and left on the ground to be torn apart by dogs.

How could these savages have turned their backs on nearly thirty years of civilization? How could they have clung to hideous idols and rejected the grace and redemption offered by the true Son of God?

Ah, answered Charles and his prelates, perhaps because the colonials did not practice the ways of Jesus as well as they had preached it. And so, agencies of the emperor continued to turn the other cheek with conciliatory edicts aimed at unlocking the secret to Indian enlightenment. In 1551 the Council of Trent declared that Indians had souls and could be converted—an attempt to quell a dispute among clerics as to whether God intended for savages to be baptized. Then the Casa de Contratación, which regulated ships and their cargoes traveling to the new world, ruled that supplies to the Indies should include Bibles translated into native tongues. But it also forbade export of romances and other works of fiction lest Indian readers question whether the Bible might also contain fiction.

In short, relations with Indians remained a muddle, as unhappy and unresolved as was Charles V himself on this day of his abdication. And it was this riddle that preoccupied Pedro as the two Menéndez brothers walked back in late afternoon to the lodgings they shared, each too stuffed with beer and sausage for much conversation. Within the month Pedro would be sailing from southern Spain with another armada of settlers and supplies. Sometime between then he would send one of his brothers to the new king to hand deliver a letter proposing a new enterprise for forlorn Florida.

His plan had to be unique and compelling. Yet, it was agonizingly ill-formed. He knew that one pillar must be conversion of Indian souls and a second one exploration of the land—especially for discovering the much talked about waterway passage across the peninsula of Florida.

The third milestone on the road to becoming an adelantado was a plan to combat the French threat in New Spain. Still clear in the mind of Menéndez was a conversation that took place in the previous week aboard Prince Philip's *capitana,* or flagship, during the short crossing from England to Antwerp. Menéndez was standing on the forecastle idly examining a new brass sextant when an orderly appeared to say the prince would like a word with him in his cabin. Menéndez had gone expecting some questions about docking and transporting the royal party overland to Brussels. But he found the young prince pensive, looking up from a large map of New Spain. On the table beside it was an open letter on imperial stationery.

"I would like your advice," he said after a crystal of sherry had been served. "You have been to these places. I have not. Thus far my father has reserved to himself all important decisions involving New Spain. Now, if I have been correctly informed, he is," the lean man paused, "*indisposed* to discuss the issue. He seems always interested in allocating the proceeds that come in from the treasure fleets, but now not in how the treasure materializes.

"First, I thought you might gain some satisfaction or amusement from reading a copy of this letter from my files," Philip said handing it to Menéndez, who had thus far felt obligated by protocol to avert his eyes from the contents. In royal calligraphy, it was a copy of a letter from the prince to his father dated November 24, 1551. After recounting the arrival of this many ducats from Honduras, that many from Peru and so forth, Philip had urged the emperor to establish an armed fleet to guard Spain from the coast of Andalusia to the straits of Gibraltar to protect returning treasure ships from French corsairs.

"Thanks to you, it wasn't necessary to activate that fleet around our shores," said the prince. "You furnished protection from shore to shore and I am happy to see you continue in that capacity. But tell me. Based on what you have observed since then, are the French still menacing New Spain and our ships? Do they have plans to establish forts anywhere in New Spain? I welcome your assessment."

Menéndez responded solely on instinct, which was to appear calm, wise and non-committal. "Having been captured by a Corsair, nearly killed and then imprisoned," he replied with a touch of hyperbole, "you can perhaps forgive me for believing the French a grave threat to the security of New Spain. However, I know that your concerns are not for one man, but for a world's security. I would therefore suggest that your majesty give me a few days to reflect on such a critical matter and send you a communiqué encompassing my assessment of the situation."

The prince nodded with a thin smile and finished the last of his sherry. But something made Menéndez add: "I do believe, your majesty, that the French are eager to test the resolve of a new emperor to defend the possessions his father worked so heroically to establish."

Philip had merely ushered him out with a polite wave. Had his selection of words been intemperate? No! They had struck just the right chord.....*anxiety*. He had secured his opening to present his plan to become adelantado of all Florida, and the emperor's fear of the French would be the wedge that drove it home!

CHAPTER FOUR

Little Heron

1561-63

At age twelve, Little Heron's favorite time was early morning. While his mother was still sleeping, he would creep away from the hut with only his deer cloth, sandals and spear. He loved the rippling current of the outgoing tide where the river swung into the Jeaga Inlet on its last push to the sea.

Just beyond the ripples, the water flattened out to a glass-like surface. The rays of the rising sun beamed between the gnarled branches of the live oaks behind the ocean dunes. They streaked the still water and painted colors on the dozen or so canoes that were pulled up on the sand. Soon the air would be alive with the cries of babies and voices of mothers as they cleaned pots, washed clothes and traded gossip; but for now the sunlit water magnified the wonders below—snails digging, minnows darting, and shells glittering.

Little Heron walked on to where the sandy beach gave way to mangroves. He waded knee-deep, sometimes to the waist, for several minutes until he reached a bend in the inlet and began to hear the sound of waves breaking at the mouth, still a half-mile away. There he stood beside a large enclosure that had been created by cutting down spindly pines, breaking the trunks into four-foot lengths, and pounding them side-by-side into the shallow water until they comprised a stockade prison for captured fish.

Although only a few occupants swam idly inside, there would be many more by late afternoon. Several yards ahead a sea grape branch topped with three broad leaves marked the site of a net that had been laid in the water by a team of men and boys. It was made of palm fiber mesh and rung with ark-shell sinkers that also served as handles. The circular net stretched forty feet in diameter. It had been made by Calusa on Pine Island and brought to Jeaga Town as a gift from King Calus at the last Great Gathering. No one used the net much because it was so heavy and required the Jeaga council to muster enough men to lift it. But they would come that day: it was now late October and both mullet and bluefish were running the inlet. A rising tide would be coming in strong that afternoon.

At that moment the tide was low and all was still. Little Heron squatted on his haunches, steadied himself with his spear and let the silence wash over him. No mother nagging him. No teachers filling his head. No boys jostling and jabbering.

And yet, the intensity of all other life around him! Sand crabs burrowing and ibises jabbing at the sand. Minnows darting around his ankles. A blue heron standing on one leg, studying the water intently. A pelican gliding inches over the water. A tarpon fin turning lazily on the surface. A ray lifting itself out of the water. An osprey diving into the water and emerging with a mullet in his talons.

Now he watched a mullet jumping…two, three, four times. Was it trying to fly? Was something chasing it? Or do mullets, he wondered, simply enjoy leaping the way boys like to see how far they can jump?

Beside Little Heron was a row of large mangroves rising twenty feet above the water line. Below the surface, its roots were hiding places for little critters. Some were nibbling at the red bark and the barnacles that grew on them. He ran his hand over the thick, knotted trunk of the nearest tree and decided it must be the oldest mangrove on the inlet. How many years? he wondered. Older than the Jeaga?

After several minutes Little Heron waded to the edge of the staked stockade and peered inside. He had decided that spearing fish in the pen while standing outside the stockade fence was actually easier than standing inside. The reason was that fish tended to huddle in clusters. When the fisherman waded where they were lurking, they darted away too quickly to establish a predictable line of travel like the vee one could see at the surface when they swam in the open river. It was worse when several boys were yelling and splashing about in what always became a contest to see who could stab the most fish. In fact, Little Heron had once spiked his own big toe in such a melee and had since figured out a better way that he hadn't shared with the others. He stalked around the outside, careful not to ripple the water inside or cast his shadow. When he located a cluster of snook dozing motionless in two feet of water, he broke the waterline with his spear before his target could even lurch.

Bright Moon looked up from her breakfast of prickly pears and sea grapes as her son ducked inside with a fat snook hanging from a hook on his belt. "Oh," she said matter-of-factly, "I was thinking I would use one of the gopher tortoises tonight and make a stew— just for a change from fish."

"Then let's make fish stew," said Little Heron.

"Fish, fish, fish," she said. "I think you just don't want to see any of your pets put into a stew pot. I told you not to give them names."

The boy was silent as he began to saw the snook's head off with a sun-ray venus clam knife. She was right, however. He had persuaded his mother to let him build a small pen behind the house. Whenever a gopher tortoise lumbered across their path in the forest, they could put their catch in a basket with a lid and tote it back to the pen. Throw in some leaves and grass and the tortoise would be content—until the day of reckoning.

The gopher tortoise served as insurance against a day, say, when it was too cold or stormy to fish. Just boil a pot of seawater, chop the flat bottom shell with a whelk ax, and plop in a tortoise. Then add coontie root flour to thicken the greasy broth. The only inconvenience, Bright Moon soon learned, was that children tended to name and pamper their gopher tortoises. They also spent hours painting their shells, organizing tortoise races, and blubbering when their favorite pet's turn came to be dinner.

The conversation ended when the old woman, White Ibis, waddled through the opening and greeted them with a grunt. Soon the two women were talking about how to twist mulberry bark and scarcely noticed when Little Heron finished gutting his fish and slipped outside.

At age twelve Little Heron and his mother had reached a new stage in their relationship. He no longer slept curled in her embrace, but on a deerskin at the other end of the room. He was now as tall as Bright

Moon and the separate sleeping quarters had come suddenly when she awoke from sleep to find him feeling parts of her that should belong to a husband.

The separation symbolically marked a new sense of independence for both. On one hand, Bright Moon went into the forest only in the May when her precious saw palmetto berries emerged. Now, she need only remark that she would like to have a jar of persimmons or was running out of sabal palm twine and Little Heron could be counted on to bring it back that day. On the other hand, the variety of his hunting-gathering chores was so great as to let him roam from forest to river-bank to beach. While most boys his age hunted game in packs, Little Heron liked to explore alone—even when it became more like spying.

One topic of his fascination was old Hawkman, the Jeaga shaman and magic maker. The old man with long white hair lived in a large round hut a few yards from the Jeaga council house. Whereas Little Heron had often seen the masks that hung from the council house walls, he could only imagine what lurked inside the small opening of the shaman's house. Because he performed so many roles—healer, medicine maker, curse maker, performer of rituals, appeaser of gods and angry souls—the house must contain the secrets of the universe.

Most curious of all was the shaman himself. At festivals Little Heron had known him only as the mysterious figure behind the fright-ening red and yellow mask with a hawk's beak for a nose. He would plant a red and white striped pole in the ground and then whirl, howl like a wolf and stomp his feet about it until all the grown-ups were moving around the pole in a frenzy of rhythmic shrieking.

Now, when twelve-year-old Little Heron crouched between pal-mettos in the sandy scrub outside the shaman's house, all he saw was a mild-looking old man with a sunken chest and long white hair parted in the middle. When the shaman sat cross-legged outside his house, pounding various powders in wooden mortars with hardened wooden pestles, he was often humming to himself with a dream-like smile.

From his shaded hideout, Little Heron came to learn that when the shaman was ready to receive callers, the red and white pole would be placed outside his entrance and the ferocious hawk mask would be mounted on the wall beside it. When people came in, they would sometimes come out wearing a necklace of three small gourd rattles.

His mother said the rattles scared away the demons that brought fevers and runny noses. If they wore a smudge on their forehead compounded from mud and soot, it meant that they had just had their fortune foretold and that no other powers could change the shaman's vision.

Others came, she said, because someone had snatched away one of their souls, or because one of their souls had rebelled and run away.

"You have three souls," Bright Moon had told her son at an early age. The first lives in the pupils of your eyes and will never leave you. The second is your shadow. The third is the image of yourself you see in the water. If any one of the souls leaves, it can be very difficult to entice it back."

In such cases the afflicted person was instructed to build a small fire at the entrance to his home and wait three days. When the time had passed and the shaman's spells had worked, the soul was willing to return. The afflicted one again called upon Hawkman, at which time he made loud incantations while stuffing an imaginary object into the top of the person's head. Only then could the fire be extinguished.

Little Heron knew that his mother often delivered a basket of palmetto berries to the shaman's house, and he suspected that she also came for advice. He himself was to visit the shaman only once, but it was enough. He was always fascinated by the dozens of lizards that scampered in and out of his hut. They never bothered anyone and they seemed to eat a lot of bugs. One day in the patio outside his house Little Heron caught a lizard in his cupped hands and wondered what it would be like to eat one. It was shiny black with a bright blue tail. He thought of Cougar Claw's story about existing on live shells in the surf and thought maybe he'd tell his grandchildren of how he survived some great peril on a diet of lizard meat.

Before he could think twice about it, the lizard was on its back and chopped in three pieces. Little Heron wrinkled his nose, shut his eyes, and down went the lizard parts with as few chomps as possible. The taste was bitter and slimy. And it felt as if the tail was still wiggling as it slid down his throat.

A half hour later he felt dizzy and his stomach burned. When he staggered into the doorway, moaning and woozy, his mother looked up from her loom with eyes wide open and rushed to him exclaiming, "Oh my poor son, is it your heart? Has someone poisoned you?"

He knew very well what the trouble was but couldn't think of anything plausible to say. Before he could invent anything, Bright Moon had him by the arm marching down the hill and towards the shaman's house.

"Help, the son of Calus has been stricken!" she yelled at his doorway.

Like it or not, Little Heron got his first chance to see inside. An old woman with shriveled breasts was sitting with a bowl in her lap—the shaman's wife?—but she quickly moved out of sight. Hawkman, no taller than Little Heron, rose silently from his bed where he had been napping. As he looked intently into the boy's eyes, Little Heron felt the room spinning before him. His eyelids were twitching uncontrollably.

Hawkman stretched the boy out on the floor of the hut and poked about his stomach. Behind him, various ornamental walking sticks were stacked along one wall. Small ceramic pots of varicolored powders crowded the floor.

"Take him outside. We must do the analysis," said Hawkman picking up a shallow clay bowl. He poured some water in it from a jug, bent over his pots of potions and sprinkled some black and yellow powders into the bowl.

"Now sit up," ordered the shaman, pushing the boy's head downward. "Stir this with your finger and drink."

Speaking to Bright Moon as if Little Heron had no ears, he said: "What he drinks now will cause him to throw up. I will analyze the contents and then tell you what medicines to take for the cure."

They did not have to wait long. Minutes later Little Heron was retching and spilling his stomach into the same bowl. The shaman waited in silence and then took the bowl, beginning to poke about slowly with a stick.

"Ha!" he said to Bright Moon. "Look here!" Lizard parts were floating on top, barely chewed.

"Fool!" he scowled at the boy.

Bright Moon looked shocked and puzzled.

"Idiot, do you know why there are so many blue-tailed skinks in the world? Because no animal will eat them. Unlike you, they are smart enough to know they could die from the poison!"

"Someone tried to poison the king's son?" Bright Moon gasped.

"No, we have a curious boy here who probably cut up the lizard to see how it would taste. Now take this boy home and let his suffering be his punishment. I will expect a basket of something extra nice for my troubles.

"And one thing more," the shaman shouted hoarsely as the boy staggered off with his embarrassed mother. "Stop spying on me from the bushes over there or I will see to it that the spirit of that lizard steals your souls!"

When they were out of sight, old Hawkman began chuckling. Then he laughed until he coughed and his chest hurt. As a boy he had also sampled a lizard. Spied on people, too.

Little Heron's penchant for spying would eventually serve him well in a more respectable pursuit. On a clear, crisp January day in his thirteenth year his uncle Deerstalker again summoned him for what he called "another important lesson." Behind the riverfront by the council house a group of a dozen or so boys his age were gathering. Waiting quietly for the last stragglers was his old teacher, Cougar Claw, wrapped in a blue-dyed blanket. Next to the teacher, erect and with a kind of coiled quiet, was the most impressive man he had ever seen. Ten or fifteen years older than the boys around him, he wore deerskin breeches and white shell necklace over his muscular chest. Atop his head was a large panther skin with the full head and fangs resting atop his scalp. Any boy there would have given his all for one like it.

At last Cougar Claw motioned the boys to form a semi-circle and spoke. "From time to time I see you in the forest hunting. And I want to thank everyone for not shooting me with one of your wild arrows."

Nervous laughter.

"Actually, I notice that many of you are good shots. And you have made yourselves good bows."

He paused and carefully scanned the semi-circle around him. "And yet I see very few tattoos or other markings of the hunt. How many of you have killed a bear?" he asked.

No hands went up.

"Panther?"

No hands.

"How about deer?"

Five hands shot up. "Screech Owl killed a wildcat," said one.

"Yes, but it was in a trap," snickered the boy next to him. More laughter.

"The reason why you have been allowed to run around in the forest shooting at things—and hopefully not each other—is so that you will realize how difficult it is unless you first acquire another skill." The teacher paused and spoke in a slow staccato. "You-must-first-learn-to-find-the-animal-before-you-can-kill-it!"

Cougar Claw paused and turned to the taller, younger man beside him. "This is Panther Warrior, who also happens to be my son. He is the best tracker among the Jeaga, be it animal or human. He is here to teach you some things you will need to know before you can wear your own panther hide or any of those tattoos you crave.

"Panther Warrior will now attempt to show you what I am talking about. Which one is this Screech Owl, the wildcat killer?"

A nervous lad stepped forward. "We will now play some hide and seek just like when you were little children," said the teacher. "Panther Warrior will cover his eyes and I will hold my hands over his ears. Screech Owl, you will run off in any direction for about a hundred yards and hide yourself as best you can. Raise your hand when you are ready."

The boy crept to the edge of the clearing then scampered down a path, zigzagged between some shrubs and hid behind a thick live oak. After a pause, the teacher un-cupped his hands from his son's ears and Panther Warrior removed his hands from his eyes. He stood erect, and then began turning his full body around and around slowly. He picked up a bow and arrow, walked to the edge of the clearing and slowly examined the perimeter. Five times he bent over to feel and smell possible footprints or breaks in the foliage. Then he strode quickly down the same path the boy had taken, kneeling, smelling, feeling and running several times before he stopped at the big oak tree. There his audience gulped from afar as he pulled the bowstring and fired the arrow...into the trunk of the oak tree.

The boy Screech Owl emerged from behind and was still trembling visibly when he returned with the expressionless tracker.

For the rest of this and the next day the boys spent under the tutelage of Panther Warrior. He offered no jokes like his father and they ceased all jawing and jabbering. "Tracking is the last of what you will do before shooting," he said. "To track an animal you must first know what kind of vegetation it prefers, what kind of path it is likely to take, which way the wind is blowing, where the animal likes to sleep at night, whether it creates an escape route when it settles on a lair. My new friend," he said pointing to Screech Owl, "tell me what you can about black bears."

"They eat plants and things, but not meat."

"Correct. So if you are a bear you will not seek the deepest part of the forest because there is not much undergrowth and little vegetation. But you wouldn't go into the open scrub because there's no vegetation and no place to hide. Instead, you would find a place probably on the edge of the forest where there is good vegetation and a wide variety of it. And how would the bear get there? By the shortest path available, just like you and me—unless someone is chasing it."

It was not until the morning of the next day that Panther Warrior began explaining the intricacies of tracking. He began by pouring water over a square of dirt and drawing various animal tracks in the mud.

"You all know this one," he said after drawing two marks in the mud.

"Deer," they all chorused.

"Correct. Now this." He drew a large four-toed track with a much smaller one behind it. "Who knows this?" he asked.

Silence.

"This is easy if you think about it. Squirrels and rabbits hop. And when they land, their larger hind feet are ahead of the small feet in front. So you have to look at this print sort of backwards to tell if the animal is going forwards."

Panther Warrior explained that four toes on both front and hind feet with triangular claw marks indicates the dog family but that four toes with no triangular marks means cat family because cats retract their claws.

Only after a brief noon snack of plums and mashed acorns did Panther Warrior turn to the actual art of stalking. The would-be hunters were told how spot where animals had eaten—and how many. They heard how to look for polished areas where animals had rubbed up against and what kind of plants were likely to snag hair or feathers from a passing animal. They learned how to spot chewed stalks, scratchings on tree trunks, snapped twigs, and dislodged stones. By bending over some broken or bent vegetation, they learned how to inspect the growth since that event in order to tell how long ago the break occurred. The larger the broken plant or dislodged stone, the heavier the passing animal.

"Now that you have identified your bear, you still face the most important question of all...and that is?"

The boys shrugged and looked about.

"Don't you want to know *when* your bear was where you are now standing?"

Panther Warrior explained that in the early morning a tracker can "read" the dew on grass because it is wiped away when an animal passes or steps on it. He showed how bent grass takes about 24 hours to recover from a squashing, and that the angle of the bending can tell how long ago the animal passed. He concluded by describing scat and how it can tell the tracker an animal by type, size and diet.

"Maybe someday soon we will discuss how to track humans," said Panther Warrior in his quiet impassive voice. And with that he walked quickly up one of the footpaths and was soon out of sight.

Cougar Claw organized the dozen boys into two groups of six in hopes of spurring some competitive tracking. The objective was for one group to hide while the other stalked them. The boys were eager to play because they naturally divided by the same clans—Mako Shark and Gray Panther—that had always contested for leadership of the Jeaga.

It was a bad idea, however. The faction that was supposed to be in hiding always jostled or whispered so loudly that they gave themselves away. Cougar Claw ended the horseplay by forming six teams of two —chosen by lot—and told them they were to practice tracking for the next three days.

It was Little Heron's bad luck to draw the boy he disdained most for a partner. Bobcat was a short, squat roughneck who lived somewhere in the Gray Panther section along the inlet. He wore black greasy paint around his eyes at all times. When he'd go swimming and come out of the water, the black paint would run in streaks, boys around him would laugh, and Bobcat would be punching out at everybody without knowing why.

Bobcat liked being the center of attention as much as Little Heron shunned it. Recently when walking alone in the forest he came across Bobcat and two other boys who had just upended a gopher tortoise who happened into their path. "Hey, he'd make great target practice," shouted Bobcat. "Why not take him home and make him a racer," suggested Little Heron.

Without a reply Bobcat took the tortoise to the base of a big pine tree and set it upright against the trunk, legs flailing helplessly. "Let's try it at forty paces," he said. "Me first."

The gopher tortoise was long dead and Little Heron could still hear the whine and thwack of arrows striking their dead target as he walked back towards home. "I hope the spirit of the gopher tortoise steals his souls," he thought.

Bobcat had little patience for tracking. On their second day together when the two had agreed to meet at the trail-head leading westward upriver, he showed up with his bow and quiver. "This time we'll be a real team," he announced. "You track and I'll shoot."

Little Heron gave a shrug and the two had soon left the last Jeaga huts behind, taking a seldom-used, narrower pathway leading to the Southwest Fork of the River of Turtles. In a half hour they were approaching the ancient cypress trees that lined the banks of the wide but shallow creek. The sun had begun to warm the cool winter day, the silence broken only by calls of birds heralding the arrival of two-legged strangers. Heron pointed to the large ferns amidst them, some patched with white, some with gray goo. "Turkey shit, this one," he whispered. "Gray shit, large owl. Many turkeys. Maybe just one owl."

He rubbed his finger over one of the white patches. "See? Not even dry yet."

"You're the shaman of shit," whispered Bobcat.

"You need light arrows," said Heron, ignoring him. "I'll circle around over there and start walking toward you and making noise. If I get lucky and come across a nest, your turkey will come up from the ground. Or maybe one will fly from a tree."

In a minute Heron was swinging a dead tree branch in front of him and yelling "Turkey, turkey, turkey!" Despite his prediction, he was soon startled when the brush broke in front of him and a large turkey fluttered up and landed on a low cypress branch. Bobcat ran towards the tree with bow pulled, pierced the bird with his first arrow and made certain of his kill with a second arrow as soon as it fell to the ground.

Both boys stared at each other with jaws open. They had tracked and killed wild game! It had all taken less than ten seconds.

Having scoured the bush and trees in vain for other signs of life, Bobcat tied a piece of long twine around the dead bird's feet and carried it over one shoulder. Soon they were balancing atop the muddy flats that lined the shoreline of the Southwest Fork, peering into the tea-colored water. The surface was glassy, broken only by dozens of cypress knees protruding from the surface like a tribe of river goblins watching their every move.

Except for one thing, the scene could have been untouched for a thousand years. Thirty feet to their left Heron spotted an unnatural rise of greenery about three feet high and six feet long. When he crept up to the clump he could see a blackish stain in the middle of piled-up grasses with some dried egg shell fragments and pieces of what was probably a shorebird. Instinctively he jumped back and in the corner of his eye saw a log drop beneath the water's surface.

"Let's move," he whispered to Bobcat. "This is an active alligator nest and I think I just saw a big gator head go under the water."

Bobcat spun around. The two held their breath watching the water. Sure enough, in two minutes the large head surfaced again only forty or so feet offshore. Soon they could see the outline of a tail. Ten, maybe eleven feet from tip to tip. Pointed toward them.

"Here's what we're going to do," proclaimed Bobcat loudly, swinging the turkey from his shoulder. "We're going to give Mister Alligator a little snack so we can take back a big dinner to Jeaga Town." As Heron was still beginning to process the scene and its consequences, Bobcat broke the two arrows that had protruded from his kill. He put the fish-bone tips in his belt pouch, pulled the arrows from the turkey and began surveying the tree branches above him nearest the shore. Finding the highest, strongest branch he could reach on tiptoe, he pulled it down and knotted the twine until the turkey swayed from the branch.

"Now we're going to go back home," he yelled to the river as if the snout protruding in the water could understand Jeaga talk.

Heron followed, swallowing hard. "How many arrows do you have left?"

"Four."

"They'd better be long and thick," said Heron.

All were for light game—turkeys, rabbits, maybe a deer if you got lucky. But Bobcat didn't answer. They found a thick cypress thirty feet from the swinging bait and crouched behind it, Bobcat holding his bow and arrow.

The vee in the water remained motionless. At last the great knobby head came out, surveying the scene. All was quiet. Two minutes. Five minutes. A mosquito landed on Heron's arm but he let it drill in silence.

The alligator log floated towards shore. Suddenly the placid water burst. A ten-foot alligator leaped five feet in the air with jaws wide open, chomped down on the turkey, swung writhing from the twine and fell to the ground with its reward—all in the gasp of a breath. As the giant began tearing at its meal with its massive jaws, Bobcat darted out from behind Heron and snapped an arrow into the gator's side with a thud. Now just ten feet away, Bobcat had no sooner reached for his second arrow when a black streak shot across his path. Suddenly a second alligator was contesting with the first for what remained of the turkey. As the two gators snarled and snapped, Heron ran out, grabbed the bow from behind, spun around the surprised Bobcat and pulled him back along the path. "Run now or the big dinner will be us," he gasped.

As they had run, half falling, panting, to a safe distance away from the creek, it was clear that Bobcat hadn't seen the second alligator and could have soon made both gators forget about their turkey dinner. His blackened eyes were streaked with what could only have been tears of fear.

But Bobcat had his own version of events. By the next morning when the young hunters again gathered around Cougar Claw, Bobcat had already told and re-told the story of the titan struggle with two giant alligators up and down Jeaga Town. "I had an arrow in one of them and would have killed the second. But then the Calusa King's knees began to shake and he begged me to run off. We all could have been eating alligator steaks for the next two months if it weren't for him."

Heron kept quiet. I know I'm smarter than Bobcat, he thought, but maybe he *would* have killed two alligators. Maybe I *am* a coward.

At this point, Heron only wanted to be rid of his tracking partner. He was relieved when Bobcat showed up the next morning with only a spear, but not for long. They started up the same westward trail as the day before, about to pass the cluster of canoes that lined the riverfront across from the buildings of the Calusa Gathering Place.

"Let's have a *real* tracking adventure," said the brazen Bobcat with a crooked smile. "You're good at tracking animals, but how about tracking the dead?"

"The dead?"

"Let's take this old eighteen-footer," said Bobcat, tossing a pouch of fruits and nuts into a neglected canoe full of rainwater and pine needles. "Nobody will miss it for a day. Let's go up the North Fork and explore. Nobody goes up there. We'll try to find The Place of the Dead and see what it's all about. We can be the first of the young warriors to do it."

Heron stood silent at the water's edge with a dumfounded expression. Few had seen the Place of the Dead. No one talked about it. He only knew that when someone died unexpectedly, the eldest sons in the family took the body and some libations to a place far upriver and gave it to a shaman or caretaker who no one seems to have ever seen. All Heron knew was that when the sons of the deceased returned, they had to remove all of their clothes and burn them as the old shaman chanted strange words and spread a smoky powder all around. But nobody wanted to be near the remains because the soul might jump out and put a curse on them.

"But how do you know where this place *is?*" was all Heron could manage to say.

"My uncle told me," said Bobcat, scooping handfuls of pine needles from the canoe. "You go upriver a mile or so past the Gathering Place, then you go up the North Fork maybe a mile or two more until, my uncle says, the river gets narrow and deep. I don't know exactly, but that's why we're exploring. You're the great tracker. All you need to do is sniff out where they drag dead bodies," he said, laughing at his dark humor.

Heron visualized the blustery Bobcat spreading another tale about how the Coward Cacique failed another test of courage. Without a word he swung a leg over the side of the shallow canoe and pushed off.

It would not be a long trip, but one Heron would always remember. It was a chilly winter morning, but the wind and incoming tide pushed the little canoe rapidly upstream and around the broad bend where opposing white beaches marked the entrance to the North Fork of the River of Turtles. From there they looked for signs of life as they continued along an unbroken shoreline of mangroves and tall pines. If The Place of the Dead lay at the end of this, it certainly wasn't announcing itself with any trails or markers.

Heron was already beginning to calculate the tough return trip against the wind and current when he saw a clump on the narrow white beach ahead to the west. A rock out of place amid the sand? A log? Maybe a marker. They paddled closer and saw it move. Closer and they could make out a human figure. Soon it focused into an old woman.

She was very old. Her straight gray hair was pulled into a bun, which held a wilted feather. Her cheeks were sunken and the rest of her face wrinkled like a prune from the sun. Hanging from her exposed collar bones was a ragged, threadbare tunic that barely covered knees so thin that they might pop out of her skin like an overcooked dove.

But Heron would always remember her eyes. They burned like small black coals, never wavering, never blinking.

"Old woman," shouted Bobcat. "Is this the Place of the Dead? By the looks of you, it *should* be."

She spat out a nearly soundless "hah!" like a cornered cat.

The nose of the canoe edged onto the beach where she sat not six feet away, propped by one hand with bony legs outstretched. In a pine tree a few feet behind her, four turkey buzzards sat silently on a limb.

Bobcat, jumped out, leaning on his spear. "Is this where you live? Are you waiting for someone?"

Again, stony, defiant silence.

"Old woman," Heron called gently, "do you have food?" He reached into his pouch of fruits and nuts, but if she was hungry, the eyes did not betray it.

Bobcat poked at her with the blunt end of his spear. She snarled again like a wounded animal.

Instinctively, Heron put his palm before the searing eyes and waved it back and forth.

"She's blind," he said.

Then the voice cracked like the wind rustling through a dried palm frond. "Go! I am here to die. I wait for Taku."

"But how did you get here?" asked Heron. "Why this place on the river?"

After another silence, she forced herself to sit up and crossed her arms. "They bring me here. All Jeaga go here one day. Now you go."

Heron washed off a sun-bleached whelk and scooped up some of the fresh river water. When he poured some over her badly cracked lips, she spat it out.

"You *go!*" she snarled.

They did—with all energies of exploring the Place of the Dead suddenly dissipated. Heron had never seen Bobcat as silent and pensive as he had on the return trip, and he wasn't about to spoil the moment.

When Heron had returned home, after a dinner of grilled snook, persimmons and coontie cakes, and when he and his mother had stepped outside to watch the stars shine into the river below on a windless, clear night, Heron calmly explained what he had seen that day.

"Who was she?" he asked evenly. "Why was she there? Who took her? Was that the Place of the Dead?" These and more questions tumbled out.

But Bright Moon was as stony as her namesake in the heavens. "It is our way," was her stoic response to almost every question. Yes, she knew the woman, but not very well. She was a member of the Gray Panther clan. She had a name once—Pink Hibiscus—but no longer. She was blind and feeble. Could not sew nor gather herbs nor care for infants nor even cook for her family. She had to be watched over like a baby. And she soiled her clothing like a baby.

"And for that she was taken away to die?" asked Heron.

"So that her souls could be freed to enter another life."

"Will this happen to you and me as well?"

"Yes, my son. That is our way."

On a brisk morning in February of his fourteenth year Heron found himself surveying the peppers and gourds and squash that grew on the sandy patch behind his dwelling. Bright Moon had accidentally broken a water gourd and had told her son to find the biggest one he could to replace it.

"Ho, what's this?" he exclaimed aloud. As he felt along the roots of vines, his fingers had unearthed a four-inch-long worm shell that had been placed upright in the sand. What most drew his attention was that the top had been painted with a face—bright brown eyes, black nose and red smiling lips.

"Mother! Mother! Look what I've found in the garden!" he exclaimed, startling Bright Moon at her loom. "Look at the strange face on the shell I found!"

Rather than being amazed or at least curious, Bright Moon snatched the shell from his hand. "It's a talisman," she said sternly. "We must bury it again before its power is broken!" She held the slim shell cupped in both hands and close to her chest, swaying as if rocking a baby.

Now it was Heron's turn to be startled. It was only after her son refused to budge—staring back as if she might be deranged—that Bright Moon softened and continued in a tone mothers use when explaining eternal truths to their children.

"This was given to me by the shaman," she said. "It is an omen of good fortune—for *you*, my son."

"For me?"

"It represents the face of Shabula."

"The god of good luck?"

"Yes, the younger brother of Taku. While Taku rules the heavens and the weather, Shabula pays attention to the fortunes of those who call upon him."

"But what has this to do with me?" asked Heron.

"Very much. The painted face of Shabula will cause my husband the Great Cacique to come for his son and bring him back to Mound Key to be raised as the next ruler of the Calusa." Her voice rose as she elevated the sacred icon with one arm.

"And my mother as well?"

"Yes," she nodded solemnly, clasping his hand around the shell. "Now go back. Bury it quickly. And remember, it must be upright."

Until then Heron had managed to banish his memories of King Calus to a dark corner of his mind, but the incident dispelled any notion that his mother had done the same. In fact, the episode seemed to have loosened her tongue and brought forth a torrent of repressed torments.

"You are becoming of age," she would suddenly erupt in the middle of sweeping or sewing or kneading a ball of coontie flour. The Great Cacique will come soon and you must prove yourself worthy of rule."

Actually, according to gossip in Jeaga Town, King Calus was preparing to summon a Great Gathering after the summer rains had passed. The number of Spanish ships passing on the horizon had increased and Indian traders from the north had reported more attempted incursions by warriors from these ships. Wild tales were circulating about shore parties of invaders armed with weapons that made a flash of great noise and shot out heavy stones with such force that they could make a man's head disappear. The council house was tense with discourse and the only conclusion of the elders was that the threat was so grave as to require a united war strategy among the entire Calusa confederation.

Bright Moon knew it and knew, too, that her moment of glory was coming—or not. Now thirty-five, she already felt herself in danger of succumbing to the comfort of her routine, her fleshy appearance and the melancholy truth that learning to be "with a man" again might be too much of a bother. But with each report that the Great Cacique might actually come this year—and who knew when again—Bright Moon seemed to wave off all such thoughts as if shaking a winter's dust from a bed blanket.

And each time, Heron felt her burst of bravado. "This is your destiny," she would say. "You must excel at the hunt." Or at canoe racing. Or shark hunting or hurling of the atlatl—whatever the upcoming sporting contest that happened to catch her attention. Eventually it all blended into a noise pattern that filtered through Heron's ears as endless nagging—made more irritating by the fact that she alone of all the Jeaga still called him "Little Heron."

But little he wasn't. Whereas the typical Jeaga was built short and lean, Heron was a few inches taller and more thickly muscled. As much as he wished to blend seamlessly into Jeaga life, anyone who passed him on a trail would be reminded that he had Calusa blood. And yet something inside him instinctively rebelled against the expectation that it implied.

The conflict came into open scrutiny with the whale hunt that same February. As usually happened sometime in winter, an entire town of 2,000 was suddenly wrenched from its daily routine by shouts from atop the dune line.

"Whales! Whales! They're here! A pod off the sand pits! Two floating into the inlet. More coming!"

Most winters from January through March brought pods of right whales ambling along the Atlantic current that flows from north to south. They had fed and fattened themselves all summer somewhere far up north. Now they escaped the cold waters by gliding south between the shoreline and the Gulf Stream. Winter in the waters of South Florida and the Caribbean were a time to luxuriate, mate and nurse their newborn. Only for a few days would they pause off Jeaga Town. Males would skirmish for mates in the sandy-bottomed blue waters that lay not quite a mile beyond the observation platform that Heron and his fellow apprentices were raising. And plump, pregnant females would nuzzle their way inside the inlet to deliver and suckle their young.

A whale sighting spurred all Jeaga to a higher calling. Right whales ranged from twenty to forty feet long, and just two or three could produce enough dried meat to feed every family until well into summer. More than that, the whales that migrated inside the Gulf Stream gave the Jeaga their special identity and respect. Whale meat could be given to the Calusa as a tribute unavailable from any other source within the tribal family. In fact, whale meat and plunder from Spanish ships were the main reasons why the Calusa bothered to include the Jeaga in their kingdom and protect them from intruders, be they Spanish ships or Indian tribes.

To a lesser extent, the arrival of the whales was a way for warriors to demonstrate their courage and for boys to enter into the realm of manhood.

Not long afterwards Heron had heard the shouts of "Whales!" passed along the ridge line overlooking the River of Turtles. A few minutes later his uncle Deerstalker was crouching at the entrance of Bright Moon's home. "Heron, come with me!" he shouted inside. "I have a task for you. Bring your quiver and arrows. Bring your large spear, too."

Soon uncle and nephew were striding quickly along the path above the inlet. As the passage to the ocean loomed in sight, Heron could see a dozen or so boys and men milling about excitedly, their spears bobbing up and down as they talked. But unlike the usual hubbub, the only sound was a low buzz. Below the crowd, a black form floated quietly in the calm waters. Heron measured the whale with his eyes and estimated it to be about six times a man's height.

As Deerstalker, the Jeaga chief, approached with his nephew, the crowd gave way, expecting his orders.

"Who is going to ride the whale?" the cacique asked mischievously as he marched along the line of would-be warriors. "Are you afraid of the big bad whale? Did you bring all those spears just to shake them at the whale like gourd rattles at a festival?"

All knew how whales were *supposed* to be killed in the inlet. The "whale rider" bravely leaped from his canoe onto the back of the slumbering behemoth and pulled a sharpened stake from his belt. Then he would quickly thrust the stake into one of the whale's two blow holes and drive it home with a second stake. The hardest part would come when the animal would awake with a start and begin thrashing. Somehow the rider had to train his eye on the second blow hole and jam it with another stake. Then he could expect a frenzied, bucking ride for a minute or two until the whale's lungs burst from suffocation.

That was the idea, but the sight of such a large, wild animal lying on the surface and extruding a great gurgle of water and air made every youth feel small.

"All right then, cowards," said Chief Deerstalker, "the honor will go to Heron, son of Calus."

Heron froze as he looked down at the whale, nestled in the crook just inside the inlet opening. *Was the whale nursing a calf or about to deliver one?* Heron saw no calf, which would explain why this animal seemed unusually sluggish. A pool of water gathered inside its blow holes, then gurgled out slowly with each rhythmic breath.

"Climb the whale!" cried Deerstalker with eyes fixed rigidly on Heron with undisguised irritation.

Heron hesitated, pondering the scene.

"*I* will," said a boy named Brown Pelican. In an instant he jumped from his canoe onto the whale's back and sat spread-eagled with the blow-holes in front of him.

"*I* will," said two other boys who jumped on the whale's back behind Brown Pelican. The skin was so slippery that only by tightly squeezing their legs against the whale's broad back could they manage to keep from sliding off.

"The stakes!" shouted Deerstalker as the crowd grew. Brown Pelican nervously dropped one of his stakes into the water. He grabbed another from his belt and furiously plunged it into one of the blow holes.

As the great animal twisted back and forth in agony, pools of purplish blood began to erupt from the blow holes. Within several seconds, spears from the shoreline were flying into the whale's soft sides. Then other youths were climbing on its back and thrusting spears wildly in hopes of earning tattoos for their meaningless bravado. Within a few minutes those onshore tossed down ropes that were fastened that were fastened to the narrow area just in front of the whale's tail and back to mangrove trunks on the shore. Once the dying whale was secured by the tree ropes, the carving and drying could begin. And as tradition demanded, the shaman arrived in time to cut open the whale's head and twist off two ear bones from its skull. The bones would be saved and at some later occasion placed in an ossuary containing the bones of a tribal chief or perhaps even a Calusa royal.

Early the next morning, as the orange sun peeked over the ocean, a cluster of right whales was spotted diving and spouting a mile offshore in the bright blue waters that covered a bank of pure white sand. It was difficult to tell exactly how many because the waves were choppy and because the whales were courting and mating. So ardent was the age-old ritual that the whales seemed oblivious to a flotilla of ten double canoes that suddenly encircled them. Ordinarily, the Calusa forbade their "sister" tribes from gathering in catamarans—a sign of warlike intent—except when whale or shark hunting. The linked-together canoes were needed to stabilize the hunt parties in the unruly waters.

It was now that the serious business of whale hunting began. In each of the catamaran canoes was a seasoned hunter, a sturdy paddler and—in the middle—a youthful novice brought along to observe what he could aspire to do in a year or two. In the front of one canoe was a warrior known to be favored by Shabula because he would identify the first whale target—namely the bull that had locked onto the object of his affections in the oblivious, blissful state of *ufuzzwi*.

The catamarans maintained their circle no more than thirty feet from the cavorting whales. After several seconds the spotter rose and pointed:

"That one!"

The next call was Chief Deerstalker's. "Gray Shark, ride the whale!"

It was but a ceremonial gesture. All knew that the honor of the first kill went to the man with the most kills to his credit. Gray Shark, a thirty year-old warrior, already had seven. It was also a practical decision because the Jeaga needed at least one more whale to assure a winter's supply of meat and oil.

At Deerstalker's command Gray Shark rose from his canoe and balanced himself on his haunches, naked except for a belt that held three stakes and a rope held in one hand. His companions waited for a wave to drive their catamaran into the side of the whale. Then in one motion Gray Shark hopped onto the whale and lightly balanced himself atop its broad back. Quickly he tossed his rope—actually a lariat—around the whale's body and pulled it tight. Then he pulled a stake from his belt and thrust it down one of the whale's blow-holes.

As the whale was jolted from its amours with a violent wrenching, Gray Shark tied the stakes protruding from the blow hole and yanked sharply backward. If the whale were allowed to plunge, the warrior would have ridden down so fast his lungs might burst. But Gray Shark held the lasso fast with his left arm and with his right hand plunged a third and fourth stake in the soft crease between the whale's skull and first rib bone.

As the whale bucked and writhed from side to side, its natural reflex was to head out to sea. But each time it turned outward the men in the other canoes would shout and shake their spears until it turned inward. Then it was Gray Shark's courageous duty to ride the bucking whale towards shore. If he was fortunate, he would finally feel a shudder that signaled its dying breath. But more often the whale would run aground in its frenzy. At that point people of all ages on the beach would charge out in the surf, attach ropes to the narrowest part of the tail and rhythmically haul the whale ashore with each breaking wave.

The Jeaga hunt party knew they could never hope for more than one or two more whales. Already, whales were making strange low groans and belches underwater. Some had roiled the waters even more and nearly sent canoes capsizing with the wake of their tails as they plunged below.

But the spotter had seen another couple still in a state of *ifuzzwi*. Suddenly Deerstalker cried out, "Now it's the turn of the Mako Shark clan. I give the honor to Heron, the son of Calus! Heron, ride the whale!"

Heads turned to show astonished glances that conveyed a single reaction: *What a rash, impulsive, irresponsible thing to do!* Tribal food supplies and reputations were at stake.

But impulsive it was not. Deerstalker had already sized up the situation before anyone else thought about it. A tribal chief soon learned to assemble facts quickly and forge them into a decision, and Deerstalker's thoughts quickly meshed in place. First, he, with a Mayaimi Lake upbringing, had no experience in whale hunting. He was nearly seasick just riding in the canoe and was not about to make a fool of myself jumping on a whale. Second, his nephew had disgraced his clan when invited to slay a slumbering whale in the inlet. He could erase all that with a sudden thrust into manhood and gain great favor with Calus the king. If he failed, well, perhaps it would wake him up to some other feat of merit by the time the Great Cacique came to preside over the next Great Gathering. Third, the Jeaga were lucky to have landed two whales already. Another one might even have involved more carving and drying than was necessary. Left to live, the same whale might return again at a time when it was needed even more.

Heron was shocked, but not surprised at his uncle's bravado. Now, all eyes were on the youth in middle of the lead canoe. The paddler behind him jabbed him in the shoulder and quickly passed up a rope and four stakes. He had no belt.

Could no one but Heron see that this was a disaster in the making? Between the waves and the blue-gray flesh ahead of him, Heron could see he was actually approaching two whales—one on top of the other. Suddenly a wave bounced the canoe almost directly into the eye of the topmost whale. "Jump!" shouted his uncle. "You're big and strong enough. Now go do it."

Heron did, but found himself quickly losing his a footing on the bull whale's slick skin, like trying to straddle a huge tree trunk with mossy bark. There was nothing to grab onto except the blow-hole and the only way to do that was to fling away the rope in his left hand. The blow-hole was slimy and hard to grip. The monster beneath him shuddered and made a loud bellow. Heron's legs worked furiously but could find no foothold.

"The stake, the stake!" someone shouted.

Heron raised the sharp stake in one hand, but before he could strike he felt himself lifted as if an arrow shot from a bow. The beast soared straight upward and Heron went flying backward, his stakes scattering in all directions. In an instant both whales had plunged back into the sea with their enormous tails slapping the surface as if spanking a naughty child.

Suddenly there were no whales, only Heron coughing and sputtering in the heaving waves. His uncle's catamaran was the first to approach. He saw the sturdy paddler in the rear look solemnly at him, then at his tribal chief in the front. The paddler was trying to show his chief respect, but Deerstalker shrugged and rolled his eyes. With that the paddler broke out laughing and all the other canoeists joined in.

As summer approached, each exhortation of Bright Moon to achieve glory sparked the opposite reaction in her son. "Stand up to a cougar," she would blurt out absentmindedly when she'd see him gazing over the riverfront, lost in thought. Or..."Go hunt the bear. That son of the canoe maker down the row is walking around in a new bearskin telling everyone tales of his bravery."

Heron's rejoinders had now been reduced to reflexes such as "Yes, mother," or "Good for the canoe boy." Truth was, he could not see the sense in ending some animal's life just to prove to others that he was brave and manly. Besides, the act of killing was often not brave or manly at all. He knew how the canoe maker's boy had killed the bear. In June the huge loggerhead turtles lumbered up on the beach and dug nests in the sand to lay their eggs. He knew that on many a summer's night a black bear would be hidden among the sea grape bushes, watching the loggerheads in the moonlight until they had finished covering their eggs. And he knew that a gang of boys his age would climb the pine trees behind the dune line, waiting until the bear ambled down to the newly-covered nest and began digging like a dog to uncover the most delicious treats he would eat all year. And while the bear was sprawled on the sand enjoying his meal, a half dozen youths would sneak up behind and spray him with arrows at point-blank range.

And this was bravery? Heron learned to stay in the background by finding ways to support the tribe—and so indispensably that it was wisest simply to let him be different than to mock or chide him. In time, for example, they would come to rely on producing the tips of arrows, knives, spears and atlatls that brought hunters game and glory. His skill came because his uncle, as chief of the Jeaga, was also keeper of the coveted chert supply. Chert was a quartz-like sedimentary rock that was extracted from outcrops by the Tocobaga and Timucua tribes in northwest Florida. It was prized by all tribes as not only the hardest of projectile points, but one that could be shaped into sharp edges by the delicate art of "flaking."

One of the ways the Calusa controlled their kingdom was to enforce a monopoly on the trade in chert. Thus, the Calusa could exchange chert with the Jeaga and other vassal tribes for goods unique to their areas. Moreover, the Calusa could in effect ration the amount of weaponry any subject tribe received, depending on its loyalty.

Chert was one of Deerstalker's levers of local power. It was stockpiled in a guarded room in the council house. One of the chief's nagging problems was that hunters were trying to forge their own projectile points. Too many arrowheads were blunt and too much of the precious material was being flaked away and lost in the sand by clumsy hunters.

Maybe it should be woman's work, thought Deerstalker. The most dexterous woman he knew was his sister, the weaver and sewer. If she could get the hang of it, the cacique would also tighten his authority by keeping the sole source of chert supply in the family.

One day Deerstalker arrived at Bright Moon's entryway with a bag of chert rocks and asked nonchalantly if she could make them into arrowheads and spear points. He described the problem, dropped the bag on the ground and left.

Bright Moon, with both hands extended entwining a cord of mulberry twine, was both preoccupied and annoyed. Heron was sitting cross legged outside about to stoke a coontie flour pancake into the clay oven that had become red hot. Without saying a word, he opened the bag, took out three large chert rocks the size of turkey-wing shells, laid them on a conch lip and put them in the oven.

Once heated, removed and cooled down a bit, Heron took a hammer made from the blunt base of a deer antler and began to chip at a chert rock. The heat had made it easier to flake, but pieces still flew in all sizes and in all directions.

Heron went to bed that night puzzled. But the next morning he had a surprise. The once-gray chunks of chert rock had cooled and changed to pink, orange and red-brown. Now it was easier to chip or flake off pieces that looked more like projectile points. For the first hour or so Heron was just as wasteful as any Jeaga hunter, but after a day's practice he could pick an exact spot in a chert rock and hammer off a long, thin flake with precision.

As Heron perfected his skill, it became known throughout Jeaga Town that when someone made a big kill or won a shooting contest, it was usually with a tip fashioned by Heron, the so-called son of the Great Cacique. And for Heron, sculpting chert gave him time away from the bantering, boasting, boring gaggle of boy warriors.

CHAPTER FIVE

The Prisoner of Seville
1563- 1564

Once after making their port calls at Cadiz and Sanlúcar in southern Spain, treasure ships from New Spain would wend their way fifty miles up the Guadalquivir River to Seville, probably the most prosperous city in Spain. There they would nudge their bows inside the medieval archways of the *Atarazanas,* or Royal Dockyard. On the second storey of the stone cathedral-like fortress, clerks and accountants would scrutinize the ships' logs and cargos to be certain they reconciled with the captain's manifesto and regulations of the all-powerful Casa de Contratación.

One floor above the government offices were tiny detention rooms for stowaways and passengers who had disembarked without proper papers. On the tallest floor above were larger apartments for distinguished guests and a few plainer but similar suites for prisoners of special renown.

In September 1563 Pedro Menéndez de Avilés, Captain-General of the royal armada, was foremost among the latter. And not even the view from his small balcony—handsome ships resting and the sun glistening on the historic waters below—could quell the rage and frustration that burned within him. Nor could his older brother's stern admonition to be civil to the "distinguished attorney" the Menéndez family had engaged to defend the charges against him before the Casa de Contratación.

The fact that his older brother, Álvaro Sanchez de Avilés, was now his chief contact with the outside world was also irritating. Pedro had been sent off at an early age to live with distant relatives and had never known his brother in Avilés during childhood. As fellow seafarers, they had become close allies, but the younger Menéndez had far surpassed the conservative Álvaro in his exploits. And now Pedro bristled because Álvaro was free to go bolstering his bank account with booty from French prizes and because Pedro was dependent on his brother's generosity in providing the lawyer.

Menéndez was already pacing impatiently in his spare but spacious medieval chamber when his heavy metal door was unlocked to admit Álvaro Sanchez and a goateed middle-aged man who was dressed exquisitely as if for a royal audience.

"May I present the eminent attorney Don Juan Gómez de Argomedo," said Álvaro Sanchez.

"You honor my wretched dungeon." said Menéndez with a stiff smile, but already suspecting that the lawyer's attire of patent leather breeches, flowing white silk shirt and calfskin knee boots was meant to contrast sharply with the prisoner's plain cotton shirt and pantaloons.

"Captain-General, I honor not the place you happen to be in, but your fame and glory," said Gómez. "My task will be to extradite you from these unworthy surroundings."

Before another word was said, Menéndez put his finger to his lips and motioned for his brother to help him move the wooden dining table and chairs to a far wall and its open window. "I could see the back of the guard's head in the doorway opening," he whispered. "The extra distance and the sounds of the harbor below should make it more difficult to spy for the Casa de Contratación—not that I would ever accuse such an upright organization of such a foul deed."

"So you are a *nortero* from Argomendo, I understand?" added Menéndez.

"Oh, yes," said the lawyer. "In fact my father knew yours, he told me. He was an importer and used to buy olive oil and vinegar from his ships at the docks when your father would sail in from the Canaries. And my sister's husband even once sailed on one of your corsair raids as a gunner. You remember Sebastian de Luarca?"

"Of course. A good man," answered Menéndez. Usually he saw only the backsides of gunners and he remembered nothing of this one, but he felt some comfort nonetheless. "So you're one of us?"

"Yes, one of us," said Juan Gómez, his slender fingers resting on a thick notebook. "But I practice today mainly in Seville on maritime matters—better to be nearer to the Casa and with an ear to *their* door," he said with a laugh. "Now, if I may, I would like to begin by hearing in your own words why you are in this predicament."

The lawyer's words were like a torch to a month of frustrations. "Being from the north, you know that this is all because the merchant guilds of Seville have forged for themselves a monopoly of steel so that they may live lives as soft as silk and lace." said Menéndez through gritted teeth. "They don't like coarse *norteros* from rocky, windy places like Asturia because they know we actually build ships and sail them and labor mightily for the treasure we bring back. All these people of the *Casa* do is sit two floors below us and" (cocking his ear to the open window) "ah, yes, you can almost hear them down there clicking their abacuses like so many hens clucking over their nests of golden eggs. And then when a captain-general from Avilés brings home his fleet, they send out three times the ordinary number of inspectors just to see what they can turn up.

"And *that* is why I'm here." Menéndez leaned back in his chair, took a deep breath and realized that his torrent had almost come in a single burst.

Juan Gómez and Álvaro had listened patiently, knowing what would be said, but understanding that a volcano could be quelled only after expelling its lava.

"Let us please remember first," said the attorney softly. "The Casa is not the judge and jury but only the plaintiff. So far they are your equal. Our judges are from the Council of the Indies and are not necessarily aligned with the merchants of Seville. They are drawn from many parts and probably reflect the king's interests much more than the guilds of Seville. So our strategy must be framed as if the king himself were the sole judge."

With that, Juan Gómez opened his black leather cover and removed several official-looking papers. "You are accused of bringing back illegal, unregistered cargo and passengers. Our problem today is that there is a record of similar charges on previous voyages. The opposition will attempt to show that this has become a pattern and I will need your assistance in proving otherwise."

Gómez pulled a slim packet of parchment from his sheaf and slowly ran his finger down one of the pages. "The first case is dated November 1555. I believe this case involved your first voyage to New Spain after having escorted Prince Philip to England and then to the emperor's abdication ceremony. That must have been quite an honor."

Menéndez grunted impassively. Inside, his stomach churned at the reminder of his long-postponed dream of becoming an adelantado with a mission to Florida. It had been eight years now, an opportunity lost at the hands of both the meddlesome Casa de Contratación and the hand of Philip himself. Partly because Menéndez was deemed indispensable to the treasure fleet and the king's personal transport, Philip had recently sanctioned the viceroy in Mexico to launch two attempted settlements in Florida—one on the coast of Pensacola Bay and the other on the upper east coast. Both missions were aborted when storms scattered their ships. The king, already battered by financial obligations, declared his interest in Florida *muerte*.

Gómez traced his finger over a long list of numbers. "I see here that even before departing, Casa representatives inspected your ships in the harbor at Cadiz and found many of them to be in violation of various regulations, including, it seems, that the lead vessel was carrying private cargo owned by its captain—he being you—that made the ship's weight unsafe. Open fighting ensued in the streets between your crews and port officials, and you, the captain, were invited into the jail at Cadiz. This is accurate?"

"Only in the eyes of the Casa," muttered Menéndez with an eye on the guard's head on the other side of the door. "The record neglects to mention that we had already left the port once. The fleet had been scattered within a few hours by a violent storm and we had to return to port to regroup. Yes, we had some broken spars, lost cargo and other things that would make an inspector cackle with glee. But not the king, I believed. I knew that with winter coming on, Philip was depending on the mission leaving and returning on time. So rather than wishing us Godspeed on a heroic journey, this army of clerks went around writing up violations that would have kept eighty one ships in port until February. Yes, that did prompt a scuffle," said Menéndez with a smile at the sweet memory of swatting one of the harbor police in the ribs with a spar of ship's rail.

Juan Gómez continued. "The record shows that in September 1556, when you returned with the fleet, you were arrested and charged with having brought 500,000 ducats worth of cochineal and sugar that were not registered. You were also charged with bringing in passengers disguised as soldiers. You were condemned by the Audencia of the Casa de Contratación, yet freed on appeal to the Council of the Indies. Can you provide details that might enlighten me in terms of this case?"

Menéndez was prepared by eight years of frustration. "Take this down," he fired back in crisp sentences. "We departed Spain knowing that in the summer of 1555 French corsairs had sacked Havana and damaged most of its crops and mercantile production. Despite the debilitating effect this had on a fleet of eighty one ships and our dashed expectations of re-supply at that port, we made do as best we could and made for Cartagena and Nombre de Dios where we collected the gold and silver bullion treasure for the return trip. Although our charter stated that we were not expected back until the spring of 1557, we brought the entire fleet home by September 1556—richly laden, I might add—with more than the crown had anticipated."

"Did you carry unregistered cargo and passengers?" asked Juan Gómez.

Menéndez answered with a question of his own. "Was it not in 1556 that the Spanish crown was declared bankrupt and Philip thrown upon the mercy of the banks of Genoa? If one were a captain-general in charge of eighty-one ships and hundreds of men expecting to be paid upon their return, would you not make some provision to cover such a contingency? I have come to realize that sailors and carpenters have a way of not understanding the complexities of royal finance."

"But somehow you were acquitted," noted Gómez as his quill pen darted across his paper. "So we can infer that the king and the Council of the Indies decided at the time that the treasure fleet and your skills as a captain-general were more important to the nation than the comparatively trifling amount involved in a dispute with the Casa."

"And I suppose it supports your theory of arguing on behalf of the king's interests," said Menéndez with his first benign smile of the day. "I was assigned to take the fleet out again the next year, but Philip decided that it was more important to secure the supply lines between Flanders and England from the French navy and their privateers. I spent two years in that service escorting troops and war supplies."

"So you were actually called into royal service?"

"Yes."

"And I see you received a commendation from Queen Mary of England."

"Yes."

"And selected for the honor of escorting Philip II back to Spain from Flanders?"

"Yes."

"And in April of 1559 you brought the king back to Spain without incident?"

"Yes." Menéndez was beginning to like his lawyer's sense of direction.

Juan Gómez wiped his pen clean on a cloth from inside his black leather case and lifted from it another packet of papers. "Well, now, we seem to jump to 1561," he said looking up with a smile. "No problems in between?"

During those three years Menéndez would captain one voyage a year to the new world. During the interim he would send his ships in search of French prizes or lend them to various commercial enterprises. His income from the latter came largely from freight and passenger charges—enough so that he now owned several ships, two galleons and four galleasses that were rowed by crews of a hundred each.

"Now we come to 1561 when the problems arose again," said Juan Gómez picking up another packet. Can you tell me more about your relationship with Pedro del Castillo?"

"A leading trader of Cadiz, as you probably know."

"And a relative?"

"Very distant, but a man with his roots in Asturia all the same," replied Menéndez. "I struck up an alliance with Señor Castillo perhaps for the same reason you are here today. He was someone I could trust, yet someone on far better terms with the merchants of Cadiz than me."

"The record here shows that upon your return Señor Castillo—not you—was arrested on those familiar charges of smuggling goods outside of registry. Remember, I am only reading the official record here," Gómez added as he saw the captain-general's face tighten again. "On the night you arrived at Cadiz, witnesses swore that Señor Castillo had come aboard your galleon after dark and that you spent quite a while in conversation. Around midnight, the witnesses said, thirty-seven chests of 'contraband silver'—their words—were removed from your ship and taken by a launch to shore and loaded onto a mule cart, which then disappeared into the darkness.

"Now then," added Gómez, "you both insisted that you had met only as two old friends and knew nothing about any silver. Castillo was put under heavy bond and lodged in detention for several weeks, after which he was released because he came down with an illness that became too difficult for his jailers to manage. Correct, sir?"

"Correct."

Gómez looked up and caught the two brothers exchanging nervous glances. He decided not to press them for an explanation when their sign language had provided all the answer he needed. "I should point out that even though you were not personally convicted," he added, "the episode would no doubt be cited by the prosecution in the case now at hand to show it as part of a pattern.

"So let us now turn to the case at hand," said the attorney spreading out the weightiest packet of papers from his leather case. "You returned with the first part of the fleet and dropped anchor near the entrance to the Guadalquivir River on June 10, 1563. I will read from the official summary:

> *Pedro Menéndez de Avilés left his ships there the evening of June 14 and went up the Guadalquivir in a small boat. With him he took a priest who was a distant relative, some servants, and a quantity of unregistered bullion. As he sailed northward through the night, the prosecutor of the Casa de Contratación was being rowed southward as he searched for evidence of the smuggling of contraband. When the two crafts approached one another on the dark river, the captain-general deliberately evaded the boat from the Casa.*

> *At dawn on June 15, the Menéndez party was seen to land on the riverbank just south of the city gates of Seville. Witnesses stated that the priest and sailors appeared to be heavily laden as they walked toward the city. Closer examination revealed*

*that they carried bars of silver and several chests. Once in-
side the city, Menéndez and his party went to the home of the
Archbishop of Seville, Hernando de Valdes, where they received
hospitality and lodging.*

"I have your written reply of course," said Juan Gómez, stroking his
silver goatee while searching Menéndez' eyes for a clue. "In general, you
had gone upriver with the full knowledge of Casa officials in Sanlúcar.
You carried only normal traveling items and enough silver for 'personal
necessities.' You saw no Casa boat on the river. Your visit to the archbishop was personal and confidential. Do you have anything to add to
this to help me prepare our defense?"

"How much time do you have?" answered Menéndez with a smirk
as he leaned back in his chair and stretched his legs under the table.
"Once again, this is the narrow perspective of a body that sees only
what happens on one river on its side of the ocean and which perceives
itself first as a policeman charged with levying fines to swell its coffers."

He was now standing, leaning on his chair, half talking out the
window as the late afternoon sun streamed in. "It all comes down to
money," he said. "Because neither the king nor the Casa had delivered
me promised sums to repair and prepare the ships for that voyage, we
had to limp out of port with seven vessels that were near being un-
seaworthy. The cruel irony is that we had to spend money masking their
deficiencies from the Casa with pitch and baling wire or we would have
been delayed and fined!

"You want more irony? On the day before we crossed the bar I received a dispatch from King Philip ordering us to intercept—not only
French—but English and Scotch corsairs who, I remember well, he
said, were 'seeking to steal what comes and goes from the Indies.' Not
only that. He now wanted them hanged on the spot as peace-breakers
and robbers. 'I *order* you to proceed with all vigor,' he said."

"I remember asking the courier: 'Did His Majesty also send the
funds to carry out his orders? Perhaps a promissory note?' The man just
looked at me blankly, as I knew he would."

"And did you give chase to the outlaws?" asked Gómez.

"Fortunately, the few we spotted stayed out of reach. Had they
engaged us, they would have had a pleasant surprise," answered the

captain-general. "By the time we reached Havana on the return trip, seven other ships were judged to be in risky condition. One of them was the *captiana* itself, which required me to outfit my own *Santa Maria* as the lead ship at my own expense. Because we had to make so many repairs in Havana, we had to return in two sections. My son Juan stayed behind and captained the second group. I am still waiting for their return—I pray every morning to see them from this window—and I hope it is only because I ordered Juan Menéndez not to depart Havana during the hurricane season."

"So you see, counselor," he said with a sigh, "it really *is* all about money—the king's lack thereof and my lack thereof. If I only could now, I would sail all my ships back to Biscay and be like Álvaro here, watching my hired captains return with French prizes fat with cognac and chenille and enough gold pieces to pay my crew. But the king calls me to his service like a spider beckoning a fly to his imperial web of bankruptcy."

He sighed again and was silent for the first time. Now it was Menéndez' turn to catch his brother and the lawyer exchanging glances.

"What!" he demanded.

"Well, I think we may have an excellent strategy for cutting the fly out from his web," said Álvaro with a smile. "We have just gotten some word about a little French undertaking that may interest you."

Menéndez sat and stared intently. "All right, *what?*"

"This is another irony," said his brother. "It seems that while your fleet was limping towards New Spain, the French were leaving Le Harve with a large contingent of warships and settlers. The king now has confirmation that they are now reliably said to have built a fort in Florida. It's well up the east coast—the inlet we know as Santa Elena."

"Oh, more irony," sighed Menéndez, shaking his head. "This would have been just after the king was swearing off any more ventures in Florida."

"Yes, but I believe it's more complicated than that," said Juan Gómez. "I'm about to make a point that may offer you great hope, but let me develop it properly. As you know, when your patron Queen Mary of England died in 1558 and Philip married Elizabeth of Valois, we were all told that the purpose was to return stability to France. But we know that the Valois regime has remained weak and that conflict between Catholics and the heretical Huguenot Protestants has divided the country. In fact, did you know that the admiral of the French fleet, Gaspard de Coligny, is a Huguenot? And it is he who is behind this immigration to Florida. They may intend to make it a haven for Huguenots."

"Protestant heretics occupying Florida," mused Menéndez. "Well, that ought to get Philip's blood up." He could see where this was heading.

"Now my theory," said Gómez, "is that Philip is being, shall we say, deceived by the charms of his wife and her French court. I suspect they knew quickly about his decision to forego Florida and that they immediately began making their plans to fill the breach. And all the while, our king is in the position of having to whisper sweetly to his wife and their people for fear of igniting an all-out war that neither can afford. So everyone in both courts pretends that what is there is *not*."

Menéndez broke in. "Perhaps I can finish your point myself. The king wants to extinguish this little nest of Calvinist Huguenots, but he can't announce that his ships have gone to sea because he wouldn't want to offend his dear wife and begin a costly new war in Europe. Ah, but he *might* just sanction a private party to lead an expedition—perhaps one with the official purpose of exploring uncharted land, converting natives to the True Gospel, finding the inside passage to the Gulf and so forth. Since he will need a few hundred men to ward off possible Indian troubles, the world would quite understand should he stumble upon and erase a secret French outpost in the midst of a land the pope has already declared to be Spanish.

"You have both brightened my outlook on life," exclaimed Menéndez beaming, "even if you took a long time to do it."

"You both have my word that nothing will be of more importance to me than working for your early release and doing what I can to see that you head the mission you described," said Juan Gómez, carefully placing his packets in his carrying case.

"I thank you," said Menéndez," but beg that you answer one question for me. You just said that the 'king *received confirmation*" of this Florida settlement. How do you, a lawyer from far-off Seville, know what was in the king's correspondence?"

Gómez smiled. "It all stems from the fact that you are very important to Spain and its crown, Captain-General. Others besides your brother have engaged me to safeguard your interests. It is not illegal for a counselor at law to have two clients supporting the same cause," he said with a cocked head and slight bow. With that the cell door swung open and he was gone.

On the early evening of December 20, 1563 Pedro Menéndez de Avilés stood alone on his small balcony gazing down the quiet Guadalquivir River stretching to the south below him. The air was crisp and he now wore a heavy llama wool parka acquired on a distantly-remembered trip to Mexico. The rising moon was full and cast undulating shadows on the ships that rocked gently in the windless night, with only an occasional tinkling of a yardarm bell to signal their presence. As Menéndez gazed down river, flickers of candles and torch lights danced in the moonlight from the houses that straddled the river. And in the spacious public square surrounding the Casa de Contratación building on three sides the sounds were not of dockworkers, but of couples on evening strolls and townsfolk briskly on their way to celebrate the season in homes and public houses. For Christmas was approaching and Menéndez, the leader of a determined clan, the great hope of northern Spain, the man who instinctively knew what to do when a ship was reefing or a corsair closing in, had succumbed to a heavy wave of loneliness and despair.

It had begun in November with confidence and hope. As the attorney Juan Gómez had predicted, the Casa de Contratación received a letter from King Philip urging rapid disposition of the case. When that had brought no result, the king sent the Casa a direct order to pay the captain-general all fees for leasing his ships on the previous voyage to New Spain.

But what power has a king, Menéndez soon realized, when the royal treasury is empty and in debt to the merchants of Seville for over two hundred thousand borrowed ducats? The Casa held fast, insisting that the ships had been leased as armed protection for the commercial fleet. How could Menéndez claim lease income for defense when his very ships were engaged in commerce? Moreover, it said, the charges involved "grave and ugly faults," including new evidence that the captain-general of the New Spain fleet had taken bribes from no less than the viceroy of Mexico and several friends to transport bullion for their private accounts. How could His Majesty mandate the Casa to enforce the laws of the crown and yet excuse a probable criminal?

As the Casa bureaucrats held the high ground, Menéndez was buffeted by more waves of depressing news.

His brother Bartolomé, upon returning with the second leg of the 1563 fleet, had been incarcerated elsewhere in the same building and was now dogged by a mysterious miasmatic illness. With him had come the news that on July 22, Menéndez' expensive new galleass, the *San Sebastian,* had been shipwrecked along with four other vessels along reefs in southwest Cuba.

Worse, no one on the returning fleet could account for Juan Menéndez. They knew only that the captain-general's son, piloting the lead ship for the first time had—no doubt bravely—disregarded his father's orders not to sail from Havana in the hurricane season. Chancing that he could make up for delays caused by the unexpected repairs in Cuba, the young Menéndez had sailed his seventeen-ship convoy north without incident until, on September 10 they were clubbed by gale force winds off Bermuda. Four ships sank the same day. The rest were blown south all the way to the coast of Hispaniola. When the eight surviving vessels finally regrouped in the Azores, no one could remember anything about the fate of young Menéndez beyond seeing his *captiana* trying to outrace the wall of the hurricane off Cape Canaveral.

On December 10 the Casa had filed its case with the Council of the Indies. Juan Gómez had filed his response December 16, admitting to his client that the case had been "compromised" by the new evidence. The Council decision should come soon enough.

Menéndez pondered all this as he gazed into the moonlight. Despite all the recent blows, he was still legally obligated to outfit the treasure fleet scheduled to depart the next March. He had no money and precious few ships. The king had no money and could get it only via the next bullion shipment. The captain-general's curly full beard had become entirely gray. He was forty four. His joints felt stiff and his muscles flabby. He decided to stake all on a personal letter to the king.

After mounting his own defense to the various charges against him, Menéndez seized upon the subject that bothered him the most.

I am especially sensitive to the complaint that I have grown rich in royal service. When I began to serve the Crown, I possessed two galleons. Now, after sixteen years, I have only three ships, and these are heavily mortgaged. I have lost two ships in the most recent voyage and I have lost my eldest son and too many friends to name, all in the service of Your Majesty. I wish to continue in that service, but I can not accomplish this in prison, and even if released cannot continue my obligations at sea unless the Crown and the Casa provide me with the means to do so.

From there he boldly addressed the subject of Florida.

The [two previous missions] *were wasteful and misdirected* [by the viceroy of Mexico]. *More than a half-million ducats and five hundred lives were expended with no visible effect. It would be far better and much less costly to plant colonies in Florida directly from Spain.*

Then he wrote a second letter to the president of the Council of the Indies. Rather than refute the charges, he pleaded humbly for understanding at a father's plight of losing his son and being powerless to launch a search for him. He proposed to take four pataches and seek the lost *capitana*.

His entreaties were rejected.

Menéndez was still pacing in his lofty confinement on January 17, 1564 when the same Council of the Indies also found him guilty and fined him one hundred gold pesos for bringing the viceroy's unregistered silver aboard ship. On March 8, with the king urging them to delay no more, the Council approved lease payments for two of the ships on the 1563 voyage—but only after deducting an amount equaling all fees the captain-general had collected from passengers and merchant shippers. He had asked for four thousand ducats to equip his next voyage. They awarded him fifteen hundred. The spring convoy to New Spain managed to sail, but with substitute captains.

It was now late June 1564 and Pedro Menéndez de Avilés faced the possibility of seeing a year of imprisonment as the Council sat upon the various appeals of the attorney Gómez. The king himself had attempted to hasten the outcome by issuing a summons for Menéndez to report to the Council of Indies in Madrid within twenty days. Menéndez feared that the Casa would not send him to the capital—even on the king's orders. After all, it had balked or foot-dragged at other royal commands.

"I cannot wait any longer," he told Gómez, who had come to report the status of yet another appeal. 'I want you to perform two tasks for me—and I implore you not to ask why you are doing them. I see in your case some letters from the Casa de Contratación. I want you to give me the most routine or least important of them. Just the first page will do. Even better if you have a blank sheet with just the Casa seal. Next, I ask that you carry that stationery and a letter I have written to my agent Castillo in Cadiz. Finally, when you receive some confidential correspondence from Castillo addressed to me, be kind enough to deliver it here personally."

"And I, your trusted confidant, am not to know the contents?" said the impeccable figure with an arched brow.

"If I *am*, in turn, your trusted client," replied Menéndez, "then you will believe it when I say that nothing you are doing will implicate you in any illegal actions—that is, as long as you have no knowledge of the correspondence. Besides, you enjoy the confidentiality of a lawyer-client relationship."

Gómez returned in a week, was admitted as usual with his familiar black correspondence case, and pried from it a slender folder. "I thank you," said Menéndez with a rare twinkle in his eye. "We will now pretend to have a routine legal consultation and you can leave whenever you feel a suitable time has passed. Either you will not see me for a spell or you will have need to see a great deal more of me very soon."

Juan Gómez was still deciphering the meaning of those words as he banged on the steel door and the guard opened it.

After the attorney departed, Menéndez bided his time. He became cordial and charming to the three guards who alternated duty outside his "apartment." He asked about their homes and financial needs.

Finally, he selected as his most likely mark one Dominguez, a round, affable Andalusian who was inclined to offer the prisoner an extra glass of wine or two at mealtimes. Menéndez was quick to establish that the guard could not read well—if at all. Dominguez had seemed especially intrigued when the captain-general spoke of offering his apparently aimless son a "profitable" position on one of his sailing ships.

On Day five of his plan Menéndez turned to the guard when he brought the evening meal and said with a broad smile, "My friend, I want to express my thanks for the many courtesies you have offered me during this long stay. Why, you have even made me feel like a guest in a commodious inn."

He withdrew a soft leather purse from his pocket and held it out. When Dominguez weighed it in his cupped hand it was more money than he ever held at one time.

Menéndez had learned from the guards themselves that they earned three ducats a month. The little sack contained a hundred one-ducat coins.

"Well, I'm not allowed to take it," stammered the guard, his eyes still riveted on the purse.

"Ah, my friend, you are not allowed only if the giver seeks something in return that would compromise your position," intoned the prisoner. "I am asking nothing. Please, you are captain-general of my quarters and it is my right to show you my esteem."

Dominguez was still staring into the open purse in his hand as he closed the door behind him. *"Madre de Dios!"* he heard the guard mutter outside.

So far so good.

Two more days elapsed. On the late afternoon of July 1, 1564, just after sunset a conversation erupted outside the cell door. Menéndez went to the small window to see Dominguez squinting at an official-looking letter. "Ah, there is the prisoner," said an officious young man in a long black cloak that no doubt covered a Casa bureaucrat's garb. "As you can see," he said to the guard in an impatient voice, "this is a summons from the president of the Casa for the prisoner to appear tomorrow morning at the *Audiencia* of the Casa. He is to be held in that building prior to the hearing. You will have him back in a day or two, but meanwhile I need him to pack a few essentials for his stay. Can you do that quickly?" he said with a head jerk toward the face in the small opening.

"Yes, I'll be but a moment," said Menéndez. He had already packed a change of clothes and some papers. "Ready," he said after a few discreet seconds.

"Well, I don't know," said the guard with eyes still scanning the letter. But the key went in the lock and the door swung open as he did so.

"Step lively, sir," said the Casa official. "I have others to round up as well. Where is the nearest staircase?" he asked Dominquez.

The guard pointed dumbly down the hall and the two men were out of the prison corridor and taking two steps at a time down four stories of stairs. Outside on a side street a carriage waited with two young, fit-looking horses already snorting as if impatient to begin a brisk ride.

The man in the black cape quickly opened the door to the cab, half-pushed Menéndez inside, and then sprang up to the driver's seat. "If need be, we can unhook these horses and ride them," he shouted back. Menéndez was too out of breath to answer that for him to ride a horse would be as precarious as a farmer riding the ocean waves.

By July 6, Menéndez had reached Madrid, where Philip II had recently built his royal palace, the Alcazar. But rather than receiving a respectful welcome, the captain-general was placed in the royal jail. In fact, he would soon complain of being thrown in crowded conditions with men "of lesser station," but he was still nearer to the king's ear.

Back in Seville, Casa officials were so furious that they the imprisoned the banker who had posted bond for the escaped prisoner. Dominguez the guard was found to be illiterate. He was demoted to two ducats a month, but seemed oddly placid about it.

CHAPTER SIX

Heron Comes of Age
1563-1564

As Heron turned fifteen in the Christian year of 1563, his main refuge from the suffocating scrutiny of family and "friends" was his skill as a tracker. Besides providing cover for almost any private excursion he wished to make beyond Jeaga Town, it led to a discovery that would at the same time change his destiny and scar his conscience for the rest of his days.

It began innocently enough with the Duck Hunt, which was actually more varied than its name would indicate. Each spring as the southern winds began to prevail, huge flocks of mallards, geese, and other birds would blacken the sky on their annual migration northward. Among their favorite stopping places were the many islands that dotted the Long River that flowed north-south between the mainland and the narrow strip of scrub that formed the barrier with the sea.

A dozen or so miles up the Long River from Jeaga Town, yet still below the territory claimed by the Ais, were several small islands. On four of them mangroves had been chopped down many years ago, leaving an open space of sand and shell. The other half of each island contained the intact tall mangroves, with one embellishment. A large fishing net of some forty feet long by twenty feet tall was draped among the mangrove branches as inconspicuously as possible. Placed on the ground below the mangroves were decoys made of wood and feathers. Once the skies had begun to fill with migrating birds, two men in canoes—one canoe at each end of the large net—would sit quietly in the late afternoon, camouflaged by mangrove branches.

As the first flocks approached, the hunter with the best duck call would begin puffing his cheeks and blowing *"scree, scree"* through his fingers. If all went right, the Vee in the sky would bend. In seconds the lead duck or goose would skid onto the island's cleared area and begin to approach the decoys cautiously. Others would fly directly into the mangroves and begin roosting.

But in a minute or two the lead ducks would be upon the decoys and sense the ruse. Just as they lifted their wings for a takeoff, the men lurking in each canoe would rise up and pull down on the net with all their strength. On a good haul they might cover a dozen roosting birds and as many more on the ground. Two weeks' work could yield enough smoked meat in summer to make up for the usual slump in fishing.

On a clear, crisp morning in April Heron and his friend Screech Owl found themselves paddling north up the Long River on an errand from Deerstalker. First, the chief wanted some advance scouting to assure him that no Ais had decided to head down the waterway and claim for themselves the sites that Jeaga had maintained for years. More importantly, Heron and Screech Owl would pull down each makeshift fish net and inspect it for dry rot or tears since the last migratory season. If flaws were found, Bright Moon and her son were the best qualified in the tribe to make repairs.

By late afternoon, the two youths had only been able to bring down and inspect two of the four island nets, so they decided that another trip would be needed. On the return trip when they entered Round Lake—actually just a wide spot in Long River—they could hear the ocean roar just over the low dunes to the east and Screech Owl decided he needed a swim to cool off.

As soon as they beached the canoe, Screech Owl took off in a run for the surf. Heron was ready to follow, but his tracker's eyes automatically swept the ground around him for intriguing signs.

And they found several. On the well-worn path from the canoe beaching to the ocean were Screech Owl's fresh, deep footprints. But a few yards down the path were tracks as if made by a thistle broom or small-leaved shrub. In front of these were a man's left foot, perhaps the ball of a right foot and a deep small round hole. They'd been left perhaps a day ago.

The image that formed in Heron's mind was that of a man—a scout from a hostile tribe?—resting on his left foot while the end of his spear balanced his other leg. But where were the prints when he walked away? Leading off into the low sandy scrub of prickly pear cactus and stunted live oak was another trail of evenly swept sugar sand. In front of it were another set of foot prints and peg hole just like the first ones.

From there the pattern repeated itself—twenty or so feet of freshly swept sand followed by the same prints. The left foot track was always followed by the ball-pole-hole to the right.

Would a scout *always* lean on the same foot while resting? And why the need to rest every twenty paces? No, it suggested someone with a lame right foot who hobbled always with the aid of a stave. Was this another place where the Ais or Jeaga sent their old people to die?

The trail led up a rise so that Heron could see Screech Owl at a distance, having the time of his life body surfing. At the top of the gentle hill was a turkey oak that stood out slightly on the otherwise flat surface. On one of its higher limbs hung the crook of a bleached old branch. It was meant to mark *something*, he thought, but no Indian tracker or scout would have left so obvious a marker. Was it indicating a camp? A grave? A stash of provisions?

When Heron reached the tree, the brushed trail ended where the partially exposed roots had been burrowed into by a gopher tortoise. What Jeaga child hadn't crawled into an abandoned gopher tortoise hole? Gopher tortoises were the home builders of the small animal world. A tortoise could burrow for thirty feet in the roots and sand, and after he decided to move on, his tunnel provided a fine home for the likes of snakes, raccoons, and mice.

Heron added it up. A limping man trying to cover tracks that led to a marked tree with a small opening at its base. Heron picked up a stick and poked inside the hole, mindful of the tale told by a friend who as a child had crept inside on all fours only to find himself facing a skunk's uplifted tail.

What he did feel with the tapping and poking of his stick were rocks so heavy he could hardly budge them. Strange for an area that was all sand and wood. Then he felt cloth with something inside that moved and jingled like a bag full of arrowheads. Heron was now on his knees peering inside, the late afternoon sun providing added light. His extended hand felt the rocks and found them to be individual slabs of some heavy substance, perhaps what chert might be when first mined and refined for trading. He grasped two of the slabs and pulled them towards the opening, thinking them the heaviest objects for their size that he had ever lifted.

Now before his eyes, they were gray in color—rough rectangles, forged by some human hand, and each with strange markings that he traced with his finger. Heron placed the two rectangles back on the pile inside the gopher tortoise den, then counted the number in the pile—nine in all.

Next to this pile was another of somewhat smaller and more uneven rocks, stacked more haphazardly. He grasped two of them, pulled them out into view and recoiled his hand as if he had grabbed a rattlesnake. When he first felt the thin, rounded, eight-inch-long rectangles and saw them glisten yellow, he knew he had grasped what Indians coveted and what had made the great cacique so angry that he had once killed a Jeaga chief for not surrendering it.

Heron jumped back and quickly looked all around. No Screech Owl in sight. No owner of this cache ready to send a spear through his back.

He had covered his tracks to the gopher tortoise hole before Screech Owl returned from his swim. That night Heron told no one, turning the matter over in his head to extract as much information as he could from his find in the gopher tortoise nest. Who had stashed away the cache? Was he Jeaga? Was he now dead? Could Heron claim it? Or did it belong to the tribe? Or the Calusa? Both the Calusa and Jeaga penalized stealing with death.

Whatever the answers, Heron felt a surge of power: He had just discovered that to be in sole possession of important information was worth far more than gaining a tattoo or thumps on the back for winning a contest or killing an animal.

The next day when the two youths returned to survey the rest of the four bird islands, Heron took a separate canoe on the pretext that they would need extra room in case they had to return with a tattered net. That afternoon, when Screech Owl had paddled for home and out of sight, Heron pulled his canoe into the palmettos on shore and lay in the sand with an eye on the turkey oak that stood atop the gopher tortoise hole.

But his wait produced nothing. No tracks. No Indian scout. No one to claim the gold. Only the buzz of mosquitoes claiming the land as the sun retreated below the tree line.

Heron had begun paddling south and hugging the west shore of Long River so as to keep the sun behind the tree line when he saw a flicker of movement from the corner of his eye.

A head ducking down beneath a saw palmetto bush. A man or animal? What animal ducks behind a four-foot bush? Bears don't duck, they charge. Deer bolt and run when discovered. A man ducks.

That night he wrestled with his thoughts again. Do I ask a great hunter/tracker like Panther Warrior to investigate? What if the trail leads to some abandoned old person and people laugh again at Heron? But what if I'm wrong about the tracks and the gold hider is stronger than me? Do I enlist Screech Owl? The same boy who bragged about shooting a wildcat when it was already in a trap? He put his faith in what the tracks had told him: a lone person, probably weak and lame in one leg.

A few days later Heron headed up the Long River with some re-paired net fragments for the island bird traps. This time when the Long River began to widen into Round Lake, he pulled his canoe into the mangroves on the west shore and began zigzagging among the pines and palmettos, his bow over one shoulder and his swordfish knife in one hand. His mind raced just as quickly: *If I were alone and living out here, I would want to be within sight of the turkey oak tree across the water, yet not visible from passing canoes.*

Heron adjusted by walking a line twenty or so feet behind the shoreline mangroves until it suddenly unfolded before him—a small clearing with a crude clump of man-made objects. Instinctively he bolt-ed backward, flattened himself in the sand behind the perimeter and made a quick survey inside the clearing. In the center were two palm trees, a rope sagging between them and thatched with a crude lattice of old, browned sabal palm leaves. Propping the sagging roof on each side were pieces of driftwood that had been jammed into the sand. Inside, barely room for a man to sleep, was a mat of leaves and soft gray tree moss known to the Jeaga as maiden's hair. By the makeshift lair was a small pile of old clothes long faded by the sun into the same dirty gray. Nearby was a cold campfire with a crude wooden bowl containing what looked like blackened bones of a small bird.

Heron might have fallen asleep on the ground in the afternoon heat if he hadn't been alerted by the voice of a man singing softly and humming. It was no language he knew, but the tone was carefree and unguarded. In a few seconds he would see the very man he had created in his mind.

The mental image was partially right. His quarry emerged into the clearing limping with the help of a large straight pine limb for a staff. But Indian he was not. The man was short, perhaps once thick-set, but now with bony arms protruding from a torn gray cloak that was fastened around his small waist with a piece of rope. His beard, maybe once full and black, was matted gray by salt and sun. He had to be a Spaniard, although Heron had only seen a half-dozen of them in his lifetime.

Over the thin man's shoulder was a ragged sling from which dropped some prickly pears and palmetto berries. As he bent to pick them up, he was so close to Heron that the Jeaga feared being discovered in a defenseless position. He jumped up, brandished his knife and in his fiercest bellow shouted "Prepare to die!" in Jeaga dialect.

The startled man was a head shorter than Heron and now bent over even more so. "Oh please spare me, oh my master, and I will serve thee to the end of thy days," he intoned in the dialect of the Ais.

He dropped to his knees with his head bowed to someone he took for much older than a fifteen year-old boy. "In the name of Jesus Christ and Taku, please grant me mercy."

Heron had no idea what to do, so he walked around the man waving his knife in the air and scowling. When the man looked up at him with pleading eyes, Heron grabbed his hair and pushed his face downward as if preparing to scalp him as Jeaga warriors had instructed their apprentices.

But the truth was that Heron had squandered all his concentration on tracking his quarry. He had no idea what to do with a captive. And here he was alone with a man who seemed old enough to be his father.

He knew without asking that this was the man who had hidden the cache across Long River, but he had no need to mention his discovery. And if he killed his captive, no one else could lay claim to the gold.

"Who are you?" Heron asked with his most menacing scowl.

"I am a Spanish *marinero*," the man answered in the Ais dialect that was largely understood by the Jeaga. "I was a sailor on a ship. My ship was passing by these shores and I fell into the sea."

"When was that?"

"Just recently. I am waiting for my ship to come and bring me back."

"Just recently? Then why do you speak the Ais language?"

"Ah, well, the Ais found me on the beach and they brought me to their council house and taught me their language to show me their friendship."

"Then why do you not live among them now?" Suddenly Heron drew an arrow from his quiver and pulled back his bow. "Tell the truth, old Spaniard, or you will not to live to see the moon rise."

The man begged that he be allowed to rise to a sitting position because kneeling was very bad for his lame leg. Soon he was seated on an old palm log, peeling a prickly pear and telling Heron what seemed more like the truth.

"Do you remember the Spanish galeota that ran aground south of Jeaga Inlet? Fifteen years ago, I think."

Heron nodded. It was the year he was born, but his captive obviously thought him much older.

"I was one of the crewmen who were on that ship. Some were drowned in the rough water and you Jeaga killed others. I was one of only eight who managed to hide ourselves. When night came we made our way up the beach until we ran out of water and out of strength. When we saw the town of the Ais we just fell on our knees and asked for mercy, as I did with you just now.

"Since then I have been a slave of the Ais. Sometimes I was treated harshly. Sometimes I was allowed to do cleaning and cooking around the council house. But over the years I had seen one and another of our original eight suddenly disappear until there were just three remaining. I knew they had been sacrificed to your gods, and knew it was only a matter of time until I, too, would meet that fate. So, not many days ago I walked away from Ais Town and came to the place where you found me."

Heron was silent as he thought hard, not knowing what to do. At last he regained his tone of authority. "Now that you have told me all this, my only choice is to take you back to the Ais. Or maybe you would find it easier if I killed you here with an arrow."

Now it was the old sailor's turn to assemble his thoughts carefully as he wiped the last of his prickly pear peel on his dirty sleeve. "There may be another choice," he said slowly, looking directly into Heron's eyes. "You could come with me to a better place and better life."

"What do you mean?"

"For you to understand fully, I would have to teach you Spanish ways," said the ragged man gazing up at his captor. "I will tell you something you may not understand now, but it is the truth. In a very short time many great Spanish ships will come. They will look for me and send men in rowed boats to find me and my companions. If the Jeaga or Ais do something to anger these warriors of Spain, they will attack your people with many more soldiers than you have ever seen. They will kill every one of you with weapons so powerful that you cannot understand now what I am talking about.

"If you will help me get food and help me stay hidden in this place until the ships come, I will take you with me and bring you to Spain. I will share with you half my fortune."

Heron knew the man must be talking about the things in the gopher tortoise hole, but he never let on. "What is *fortune?*" he said. There was no Jeaga or Ais word for it. In a matter of minutes, Heron and the man with the sun-bleached beard were in earnest discussion, seated on opposite ends of the old log, Heron's knife jammed upright in front of him as his symbol of domination. But it was all but forgotten in the boy's hunger for learning about things he had never imagined a scant hour before.

The man, who gave his name as Marinero, explained that one reason the eight shipwreck survivors were so exhausted in their night march up the beach fifteen years before was that each carried all the treasure he could manage from the abandoned ship's hold. Only when they knew that they would die with their heavy loads still on their fallen bodies did the survivors agree to bury their treasures separately. Then they regrouped and surrendered to the Ais.

Marinero seemed to be telling the truth, but Heron felt almost disoriented by what he was hearing.

"Why would they carry this heavy load if they knew it would make them get weary and fall down?" he asked. "This is the *fortune*? What is it?"

Marinero, too, felt frustration in making this Indian understand, as bright and curious as the young man seemed to be. "The fortune is gold and silver, he explained. "They are why we come to your land—to find it in the ground and bring it back to our homeland in our ships."

"But why? They are just heavy stones."

The gaunt sailor scratched his head and thought. "Am I correct? Your tribes trade things, such as chert, for whale meat. We are the same. When we bring these 'heavy stones' back to our land, we can trade them for many things beautiful and grand beyond what your people have ever seen."

"Such as what?"

"Jewelry beyond the finest shell necklaces that your women have ever worn. You can trade these stones for land that will be yours alone. With enough of these gold stones you can build a home to live in that has walls thicker and a roof higher than even the largest council house."

Understanding seeped through Heron's brain like water through cupped hands. "Land for me alone? Only *I* can walk on it? But if someone else gets *his* own land, does that mean I can't walk on it? If I have only one piece of land, how would I hunt if animals run onto to another man's land?"

They talked about the place Marinero called Spain. The king was so great that his lands were many times larger than those of Calus. The palace of the king was taller than twenty men standing on each others' shoulders, and made of rock so hard that the most powerful Jeaga arrows would bounce right off. The king dressed in robes so resplendent that to look on him was like staring at the sun. And when the king traveled, he would laugh at the suggestion that he do so by canoe. No, he went in a large sedan pulled by trained animals that were much bigger and more powerful than deer.

Large thunder clouds were rolling in with late afternoon and Heron knew that the discussion must somehow be brought to an end. He didn't know how much to believe of this escaped slave, but he found himself eager to learn more of things he had never thought of before. He wanted to learn more of the Spanish words he had heard, such as *castle, horse,* and *treasure.* Convinced that Marinero was not going to wander far from his gopher tortoise cache, Heron agreed that in a few days he would come again in his canoe and bring the old man some smoked fish, fruits and nuts. In turn, the Spaniard would give him evidence of the treasure that he had promised to share.

A week later Heron paddled up the Long River with the bow of his canoe piled with repaired nets for the coming bird hunting season. Buried in the woven twine was a wooden bowl of dried snook and smoked pompano. Also covered over were two broken gourds from the family trash pile—one with shelled acorn meat and the other with a mix of elderberries and grape raisins.

Marinero placed the containers under the thatched roof that protected his bed of leaves and maiden's moss. He grabbed a handful of each and again straddled the log. Again, Heron sat at a wary distance away on the other end and drove his knife into the log to show that nothing had changed in their relationship.

"I thank you, my master. You are very kind," said the balding, sun-burned sailor chomping eagerly on some shelled acorns.

"And what do you have for me?" asked Heron.

Marinero wiped a hand across his threadbare shirt and reached into his trouser pocket. He produced a flat round gray metal and flipped it to Heron. It made a *ping* as it turned in the air. Part of it was covered with black mildew, but part was cut deep with carvings and pictures. .

"This is your treasure?" said Heron with a smirk.

"It is but a small part of my treasure—*our* treasure."

"But what *is* it?"

"A silver coin, my master. We call it a *real.* It is actually a coin worth eight reales, which we call a piece of eight."

How stupid of me. He has no idea of what I am talking about.

"It feels heavier than stone," said Heron after staring at the coin in silence.

"Yes. To make this *real* we sent ships to a place called *Mexico*—far south of here—and people dug deep into the earth until they found this silver in big pieces. They heated it like you do chert. And when it became very hot they could cut it into round pieces like these."

"But what are these carvings?" asked Heron, turning the coin over in his hand. One side showed the family crest of Philip II, with two lions and two castle turrets. The reverse side showed a large cross and the markings of the mint in Mexico.

"What do they say?" asked the savage.

Marinero pounded his fist to his head, imploring his brain for a way to explain to an ignorant Indian what every Spaniard knew from childhood.

"The one side shows the mark of Christ, our God," he answered, quickly turning the *real* it to the other side. "Over here you see the shield our soldiers use for protection in wars. It shows our king's strong house and some of the ferocious beasts that protect the king's great house from invaders."

Heron pointed to an M and the letter G on the reverse side. "What are these"" he asked with a frown.

Marinero thought he had explained well enough, but this lad's curiosity was insatiable for a savage. "The first letter [M] means that the *real* was made in Mexico, the place I just told you about. This marking here [G] is the name of the man who actually carved the coin." *Carved* was not the proper word, but Marinero had no idea of how he could describe the process of die casting.

Heron continued to study the coin as he turned it over in his fingers.

"But why do you go to all this trouble?" he said at last. "All these reales do is make you heavy and tired when you try to walk any distance. You said so yourself."

"Ah, but you must remember, my master, that this real is worth keeping because it can be traded for so many things. As I said, you Jeaga can trade chert—or arrowheads made from chert—for fish nets or canoes or whale meat or many other things. In my country this coin can be traded for a boat or a fine house or even a beautiful wife. And when you go to Spain with me you will have many of these doubloons."

Actually, the real Heron held in his hand might have bought a night's cheap lodging or two drams of rum in Havana, but the old sailor's objectives were riveted on avoiding sudden death and obtaining enough food to survive another week. This, in turn, depended on keeping the young Indian intrigued, entertained and susceptible to the scheme he was ready to propose when the time was right.

And so, once a week throughout the rainy, wet summer, Heron would arrive with his smuggled subsistence. The master would straddle the same log, extracting from his captive all he could assimilate about Spanish words, Spanish ways, and the dazzling life that existed on the far side of the ocean.

On the highest ridge overlooking the ocean near the inlet stood a clump of the tallest, oldest pine trees in Jeaga Town. Everyone knew them simply as The Ten Pines. On one of them the branches had long served as a ladder to a platform near the top that was covered by hanging maiden's moss. Beginning in August the lightest, most agile youths would scamper up the tree to maintain a watch, camouflaged in the hanging moss. They watched for stray frigate birds blowing in from the Caribbean islands that would signal an impending tropical storm or hurricane. The more frigate birds, the greater the storm threat.

More importantly—at least to King Calus—the treetop scout would be watching for a sign of a Spanish convoy. This was the time of year when a line of ships would head north in the Bahamas Channel, laden with treasure and passengers headed back to their homeland after a year of digging into the earth. Three or four groups like this might pass in a fall. If there were no storms or high seas, the convoys were apt to sail in the middle of the channel, usually out of sight from shore. But if the storms blew, the fleets would attempt to sail close to one shore or the other. If a storm swirled in from the west, for example, the ships would sail as close as possible to the Florida shore because the wind and waves would be diminished somewhat by the shoreline's protection.

But keeping a fleet intact and in formation was another matter. Storms—especially hurricanes—could scatter ships. Some would run aground and some might lose their supplies and be forced to seek shelter in places like Jeaga Inlet. In these rare cases all tribes were under orders from the Great Cacique to lure a ship's crew ashore with the promise of trading, then destroy or enslave them.

The old Spanish sailor, encamped a dozen miles north, knew all too well about the convoy season, and all of his hopes of ending his precarious life as an escaped slave were pinned on somehow going out to hail a passing ship. For that he needed a seaworthy craft and a willing partner in his enterprise.

And so, his meetings with Heron became all-important and his entreaties more earnest. On a muggy day in late August, Marinero finished stashing his weekly supply of fish and fruit, took up his place on the old log, and leaned forward with a solemn gaze. "My master," he said, "I have told you that the Spanish ships were searching for me. The reason is that I am a nephew of the great king of Spain."

He paused. The Indian remained impassive. "I have vast estates— whole forests and gardens and many servants. They eagerly await my return. Besides sharing the small fortune I have here, I will take you to live in my great house and share all that is in it. You will have my lands in which to hunt the many deer and bear and many other animals that abound there. And when you return from the hunt, your servants will array you in fine robes and perfumes."

"Perfumes?" interrupted Heron.

"Ah, yes," exclaimed Marinero. "Your servants will show you a hundred different pleasing scents." He held an imaginary vial to his neck as if shaking it. "They will make you irresistible to the many young ladies who adorn the king's court."

Perfumes? The new term had a way of jarring Heron to his senses. How could he appreciate something he simply couldn't understand? He looked over the weathered face with its matted beard and tried to imagine it as part of a splendid royal family. Besides, he had long since learned that *Marinero* was simply the Spanish word for "sailor." The man had never offered his name. But then, neither had Heron.

"We need but one more thing to make all this happen," Marinero continued leaning forward again. "We need your canoe plus one more that we can lash into a catamaran. Then we need some water and provisions so that we can go into the ocean. In a few days we will be safely in Cuba. Or if we get lucky we will spot a passing convoy of ships. When one of them picks us up, will be treated like kings on the ship and in just thirty days we will be across the great ocean and home on our estates! "

Heron had retained the same frown he had expressed at the word *perfume.* "And you will take your treasure on these canoes as well?"

Yes, yes!"

"You want me to leave my people and acquire—steal—two canoes and much food. The Jeaga penalty for doing that is death. How is it then that you have not given me my half of the treasure—or even shown it to me?

"Oh, but I *will*," said the bearded one, nodding his shaggy head vigorously. "When you bring the canoes I will have the treasure ready to pack in them."

"But you promised to share your treasure if I would feed you. That was *before* you talked about canoes and flagging down ships."

Marinero was silent, looking at the ground. "Well, if you don't trust me...." he stammered.

Real power is the possession of important information.

"What if I told you that I already know where your treasure is?" said Heron evenly.

The bearded face remained fixed on the ground, but Heron could see the shaggy eyebrows jerk upward.

"How would you know *that?*"

"I knew where your treasure was before I ever set my eyes on you, Marinero. I told you I was a tracker, and it was your poorly covered trail that led me there."

More awkward silence. "Then tell me—show me—where it is."

"No," said Heron. "Here is what I have decided. At some time soon, unknown to you, I will return myself to the place where your treasure is. If I find it still there, it will be my sign that you are sincere in sharing it with me. If it is not, then I will assume that you plan on keeping your treasure and my canoes—and your great estates—all to yourself."

Heron rose slowly and backed away as one would from a dangerous animal. "I will now leave you to decide for yourself," he said. "I may leave you with your thoughts for more than a week and return at a time of my own choosing. If there is a fleet of ships passing by, my people will know about it before you do and I will have time to join you. Meanwhile, you may want to use all the time you can to learn to hunt your own food."

Heron was stepping into his canoe when he heard "Wait! Wait!" The old sailor hobbled to the water's edge and said "I just wanted you to have this as a show of my sincerity," He handed Heron a large gold coin that was much heavier than the gray one that now lay buried in his gourd garden next to his mother's talisman. Soon the carved image of the king of Spain would be lying near the painted likeness of the god Shabula.

September was muggy and rainy as usual, but without the bluster of a hurricane. The boys who swayed and snoozed in the pine tree lookout loft saw neither a frigate bird to signal a coming storm nor a sign of any Spanish ships out on the Gulf Stream. No doubt ships were sailing, but probably too far towards the Bahamas side of the channel to see.

If there were to be no major storms, the most reliable confirmation would come soon as the first migratory flocks flew over the Long River on their way south for the winter. Once again, the nets on the duck islands had to be made ready and Heron offered to take the first inspection trip.

He had his own reasons as well. One was that Heron was curious to test a canoe in the ocean current that ran in the mile or so between the shore and the Gulf Stream. The prevailing current still ran from south to north, but in just a week or so it would begin reversing as northeastern winds scoured the sand from beaches, leaving only cliffs of sand until another summer came and the beaches were replenished with sand again.

One morning as the sun rose, Heron climbed into a canoe made for ocean fishing. Its prow was raised slightly with a foot-long wave cutter the fishermen called a "heron's beak." The occupant Heron felt no fear as he paddled out Jeaga Inlet. The tide was behind him, the waters were gentle, the wind and current in his direction, the beach only yards away, and no whales around to upend him.

He had calculated the distance to his first destination at just two hours when taking the Long River and reckoned it about equal by sea. As his paddling settled into a trance-like rhythm, he found himself in a blissful state of just being alive. It seemed like time had scarcely passed when the sun's position told him to begin knifing through the barely undulating waves and beach his canoe. As the sun transformed the morning sky from gray to bright blue, the only animation Heron could see on the flat horizon were pods of dolphins bounding in the sun's shimmering rays.

He knew from the stunted scrub that he had reached the targeted area because he could look across the narrow strip of sand he stood on and see the wide expanse of Round Lake to the west. The Jeaga was confident that the old slave was still sleeping in his lean-to on the other side or off in search of fruits or field mice or whatever it took to keep him alive.

Still, Heron walked the beach below the line of vision from Long River until he spotted the weathered turkey oak with the bleached branch elbow hanging over a limb. "Thank you again for the marker," he said to himself.

Now he was in a crouched scamper towards the tree. Suddenly he was treading over a jumble of footprints going back and forth that no one had attempted to erase. They grew heavier towards the tree, and when Heron stood before it he already knew what waited when he reached into the gopher tortoise hole. He knelt and did so anyway, but every direction in which he groped yielded only a fist full of sand.

The footprints led north into the scrub hills, but Heron had no interest in following them. Old Marinero had given him the answer he had sought. The clarity gave him a great sense of relief. He returned to his canoe, portaged it across the narrow strip that separated the sea from Long River at that point, and continued up the next mile or so to the first of the duck islands. Heron kept his knife and spear near his lap, but he knew that the old man would not appear on the shore or challenge him.

Thanks to the unusual lack of tropical storms that year, the net traps on the duck islands appeared to be in fine working order, needing only men, canoes and camouflage to begin the bird hunt. After replacing parts of nets that sagged to the ground and tucking them back into the mangroves, Heron headed south down Long River for home. The sun was just finishing its morning arc.

Uncle Deerstalker and the elders will be pleased that the bird hunters can begin camping out soon after the first fly-over, he thought. Then he wondered how the chief might receive information about an escaped slave to be tracked down and a treasure to be obtained along with him. He felt no rush. No Spanish ships were coming to rescue the wretch.

Heron was still in possession of valuable information and needed only to decide how best to use it. The mounting heat and the rhythm of his paddling created a somnolent state of mind and Heron allowed himself to succumb to it as he glided in the shallow estuary over oyster beds, conch, lobster and scurrying fish. At one point he passed two deer lapping water on the shore. The deer scarcely noticed and Heron let his atlatl and spear rest where they were. "Another day, perhaps," he said to them with a wave.

By mid-afternoon Heron slid his borrowed ocean canoe into position by the inlet mouth. He jabbed a red snapper from the stockade trap he had helped to build and thought he'd stop at his uncle's hut on the way home to report the good news about the duck traps. As he passed the council house to his left Heron was startled to see a tall, muscular Calusa warrior standing at the entrance with his arms crossed.

"Where's your brother, the chief? he asked his mother, hanging the fish on a hook inside. "Are they having a meeting or something down in the council house?"

"Yes," she said brightly. "All he said on his way there was that three messengers from King Calus had suddenly arrived and that they wanted a meeting about the Great Gathering next month."

"What about it?"

"Well, I should think it would be about advance preparations. What events will be held and that sort of thing."

Not more than twenty minutes later Deerstalker himself came striding swiftly along the river ridge with a scowl on his face. When Heron mentioned trapping ducks he was waved off. "Sometimes I wonder what I got myself into," he grumbled. "Now I've got to spend three days going to Mound Key—and for what? They send three so-called *ambassadors* here who are no more than armed thugs to tell us the king wants us. When we ask why they say only that he wants to discuss the Great Gathering. When we say let us know what we're supposed to discuss, they say that only the Great Cacique can tell us. In other words, he doesn't trust his own people to communicate his orders and doesn't want anyone else to discuss something in a group that he can't be there to influence. Bah!"

But that was not even the half of it. "Do you think Calus would travel in September when the rains make it so that you sit in your canoe all day with water squishing up your crotch and then have to find some tiny muddy island to sleep on?"

Since he had an audience, Deerstalker let it all out. He hated the "Rule of Four," a clever lever of power that the Calusa had fashioned over a thousand years of controlling vassal tribes. The Rule of Four meant that whenever the king summoned the elders of a vassal tribe to Mound Key, the delegation must be limited to the heads of the four largest clans. Four men weren't numerous enough to pose a threat on Mound Key—and having the largest four clan leaders together assured that no one clan would rebel against the other in their absence.

Deerstalker worried that he might be the exception to the rule. Despite all the years that had passed, he still felt himself an outsider from Mayaimi Lake. The Jeaga clans might tolerate him well enough in a two-hour council meeting, but facing a three-day trip left Deerstalker uneasy. What if they appeared before the Great Cacique and reported that their chief had suffered a "fatal accident" along the way?

Equally unsettling, Deerstalker dreaded visiting people who were a foot taller and required slavish pomp. "I don't like bowing, kneeling and avoiding looking directly at the Great Cacique as if my gaze could put a hole in his head," he bellowed.

Bright Moon had withstood all this standing before her brother with her hands on her hips. "Now you've said quite enough about my husband," she said stiffly. "Will you please tell the king about his son?"

Deerstalker looked at the silent boy with a frown. "What *about* him?"

"That he is growing into a strong, handsome young man who is ready to take his place next to his father."

"Maybe strong," said Deerstalker. "I suppose good-looking. But *man?* I should tell the Cacique how his son rode the whales? Killed a bear? Maybe he scalped a Tocobaga warrior when I was out fishing. Maybe if he were a woman I could show the king how well he brews berries or dresses a deer. But right now I would have a better chance of impressing the Cacique if I told him the boy could make gold."

Bright Moon smoldered silently until Heron could take it no more. "I *can* produce gold," he said softly to the chief of the Jeaga, indicating for him to wait a moment. He disappeared around to the gourd patch in back of the hut and re-appeared brandishing between his fingers the large Spanish gold piece he had unearthed. "I have this and know where to get more," he said.

Instead of impressing his uncle, Heron's revelation produced a long moan. "All right, tell me about it," he said at last, easing himself onto a wooden bench.

Heron recounted everything: the Spaniards' escape from the wrecked ship, the desperate trek into Ais country, the gopher tortoise cache, the meetings with Marinero, the "escape" plan and where the old slave and his treasure could probably be found. With each new discovery, Deerstalker would groan and shake his head until at last he raised his hand and cut off the lad.

"So you think we should take all this gold to the Great Cacique and that he will think well of you and me and your mother because of it?" His voice became strained but quiet. "Perhaps your mother has forgotten to tell you about something rather important that happened just before you were born. The chief of the Jeaga found some Spanish treasure and did not report it at once to the people on Mound Key. For that reason they sent soldiers to Jeaga Town and lopped off the heads of those leaders.

"So now we are going to bring the king some Spanish treasure that has been buried on our land for *fifteen* years and tell him we just found it? Not me. Not you. I do not know where this treasure is and do not want to know. I command you to forget you ever saw this gold and whatever else was there under that tree. And I command both of you not ever to mention it again."

Deerstalker rose to leave, then sat again. "You have also presented me with a second problem," he said heavily. "You have reported a runaway slave that must be re-captured. Before I depart for Mound Key I am going to find the tracker Panther Warrior. You will guide him up the Long River so that this slave is our prisoner by the time I return. Surely the two of you will be able to find an old man who limps on a cane."

With that, Deerstalker shook his head in Heron's direction, muttered something unintelligible and trudged along the ridge to his hut to gather his belongings for the trip. He would need his best paint, whitest shell jewelry, his red fish bladder earrings, a deerskin to sleep on and shelter him from the rains while traveling. His wife, Morning

Dove, was equally busy packing pouches of smoked fish, dried venison, persimmons, coontie flour, and prickly pear meat that could be stored in a canoe. For the rest of his needs he could catch fish or pluck apple snails and pond apples along the shorelines of Lake Mayaimi and the Calusahatchee River.

Three afternoons later Panther Warrior and Heron lay hidden in the scrub watching a pathetic sight on the beach. Marinero was busy tying grapevine twine to bind together a raft of thin pine logs that were obviously meant to take him out to sea. A single sapling held up a ragged sail that had been made from a shirt and pantaloons. The whole contraption was no more than a dozen feet in length and would probably come apart in the slightest tropical squall.

The gaunt fugitive was startled when the two Jeaga rose up from the sand and approached him, but in an instant he forced a smile. "Hello, my friend and master," he said in Spanish. "You have brought help so that we can take our great journey."

"No," replied Heron in broken Spanish. "We come to take you on a great journey to Jeaga Town."

Panther Warrior ordered the captive to lie on his back in the long canoe, then bound him with thick strips of mulberry bark. Marinero asked only for a drink of fresh water, then seemed content to remain inert with his eyes closed for the entire journey.

In a week, when Deerstalker and his colleagues returned to Jeaga Town from Mound Key and approached the Council House, they could see children standing on each others' backs trying to peek into one of the tall air vents. Some were laughing as they tossed stones and pebbles into the open space above them. Once Deerstalker entered the thatched building he soon realized that the children were trying to get a peek at the Spaniard who sat inside a small, stuffy cubicle, strapped by his hands and feet.

"Our report will be rather brief," said the Jeaga chief once the elders had assembled. "There will be no Great Gathering here this year. The main reason we were summoned was that the Great Cacique wants us to send warriors to him to fight the Tocobaga. It's probable that the threat of an invasion from the north is why the king and his warriors could not leave their homeland at this time."

Much muttering and consternation. The Tocobaga of Tampa Bay meant nothing to the Jeaga. In fact, they controlled a large quantity of chert mining. The Jeaga yearned to trade with them directly, but were forbidden by their masters on Mound Key.

"Wait." Deerstalker raised his hand to quiet the discontent. "It is not so certain that we must actually go to war right now. The Ais delegation asked for the king's help in attacking the Jororo on their northern border. But the Jororo have allied themselves with the Timucuans and my colleagues and I doubt that the king wants to face both the Tocobaga and probably other Timucuan tribes at the same time. In any case, he said he and his war council would have to discuss such a move and get back to us later.

"It may be that one request will cancel the other," said Deerstalker. "But in the meantime we have told the king that we would show our support by holding a festival in his honor beneath the Place of the Sun and the Moon. We can conduct war training and hold competitions to show that we are ready to fight if needed. And we can combine this with the Coming of Age ceremony, which will add more young warriors to our ranks."

When the council broke up, Deerstalker was relieved for two reasons: he had attained a consensus for doing nothing at present and hadn't been asked to tell the elders something else the Jeaga delegation had learned on its visit. But he knew he would have to do so in a few minutes when he passed by the hut of his sister on the way home. And this, as weary as he was, would be unpleasant and delicate.

Deerstalker was bone tired. His arms and lower back ached from three days of steady paddling and his tailbone was sore from the canoe's hard, rough seat. He thought fleetingly of his days on Lake Mayaimi when he could hunt and fish while his father worried about tribal conflicts and settled people's personal problems. He wanted to collapse on his bed, but already he could see his sister standing on the ridge line, waiting in the middle of the path with her arms.

As he climbed the hill, Deerstalker could compare the woman in front of him to another one he had seen on Mound Key. It was now October and the early evening had turned clear and cool. Bright Moon had taken the trouble to dress in her best, as if expecting a festive occasion. A dyed white doeskin hung loosely around her shoulders and the long golden Spanish chain was double-wrapped around her neck—her symbol of royal marriage. A second necklace of blue and white shells matched the ones she wore on her ears.

But time had taken its toll. Her black hair now hung down almost to her hips in an almost careless, disheveled way. Her large breasts had begun the inevitable middle-age sag. Her nose seemed larger. The tunic that girded her hid a puffy belly and hips that childbirth and time had widened.

Bright Moon's eyes searched for a hint of expression that would tell her that the Great Cacique was coming or that she was going, but Deerstalker said only, "We're lucky we don't have to climb those hills on Mound Key every day. Our little mounds are better."

She began to bore in at once. "Did you see my husband? Did he ask for me?" But Deerstalker cut her short.

"Is the boy in there?" he motioned to her hut.

"No, I think he's over at the fish traps."

"All right then, let's talk while we can." The two sat on the sandy mound facing the River of Turtles and the taller Place of the Sun and Moon on the other shore.

"First, he said, "there will be no Great Gathering again this year. The king is facing an invasion from the Tocobaga and his war council thinks it's too risky to leave. Just between you and me, some of the Calusa hinted to me that the king might also face an uprising from within. Perhaps another reason he doesn't want to show up here is that he might have to deal with you, which would be awkward."

"Awkward? How could that be?" Her face had already begun to redden.

"Well, you see, sister, we learned on our trip that Calus now has another wife. And a child, I'm afraid to say. A baby boy."

"What? A child with one of his flute girls? He's had several of those, I've been told."

"No," said Deerstalker. "This one is like the official queen. Her name is Neemba. She may have been forced on the king—I don't know. But I do know that she is the daughter of his chief war counselor." He spared his sister from knowing that Neemba sat prominently beside her husband when the Jeaga delegation appeared in his Great House.

125

"I suppose she is young and pretty," Bright Moon said after a stunned silence.

Again, Deerstalker spared his sister from a cruel comparison. In fact, he had been captivated by the young woman's simple dignity and dress. Whereas Calus had been a tree trunk of red paint and black grease, his slender, stoic wife had been adorned with all-white matching shell jewelry and her black hair topped with a single egret plume. She looked every inch a queen.

"Oh I suppose she was fair enough," he said.

"And how old?"

"Oh, perhaps approaching twenty."

"So the other Jeaga elders know this as well?"

"Oh, I'm afraid so," he said. "After all, they were with me. And you can expect that by tomorrow everyone on this river will know it."

Bright Moon sat with her hands cupped around her ears, chin on chest. Then she began weeping convulsively. Deerstalker stared out at the first of the fall mullet run diving and leaping their way upriver. It would be a good year for the netters at the inlet.

"What does this mean for me?" she said at last. "What of Little Heron?"

"What about me as well?" he replied, relieved that her thoughts had advanced beyond pure grief. "All this presents important questions that we must answer. As cacique of the Jeaga, I must continue to show that my authority stems from the king himself. I am convinced he will not want to change the Jeaga leadership when war threatens as long as he believes in my loyalty.

"But you and the boy present a more complicated situation," added Deerstalker. "Heron is still the oldest male offspring of the Great Cacique. If something should happen to this infant he has now, or if Calus should not be able to father other children, or if another faction is looking to replace the king with a logical male heir, then your Heron could be the next Great Cacique. Besides, should something happen to *him,* it could weaken my—our—own authority among the Jeaga."

Bright Moon looked at her brother and shrugged with palms up. "But how can we know which one of these things will happen?" she asked.

"Ah, that's what I've been thinking about in a canoe for three days," he said with a foxy smile. "You see, uncertainty is our best friend in this case. No one else knows, either. And for that reason the Jeaga will continue to treat Heron with a distant respect because there is always the possibility that he could one day have the power to lop off the heads of those who weren't nice to him back in Jeaga Town. Then, of course, we have on our side the ancient Calusa custom in which case if a Great Cacique's son dies, each village chief must sacrifice his own son as well. Would this apply to Heron? I don't know, but I doubt that anyone wants to find out.

"At the same time, I will no longer thrust your son into the faces of everyone here. I am done forcing him to become a mighty warrior. The more glorious his reputation, the more Calus or his wife's family might feel threatened. No. Heron just needs to....needs to *be* for now."

"And what about me?" She said softly.

"Right now, I don't know the whole answer," he said looking into her moist eyes. "But I do know that we can't thrust *you* into the faces of the Jeaga either. By that I mean stop telling everyone you see that the Great Cacique is going to come and take you back to Mound Key. Maybe you need to be seen less wearing that long gold chain."

Deerstalker rose stiffly and began to retreat along the pathway. "And I'm to become the Weaver Widow again?" she called after him.

"Is it so bad to be the chief's sister?" he answered. "Most women here would gladly trade places with you. Now I must go and deal with *another* woman and some children who think I will want to play games with them."

It was now mid-October and the Great Gathering Place would now be co-opted for an all-Jeaga Festival of the Sun and Moon—a full day of games and competitions capped by some weddings, a feast, and dancing through the night. For most of the Jeaga it would be a happier occasion than a Calusa Great Gathering simply because only elders and their families attended the multi-tribal conclave. The Jeaga rank and file swept the Great Hall, prepared the food, then watched from canoes or from across the river while an elite group mostly of strangers endured somber rituals followed by a contrived levity under the wary eyes of a king and his warriors. On this occasion, a thousand or so Jeaga men, women and children could simply celebrate who they were.

However, for twenty boys aged fourteen and fifteen, the festival day would be preceded by a trying, secret ritual known only as "The Birthing." Every living adult male in Jeaga Town except the crippled and feeble of mind had gone through The Birthing. All had been sworn to secrecy from divulging what went on at the ritual.

Two mornings before the Jeaga festival, Heron was helping his great uncle Red Hawk smoke mullet in his large steam oven when he saw his old mentor, Cougar Claw, approaching with a serious look on his face. "Oh, no," Heron thought at first, "he can't be organizing some garbage squad." Instead, the old warrior took him aside and placed in his palm a large flat gray stone that might have been prized for skipping on in the water. On its surface was carved the crude outline of a ritual mask.

"Heron, you are called to the Birthing," he said stiffly. "Tomorrow as the sun is highest, you are to go down to the canoe beach across from the Gathering Place and present this to the man waiting there. You may not discuss this with your friends beforehand. And I would suggest that you be sure to get plenty of sleep tonight."

Cougar Claw, who seemed to have other stones to distribute, began continuing along the path of huts, then retraced his steps. "One thing more. You are to see the shaman Hawkman at his house as soon as you can."

In the "square," the clearing below and behind the house of Bright Moon, stood the old Jeaga council house with the shaman's hut a spear toss away. The red and white striped pole had been placed outside and the outer perimeter of the hut had been lined with several large baskets, which, Heron speculated, might have been assembled for use in the ceremony in which he was about to take part.

The old shaman bent himself through the opening and stiffened so that his eyes faced Heron's shoulder. "So...you haven't been spying on me lately," he said. "You must be very busy." He quickly got to the point. "Your uncle the cacique has asked me to tell you something. The Spanish prisoner you brought here says that you have cheated him and stole from him. Do you know that the penalty for stealing is death—from a Jeaga or *anyone?*"

Heron's mouth dropped open. No words came out. "Come with me and we will settle this," the shaman said tersely. He took a gourd of water, a piece of coontie bread, and strode toward the thatched council house, Heron following haltingly.

Behind the large stone grill used for feasts was a small supply room separated by a hanging rattan mat. When Hawkman pulled the covering to one side, he saw old Marinero slumped in the dark and still bound tightly. His tongue licked around his swollen, cracked lips. His eyes scarcely took note of his captors, much less of the ants that crawled over his hands.

"Now," said Hawkman, leaning over the prisoner, "tell me again what you said to the cacique and me earlier."

The old man opened his mouth and worked his lips up and down like a baby squirrel begging its mother for a meal. The shaman read the universal language for thirst and poured water in the Spaniard's mouth from the gourd. After a piece of bread and another swallow from the gourd a faint light seemed to shine in Marinero's eyes. Heron could already tell that the prisoner was preparing for another appeal to his new "lord and master," perhaps the last and most important one of his life.

"Ah, I remember it clearly," he said as the shaman cocked his ear to understand the more guttural Ais dialect. "One day I was out on the Long River gathering clams, totally unarmed. Suddenly this boy here came out from behind a tree with a spear and threatened to kill me. He is large and I thought he was much older."

The old sailor begged for another swallow of water and cleared his throat. "This boy here said he was going to kill me. All I could think of to save my life is that I knew where to find some of the gold that was taken off the shipwreck that brought me here some fifteen years ago. This is the same ship whose skeleton still lies on your beach. I led him to where the gold and silver were buried. He took it and put it in his canoe and then tied me up to a tree. A few hours later he came back with the older man and they took me here.

"But I know where more is buried," said Marinero, straining to use his bony bound wrists to gesture. "Let me live and I will serve thee well, oh master. I will lead you to a treasure that will find you great favor with your king. But if you take my life, the Ais will find out what happened—for they are looking for me, their favorite slave, and there will be hostility between your tribes. And they will also claim the gold that should be yours."

Heron had paused to begin weaving a defense in his mind when the shaman nudged him out of the airless cubicle and pulled the covering closed behind him. They went to the far end of the council house and sat on opposing benches. "And now *you* tell me," he said in a low tone.

"This didn't happen all in one day," said the youth, still feeling the dread of death hanging over him. "I was practicing my tracking up on Long River early last summer. I found the camp he had made for himself in the woods, then I watched for a while trying to figure out who he was."

"Just like you enjoyed watching me," said the shaman with a pointed figure.

Heron felt he was on trial for his life. His mind raced for the right answer. "When I showed myself with my spear, he did say that he had a buried treasure and he said he would share it with me if I brought him some food. So I did bring back some food, mainly because I was already going up the river each week to repair the nets on the bird islands."

"If that was early summer, why did you wait so long to tell your cacique and capture the fugitive?"

Your cacique? Heron froze at the thought that his uncle might have left to the shaman the unpleasant task of punishing his nephew. "It is true that I would bring him nuts and dried fish from time to time," he continued. "The reason I took so long is that I...is that I am curious by nature. When he told me he was Spanish I found myself wanting to know more about where he came from and to learn his language."

"I will agree that you *are* a curious fellow," said Hawkman with the first twinkle of mirth Heron had detected. "Well, *did* you learn his language?"

"Some, but not as well as I would have wanted. Something happened that made me realize that he might not always stay in the place where I was meeting him. Last month he said that the Spanish ships would soon pass on their way to Spain and that he would give me his treasure of gold and silver if I helped him build a raft and bring him some provisions. That is when I went back and told my uncle, the cacique, and got the help of Panther Warrior to bring him back to where you now have him."

"And this buried treasure of gold and silver...you never saw it and he never produced it?"

"No."

By now thoughts were clanging together inside Heron's head. If this was a secret trial, he had already said things that conflicted. He had told his uncle of finding a treasure in a gopher tortoise hole. Now he told the shaman he saw no treasure. He hadn't talked of stealing two canoes and joining Marinero, but then wouldn't Marinero surely bring it up in his desperation? Then they would ask why he *didn't* tell. Oh, Taku, he was a fish in a trap of his own making.

But the shaman was, at the same time, silently thatching together his own thoughts. The treasure was uppermost in his mind, but not in the way Marinero or Heron might have thought. To the old prisoner, the lure and promise of gold was all that might keep him alive. To Heron, the fear of being exposed in a lie about not ever seeing the gold or plotting to sail off to Spain with it were enough to make his heart race and hands shake. But to old Hawkman, the treasure mattered only because he and Deerstalker had already decided that the Jeaga wanted no part of it. If the old slave died, the gold's secret whereabouts would vanish with him unless some other Jeaga tracker discovered it years later. Heron had denied any knowledge of it, as they had hoped he would. And even if he were lying, today's stern lesson would surely seal his silence. Maybe the experience might also put a halt to his confounded curiosity.

And what of the Ais? Well, a freed and/or talkative slave could indeed kindle strife among the Ais and Jeaga. However, if the Ais heard news of a dead slave several days or weeks later, the Jeaga could always shrug their shoulders and profess ignorance of his identity. And perhaps a few baskets of fresh oysters might appease their cacique?

Hawkman now sized up Heron and concluded that he had succeeded in producing enough fear. After a few seconds of silence to be sure that terror had saturated the boy's every pore, he said in the same low tones: "I do not think we need to take this matter any further. However, there is one thing you must do. You must vow to Taku that you have spoken the truth and you must at the same time purify your souls. Therefore, I will tell you alone—and not for the ears of your friends—that part of the birthing ceremony tomorrow night will be to conduct a sacrifice. You will learn to defeat the devil Catalobe by destroying the souls of the evil ones who do his bidding on earth. To do that you must destroy the eyes, where the souls reside. Remember that. You will be the first to strike, and you must not fail to do so *convincingly* or the gods will know that you are untruthful and command that you be thrown into the fire."

When twenty boys assembled at the canoe landing in the noon sun the next day, they nodded at one another stiffly, even though they were family or clan members or had hauled garbage or tracked animals together as part of the training that led up to this event. Ordinarily they would be jostling or wrestling. Now there was no bravado as they stood still like so many cypress knees in a swamp of unease. But Heron was more than nervous. He was scared, with a gnawing dread in his stomach, because he knew some things the others didn't. And he had hardly slept the night before as he churned the previous day's events over in his mind.

The scene became more ominous when the men showed up: elders, hunters, warriors, fishermen. All were silent and solemn, and they looked right through the inquiring glances of the young novitiates even though they were fathers, uncles, cousins and brothers.

They soon were paddled silently across the River of Turtles and were then led in single file towards the Great House. They were surprised to see along one outer wall a long table with jars of palmetto tea and large baskets of foods. Their silent custodians motioned for them to eat all they wanted. As they grabbed hands full of raisins, nuts, sea grapes, prickly pears and coontie cakes, one could see the novitiates slacken their posture and exchange friendly glances as if to say "this isn't going to be quite so bad after all."

Heron ate, too, but something didn't seem right about all the gracious generosity. Also strange was that despite the heat of the day, a fire was burning at the far end of the Great Hall. And as everyone ate, men were filing into the building with masks, drums, flutes and rattles. Others were lighting pipes.

In the center of the building stood old Hawkman, leaning on his striped pole. When the meal was finished, the twenty boys were told to sit in a circle around the shaman, who announced that the ceremony would begin with the Dance of the Masks. They were about to see, for the first time, he said, painted face masks that had been carved from mahogany and cypress so many centuries ago that they were now the tribe's most sacred possessions. "Each represents what you must become to win the favor of Taku and Shabula," said the shaman.

As the drums and rattles began beating a steady rhythm, the Dance of the Masks began. And so, whirling past the shaman in the center circle, one at a time, came the man in the wolf mask chanting of how they must stalk as stealthily as the wolf. Spinning about behind him was a man in a toothy barracuda mask, urging them to control the sea as the barracuda did the fish on his reef. The alligator preached patience and vigilance. The whale mask represented abundance of the sea. The man in the eagle mask promised them eyes to see their enemies coming from all directions. Another mask had a long *parrata* in place of a nose and the wearer preached the need to produce many children.

Next, chanting men wove their way through them wearing their own personal warrior masks and extending them to the novitiates, then pulling them away as if to indicate that they weren't yet ready to become brothers in the tribe.

By now the Great Hall was thick with smoke from the fire and tobacco pipes burning leaves of the powerful nicotina rustica. Over Heron's left shoulder a hand extended a lit pipe. Some of his fellows already smoked, but Heron had never been able to endure the first bitter puff. Seeing all those about him sucking on their pipe stems, Heron began puffing, trying to keep the smoke out of his lungs. But a warrior in a mask was watching and made motions for him to suck in the smoke. He nodded and instantly there was a sharp pain in his lungs, followed by dizziness that nearly made him pass out. The warrior urged him on again and soon Heron had sensation that he was floating in air. Instead of passing out, he now felt pleasantly insulated from the people and noises around him.

As the dancing continued, a large basket of palmetto berries was passed among the boys. Heron had picked thousands of them and drank the tea every day, but, when he tried them in undiluted form, as did many Jeaga, he had told his mother he would rather chew a plate of deer scat. Now he was told to hold out a cupped hand and fill it with the shiny black berries. They tasted as rotten as he had imagined. But after he'd swallowed the whole horrid handful, he saw one of the drummers smile broadly at him. He smiled back. He felt less anxious.......even powerful. But the smoke and berries had also produced a powerful thirst.

After two or three rounds of the palmetto baskets, the shaman raised his striped scepter and the drums and rattles faded away. "And now you are about to begin your re-birth as Jeaga men," he pronounced. "You will take part in the tradition of the black drink."

Every boy the age of seven had known of the black drink. Warriors partook of the dark brew before going into battle. One tribe served it to another as a show of hospitality. It was passed around at funerals. But never by women and children, which is why boys would pick strange plants and pretend their concoction was the real thing. But only the shaman was entrusted with the secret recipe.

Now they would taste the black drink for the first time. One of the warriors struggled to carry into the circle a three-gallon gourd. It had a long neck and a small hole on top that could be covered by a single finger. At one side was a round hole of two inches in diameter. When the dark brown liquid inside was poured out the side hole into a large conch shell, a low whistle-like noise would erupt from the top hole.

The secret of the black drink was disarmingly simple. One picked both leaves and twigs of the yaupon holly, or cassina plant, parched them in a ceramic bowl, then boiled them until producing a strongly caffeinated tea. In this case, however, old Hawkman had added a few powdered herbs to be sure of inducing a special reaction at the re-birthing ceremony.

Now the pipes and palmetto berries were joined by passing around whelks of black drink. All of the youths were prodigiously dry and each one was more apt to gulp down a swallow first and consider the taste later. Again, the earthy bitterness of leaf and twig extract soon gave way to euphoria and a desire to partake of the next round.

Heron had hardy noticed at the time, but some large clay bowls had been placed near the shaman, perhaps to contain some other ritual concoction. Out of the corner of one eye Heron could see men in the hazy background looking on and whispering, as if suppressing amused expressions or expecting something to happen. Within a few minutes he realized why the novices had been treated to a generous mid-day meal, followed by pipes, berries and the bitter black drink. The euphoria yielded again to dizziness and his stomach began churning. When the symptoms became evident among those all around the circle, the shaman raised his painted pole again.

"Now listen," he croaked at his loudest. "You are about to purify your inner selves for a re-birth as Jeaga men and sons of Taku. You are to empty yourselves into these vessels. Your past lives will be intermingled and then tossed together into the river and carried away. Now come forth or you will drink again until you do."

The dancers and servers quickly scattered into the background and the scene became one of boys gagging and retching into the clay crocks. Heron was in the middle of them and soon fell to the ground and doubled up. Vomit stained his buckskin shirt and mixed with the sand he laid on. He cared not. He saw others get up and bend over the clay pots again. He knew he would as well, but for the moment he just wanted to close his eyes—or die.

The moaning and dry heaving continued for several more minutes. None of the spectators interfered with those who had "purged" their insides. The boys lay mostly soundless, some trance-like with eyes rolled up, some quietly convulsing. When Heron managed to raise an eyelid, he looked out beyond the thatched roof of the Great House and could tell that the sun was low on the western horizon. He could sense that the men behind the masks were conversing again, becoming more active.

Suddenly the air was pierced again with the shaman's scratchy voice. "You have now purged yourselves of the children that have lived within you," he said. "Now you are about to be reborn into a new life. But first your body must die to its old ways. You will die so that the ancient masks can instill within you the persons that you need to become. You must now submit to your spirit guide."

With that, one of the mask wearers stepped up behind each inert initiate and forced him up to his knees. He then put a black fish bladder over each eye and fastened it in place with a cloth blindfold. Heron was blindfolded, helped to his feet and led on a maze-like walk of twists and turns that was probably meant to confuse him as to distance and destination. In a few minutes he knew he was outside the Great Hall because he could feel the cool breeze of early evening.

More prodding, stopping, starting. He was obviously in a line, and in time he was pushed nearer to where low voices were doing something to the boy in front of him. Suddenly a powerful arm slapped him behind the thighs and his knees buckled into the kneeling position. His ankles were bound and hands strapped and crossed in front of him like a corpse. Then he was picked up and put down in a sitting position with his knees to his chest. A moist rag was shoved in his mouth.

The floor was of broken shells and his back leaned against a wall of hard protruding points that was probably coquina rock. The sheets of ancient, compressed, pebble-like shells were usually found in caves. Maybe this was a place where bodies decomposed before being taken to The Place of the Dead. He knew from the moans and thrashing about him that the others were all there, too.

Despite his tight fish bladder and cloth blindfold, Heron could still make out a faint orange light from the entrance and the sounds of men muttering. A loud voice from that direction announced: "You will now experience your death in silence. Your spirit guides will be listening, and each murmur or noise will signify that you are still alive in your child's body and not ready to be re-born."

With that all light was extinguished and the twenty sat in the black stillness, each alone to overcome his fears and lingering nausea.

Despite a cramped leg and aching back, Heron fell asleep. He had no idea how long he had been in a state of dreamless nothingness when he was startled awake by the sounds of the entrance covering being removed and a cacophony of sounds flooding inside. The rattles and drums were shaking and beating again. Men were rushing into the dank crypt and dragging out each "corpse." When Heron was picked up and deposited outside, he could hear voices all around him chanting.

> Devil wants you.
> Chase the devil.
> Kill the devil,
>   or the devil gets YOU.

Arms and hands were working quickly to unbind his hands and feet. He stood, ripped the blindfold away, and he realized that he had emerged from a cave behind the base of the wooded dune. It had probably been dug out generations ago to store firewood and artifacts for rituals atop the Place of the Sun and Moon. There was no time to stretch or rub an aching muscle. The drums, rattles and chanting grew louder.

> Devil wants you.
> Chase the devil.
> Kill the devil,
>   or the devil gets YOU.

The same voice in the cave now emerged in the form of a man wearing the mask of Taku. "The devil wants *you*," he shouted in the faces of the groggy initiates. "Taku wants you, but you must first chase the devil's agent and kill him so that you can live." The chanters, all in warrior masks, huddled closer around the youths exhorting them to join the chant. Soon all were yelling at the top of their lungs.

Just then in the doorway of the cave came a great shout and there appeared a man wearing the largest mask of all—a hollowed out tree trunk that surrounded his head and rested on his shoulders. The eye holes were large, rimmed by thick red circles. Great horns protruded from each side. Hideous faces were painted in red, white and black all over the trunk.

"Ooooooaaaaaaaagh. The devil wants YOU," a voice behind the mask shouted. He jumped forward and began whirling about the stupefied youths.

"No, no," shouted back the Taku voice. "He is the devil's messenger. You must kill him before he can tell the devil to steal your souls!

> Chase the devil's man
> Kill the devil's man.
> Before he gets YOU.

The devil man spun away from the group and next appeared at the foot of the path leading up to the Place of the Sun and Moon. "I go to capture Taku's temple," he shouted with arms raised. The stunned boys paused.

"Go, go, go!" said the Taku mask. "Chase the devil's man!"

The twenty were now off climbing the stony pathway with the gourd rattlers and drummers right behind.

> Chase the devil.
> Kill the devil's man.
> Before he gets YOU.

All the way up, the stiff and exhausted novitiates saw only glimpses of the nimble, fleet devil man. When they reached the top, they froze at the entrance to the circular ritual arena and tried to take in the sight. In the middle of the mound stood Hawkman, the old shaman, again with his striped scepter but now wearing a mask of Taku. Behind him, much like a child emboldened when hiding behind a parent, the garish devil man danced back and forth, making menacing gestures at his assailants. In the shadows opposite where the chasers stood was a rectangle covered by a large blanket.

"I fear the devil's man is too clever for you," announced the shaman. "Stay where you are and I will work some magic to help you."

He turned his back, raised the blanket and held it high. The devil man darted behind it. The shaman uttered some inaudible incantations. A commotion took place behind the large blanket. Then the shaman pulled away the blanket with a flourish and lo, the devil man was lying in his huge tree trunk mask, his arms and legs pinned to stakes. The pursuers uttered a collective gasp.

Their attention now riveted on the nearby ritual fire pit with a roaring blaze that sent sparks flying into the crisp November air. Many wooden spears had been laid on logs near where the fire flared. Their tips were either red hot or actually burning.

What Heron saw next made his heart race and his head go dizzy again. The devil man who lay pinned to the ground beside the burning spears was not the fleet-footed devil man they had chased. The trunk mask must have been thrust upon someone else who was then pinned down and tied to the four stakes. Heron recognized the ragged trousers made from Spanish sail cloth. The others were still in awe of the shaman's magic.

Hawkman now raised his hand. "Through the power of Taku, I have captured the devil man, but only you can stop the devil man from stealing your souls," he intoned. "You must extinguish *his* souls tonight, like *this.*"

The shaman picked up one of the spears from the fire. He walked directly to where Heron stood in the front row and placed the shaft in his right hand with a subtle nod. "Strike for an eye," he said in barely audible tones.

Heron looked at the spear, its tip aflame. *"Kill the devil's man, before he gets YOU,"* intoned the chanters and drummers. Their rhythm suddenly quickened. *Kill-the-devil-man-before-he-gets-you. KILLTHEDEVILMANBEFOREHEGETSYOU!*

Four, five seconds seemed forever. Heron was now above the man in the tree trunk mask and through the two red-rimmed holes stared eyes opened wide.

No more time to think.

"Ah, decided not to go to Spain?" said the voice inside the mask. Heron was so startled that he quickly aimed for an eye socket and thrust the spear down into the souls of old Marinero. A scream. A spurt of blood. Heron staggered away as the next lad raised his fiery spear and aimed for the other eye socket, his face the picture of cruel lust.

On and on it went, each youth finding a new place where the blood-soaked, twitching body had not yet been pierced. In time the chanting gave way to another row of onlookers wearing animal masks. For over an hour, in constant cacophony they bayed at the rising full moon like wolves and screeched like owls. The ear-splitting commotion was required to assure that the devil would not hear the pleas of his fallen agent and return to revive him. The initiates were prodded to join in the yelling and yelping even though their throats were raw from smoking and vomiting and lack of anything to drink.

As the howlers' stamina eventually waned, the shaman signaled it was time for the final ritual. The large devil mask was removed and quickly spirited away to be stored where the devil couldn't find it. The head of the sacrificed slave was severed from the neck and the body dragged into the fire pit. Now the drums beat more slowly and flutes played a slower, melancholy melody as Jeaga men took turns whirling slowly with the head of the "devil man."

Heron remained slumped in the shadows, not sure he had performed up to the shaman's expectations. Poor Marinero, he thought.

Maybe if he had shared his treasure with me, would I have gone with him and hunted on his great estates? Or were there any estates at all? Or a castle twenty times a man's height or a hundred potions to make one smell better?

"Ohhhh." He started and shuddered as the bellicose Bobcat whirled by and suddenly stopped. Bobcat was holding the bloodied, sightless head of Marinero in both hands. "You see? This devil's man was no Jeaga," he exclaimed. "I knew that no Jeaga could work for Catalobe!"

In the final test of the ceremony, the re-born were made to stay up on the Place of the Sun and Moon to assure that Catalobe himself would not come looking for his lieutenant on earth that night. Most of the initiated, too exhausted to exercise their new manly rights, were content to find a place by the ring of the smoldering fire where they could warm their feet and sleep until the sun came up.

Only Heron seemed bothered by the acrid smell of singed clothing and burning flesh in the fire pit. He lay near the rim of the great mound, his face to the stars, afraid to sleep lest the angry spirit of Marinero lead the devil to him.

He was now a *man* but he felt no euphoria—only shame.

CHAPTER SEVEN

Menéndez and Philip
1564-65

When Pedro Menéndez had time to contemplate his bold escape from prison in Seville, he realized that it had been less than a heroic cavalier's welcome at the royal palace in Madrid. Escorted to a common barracks, he was quick to write Philip II to complain that neither the dank, windowless quarters nor his nearby neighbors were suitable "for a man in my position."

When the Casa de Contratación and Council of the Indies learned that Menéndez had found sanctuary in the very palace of the king, the only way they could show their pique was to delay the scoundrel's case even more. Finally on November 23, 1564, after the king had accused it of "malicious and capricious" delay, the Council of the Indies issued its ruling. Menéndez, despite now being in the king's embrace, was found guilty on nine of fourteen charges. He was fined three thousand ducats and would be denied his "office" for three years.

This might have been his nadir of despair, but Menéndez was not destined to suffer much longer. First, after lawyer Juan Gómez had filed an appeal, Menéndez was admitted to the royal court and assigned chambers befitting a captain-general of the fleet pending final outcome of the case. Secondly, just a few days after the Council's ruling against Menéndez, a royal courier had delivered Philip shocking news. The rumors about a French fort in Florida could now be confirmed!

It seems that in the summer of 1563 a group of 150 or so French soldiers and settlers had begun a colony at Santa Elena near the thirty-first parallel, well north of the main channel for Spanish ships and out of their sight. In charge of their mission was Jean Ribault, who was already feared by the Spanish as a daring corsair captain. A Spanish reconnaissance ship had captured a sixteen-year-old French boy on a nearby beach, who had reported that Ribault had erected a large stone column on the landing site and intended to build a fort there. Another report had it that Ribault was now back in Le Harve preparing a massive flotilla of soldiers, tradesmen, farmers and domestic animals to consolidate the French gains in Florida. Meanwhile, other reports were returning with winter passengers from the Indies that the new French fort had already been used as a base for raids on port towns in Santo Domingo and Cuba.

Suddenly Menéndez and Gómez could witness the ice thawing in the halls of the Alcazar and the king's drawing room. The "French threat" was on the lips of everyone passing time in the salon, and those who wanted to be in the know bowed when greeting the captain-general and sought his expert opinion. Who was this fellow Ribault? Had any of Menéndez' ships encountered him before? Could the French survive in such a wild place as Florida? Did he think Lutherans will be settling in the Caribbean? Will he be sailing to intercept Ribault?

Menéndez, the man who had been shunned by the same court notables during his battle against the Casa de Contratación, now accommodated all of his flattering inquirers because he never knew which one might slip in a favorable word to the Council about his appeal or —dare he think it—invest in an expedition to Florida.

And somehow, the wheels of justice began to grind more quickly. On February 3, 1565, the Council of the Indies terminated the last of its cases against Pedro Menéndez de Avilés. Two disputed bars of silver were ordered returned to him. And finally, he was to receive all 20,000 ducats due for having housed soldiers aboard his ships during the 1563 voyage to New Spain.

Menéndez was finally free to serve his king. And Philip, having disentangled himself from the hidebound legalities he had imposed on the Casa, could now feel free to consult the one man most qualified to answer his pressing questions about the French in Florida.

Within a few days Philip II asked Menéndez to study and report on the "problems of Florida." What did he believe could be done to settle there when so many Spanish expeditions had failed in the past?

What measures could be taken in the event that the French had already established a strong base for raiding the gold and silver-laden armadas that traveled north from New Spain?

The quarters in the Alcazar were not much larger than the "prison" in Seville, but the occupant had been allowed to bring in his sea chests and outfit it with a few tapestries, paintings, tableware and clothing more in keeping with his status. Now, on this cold afternoon in late February, Menéndez and Gómez met to draft their memorial to the king about Florida. They had poured goblets of Madeira to keep themselves warm. The captain-general paced, dictated, and muttered to himself. Gómez sat at a table scratching on parchment, having to decide which sentences were idle ramblings and which deserved to be in the written analysis of the "French problem" that the king would read.

"We need to say that the French aren't the only threat," said Menéndez after a sip of wine. "If it's true that the French are using Florida as a raiding base, then we can expect the English to follow. I had a letter last fall from a merchant in Galicia saying that five heavily armed English galleons were seen at Tenerife in the Canaries. They could be in Florida by now."

"But you don't know that they actually *are*," said Gómez, his quill suspended in the air.

"Put it in," said Menéndez with a wave. "Besides I've heard that the infamous Portuguese corsair Mimoso was seen off Santo Domingo. The point is that someone besides the French will set up his own operations on Florida if the king doesn't act."

The Madeira wine was warming him to the task. "I also wish to raise the specter of these enemies inciting slave insurrections in all of New Spain and the Indies. And such establishment, if not extinguished, might take root quickly and wipe out our strongholds of supply."

Gómez looked up again, cocking his head. "And this is because....?"

"I am convinced that Protestant heretics and aboriginals in Florida hold similar beliefs—quite probably satanic in origin. These shared beliefs could naturally lead them to an affinity unless they are kept apart."

Gómez said nothing, kept scratching with his quill.

"Now let us turn to some geographic features of the Florida mainland," he said. "There is strong anecdotal evidence that an arm of the sea extends westward from Newfoundland and joins another waterway that leads to the mines of Zacatecas in New Spain. This, in turn, may be a watery gateway to the South Seas and China. There are similar reports that the St. John's River much further south flows into a great inland sea, and from there through a river to the west coast of that peninsula. Both possibilities need to be explored."

He glanced at Gómez and decided the lawyer-scribe needed time to catch up with his words. After another long draught of Madeira, Menéndez continued. "Under no circumstances can the French be made aware of these possible trade routes. As his majesty knows, French fishing vessels are already using the Grand Banks near Newfoundland.

"That reminds me," he added. "Find somewhere to say that French or English settlements could also establish sugar growing and sheep farming and undercut two industries that are just becoming profitable for the crown."

By this time rumors had come to Madrid that the first French fort at Santa Elena was not active—perhaps even abandoned. Some reports had it that the French marauders who had sailed from that settlement were actually the last remnants of the colonists who had mutinied for lack of food and headed to the Indies in search of it. But Menéndez was a fast coach on a downhill run.

"The Spanish expedition should include 500 sailors, soldiers and farmers," he dictated. "If upon searching the coastline no intruders are discovered, the expedition should land at Santa Elena and begin the process of settling and farming. And it should include say, four Jesuits to establish *doctrinas* and teach the faith to the sons of the native chiefs. And while the settlement is nurturing, smaller vessels can depart to map the coast north to Newfoundland."

"And perhaps to search for the whereabouts of Juan Menéndez?" said Gómez peering up at the captain.

"Yes, of course, but don't put that in. Now let us address the king's favorite subject: money. I will suggest that the first expedition be estimated at 80,000 ducats for initial outfitting and a year's supplies. If it turns out there are Frenchmen in the area, a punitive expedition of, say, four well-armed galleons can be mounted at an additional expense of 50,000 ducats."

"I wonder about *that*," said the attorney. He paused to wipe his pen for effect,

Menéndez paused to fill his goblet. Without comment he waited for Gómez to finish scratching and continued. "I need the right diplomatic language to suggest that the crown bear the cost of the entire undertaking because it would enable the king to act more quickly and secretly. All profits, glory, etcetera, etcetera, would flow to the crown, of course."

"You don't *really...?*" Gómez said.

"Well, perhaps not," interrupted Menéndez with a sheepish contortion. "But see here. With all that's transpired with the Casa and the Council, I don't think they would appreciate the idea of making me Adelantado Menéndez. No, the idea must come from Philip—and in the form of a royal decree."

Within a few days of filing his "analysis" with the king's secretary for correspondence, Menéndez left for a brief trip to Avilés. It had been a year since he had last seen his wife Ana Maria. Although she had been betrothed to him when they were both ten and then wed for more than thirty years, Ana Maria had long understood that her husband's true mistress, the sea, would claim him for all but a few sporadic weeks each year.

In fact, this visit, like the others, would be punctuated by many discussions with bankers and other backers in the port towns of Asturia. It was in these beehives of gossip that Menéndez heard from several captains of Basque fishing boats that the feared Jean Ribault was at this time in the French port of Le Harve outfitting a major expedition—not to Santa Elena, but to somewhere else on the Florida coast.

Menéndez hastened back to Madrid in mid-March with this news and asked for an audience with the king. However, when he was ushered into Philip's study, the Castilian ambassador to France was also present. The latter said he had heard nothing whatever about any Ribault expedition preparing at Le Harve. Yet, the king was inclined to believe Menéndez' report because he had recently received another piece of valuable information. Another winter arrival in Seville carried correspondence from the governor of Cuba stating that several of the French marauders in the Indies were indeed mutineers, but not from Santa Elena. That settlement had been abandoned the year before and Jean Ribault had returned to France. No, these men were from a second French settlement that had been established much further south, near where the St. John's River met the sea. There they had already built a triangular fort named Caroline. The mutineers insisted that they were good Catholics who had rebelled at the harsh duties imposed by their "Huguenot Lutheran" officers and because supplies at the settlement had become unbearably short. Ribault, they added, was expected to return and re-supply the hungry occupants of Fort Caroline.

It still lacked confirmation, but it all fit. King Philip decided it was time to act. He informed Menéndez that he would appoint three members of the Council of Indies to negotiate terms of an *adelamiento* for the Florida expedition. Rather than take place in some chamber of the royal palace, Menéndez and Gómez were directed to meet with the judges at 10 am two days hence in the same *Audiencia de Grodos* hall in which they had faced so many charges a few months before.

On March 15, 1565, still smarting from his appearances as a prisoner before the Casa in threadbare clothing, Menéndez strode into the large near-empty courtroom resplendent in ruffled outer cloak with gold and red striped sleeves. He carried the sword of an admiral. Gómez the attorney was at his side, impeccable as usual in black suit with white ruffled shirt.

Menéndez recognized the judges from his earlier trials and quickly realized that the king had not selected the most punitive and pernicious of the lot, as he might have done to show intimidation. The president of the proceeding was Dr. Juan Vázquez de Arce, a professor of law at the University of Valladolid. The other two were a wealthy sheep raiser and a sugar broker. None were from Seville or Cadiz, another sign that the king had taken pains to select negotiators who were neither tools of the Casa nor prejudiced against northerners.

Yet, two irritants gnawed at the mind of Menéndez.

Why hold an intimate negotiating session in such an ornate, cavernous, yet empty chamber? Answer: to remind us of the power and majesty of the crown. Why were Gómez and I seated at the petitioners' table where we have to crane our necks looking up at the judges seated en banc above us? Answer: to intimidate us.

After proper introductions, Dr. Vázquez, the presiding officer, cleared his throat. "After receiving and studying your memorial to Philip II," he read stiffly, "the king and Council have determined to carry out the Florida enterprise as an *adelantamiento* with Pedro Menéndez de Avilés as adelantado." You have well described the many political and economic reasons. However, we should also stress that the winning of souls for Christ would be an enterprise of great spiritual merit for the Crown of Castile and its adelantado. Conversely, for those souls to remain in their heathen state or even worse, to become afflicted with the plague of heresy, would be a greater sin before God.

"Alas," continued Dr. Vázquez looking straight down his nose at the two men seated below him, "the Crown is unable to contribute any monies from the royal treasury directly to the enterprise. You must understand that we have had several previous unsuccessful attempts at settling Florida. We have also encountered situations where funds of the Crown have been, ah, misdirected. These reasons are why in 1563 the Council and king determined that all funding of exploration should, as a general rule, be private."

The professor droned on. The king had spent heavily to repel Muslin assaults on the North African bases of Oran and Mazalquivir. Now, with the Turks invading the Mediterranean and seizing Malta, Philip had to borrow again from the merchants of Seville to raise a navy to repel them. "After all," he added, "you do own the nucleus of a fine fleet and there are as yet no proven French hostilities in Florida."

Menéndez had anticipated every word and had already charted his response. He would risk all. "Distinguished Council members," he said, rising slowly to his feet. "I will excuse myself for a few minutes of consultation with my attorney. When we return, I would appreciate seeing you three sitting at the same table we now occupy. There is ample room. This is not a trial or inquisition. It is a negotiation between equal parties. Thank you."

Gómez followed Menéndez out into the hall barely disguising his agitation. "For the love of the saints," he said as they found a bench, "that is no way to address members of the king's Council."

"On the contrary," said Menéndez smiling indulgently. "This is an historic moment. The king must have an adelantado in Florida to repel a grave threat. Since he has no money and Seville is a rusty lockbox as usual, we will turn to the merchants and bankers and shipbuilders and sailors of the north. And with the finest fleet ever sent on an exploratory enterprise, we will settle lands and enrich our investors and break the monopolistic back of Seville and its Andalusian merchant princes. Oh yes, in the process we will enrich the Crown as well."

Gómez said nothing but thought his client a reckless gambler. But Menéndez thought of Hernando Cortés in Mexico. Starting as a hopeful conquistador in 1519, he and his heirs had over thirty-five years founded an economic empire on Indian labor that produced over thirty thousand pesos a year from mining and agriculture. Cortés had become a marqués. Menéndez envisioned all that *in addition* to a rich income from shipping.

"Well, my good friend, let us return to this august body," Menéndez said rising from the hallway bench with a wink. When he opened the door, the three negotiators were still seated on the judicial dais. "We will now see how much they want this *asiento*," he whispered. "When I open the door, don't move forward until I do."

Menéndez closed the door behind them and the two stood silently in the rear of the chamber with arms folded. A minute passed. Then the three men whispered to one another, gathered their papers, stepped off their dais and sat at one end of the long lawyer's table. "This should be enjoyable," muttered Menéndez as they strode forward. "Just remember, the more they want of us, the more we will extract from them."

The first half of an *asiento* spelled out what the king expected from the expedition. In this case the negotiators required that Menéndez provide his own 900-ton galleass, the *San Pelayo,* as the nucleus of a fleet that would include four fast zabras and six shallops—the latter to be used chiefly for fishing and exploring shallow waters. The enormous *San Pelayo* would be used to transport the bulk of 500 men, including a hundred sailors and a hundred farmers plus several tradesmen and up to a dozen clerics. Menéndez was also to provide livestock: a hundred horses, 400 hogs, 200 calves and 400 sheep.

The great galleass would also carry a cargo of trade goods for New Spain. Thus, once the ocean were crossed and the fleet safely in the Indies, men, animals and supplies would be transferred to the smaller ships, with the *San Pelayo* then free to unload its trade cargo in some Indies port take on more supplies for the new settlement.

Menéndez cheerfully and quickly assented to all of these requests, so that within a few minutes the tension that begun the morning was lost in an affability unknown when he had faced the stern and stultifying Casa. The area assigned the adelantado had no limits save the boundaries of the viceroyalty of New Spain. The only constraint was that the mission had to be completed within three years.

Menéndez also agreed quickly to the proposed details of settling. He was to form two to three townships and fortify each one with a "strong house" of stone or wood, surrounded by a moat and drawbridge. Five hundred slaves would be acquired to build the fort and then work the fields. The *asiento* ignored the fact that the king's father had forbidden all forms of slavery. It simply granted Menéndez a license to acquire up to 500.

And the native population? Not much was said about it *per se* except when one of the judges read aloud to the new adelantado: "Every attempt shall be made to bring natives to the Christian faith." The mission, he read on, "must be carried out in peace, friendship and Christianity."

In the very next clause, Menéndez and the Council members agreed that the adelantado and his heirs for three lifetimes could require the services of Indians within his chief settlement for building, harvesting and whatever else served the good of the community. He was also empowered to grant *encomiendas* to settlers in other towns as inducements or rewards. Thus, a farmer favored by Menéndez would be entitled to claim the labor of so many Indians for his lifetime and that of his first heir.

In light of taking on such enormous responsibilities, the judges assured Menéndez that the king would be lavish in his generosity. Menéndez could lay claim on fifteen thousand ducats instantly and an annual salary of two thousand ducats—provided that he swore to return the money if his fleet did not sail by May 31. The title, Adelantado of Florida, could be bequeathed to his heirs. He could instantly claim up to 5,500 square miles of land and be entitled to all of its bounty except minerals. Unlike all other adelantados before him, he could trade on his own behalf anywhere in Florida, the Indies or New Spain. Upon returning to Spain he could bypass the customs inspectors of Cadiz and Seville and go directly to a port in his northern Spain homeland. And when he arrived, he would pay only ten per cent of the normal customs duty. Along the way, if he captured any corsair prizes, all of the booty would be his without the king extracting his usual twenty percent. And after three years, if the mission were declared a success, the coveted title of *marqués* would be his!

It was approaching time for the mid-day meal and the entire deal to settle the remainder of the unexplored world had been conducted in less than four hours. The men shook hands and departed, Menéndez and Gómez to the adelantado's quarters. In a few days the king would issue and official decree, but they expected no surprises.

When they walked in, they were greeted with an anxious look by Bartolomé Menéndez, who had been released from his custody in Seville and gone to Avilés to shake off his mysterious ailment. Now he was in Madrid at his brother's behest and looking better.

"Well?" he said when they appeared.

"Well, what?" said Menéndez with a playful poke in the ribs

"Perhaps you should bow or genuflect to the new adelantado of Florida," offered Gómez.

"You really *did* it after all? So I am now the *alcaide* of some important place, correct?"

"Yes," said his Menéndez struggling out of his scratchy lace collar. "Only so far there *are* no important places. We have to get there first, which is why you will be a lowly admiral for the time being." He poured three goblets of Madeira and handed one to each for a toast.

"Let us toast to my new estates," said the jaunty Bartolomé.

"To be sure," said Menéndez. "I hereby grant you ten times the land you now own." And with a wink to Gómez: "All he has is a small house on the plaza in Avilés. The patio in back barely has room for a fountain."

During the frivolity it was evident to Bartolomé that the lawyer was less than jovial in return. "There's more sparkle in these glasses than in your eyes," he said. "Is my brother holding something back on me?"

"No, maybe it is me," said Gómez. "Forgive me, but we lawyers are trained to look for scorpions in a chest of gold," he said with a faint smile. "I just have some fears because it is such an enormous undertaking, starting with the fact that the contract calls for you, admiral, to be off at sea by May 31. And I do think, Don Adelantado, that you may not realize the full extent of what you signed today. You may have been talking to these Council people as equals, as you said so directly this morning, but you must realize that this is a contact between a king and his subject. And when your sovereign issues his formal decree, I assure you it will state that your failure to comply with its terms will not be a mere contract violation. It will say that it constitutes "treason to your natural Lord."

"Well, it's still better than rotting away in Seville," said Menéndez before tilting his goblet again.

"There is one thing more, as long as I've ruined the occasion," said Gómez. "Philip is sending you because he thinks he is thwarting a major French incursion of Florida. Well, suppose it's now late May. You've spent all that money loading your ships and Philip beds his wife, the French queen. He utters some sweet things in her ear and she promises never to set foot in Florida again. Can you imagine trying to sell everything from those ships at auction prices and sorting out hundreds of invoices with the Casa?"

But Menéndez was simply too jubilant, too relieved that after two years of suspense, he once again had the same rush of hope that went with him every time he left a harbor and the wind propelled his sails toward the open sea. "My esteemed counselor," he said waving his goblet of wine, "I promise you that if the queen relents I will simply sail away with the fleet to the South Seas. Or maybe I'll become the first adelantado who never returned, creating my own pirate's island somewhere in the Caribbean.

"But I do agree with your concern about the May 31 deadline," he said, "and that is where you come in, brother. Bartolomé, I need you to go to our friend Pedro del Castillo in Cadiz at once. Do not stop in Seville for ten seconds. Leave as soon as we can obtain a copy of the contract for you to give Don Pedro. Emphasize to him that the king has pledged fifteen thousand ducats upon departure and that we need an advance to begin lading. After that, I will need you in Seville to organize the mission until I arrive. I myself must first go to Asturia to recruit sailors, ships and investors. This will be a great new era for Asturia, I tell you!"

Then he abruptly turned again to Gómez, who stood silently by looking into his goblet. "My friend, I know you think that king spider has caught the fly in his web again."

"Oh, no," said the lawyer slowly. "Now you're too big to be a fly. It's more like he's trying to snare an eagle in mid-flight. You can probably break free of the web, but you might destroy it in doing so."

On May 12 Pedro Menéndez de Avilés approached Seville in a jaunty mood. When King Philip had proclaimed the *adelantamiento* in March, he had also ordered the Casa de Contratación to comply with the terms of the *asiento* and accommodate Menéndez' requests. A similar order had gone to Casa officials in Cadiz, Galatia and the Canary Islands.

The trip to his northern homeland had been a rallying cry for the network of merchants and ship builders that lined the Bay of Biscay. Menéndez was greeted as a hero wherever he went and used every gathering of well-wishers to stress that "every family of means should be proud to send at least one of its blood or part of its treasure on this enterprise." He left confident that at least 200 farmers and seamen would depart Avilés by May 31 and join the main fleet from Seville in the Canaries. On the overland return route to Seville the adelantado had posted copies of the *asiento* in town halls and had attracted a straggling of volunteers like a Pied Piper.

As his carriage finally bumped along the cobblestones of Seville and into the great plaza facing the harbor, Menéndez swept the scene with his eyes and instantly concluded that something wasn't right. To his left the primary lading areas A, B, and C were a bustle of men painting and hammering and over-stuffed carts being pushed up gangways. He recognized the ships as the armada for New Spain, all but ready to deliver trade goods and gather bullion.

To the right, at wharf D, usually reserved for local transient ships, wallowed the great *San Pelayo*, its gangplank down but nothing moving up or down it. Two pataches were tethered behind it, also quiet. All along the strand were clusters of aimless-looking men idly chatting or shooting dice. As the carriage stopped and Menéndez emerged, the men jerked their heads up and one said "Are you the....?" But the adelantado had already bounded up the gangplank and was striding astern to the captain's quarters.

He threw open the door and saw Bartolomé sitting at the chart table with his head in his hands. All about were disheveled piles of paper. An inkwell had recently been spilled and clumsily sopped. A half-empty clay mug covered part of the ink stain and another sat by the bedside. Menéndez picked it up and sniffed.

"So you've gone to rum now?" he thundered at the startled Bartolomé. "What in the devil's infernal hell is going on? Or not?"

"Maybe this *is* the devil's infernal hell," said Bartolomé, still slumped in his captain's chair. Menéndez recognized that what he first took as a look of lethargic resignation was actually one of a man coiled and ready for combat.

"All right," he said more evenly to his younger brother. "Can you bring me up to date on where we stand? Did the Casa release the fifteen thousand ducats? Do we now have the money due us from the last voyage?"

"We have neither," said Bartolomé again without moving or looking up. "I don't care if his majesty Philip II came down here and threatened to behead every one of them with his own sword. They won't issue a ducat until you give collateral that you'll repay it in full if we don't sail by May 31. And they won't release the other twenty thousand ducats from 1563 until they have in hand all the receipts for everything spent. Now you tell me, Señor Captain-General," he said looking up for the first time, "where are these missing receipts? I've had fiscals looking all over five ships for them and all I have are a few shards."

"A great many went down with your nephew's ship in the hurricane. Some others are probably on the bottom of the Caribbean with the *San Sebastian*."

"Well, now you see my problem," said Bartolomé running his hands through his thick black hair. "No money means no supplies, no lading. Oh, and the Casa says that the supplying of the treasure fleet must take precedence over our mission to Florida. But that's hardly our only problem. I can occupy you with many more."

Menéndez 's eyes searched for the rum bottle. He was dusty and thirsty from the long trek and needed something, but discovered the rum bottle standing empty in a waste barrel. "Yes, of course, tell me," he said, settling into the other chair at the chart table.

"A week ago a royal courier delivered a sealed letter from the king addressed to you. I said you had been delayed and broke the royal seal before he could say 'Mother Maria.' The king says that he has further evidence that the French are indeed outfitting a mission to Florida at Le Harve. He has sent a 'personal representative incognito'—I suppose that's what kings would call a spy—to conduct an eye-witness survey of the scene and report back personally to him. He expects that in two or three weeks we should know more as to the number of ships and men, etcetera."

"That doesn't sound like a problem," said Menéndez. "Can you get your poor brother glass of Mazuelo? Maybe a Viura? I don't care if your cabin boy has to crush grapes with his boots on."

Bartolomé clanged a bell and the two were soon sharing a bottle of the black-graped Mazuelo. "You say no problem? Let me finish. Philip said he is so sure of the French intentions that he is mustering another 500 men to Seville to climb aboard our ships. They are arriving by the dozens right now and expecting to be quartered on board until we sail. I have no money for food, so I did the only thing I could think of. I have told all of the passengers—soldiers, farmers, whatever—that they must pay for their own food and lodging in Seville until we sail."

"Yes, and then?"

"Well, and then they will be reimbursed upon sailing," said Bartolomé with a crooked smile. "You know we could always hang ourselves from the main mast right now. It would be much more pleasant than being drawn and quartered by an angry crowd in a few days."

"There is more?" Menéndez asked. By now the elation of his visit to Asturia had faded into the present.

"Yes indeed. The same letter from the king also said that because the French fort is said to be strong, he will supply us with heavy artillery to batter its walls down. He promises a dozen heavy cannon and a hundred hundredweight of gunpowder.

"Now the tricky part," added Bartolomé, "is that the king promises to pay for it but has not. Meanwhile, he instructs us to employ carpenters *now* to buttress the decks and secure all this rolling iron. They are just finishing now and think they are going to get paid. Imagine that!"

"It's even worse," said Menéndez, his new title beginning to wear like an anchor around his neck. "I have expected to net twelve thousand ducats from freight charges on the outbound voyage. With all that artillery and five hundred soldiers, there won't be any room at all for extra freight. And the king's soldiers will take another seven thousand ducats to feed on the way."

On May 26, with still no funds forthcoming, Menéndez again pled before the Casa de Contratación. If the Casa would pry loose the fifteen thousand ducats promised by the king, he would offer a bondsman to guarantee its return if he failed to sail by May 31. Still smarting because Menéndez had jumped bail when disappearing from its prison, the Casa smugly refused.

Menéndez returned the next day and offered to accept six thousand. He had his money the next morning. Sailors and suppliers were ready to begin lading, but the adelantado held them off. On the same day he sent King Philip a letter by courier stating that he would miss the deadline set by the *asiento* and would not be able to depart at all if he did not receive the twenty thousand ducats for leasing his ships to the armada in 1563.

Now it was time for fortune to smile once again on Pedro Menéndez. His letter arrived the day after the spy from Le Harve had reported personally to the king. And the report was more alarming than Philip had even imagined.

The king's *incognito* was a charming French physician named Enveja. When he had strolled about the harbor at Le Harve on May 17, he had seen a large fleet in advanced stages of loading men and cargo. Leading the mission to Florida was none other than the swashbuckling corsair captain Jean Ribault. He had indeed founded Fort Caroline on the St. Johns River, and had now returned to France for a second wave of settlers and supplies. His flagship was a mere 150 tons compared to the *San Pelayo's* 900 when loaded, but it was also rigged with oars for speed and close combat. And two of the six remaining vessels were of similar size.

Dr. Enveja estimated there were already 500 soldiers aboard the ships, almost all from Normandy and all smartly outfitted with matching wool tunics, shining helmets and new arquebuses. Moreover, the ships were said to carry 200 cannon to defend the fort. As the spy strolled about unimpeded, he saw women, children and one ship that had been converted to accommodate horses, sheep, and cows—essentially a mirror image of the Spanish expedition. One thing that was *not* a copy was the presence of eight or so Lutheran ministers, all preparing to infiltrate the new world with the Huguenot Heresy!

So casual was Dr. Enveja during his visit that he even obtained an interview with Jean Ribault himself and was amazed to see a remarkable similarity between the competing captains. Both were the same age and with all their lives spent at sea. Ribault as well had been given broad license to settle all of Florida. And he volunteered that King Charles IX had personally pledged 100,000 francs to the expedition.

At one point King Philip had seen himself as sponsoring a precautionary expedition to expunge a small French outpost. Now he saw himself in an undermanned, out-raced struggle to save the Spanish hemisphere from a foul pollution. He quickly sent Menéndez word to recruit as many new soldiers as he could and sail immediately. The crown would pay.

Meanwhile, the king had one diplomatic card to play if he could. Philip would send the Duke of Alva, his must trusted adviser, to Paris on a supposedly routine diplomatic visit to Charles IX. If he could determine that Ribault's fleet had not yet sailed, the Duke was to lodge a formal protest before the French king and demand that the expedition be halted immediately. But if he learned that Ribault had sailed, he was to say "not one word" about it.

By June 25 the dozens of sailors and farmer-passengers were out of patience as well as money to keep paying for their own quartering in Seville and were packing to return home. Menéndez was in the same state of mind. The Duke of Alva had sent word that Ribault had departed for Florida nearly a month earlier. The cannons of Fort Caroline would be in place and well-oiled. The adelantado's own artillery had arrived in wagons but had been kept on the dock because the king still had not provided the money he needed for survival.

It was decision time, and just then three things happened at once.

First, the Casa, responding to yet another pressing demand from Philip, announced that it would disgorge three thousand of the twenty thousand ducats Menéndez claimed as due.

Second, Menéndez himself gathered his captains and officers on deck of the *San Pelayo* and exhorted them to go forth among their soldiers and sailors and preach to them the challenge of adventure, the riches of discovery and the rewards in heaven from being God's missionaries in the struggle against the heathenism of both Huguenot and Indian. In short, all were to ask each member of the expedition to forego their shipboard pay as well as the reimbursement due them for lodgings in Seville. In the bargain would be far greater rewards of land in Florida and other vaguely-defined riches. To leaven the odds of approval, each captain put the question to a majority vote among their crews. The result was unanimous—among the ships, that is.

The third and decisive factor was the power of the *poder.* Because travel across the ocean could consume thirty days or more—and then another thirty returning—anyone with business in the Indies or New Spain had to have an agent on the other side of the Atlantic to represent him when rapid decisions were required. The person holding this power of attorney from, say, a merchant in Seville, was authorized to buy and sell goods on his behalf, collect debts and even invest his money in new ventures. A successful agent had deputies in all major trading cities to whom he could delegate the same poder on behalf of its original grantor.

Pedro de Castillo of Cadiz already had agents everywhere in New Spain and saw the advantage of being the first to extend his connections to the northern half of the hemisphere. Hence, he had been an eager participant when Menéndez had offered him *poder* during his absence on the Florida expedition. Castillo had been persuaded that the king and Casa would sooner or later make good on their obligations—maybe even sooner with the impatient and abrasive Menéndez out to sea.

No doubt Menéndez sensed it as well. In any case, the decision was made. On the afternoon of June 27, 1565, the last of the big guns were locked onto the deck of the *San Pelayo,* and the huge tub of a floating armory, barracks, cargo hauler and Noah's Ark of animals wallowed down the Guadalquivir River towards Cadiz and the open sea.

However, the wary, implacable Casa de Contratación had posted observers along the river. One of them reported that as soon as the convoy was out of sight of the dockyard, it dropped anchors near an isolated riverbank. There, launch craft ferried aboard more than 150 extra passengers who had paid the adelantado of Florida for his private account.

Menéndez spied the spies and cared not. In a few more miles he would be leaving the orbit of Cadiz and surging into the glorious, un-regulated ocean blue. He sailed with a heart full of boundless enthusiasm that with the bureaucrats behind him and only his own skills to rely on, the enormous diversity of Florida would provide riches to overcome all adversity.

Chapter Eight

Lujo

Summer, 1565

W hen a Jeaga male was re-born into manhood, he was soon given a new name more in keeping with his true persona than the one casually bestowed in early childhood. Heron received his new name from his uncle Deerstalker, chief of the Jeaga, and it came in a burst of exasperation.

It happened the previous winter after the whale hunt. Each household had received its share of meat and blubber. Some of the meat was cut into steaks. Some was sliced into thin strips and left to dry in the wind so it could be eaten throughout the summer. Blubber, a yellowy, foot-thick fat just inside the whale's skin, was boiled into oil for many purposes. Although sometimes used as a rubbing balm or for treating a burn or mixing with coontie into a flour paste, blubber was prized above all for mixing with plant dyes to make body paints.

On a cloudy moonless evening Heron squatted outside his mother's hut cutting whale meat into thin drying strips. He kept one eye on the low cook fire inside as he waited for a thick glob of blubber to begin boiling into a floating layer of oil. After staring into the fire for several minutes, Heron cut out a large slice of blubber and placed it in a small clay bowl. Then he held the end of a dry stick in the fire until it flared into a low orange flame. He touched the flame to the blubber in the bowl and it quickly went out. He placed two larger kindling sticks in one hand and ignited a much larger flame. This time the blubber began to burn with a dull orange-like glow.

Bright Moon had been threading twine in a corner illuminated only by the dim cook fire several feet away. "Look, Mother," said Heron bringing the clay bowl under her gaze. "With such a light you can actually see what you are doing."

"It's not very bright," she said, barely noticing. "And it's not what blubber is for."

The blubber in the larger pot soon began to boil off, and in a few minutes Heron had scooped some of it into another small clay bowl. This time he lit the pure oil and a low blue and yellow flame quickly danced over the surface of the bowl. "Now you should be able to see perfectly!" he said with a triumphant smile.

Before long Heron had two bowls brightly aflame inside the hut and passers-by had been attracted by the dancing flickers of light that projected from the entranceway. Bright Moon had been startled at first, frightened of the magic that might have been unleashed with this strange discovery. But she was actually beginning to enjoy the attention of her neighbors when the greatest of them bent over at the entrance and surveyed the scene.

"What are you *doing*?" thundered Deerstalker with a scowl.

"Brother, it seems that my son has discovered a way to keep his mother from going blind doing the work of your people."

The chief stared at the floating flame for several seconds. Then he stirred the oil with a kindling stick and watched the flame continue as it swirled. He looked at the half-consumed piece of blubber on the carving table. Then he trained a frown on Heron, who had been standing in a corner with a smile of satisfaction. .

"So this boy here is using up half your supply of blubber to produce a light that might last—what, a few days? Then you will be in the dark again for the rest of the year. And you'll be without any oil for the purposes it is supposed to be used for. That is, if your son doesn't burn down your hut and the village first."

"No," he said pointing a finger at the other women standing by. "I don't want any of you trying this. Or *your* friends," he said pointing directly at Heron.

That ended the blubber experiment. And it had almost been dismissed in Deerstalker's memory until he had reason to pay a more anxious visit to Bright Moon's hut a month later.

It was April, the month when all Jeaga went into the woods and collected palm fronds and other thatching for their hut roofs. Over many months the sun could shrink and dry the old thatch, creating fissures big enough to let rain drip inside during the next wet season.

Another reason for re-thatching was bugs. Insects—especially cockroaches and chinch bugs—laid their eggs in roof thatches when it was warm and muggy. As the following summer season approached the typical family could expect a cornucopia of crawly things to drop onto their food by day and beds by night unless a fresh, green roof was erected.

Heron had another idea, and it came from watching his mother at work. No one was better than Bright Moon at preparing soft fibers for women to weave into skirts or use as menstrual absorbents. It was said that in olden days mothers and daughters pulled down the silvery green strands of maiden's hair from live oak trees and used them untreated even though they were rough to the touch and often infested with biting mites. But now the lives of women were easier because people like Bright Moon had learned to soak the raw maiden's hair for up to two weeks until it became soft, pliable and mite-free. They had also begun to use the soft reddish fiber from where the trunk of a sabal palm joins a branch. And to kill any insects that might be in the raw fiber, she and women helpers would hang batches over a smoky fire of green mangrove or buttonwood branches.

All of which Heron had been observing for years. One bright April morning he greeted his mother at breakfast with an idea. "Everyone is starting to talk about the spring thatching," he said. "But I don't see why *we* should have to do it."

"Why not?" said Bright Moon. "We always *do*."

"It takes too much time. And it's boring."

"Those are not good reasons."

"All right, Mother, here are good reasons. Our roof has not leaked all last year and it is probably because you are the best weaver and thatcher in Jeaga Town. Just because everyone else does it does not mean the best weaver in Jeaga Town has to do it."

"Well, I appreciate the compliment," she replied, "but you forget about all the insect eggs up there waiting to hatch."

"No, I haven't forgotten," he said, "and this is my idea. We could build a smaller, smoke fire on the pit inside the house. We'll have a lot of smoke for a few hours, but then we'll douse the fire and I'll use our woven mats to blow the smoke out. All the bugs up there will be dead and we will have saved hours of boring work."

Bright Moon had simply rolled her eyes at the time and Heron hadn't pressed the discussion. A few days later she was dumfounded when he returned home with an armload of mangrove branches. She was still staring open-mouthed as he put the limbs in the inside fire pit and set a bowl of water on them. "See?" he said, "a much smaller fire. Just enough to kill bugs. Now you go out for a walk and let me do this."

Bright Moon was now standing outside peering in. Her son would soon be sixteen and was already acting like head of the household.

Heron tried a small fire of pine kindling but couldn't get the rubbery, green mangrove branches to smoke.

He threw on more kindling. Suddenly the mangrove twigs caught all at once and produced a plume of smoke so thick that Bright Moon could no longer see Heron in the middle of the hut.

Nor could Heron see the doorway. Sparks had flared from the pine wood kindling, catching on a clump of grape vine and maiden's hair on a nearby table.

Whoosh. The dry thatching on the nearest wall began to crackle as yellow flames ate their way upward.

"Help! Help! Fire!" cried Bright Moon, running down the pathway to the neighboring houses. Heron staggered out the entranceway, coughing convulsively.

Fortunately, the cry of "*FIRE*" from any hut along the river ignited the same centuries-old response in every Jeaga. Neighbors grabbed their sharpest knives and gourds of water and moved quickly down the path. Men reached with their knives to carve away the thatched wall just beyond the fire's reach while women poured their gourds of water over the flames below.

The fire was stanched with only part of one wall lost. People had doused the mangrove smoke with more water, but the floor of Bright Moon's hut was boggy with pieces of twig, charcoal, and torn thatching. Heron's bedding was soaked.

Outside, Heron sat on a low bench with his head hanging. When he finally looked up, his uncle Deerstalker was standing over him. A crowd of men and women hovered behind the chief waiting for what was sure to be an explosion.

"I don't have to ask who did this," sighed the Jeaga chief. He looked at Bright Moon, who looked away. It was acknowledgement enough.

He looked down at Heron and set his jaw. "The first thing you will do is go to the spring and replenish every water gourd that was used to put out your fire—even if it takes you all night.

"I don't know what to say to you," stammered Deerstalker. "All I know is that you are no *Little* Heron. You are no *Big* Heron either. From now on you will go by the name I give you...*Lujo!*

Much later, after the crowd had left, after he had made nine trips to the spring and apologized to the families who had used up their water gourds, Heron—Lujo—walked to the beach with a sooty deerskin blanket because there was no place inside his hut dry enough to sleep. There, listening to the softly undulating waves looking up at the cascade of stars, he contemplated his new name. *Lujo* in Jeaga meant a "riddle" or sometimes "strange." It could also derisively describe someone as "from another world."

It really wasn't all that wrong, or bad, he thought.

He also remembered what he observed when re-entering his mother's hut after everyone had left. The floor was covered with dead bugs.

One benefit of the name Lujo was that he was left alone. His own mother no longer nagged or implored him to achieve lofty goals. The young men of his age became aloof. Adults were confused as to what the Calusa might think of this alleged son of Calus, so they paid him respect but kept their distance.

It was now July and Lujo liked to wander the beach. It was nesting season for turtles, and each morning young boys and girls from the village would scamper off to the beach in search of eggs laid the night before by lumbering Loggerheads. But the night before, Lujo would have walked the same beach and watched the pregnant females struggle up the sand and scrape away the sand for their nesting places. Lujo would be lying in the sand a few feet away observing the giant turtle grunted softly as each small white egg plopped into the sand.

It was on one such night that Lujo saw something that boys had only bragged about in his days with the work gangs. The night was almost moonless and gathering thunderclouds had almost obscured his vision down the beach. He was approaching from behind the dune line when in the darkness he thought he saw three—no four—Loggerheads all nestled in the sand, But almost on top of one another? And one of them was moving strangely.

Assuming the tracker's crouch that he knew all too well, Lujo crept forward several yards and squinted. Now he could hear voices. Low laughter. A smacking of skin. A crying out. Groaning. Now he could make out the forms of three young males. Two were motionless while one was bent over, moving back and forth over a fourth form.

He had heard much talk of sex, had spied on girls bathing naked in the inlet, but had never seen a girl bent over as men swarmed over her like male manatees clustering around a cow in her season.

When it was over the young warriors—he knew them all—plunged into the still water and splashed each other in a fit of exuberance. Then they walked up the beach and disappeared.

Lujo remained motionless throughout. So did the lump that remained in what was probably an abandoned turtle nest. *Could they have killed her?* Lujo straightened to a walk and was soon gazing down at a girl his age who he knew only as one of the Gray Panther clan that lived along Jeaga Inlet.

"Are you all right?" he asked.

She had been crying softly, hadn't seen him standing above. She thrust both hands up in a defensive posture. Her skirt of maiden hair was still askew around her midriff. "No more," she begged.

"No. There will be no more," he said softly. "Give me your hand."

He reached down and pulled her up. She averted her eyes. And as she turned her head away he could see three streaks of red paint smeared across her cheek. She began straightening her skirt and walking away when Lujo surprised himself with his boldness.

"Don't go to your home like that," he said in an almost fatherly tone. "Come walk by the water until you are feeling better."

She felt just as awkward but knew he was right. So they walked slowly in silence as the surf nibbled at their feet. In the rising sliver of moonlight Lujo could see that she had been wearing ceremonial garb—four necklaces of small white shells, the three smudged streaks of red paint on each cheek and remnants of torn egret feathers perched in black hair that flowed past her shoulders.

Finally it was she who broke the silence. "You will not tell about this?" she asked.

"No," he said gently. "But tell me, you look as though you are dressed as for dancing. Were the Gray Panthers having a festival tonight?"

"No," she laughed, looking at him for the first time. "My sister and I were practicing. We have the festival of the full moon next month and this will be our first time in the chorus. So we were trying to learn the songs. It's difficult to sing and dance at the same time. I guess I must have done it too well." Her voice cracked and she turned her head away again.

"What do you mean by *too* well?"

"I was hot from all the activity, so I walked down to the beach just to stand in the water and cool off. But I was singing the whole time and I didn't notice *them* following me. They must have been watching us the whole time."

Lujo walked into the water and snatched up some golden brown sargasso weed that had been floating in the surf. "Hold your head still," he said. "If I can rub off the face paint, you can tell your family that you went down to the water to wash it off after your dancing."

They walked again in silence and Lujo searched his uncooperative brain for something more to say. Out of the corner of his eye he spotted the golden glint in the eyes of a raccoon prowling where the beach met the dune line. "Do you like to hunt for turtle eggs?" he found himself asking lamely.

"My little sister does," she said. "I've never been too good at it. It's hard to find one that hasn't already been robbed."

"It's true if you look by day," said Lujo. "But not if you go out at night."

"I'll never go out at night again," she answered.

"Well, tonight you're already out here," he said. Just then he saw the raccoon on the beach digging industriously. "Follow me," he motioned. He grabbed a driftwood stick and broke for the spot where the raccoon had begun his work.

"Go away!" shouted Lujo brandishing his stick. The raccoon hissed in anger and stood swatting at the stick. Then it slunk into a hedge of sea grapes, its sulking presence seen only by the flickering glint of its eyes as watched its evening being ruined by bigger robbers.

"You see," said Lujo as the girl bent over him, her humiliation perhaps receding. "You can't just look across the beach for every little sand hill that might be poking up. You have to let animals do your work for you. Raccoons and bears and owls can smell where the turtles have laid eggs."

The raccoon had barely scratched the top of the nest. With a few strokes of his cupped hands Lujo had uncovered a trove of thirty or so little white balls and handed one to the girl with the flourish of a shaman making magic. Soon she had scooped up the contents of the nest in some large whelks that Lujo had gathered in the sand.

"Now you can really say you went to the beach for a purpose," he beamed. "Some day perhaps I will show you something about the Loggerhead you won't forget."

Her eyes brightened. "And that is?"

"Sometimes at night I get lucky and actually watch one of these giant turtles laying her eggs in the nest. After she rests a while, she crawls back to the sea just as if she's pushing water back with her flippers. Then as she eases back into the sea, I lay my arms across her big back so softly that she carries me along in the water."

"Then what happens?"

"She goes deeper and I have to let go before I run out of air and drown."

He laughed loudly and she joined him. As her head tilted back, her eyes and lips made him wish this had happened on any other night. And he knew for all eternity that the way to any woman's consent was not brutish dominance, but warmth and gentleness.

She knew, too, and knew his mind. "Well, someday perhaps we will swim with the Loggerhead," she said starting to stride homeward.

"One moment," he called after her. "I don't know your name."

"Scrub Jay," she answered.

"And how did you get that name?" he shouted.

"One day I will show you," she called back, her arms full of whelks and turtle eggs.

His recent disgrace aside, Lujo continued to get ideas. He questioned why things were done as they were. He wondered why no one else ever did as well. He even wondered if some shaman or devil spirit was putting these thoughts into his head.

Canoe making, for example. Ever since he and the work gang of boys had watched the long, cumbersome process of burning and chipping out logs, he had thought that there must be a better way to float people on rivers than the crude result of all this effort. A canoe was uncomfortable to sit in, couldn't hold many supplies, and could roll over as easily as the log from which, after all, it had once been.

This is what compelled Lujo to walk down the beach in July of 1565. A mile or so south of Jeaga Inlet lay the skeleton of the big wooden ship that had brought old Marinero and his fellow Spanish slaves to these shores the year before Lujo was born. All the cargo and everything metal had long been scavenged—even the timbers above the water line. But ribs and planks still exposed themselves in the sand with each receding wave.

To the occasional passer-by the boy standing in the surf and staring at the old wreck might have seemed demented or disoriented. In reality, Lujo was studying the smoothness of the ship's timbers and how they still fit together to ward off the salty surf after so many years.

One day Lujo arrived prepared to find answers. He used a sharpened whale rib to scrape away the barnacles and slippery seaweed. Seeing that the timbers were joined by a thin black strip, he began using a shark tooth scraper to gouge between two of the planks. After a few strokes he would have to halt while the next wave rushed in, forcing him to grab the hull to steady his feet. When the wave receded, he would resume.

After two hours Lujo had managed to gouge holes in the wood above and below the black seam. After using a sharpened antler to work bigger holes in the softened wood, he switched tools. Using a heavy shell hammer, he drove a sharpened wedge of thick bone, made from a human femur, between the gouged holes.

In four more hours Lujo had managed to drive the wedge through all four sides of a crude rectangle and extract a piece consisting of parts of two planks still held together by a black seam.

Next, he sat in the sand and dug the shark tooth scraper at the black seam. Was it paint? Some sort of glue? A thin strip of wood? After more scraping Lujo managed to pry loose a six-inch-long strand of black fiber. When he rubbed the strand, sticky black goo came off in his hand, leaving a thin cord of rope. It came from across the sea, to be sure, but it had the same feel as fiber from the sabal palm or century plant.

By late afternoon, Lujo was still sitting on the beach lost in thought, oblivious to the fact that the tide had receded many yards beyond him. A complete picture had formed in his mind and he was just double checking all of its parts. Lujo, the strange and mysterious, would find an isolated thicket on the river's edge that had an ample supply of young pines. The pine resin, when heated, produced one of the best glues available to the Jeaga. If it was strong enough to keep animal bones fastened to wooden handles, pine resin could probably seal small logs to keep out water. He would find out by tapping some young saplings and felling others. He would lay a dozen or so thin logs together, about twenty feet in length. Because none of the logs would be perfectly straight, he would press in strands of sabal palm fiber and cover them with hot resin. .

If the raft floated, Lujo would lash small logs together and erect four sides to his vessel—each perhaps four feet high. He figured that a river boat twenty feet long, six feet wide and four feet high could carry more trading goods than several canoes. The log sides could afford protection against anyone firing arrows from shore. The users could even sleep while moored in the water, thus avoiding any animals and hostile Indians who prowled on land at night. And if it rained, hides could be stretched between the sides to create a covering.

All this would be done in secret. No fires or smoke to alert the elders. When done, the revolutionary boat would be floated down to Jeaga Town and magnanimously presented to Chief Deerstalker. Or perhaps it could be proudly presented to King Calus to lead his next trading mission.

In the end, Lujo would have his respect back and his mother her pride. The old name they could keep.

By August Lujo had canoed about seven miles up the river's Northwest Fork where a creek veered off to the right and was lined by tall cypress. Behind the protective screen of the cypress was a grove of young sand pines of just the right diameter. He set up camp and began to go to work. He had told his mother he would gone several days hunting, but promised to bring back several kinds of fiber for her loom. Bright Moon, however, suspected that the real reason for Lujo's absence was the recent arrival of her family from Lake Mayaimi for their annual get-away from inland mosquitoes and soggy ground. When Bright Moon's parents weren't crowding the hut or creating smelly pipe smoke or sending him out for more fish, they would argue over which Mayaimi maiden would make him the best bride.

So Lujo was off "hunting" when Jeaga Town was stirred by the arrival of three young men who had come down the Long River in a large warrior canoe. As they began crossing the River of Turtles those on shore could see the man in front holding a bright red staff. Traders, strangers and enemies alike displayed the staff as the universal symbol of peace or truce. They glided into the town canoe landing. got out and stood on the shore with their arms folded to reaffirm their peaceful intent.

Although a gaggle of children and curiosity seekers had gathered by the water, they stayed respectively distant. Deerstalker and two elders stepped forward to greet them, protocol dictating that the visitors not feel threatened by overwhelming numbers on shore.

All three were well-muscled and in the prime of life. The first to talk introduced himself as Red Wolf, oldest son of the Ais cacique. With him were a fellow Ais warrior and a high-ranking warrior from the Timucua, normally enemies of the Ais on their northern border. The Timucuan had come with important information and asked for a river canoe and an escort so he could deliver it to King Calus on Mound Key as well.

Deerstalker and the elders with him were stunned to learn that a great many white people had recently come ashore from five great ships in northern Timucua. They had come with many supplies and many animals, some taller than his own head and longer than two men lying end to end. They had already built a large enclosure. Red Wolf drew a crude triangle in the sand and the Timucuan, who spoke another language, took the stick from Red Wolf's hand and drew a larger version with various buildings inside.

"Spanish?" asked Deerstalker.

"No," interrupted the Timucuan, who had known that word like every other Indian. "*Frawn-say.*"

"*Frawn*-say," he repeated to the shrugs of the Jeaga.

"He says they are different people," said Red Wolf. "They come in big ships like the Spanish, but they hate the Spanish. Big enemies like the Ais and the Timucuans," he added with a laugh, pointing to the stranger. "But we are not enemies in *this* case."

"How do you know so much about these *Frawn*-say people," said the Jeaga chief.

Answered Red Wolf: "He says the *Frawn-say* people met with his chief and tried to trade some jewels for their food. When the chief allowed it they said the Timucua would also have to pray to their gods. Then he says the *Frawn-say* warriors made them take supplies from the ships and carry them into their great house. He thinks they are going to stay and that other ships will bring even more people and animals to build other places like it all down the coast."

Deerstalker's brain was churning the whole time. *Could this be some sort of ruse? Have the Ais formed an alliance with the Timucuans to wipe us out once we let down our guard? Or maybe this Timucuan fellow is just another Ais warrior and that somewhere in the dunes on the other side of the river are hundreds of Ais ready to attack.*

"My friends, you deserve our praise for coming here to visit us with this information," he said decorously. "But I ask you, Red Wolf, if you were in my position would you not like to have some proof that all this actually happened?"

"I would," said the Ais. "We asked the same question. It seems that while our neighbors were being pressed into hauling supplies like slaves of the *Frawn-say*, they were able to leave with a few souvenirs. He nodded to the Timucuan, who walked over to the beached canoe and returned with a covered deerskin in his arms. He pulled the hide aside.

"Here we have some of the jewels that were traded for," pouring some blue beads from a leather pouch into his palm.

"Here we have a pan that they use to cook things over a fire." He passed around a black cast-iron frying pan, so heavy that one of the Jeaga elders almost dropped it.

But by then all eyes had been on the arquebus held by the Timucuan. "And this," said Red Wolf, "is a powerful weapon. You put a stone ball in this slot here and" (the Timucuan raised the gun to his shoulder and clicked the trigger) "and out this end the ball flies so fast through the air that it can go through a man's heart and come out the other end. But," he added, "I have none of these stone balls to show you."

The Timucuan drew a long, narrow rectangle in the sand. He cupped both hands into a large circle. He pulled an imaginary trigger and held his ears.

Explained Red Wolf: "He is trying to say that they have much bigger weapons on their ships and now on land. They shoot stone balls so large and with such power that they hurt your ears just to hear them."

When the meeting was over, the two Ais returned to the inlet in their ocean canoe and the Jeaga, as promised, sent the Timucuan and two of its own warriors upriver on their way to Mound Key.

In early September a Calusa messenger brought word that King Calus would be sending a delegation within one week to conduct a War Council. It would be held at the Great House beneath the Place of the Sun and Moon. But this would be far different than the festive Great Gatherings with their women, dancing and marriages. The Jeaga were told to prepare for only forty to fifty—all men—from the Calusa, Jeaga, Ais and Tequesta. No one but they would be even allowed on the sacred peninsula beside the converging rivers.

The Calusa had again taken the trouble to maintain their ratio of superiority. Only a chief and four elders were allowed to attend from the vassal tribes. The Calusa were headed by Escampaba, the king's cousin and chief of warriors. Whereas the other tribal delegates included many older men, Escampaba's entourage consisted of twenty-five tall, muscled warriors. With them came the Calusa shaman, the Timucuan and a man who was an oddity in Jeaga Town. This is the first time they had seen the cacique of the Matacumbe, a sparsely-populated archipelago of settlements in the Florida Keys.

Five elders from each tribe sat around a large circle smoking pipes and drinking palmetto tea—a magnanimous display of democracy by Escampaba were it not for the fact that his remaining warriors rung them in an outer circle with stern faces and darting eyes.

Escampaba, forty-eight years old and a head taller than the rest, began by having the Timucuan re-tell his story to underscore the urgency of the moment. "We have a second source of information," said Escampaba when the Timucuan finished. He introduced the Matacumbe cacique White Flamingo, a spare, weathered man who reported the following:

"Two months ago a nephew of mine and his friend decided to see how far they could go in their canoe—as young men so often do. They wound up in the open sea going all the way to the island of Cuba, which is almost all controlled by the Spanish. There they were fed well and treated kindly, but only for a few days, it seems. Then they were tied up and sent off as slaves to spend every hour of sunlight using heavy metal knives to cut down tall plants with stalks like cat tails. There were many slaves with them doing the same thing. They called it *sugar cane* and said the Spanish crush it into liquid and send it back to their land across the great sea.

"These two youths of ours may have been fools to begin with, but they proved themselves brave in the end," said White Flamingo. "One night as they were being led away from work, they used their big knives to kill their guard. Then they walked all night until they reached the shore and found a canoe that took them back to our homeland. They say there is no doubt the Spanish want to make all of us slaves and take us to Cuba to cut this sugar plant," continued the Matacumbe cacique to a hushed audience. "And they say that Cuba is full of talk that the Spanish are planning a big invasion of our land."

Next to speak was the Calusa shaman, Black Cormorant. Most of the vassal tribes were accustomed to their shamans being gaunt, wizened old men. Cormorant stood almost as tall as Escampaba. He wore a glistening white Busycon shell gorget, a carved bone bracelet and a deerskin breechcloth with a deer antler knife tucked in. He carried a hardwood mace curved into a snake's head. Earlier in the morning he had invoked the wisdom and war powers of Taku while wearing a fierce blue and white mask. Now, without the mask, he was just as imposing with his square facial features and long black hair that flowed to his shoulders.

"We know that the Spaniards want to make us worship their gods," he said. "That was the case when they first tried to invade our shores in my grandfather's time and it is no different now. "

"Just what are their gods?" one of the elders asked.

"I have made it my business to find out by asking some of our Spanish captives," answered Black Cormorant. "You must realize that I have to do this with the help of an interpreter, who is another Spanish slave. But here is what I can understand. They worship a man who was much admired during his life many years ago. And yet he also made enemies, and these enemies captured him. They tortured him and hung him on two pieces of wood" (and here the shaman made a cross with one arm and his mace). "After he died while hanging there he took revenge on his enemies by coming to life again and walking among his friends to prove he was still alive."

"Taku is more powerful," blurted out another elder. "This Spanish god died. Taku is stronger because he never dies."

"Yes," said the shaman. "Never doubt that Taku has the power. But let me continue. You have all probably seen little crosses of gold or wood. The Spanish carry these crosses everywhere because they believe they bring good luck. They also worship the dead man's mother as a goddess."

"Did she die and come back to life as well?" said one of the Tequesta to laughter and snickers.

"It isn't clear to me," answered Black Cormorant with a smile. "But there is something else you should know. Our friend here from Timucua feels strongly that the people who invaded his land—the Frawnsay—are at war with the Spanish because they disagree about this man who came to life again."

"Do the Frawnsay have these crosses, too?" someone asked.

"Yes, apparently they do," said the shaman with a shrug of the shoulders.

"Then one of the two tribes carrying the same crosses has to have bad luck," said the voice to a chorus of laughter.

"Well," answered the shaman, "all I can say is that we didn't have much time to find out everything because we had to leave for this meeting. But what you need to know for now is that the Frawnsay and the Spanish worship this man who came back from the dead but hate each other for reasons we don't yet know."

Escampaba took the floor again and cited other concerns. Calling Red Wolf, the Timucuan chief's son, to the center of the circle, he described through an interpreter the strange animals that the Frawnsay had brought to Florida. He did his best to describe horses, cows, pigs and sheep, each time evoking cries of disbelief or the question: "Can it be hunted and eaten?"

"Now let me discuss something more important than animals," said Escampaba. "They bring new weapons, and some of you have seen them." The Timucuan again described the power of the arquebus and cannon. The Matacumbe chief reported that his nephew had seen soldiers in Cuba marching up and down and shooting. He added that the cannon indeed was so loud and powerful as to hurt a man's ears.

"I will have something to say about this later," said Escampaba, "but there is an even worse threat from these invaders. We have concluded that wherever they come in contact with our people, many of us get sick or die. Our friend from Timucua believes this as well. White Flamingo from Matacumbe says that the slaves in Cuba are also becoming sick after they go among with Spaniards. I leave it to our high priest to explain."

"Right now I cannot fully do so," said Black Cormorant rising to his feet. "We have known for years that when our people spend a lot of time around our Spanish slaves they often develop sores and pockmarks around their faces. Some of our people have spit up blood and coughed so hard that they shrivel up and die. It could be that their god is trying to cast a spell on us. I think it could also be because these people do not bathe and they smell bad like bears. The smell may carry bad air to others and then they breathe it in. But in any case it is another reason why we should never let these people invade our shores."

"Then it is clear," said a Tequesta elder. "We must kill them all!"

"Death to the devils! Death to the devils!" the men began to chant as the Calusa warriors joined in. "Death to the devils!"

When the chant had risen to the level he wished, Escampaba, the Calusa general, rose again from his bench in the circle. He had accomplished his purpose—to create alarm—and now it was time to create a strategy. "Now hear me," he shouted. "We say we will repulse the devils from our land, but how can we do this when they bring many men and powerful new weapons? No, my friends, it cannot come through a single battle or a single week.

"Now think along with me," he said as the noise abated. "They have big ships and bring many days' supplies. But supplies run out, don't they? And when these smelly little men little grow hungry they know nothing about oystering or making coontie flour or picking prickly pears unless we show them. We wait until their supplies run out, and *then* we kill them after some of them have already grown weak from hunger.

"Meanwhile, what can you do to weaken them? For one thing we can isolate them so they don't live among us. Then we can divide one against the other. We can burn or steal their supplies. We can lie to them and make false promises. Tell them you will worship their gods and thereby give them false comfort. If they ask where they can find gold, send them off on a long trip to some imaginary place.

"Oh, and let me tell you about the Fountain of Youth," added Escampaba with a smirk. "Some of our slaves on Mound Key came from ships that were seeking a lake or spring somewhere on our lands that is supposed to make a man live forever if he bathes in its waters. Are any of you hiding a Fountain of Youth somewhere on your land?"

More laughter.

Added Escampaba: "I think it's fine that these people bathe and I urge all of you to encourage them to go searching when they ask you about the Fountain of Youth."

"But what about these weapons?' It was Deerstalker, breaking the bravado and asking what was in the back of everyone's mind.

"Yes, they are powerful, but that is not the whole story," answered Escampaba. "The two Matacumbe boys saw soldiers practicing with these long shooters in Cuba and they say that it takes several seconds to reach into a supply of metal balls and place one properly before firing. They say that any of us here could shoot an arrow four times during that time. And the bigger the shooter, the more time it takes to put in the next ball. I should think our warriors could overpower them while they are fiddling with their shooters and metal balls."

"One thing more," said Escampaba. "Both the Timucuans and our young 'scouts' from Matacumbe say that the Spanish and the Frawnsay wear armor of woven metal strands so that they can't be killed by these metal balls. This is true because it is the same armor worn by the soldiers in the ships that tried to invade our Calusa Bay when I was a young boy. Now I want you to see something."

He motioned to one of the warriors standing behind him. The man went to a large wicker basket and returned with a rusty, bulging chain of mail as if still containing the torso of a slain Spaniard.

"At that time in my youth," Escampaba continued, "we sent so many warriors out to their ships in canoes that they forgot about their invasion and sailed away. But as our canoes were circling their biggest ship, one of their warriors leaned over so far that he fell off the ship and sank at once with all his armor on. After they had sailed away we raised up his body and saved his clothing—including this armor.

"Now then," said Escampaba. "I want you to observe something." He walked around the circle holding the rusty chain of mail. "This armor is not solid. It consists of strands of metal almost like sabal palm twine only heavier. I had this armor stuffed with soft clay because I wanted to show you something."

Escampaba set the bulky coat of mail on a bench beside the furthest wall in the Great House. He summoned another Calusa warrior. The soldier produced a bow and arrow, took aim from about forty feet and—*thwack!*—the arrow pierced the coat of mail.

Escampaba walked over to it and yanked twice on the protruding arrow. "You see," he exclaimed triumphantly, "the arrowhead is embedded so far into the clay—which is harder than a man's heart—that I can't get it out. These strands of metal may be able to repel a round metal ball, but a slender arrow tip can penetrate them easily."

There were more shouts of "Kill the devils," followed by a ceremonial passing of the black drink. The Calusa had again coaxd, convinced and coerced their vassals into forming an alliance and pledging their lives to repel all enemies from the sea.

CHAPTER NINE

Menéndez in Florida

September-December 1565

W hen the Menéndez fleet sighted the coast of southeast Florida in early September 1565, it was not with jubilation but anguish and caution.

Before leaving the Canaries in early July, the adelantado had reckoned that the French expedition led by Ribault had a twenty-two day head start on him. When the expected contingent from Asturia had not appeared in the Canaries on schedule, Menéndez left instructions to rendezvous in Havana and impatiently sailed away with eight ships and 1,504 souls. The *San Pelayo,* 600 tons when empty, now creaked and groaned with 300 tons of cargo. A glance down its manifesto showed sixteen large bronze cannon, thirty crossbows, 250 arquebuses, 450 shovels, harnesses for fifty horses, fifty-five pipes of wine, 6,000 pounds of sea biscuit, eight church bells and other indicators of a complex civilization about to be planted deeply in Florida soil.

The armada that sighted Cape Canaveral in September consisted of five ships, 300 fewer passengers and shortages of several key supplies.

Its troubles had begun just two weeks after leaving the Canaries when turbulent winds began to separate the ships. As the heavily-laden *San Pelayo* floundered in the high seas, two of its masts were carried off. The bronze cannons, mounted in the upper decks in order to bombard the French fort, broke loose and battered everything in their way as they careened back and forth.

As the storm raged on, another of Menéndez' ships was leaking so badly it that it lurched back towards Africa in hopes of reaching the

---

177

Canaries. On another beleaguered supply ship crewmen pushed overboard cannons, granary millstones and precious casks of water in a desperate effort to stay afloat. After being blown down to the Grenadines, the flooded ship capsized, its entire crew either drowned or killed ashore by Carib Indians.

A third ship was about to limp into the Port of Santo Domingo on Hispaniola when French corsairs captured it with a hundred Spanish soldiers and great quantities of supplies.

Weeks after the storm abated, the survivors managed to rendezvous in the harbor of San Juan, Puerto Rico. There, as ship repairs went on at a feverish pace, the adelantado used the delay to re-organize his fighting force. His first decision was to integrate the king's soldiers with his Asturian mercenaries so as to dissolve any possibility of factionalism. All were divided into fifteen companies, each commanded by a captain, as was the Spanish tradition in centuries of European wars. Each also had an ensign, chaplain, sergeant, piper and drummer.

For the role of *maestre de campo,* Menéndez bypassed all of his seafaring brethren and chose Pedro de Valdés, who was betrothed to his daughter. Although only twenty-five, Valdés was already battle-tested as an officer in the Italian campaigns. He was also from a powerful Asturian banking family and a relative of the archbishop of Seville. And to complete the circuit of interdependent relationships, this was the very archbishop whose house the Casa spies had observed accepting ten chests of contraband silver and gold just after Menéndez brought the treasure fleet back from Mexico.

On August 15 the refurbished little fleet of five had made its way out of San Juan harbor with a plan that called for meeting the Asturian fleet in Havana as well as some troops promised by the governor of Santo Domingo. But Menéndez already feared that the stopover would end his chances of beating Jean Ribault's re-supply fleet to Florida. He also began to sense that if he made his way north through the Florida Straits and up the Bahamas Channel, he could be ambushed and destroyed by French corsairs. So Menéndez again combined instinct and boldness: he bypassed Havana and sailed along the southern coast of Grand Bahama Island until he crossed the Bahamas Channel for Cape Canaveral.

At around 2 pm on September 4 the little Spanish fleet was creeping its way northward along the Florida coast when a voice from the crow's nest called out "Four masts ahead." From about two miles away all that could be discerned was that the ships lay off a great river and that they were bobbing in the sea as if anchored.

"Continue until we can identify." Menéndez shouted to his helmsman. "Look for the *Trinité*, the flagship of Ribault."

As he spoke the skies were blackening with the arrival of another afternoon tropical storm. Soon heavy winds were upon them, driving the ships eastward and away from the anchored vessels. But amidst the gale the sailor swaying in the crow's nest shouted "Confirmed! The *Trinité*!" As the rains lashed the *San Pelayo*, Menéndez' mind roiled as well. Every decision he had made thus far had been to beat the French to Florida and block the entrance of the St. Johns River to prevent reinforcing Fort Caroline. Now he had lost.

As the summer squall abated, the French ships were still within distant sight, but the sea was now so becalmed that the Spanish fleet could do little more than wallow in place. Menéndez used the interregnum to summon a hasty council. Seven of his captains were on board the *San Pelayo*, including Bartolomé Menéndez, who would be named governor and alcaide of the new settlement if the mission succeeded.

After a brief discussion, the consensus was to return to Santo Domingo. There they could re-group with the contingent from Asturia, which supposedly included a large galleon and many more cannon. Moreover, the governor of Santo Domingo had been under the king's orders to muster 300 soldiers for Menéndez and might at last be ready.

As the council of officers stood hunched around the chart table in the adelantado's quarters, Menéndez had been sitting silently with his head resting on his chin.

"Wait," he exclaimed at last, both arms fanning the air as if to blow away smoke from a burning cook stove. "Think with me. What if Ribault has only just arrived? Did they not face the same hurricanes and storms that we did? Did we not make up some ground with our dash through the Bahamas?

"Caballeros, let us all become Jean Ribault for a moment," said the adelantado. "Your goal is to bring all of your ships over the bar and into whatever harbor exists by the fort. But your four largest ships are still too heavy to cross. This means you have just arrived. So, Bartolomé, what is the first thing you would do?"

Bartolomé drummed his fingers on the chart table while he thought. "I would take as many men off my large ships as prudent in order to help unload the ships already in the harbor," said the brother at last. "Then, as soon as possible, I would send those men in the smaller ships out to lighter the galleons so they could cross the bar."

"I would, too," said Pedro Menéndez. "Therefore, we may assume that not enough time has passed to allow this to happen. In fact, many of the cannon needed for the fort may still be stowed on the big ships."

Men were beginning to nod their heads. "Now think about conditions at that fort," added Menéndez. "The people there must have been half-starved, and at this moment they may well be loading their bellies more than unloading cargo. In any case, there hasn't been enough time for the new and old soldiers to get acquainted much less organize into units."

Within minutes the adelantado had turned disappointment into a bold stratagem: determine whether the four anchored ships were indeed undermanned and, if so, destroy these workhorses of the French expedition at once.

Well after night had fallen, a breeze began filling the sails of the Spanish ships. With scant moonlight to guide them, the *San Pelayo* and its smaller companions glided amidst the anchored French ships and lowered their own hooks. When the *San Pelayo* swung about, its stern actually lightly kissed the bow of the *Trinité*.

A Spanish voice called out in the blackness, asking the *Trinité* to identify its commander.

"Jean Ribault," came the answer, "as authorized by the King of France."

When asked in turn, the French heard what they already feared: "Pedro de Menéndez de Avilés, designated adelantado of the province of Florida."

He shouted again. "We come from the rightful ruler of these lands, King Philip II, with orders to burn and hang any Lutheran French we might find here. In the morning, your vessels will be boarded, and if such people are found, the justice of King Philip will be carried out."

The "official greetings" soon gave way to a cacophony of taunts and fist shaking. "Spanish bastards, why wait for sunlight?" hollered several sailors over the ramparts. "Come over now and we'll give you your last rites!"

Menéndez had already decided on doing just that. He ordered the *San Pelayo's* anchor line paid out so that the current would swing it alongside the *Trinité* for boarding. But before he could give the order to his other ships, the French confirmed his suspicion that the four ships were undermanned. They cut their anchor lines, raised their sails and began to slip away with the current.

All night long, Menéndez' ships chased the French, even taking five cannon shots at the nimble *Trinité.* However, the Spanish ships were too heavy with cargo and still bore damages from the July hurricane. By morning Menéndez had determined to sail inside the river and attack the fort directly, but the giant galleass *San Pelayo* could not cross the bar. Besides, Fort Caroline was said to be seven miles inside the inlet, which could be full of shoals.

Instead, the adelantado sailed south to find a suitable site for a settlement and prepare for a long campaign to dislodge the French at Fort Caroline. The first inlet lay some forty miles away at the mouth of the Matanzas River. On September 6 a shore party headed by two captains landed on the mainland where a creek flowed into the St. Johns River and were received in friendly fashion by the chief of an Indian village there named Seloy. Having found the land and the reception hospitable, the shore party began preparing for an elaborate ceremony.

On September 8 Pedro Menéndez himself disembarked with two companies of infantry, trumpets blaring and banners flying. He was approached by Father Francisco López de Mendoza Grajales, holding a cross before him and singing *Te Deum Laudamus.* After Menéndez and all of his followers kissed the cross, they celebrated a solemn mass on an altar brought from the *San Pelayo.* They christened the settlement the parish of St. Augustine. Then they invited the crowd of gawking Seloy Indians to a large feast of thanksgiving.

Later that same day Menéndez executed some bureaucratic duties that would lay the groundwork for ruling all of Florida. Even though the new colony consisted of no more than five ships that had yet to unload except enough for a large picnic, it was important to lay a political foundation before a single brick were in place. Thus, Menéndez was now officially confirmed adelantado on a parchment that would be sent to the king. Bartolomé Menéndez was named governor of the new settlements and *alcaide* of the fort to be built there. St. Augustine was declared a municipality and a court was established to hear appeals of decisions made by the alcaide.

With these institutions in place—a microcosm of Castile—the adelantado could now begin to parcel out land to his settlers. But their survival and success would depend on upon being supported by peaceful Indians. Would they remain so when the cross was thrust upon them? That it would come soon was evident from a letter Menéndez wrote King Philip the same week. "Your Majesty may be assured," he wrote, "that if I had a million ducats I would spend it all upon this undertaking because it is of such great service to God Our Lord, for the increase of our Holy Catholic Faith, and for the service of Your Majesty. And therefore, I have offered to Our Lord all that He may give me in this world in order that I might plant the Gospel in this land for the enlightenment of its natives...."

The break in military action also gave Menéndez time to assess his strength vs. the French. The Spanish could count on 500 soldiers, 200 seamen and a hundred tradesmen of various disciplines—all reasonably healthy and rested. According to spies and Indian reports, the French had an equal number. However, 200 or so were survivors of the original Ribault garrison. One could expect them to be emaciated by disease and starvation. Moreover, several of the fighting force had to be aboard the four French ships that Menéndez had scattered, and they had not yet returned to their moorings, probably due to the strong winds and rough seas that had flared up in the past week.

Again, Menéndez lived up to his reputation for imagination and boldness. He would not send his ships to attack Fort Caroline seven miles up an unfamiliar inlet. Instead, he would dispatch a force of 500 by land to attack the fort from its neglected rear.

In the gray dawn of September 20, the wet, bedraggled Spanish force finally came within sight of Fort Caroline. In normal times the soldiers would have walked easily through level scrub land with only narrow, shallow tidal streams to impede them. But three days of driving rain—the same storm that had scattered the French supply ships at sea—made the forty-eight mile march a slog through wetlands so swollen that finding a dry patch on which to sleep was nearly impossible.

Fortunately, several of the guards at Fort Caroline had sheltered themselves inside from the rain. As the sun began to turn the sky pink, the Spanish quickly captured the only sentinel they could find. In a few minutes Pedro de Valdés, the *maestro de campo,* was leading the way inside with two battle standards at his side. As day broke, and when a French trumpeter managed to climb to the top of the fort and blare out the call to battle, soldiers began pouring out of their lodgings in various half-dressed stages. But they could scarcely begin to load their crossbows and arquebuses before they were cut down.

Later, as Spanish officers sauntered about inside the triangular fort, they counted 132 dead bodies sprawled in the rain-and-blood-soaked parade ground. They had spared about fifty women and children as well as three drummers and four trumpeters. Nearly fifty defenders had escaped into the woods and were being pursued.

Menéndez' prize, aside from capturing a serviceable ship, was in being led to Jean Ribault's bedroom and finding a metal chest containing orders from the King of France that removed all doubt that Fort Caroline had been a bold attempt to make Florida a French colony. Also discovered were "books and symbols of the Huguenot religion"— proof that the dreaded heresy was already being used to pollute the native population. Worse yet, the Huguenot heathens themselves had many packs of playing cards with the figure of the Host, the Holy Grail and other cards "burlesquing things of the Church."

The adelantado's biggest worry, however, was that the four French ships that he had chased might return to destroy the barely organized, lightly-defended settlement at St. Augustine. Most of his invading force was quickly marched back inland.

When the Spanish detachment returned to St. Augustine they soon learned from Indian scouts that Jean Ribault and his long-missing ships had been driven south by hurricane winds and either sunk or scuttled. One cluster of survivors was reported camping near Matanzas Inlet and another—including Ribault himself—somewhere on a beach near

Cape Canaveral. Both groups of survivors were headed north up the beach, expecting to find refuge at Fort Caroline.

Menéndez was able to track their whereabouts because friendly Indians had stalked both parties, sometimes harassing them, sometimes extracting "trades" of metal tools for fresh water and balls of coontie flour. On September 28 an Indian reported that many Frenchmen were gathered on the south shore of a small inlet eighteen miles down the coast from St. Augustine. By midnight Menéndez had arrived on the north shore of the inlet with forty soldiers, a priest and a French prisoner as interpreter.

When day broke and the French squinted across the inlet they saw a lone figure, dressed in a French uniform with a cape across his shoulders and carrying a short lance. It was Menéndez, dressed that way to show his simpatico and respect.

After shouting introductions, the French survivors pleaded for help in reaching their fort. After all, they insisted, Spain and France were not officially at war.

The adelantado shouted back that the fort was theirs no more. He said he was their sworn enemy by reason of "disseminating the Lutheran religion in the provinces of his Majesty, Philip II." He was bound by the king to "pursue you to your extermination."

The survivors sent across a nobleman to negotiate for their lives in return for their surrender. Menéndez would offer only his "mercy." Parched, sunburned and exhausted, the Frenchmen at last agreed to be ferried across the inlet in small groups. On arrival, their hands were bound on the excuse that "it is a long walk to our headquarters and there are too many of you to keep track of." Menéndez and his interpreter then questioned each in the style of the Inquisition to determine their faithfulness to the Roman Catholic Church. A mere half-dozen were found acceptable. Four caulkers and carpenters were also singled out and spared simply because they were needed in shipping and fort building. The rest, probably 150 men, were marched out of sight beyond the dune line. There they were stabbed while still bound. Then their heads were cut off and bodies piled high for seabirds and human scavengers.

Menéndez had no qualms about it. He was under orders from the king to do exactly what he did. He had actually shown mercy because he was legally obligated to burn heretics at the stake. Besides, he lacked provisions to feed so many prisoners. A few days beforehand, The *San Pelayo* had been sent to Havana for more supplies and had not yet returned.

Back at St. Augustine, the adelantado began to focus on his next conquest. He would sail north to Santa Elena and found a colony that would be a seaport for yet another settlement. The inland settlement—now only a vision by the adelantado—would be at the base of the Appalachian Mountains where it might be a base for mining whatever precious metals Florida was ready to yield. There, rather than on the less productive sandy coast of Florida, he would establish vineyards, fatten cattle on lush grasses and fell a bounty of hardwood trees for lumber. Transported to the equally visionary seaport of Santa Elena, the lumber would be used to build ships for the colonies of Florida and New Spain!

On October 9 Menéndez was describing his exploits in a letter to the king when Indians again reported another gaggle of French shipwreck survivors at the same inlet eighteen miles south. This time Menéndez took 150 men. On the dawn of October 11 his guards spotted a large group of ragged men on the southern bank attempting to launch a hand-made raft. Upon spotting the Spaniards, they hoisted a white flag. After a futile effort to coax Menéndez across, one of them came over in an old Indian canoe and identified himself as the sergeant-major of Jean Ribault, viceroy and captain-general of Florida for the King of France. His commander had been wrecked on the coast with 350 of his people and had come to ask for boats with which to reach his fort.

"I to whom you are speaking am the Spanish captain-general and my name is Pedro Menéndez," said the adelantado nonchalantly as if ordering stuffed cabbage in a pub. "Tell your general that I have captured your fort and killed your French there as well as those who escaped from your other ships." And with that he had a soldier lead the man to where the headless decomposing bodies of his comrades were still stacked in the sand. When the sergeant-major returned ashen-faced and speechless, Menéndez added that "If your general wishes to talk to me, I give my word that he can come here with five or six companions and leave in safety."

In the afternoon Ribault crossed over with eight officers and faced his rival for the first and last time. If not apparent to each man, it was to those in their company. Ribault, though now in tatters, was the image of his captor: thin lips, full black beard, and now, at forty-five, just a year younger than Menéndez. One could imagine them as affectionate brother-comrades in another time and place.

Invited to share the adelantado's table, the French contingent accepted only a little wine and nibbles of cheese despite their gnawing hunger. They were too repulsed at learning the fate of their countrymen—and with it an inkling of their own. Ribault wondered aloud if they were being tricked into believing that Fort Caroline was now Spanish. But Menéndez invited him to interrogate two of the captives from Fort Caroline whom he had brought along for just such a purpose.

A somber Ribault returned from his private interrogation and played the only card he had left. "What has happened to me may happen to you," he said searching Menéndez' eyes for a sign of empathy. "Since our kings are brothers and friends, I implore you to play the part of friend and give me ships with which to return to France."

Menéndez was implacable. They must trust his mercy. Ribault was ferried across to report to his men.

In three hours he was back before Menéndez. Only about half the men were willing to trust the adelantado, he reported. The others were ready to submit their fates to Indians or the wilderness and the sea. He offered 100,000 ducats to transport the survivors to France safely.

The adelantado paused for a thoughtful moment. No, he answered, "no price could ransom heresy." They could only place themselves at his mercy.

Ribault crossed the water again, promising to deliver a final answer early the next morning.

When daylight came, Ribault returned with six of his captains. He surrendered his arms, the French royal standard and his seal of office. He reported that about seventy of the survivors—including most of the nobles and officers—were willing to cross the inlet into Menéndez' control. But the remainder, he said, had mutinied and had even tried to kill him that night. More than a hundred were already making their way down the beach.

Now the same gruesome ritual was repeated. The French were

ferried over in groups of ten. Their hands were bound and they were escorted behind the ridge of dunes. Ribault, accompanied by two of the adelantado's captains, was subjected to the same Inquisition as his comrades. "Are you Catholic or Lutheran?" he was asked. He answered with a passage from Genesis: "From earth we come and unto earth we must return." Then he sung a psalm, *Domine memieto mei*.

The three walked a while in silence as the mid-morning sun began to beat down and the first breeze wafted in from the sea. "Well, you know how captains must obey their generals' commands," one of the Spanish officers said matter-of-factly. With that, one captain whirled and buried his dagger in Ribault's stomach. The other thrust him through the back with a pike he had carried as a walking staff. Then, in the name of Jesus Christ and the True Gospel, they cut off his head and dragged to the putrid pile of rotting corpses the body of the viceroy and captain-general of Florida for the King of France.

The next day at St. Augustine the adelantado was able to finish his much-delayed letter to the king. "I think it is a very great fortune this man is dead," he wrote, "for the King of France could accomplish more with him and fifty thousand ducats than other men with 500,000 ducats. And he could do more in a year than another in ten, for he was the most experienced sailor and corsair known."

In late October, 1565, Pedro Menéndez received two important pieces of news within a day of each other. Fort Caroline, now renamed San Mateo, had burned severely after a captain's mulatto servant had left a lighted candle in the storehouse. Gone now was most of the grain that had been expected to last until January. Menéndez had already been worrying that the supplies of flour and biscuits at St. Augustine were spoiling in the humid Florida weather faster than they could be consumed.

Next came news from friendly Indians that the eighty or so rebellious remnants of Ribault's crew were back at Cape Canaveral erecting a wooden fort and trying to build a seaworthy ship from the timbers of the beached *Trinité*.

On November 2, after summoning reinforcements from San Mateo, Menéndez headed south. A hundred men were aboard three light boats along with provisions for forty days. Marching down the beach within sight of their supply convoy were another 150 soldiers led by the adelantado himself.

Their numbers far exceeded what had been mustered to subdue Jean Ribault three weeks earlier. The reason is that Menéndez had other objectives in mind as well. Thinning out the populations of San Mateo and St. Augustine would ease the food shortage. Once the French fort at Cape Canaveral was snuffed out, the expedition would move down the coast to the land of the Ais Indians where they would hopefully find new food supplies and built a fort devoted mostly to providing salvage and safety to ships on the route from New Spain.

Not mentioned often but equally important to Menéndez was continuing the search for his lost son, Juan. His ship had last been seen floundering opposite Cape Canaveral nearly three years before. The Timucuans around St. Augustine had offered no clues. Perhaps Juan would be among the Ais to the south.

On the morning of November 4, when the Spaniards first sighted the settlement at Cape Canaveral, the last of the occupants had already fled into the surrounding woods. Menéndez found the crude fort rather ingenious. Made of hard packed sand with a barrier of sharpened stakes, it sported six fine bronze cannon from the *Trinité*. Resting on driftwood timbers near the high tide line was the beginning of a ship's hull.

Within a half-hour the boat was ablaze and soldiers were burying the cannon in the sand—too heavy to carry in the three small Shallops brought down from St. Augustine.

Menéndez next sent one of his captured French trumpeters from Fort Caroline into the woods blaring for attention and shouting that all who came forth would be spared and well-treated. Within an hour, all of the near-starving survivors but their captain and four officers had emerged, and this time the adelantado kept his word. He seated the noblemen at his own table and gave them clothing. The French sailors shared mess with their counterparts. From then on they would be treated generously as equals because they could be useful in building a new fort and because this time the Spanish felt secure in their over-whelming numbers.

But equality also meant equal hardship. That same afternoon, the combined group set out down the beach to reach the main Ais village, still over forty miles south. Rations were now cut by two-thirds to a half-pound of bread each. This was supplemented along the way with hearts of palm, prickly pears and coco-plums.

They rested when dark came but were walking again in the moon-light at 2 am. After a stop for a meager breakfast, the march contin-ued through the hot, windy day until sunset. All the way, Menéndez strode stoutly in the vanguard while weary and hungry men straggled far behind. One of the men, who had been one of the first to break through Fort Caroline and lead the struggle inside, fell from sheer exhaustion and died.

Late that night they reached the inlet overlooking the northern tip of Hutchinson Island. The three small ships went scouting inside the inlet and soon found the large Ais village Indian guides had told them about. What would be their reception? To his surprise, the Ais chief greeted Menéndez with an embrace and a kiss on the lips, which inter-preters assured him, was the custom to show friendship. The cacique's face was painted in many colors and, like his elders, he wore a necklace and bracelets of Spanish gold.

The next morning the Ais chief nodded enthusiastically as Menéndez described as best he could in sign language the terms of a "friendship treaty." The cacique swore fealty to Philip II and promised Menéndez peace and obedience. And to seal the bargain he gave the chief gifts of clothing and jewelry. He also lectured his men to respect the private property of his hosts.

Still, Menéndez remained uneasy. There was no abundance of food at the Ais village and the adelantado feared that the Indians might attack if the Spaniards threatened their food stocks. Moreover, he could find no nearby site suitable for a Spanish fort. So after a four-day visit the adelantado and his men moved about nine miles down the intracoastal lagoon where there was a small harbor he would name Puerto de Socorro. There were more fish there but Menéndez began to fear that the forty days' provisions—now but thirty—would run out all too soon.

So another bold decision was made. He left 200 men and fifty French captives there to build a third settlement. The adelantado himself would captain two of the small ships with fifty Spaniards and twenty Frenchmen and head for Havana to secure provisions for the winter.

They were helped by a north wind and the fact that Menéndez had found that rowing nearer the shoreline nullified the strong current of the Gulf Stream. But a storm soon separated both crafts and Menéndez' compass broke. In three days, Menéndez was sharing the tiller with a Frenchman when they spotted a Cuban harbor. Without a compass they had drifted forty five miles east of Havana, but the salt-streaked and half-starved men were elated to be anywhere on land.

As soon as they had kissed the sand, Menéndez gathered the Frenchmen and charged them to behold the power and goodness of God. He said that if they would repent and turn Catholic, he would continue to treat them "like brothers" and even give them liberty to sail for France. Some, he would write later, "fell to their knees weeping, crying that they had been bad Christians, would abandon their evil sect, confess their sins and keep the faith which the Holy Mother Church of Rome held and believed."

The first reception in Havana made Menéndez jubilant. As the re-energized crew of Spaniards and Frenchmen swung their craft into the harbor, they were greeted by trumpets and shouts from the anchored ships of the Asturian fleet, which had been reduced to three after a stormy crossing. Likewise, the moored ships of Cuban governor García Osorio hailed him with salvos of artillery. Next to be seen waving was Diego de Amaya, who had skippered the second shallop from Florida and who had feared the adelantado to be lost at sea.

But once on land, Menéndez' fortunes began to spiral in a whirlpool of circumstances beyond his control.

After mass the next day, Menéndez called upon Governor Osorio and presented his *cédulas* from King Philip, including orders for the governor to furnish him with a vessel, 500 soldiers and twenty horses for the conquest of Florida.

The governor had a scowl on his face that never melted. Perhaps, thought Menéndez it was put there because one of the captains of the New Spain fleet had recently brought into the harbor a handsome Portuguese man-of-war as a prize. It seems that Osorio had seized the ship for himself and thrown the captain into a dungeon where he was still in chains. "The governor forbids anyone to discuss the subject," Menéndez was told.

So he didn't. Maintaining polite veneer, he offered that he really didn't need all the men and armaments called for by the king. One-fifth would do nicely.

The governor remained sternly impassive, often covering his face with his lace cuffs as he pretended to fan himself. Menéndez found himself shifting in his seat like a small boy asking for an allowance for candy. "Well, as an alterative," he broke the silence at last, "perhaps I could sell that Portuguese prize. It ought to fetch, say, 11,000 ducats, and I could make do with half."

More icy silence.

"Even 4,000 ducats would be sufficient," he added at last.

Menéndez had begun to perceive that the governor's silence had been caused by a slow boil, and now Osorio erupted. "You will not receive a ship, a soldier or a loan!" his voice crackled. With a flick of his lacey wrist, the governor bid his astonished supplicant good riddance from his audience room.

The adelantado of Florida was suddenly out on the street without knowing why, but determined to write the king about it that very night. Meanwhile, he was entirely on his own in finding a way to save the Enterprise of Florida. The first thing he did was sell a prize ship the Asturians had captured on their way over from the Canaries. With the proceeds he outfitted two small ships with enough food, he hoped, to last his Florida settlements until January. At the same time, he dispatched two larger ships to Santo Domingo to acquire enough supplies to carry the Florida settlements for many months after the December re-supply was exhausted.

As he waited for the ships to report the status of the outposts in Florida, news arrived in Havana harbor that sent Menéndez into a turmoil. From captains of one ship he learned the reason his chief asset, the *San Pelayo,* had not returned. When en route from San Mateo to Havana for supplies, the great galleass had been captured by mutineers led by French captives from San Mateo. It was last seen off the coast of Flanders and was presumed lost somewhere in the English Cannel.

Menéndez was reeling from the loss of his only remaining evidence of wealth when a royal dispatch ship entered the harbor at Havana with an urgent message from the king. Because Philip had heard that a French fleet was being readied to attack San Mateo and regain the fort, he was sending reinforcements of no less than 1,800 men to Havana. The adelantado was to use his available cash to obtain nine months' supplies of meat and fish as soon as possible.

Available cash? Menéndez cursed the month-long delay that would prevent the king from learning that he had no funds and that the governor of Cuba should be hung for treasonous parsimony. His only available ship had already been sent to Mexico to obtain corn, chickens, shoes and winter clothing for the Florida outposts.

Worse, he fell ill and took to the bed in his lodgings. He had lain there for ten days, weak from fever, when he learned that a hundred men had deserted from the Asturian fleet, followed by forty of the men who had been with him on the harrowing journey from Florida—the same ones who had fallen on their knees and renounced their heretical past. He importuned the governor to track them down, but was refused. Then, in the worst throes of fever, a secretary at bedside reported solemnly that the two ships he had sent to Santo Domingo had just embarked with supplies for Florida when a storm north of Cuba sank them both. The entire cargo was lost, and a flotsam of sailors and soldiers were stranded 350 miles from Cuba expecting to be rescued.

At this point the adelantado had but two available ships. The first was a caravel in the port of Matanzas, Cuba, carrying some 2,000 hides. He offered it for sale but no one would buy it sight unseen. Finally, up stepped Francisco de Reinoso, a Menéndez captain who had already loaned the adelantado 2,000 ducats. Reinoso agreed to buy the ship and hides, pay the crew back wages, cancel the debt and give Menéndez a thousand ducats cash. With that money the adelantado's team could outfit their second asset, a captured French barc named *Benaventura,* with 10,000 pounds of sea biscuit, meat, cassava and corn and send it to the fort that had just been established south of the Ais village.

Menéndez, though always forced to innovate on the spot for economic survival, never lost sight of his vision for Florida. He would protect the gold fleet from New Spain by establishing forts from the Florida Keys to the Chesapeake Bay. He would build warehouses in

Havana to keep his outposts supplied. He would protect Spanish fishing interests as far north as Newfoundland. He would discover the inland stream that surely led to Mexico on the other shore and create settlements in ports where inland rivers met the sea. He would convert heathen Indians to The True Gospel and root out the Huguenot Heresy wherever he found it. And along the way he would find his son Juan.

The starvation and malcontent in Florida was just a squall that would soon give way to the tranquility of order and prosperity.

CHAPTER TEN

Escape to Jeaga Inlet
November 1565-February 1566

Each day the men in the Florida outposts scanned the eastern horizon and wondered aloud: "Where is the *San Pelayo?* How could it have forsaken us?"

When Pedro de Menéndez left St. Augustine and its nearby fort of San Mateo, he had promised to return with supplies within twenty days. He had said the same to the soldiers who had settled south of Cape Canaveral, even though they had been left with only fifteen days of rations. But little did the anxious settlers know that their floating warehouse, the *San Pelayo,* would be lost at sea. Scarcely had they anticipated that two ad hoc supply ships would perish on their return from Santo Domingo, or that the adelantado would take sick in Havana, or that the obstinate governor of Cuba would inexplicably harass his every effort to further the Enterprise of Florida.

Diego de Amaya, the officer who had captained the small oared boat that had accompanied Menéndez to Havana, now was hastily pressed into bringing the first relief supplies back to St. Augustine and San Mateo. When he arrived at St. Augustine, one month after Menéndez' departure, he was shocked to see the emaciated, shivering people who swarmed about the dock. Nearly one hundred settlers had already starved to death. The survivors snarled that they didn't care how many supply ships came. They wanted out of Florida at any cost.

When Amaya's ship sailed north to San Mateo, it grounded on the bar and all but a few of the provisions were washed away in the roiling surf. At that point the starving settlers began writing letters to their counterparts in St. Augustine about joining in mutiny.

Amaya commandeered another small ship at San Mateo and headed south with a pittance of provisions that he would be able to offer the settlers in the land of the Ais.

For hours he tacked back and forth, trying in vain to locate Matanzas Inlet, which led to the Spanish settlement inside the intra-coastal waterway.

He might have saved the effort because the fort was no longer there.

An hour or so later Amaya was headed south for Cuba, hugging the inside shore so as to avoid the powerful Gulf Stream's reverse current. Suddenly he spotted a short-masted zabra with men at the oars. As he approached it, he saw many more figures moving about on shore.

Obviously Spanish. Obviously the contingent from the land of the Ais. But why straggling down the beach so far from the settlement?

The captain of the zabra was Juan Vélez de Medrano, who had once rescued Amaya at sea and fought alongside him at Fort Caroline. As they lowered sails and came abeam, Vélez, commanding officer of the Ais colony, grimly described the same scene Amaya had already witnessed up north. By late November all rations at the Ais fort had run out. At first the 200 soldiers and fifty French prisoners were able to subsist on fish, shellfish, coco-plums and palmetto berries, but these grew so scarce in the immediate area that they broke into small groups and foraged even further into the wild. The fragmentation made it easier to form small bands where the woes of embittered men fed upon one another. It also emboldened the surrounding Indians, already seething because the Spaniards were infringing on their own food supplies. Soon men were dying of hunger and Indians were ambushing foraging parties.

Also emboldened was a rank and file soldier named Escobar, who preached all-out insurrection. One night Francisco López de Mendoza Grajales, the same chaplain who had planted the cross on shore at St. Augustine, whispered to Vélez that Escobar and a hundred or so men were planning to kill him. Then they would seize the one ship Menéndez had left behind and take their chances on reaching Mexico.

Enlisting a few loyal men and some French prisoners, Vélez and the friar Mendoza slipped away in the ship. When Escobar learned of it, he reckoned that it would be only a few hours before Ais Indians would be swarming over the remaining Spaniards. So they started marching southward, hoping that they could find safety once they outdistanced the territory of the Ais.

On a cold and windy day, the insurrectionists had trudged forty-five miles down the beach and could go no further. They were now encamped on the north end of a broad inlet. It was too shallow for an oceangoing ship to enter, but too wide and treacherous to cross without sweeping away men, provisions and weapons in the swift current.

Because the men included an unruly collage of loyalists, mutineers, and the French prisoners Menéndez had sworn to protect, Vélez wanted to be sure they heard and understood a message. He waved his arms at the side of the zabra and shouted over the noisy surf that he was headed for Havana and would return soon with supplies.

But he also knew it would be a hollow promise unless he could solve some other problems. Where would nearly 200 Spaniards and fifty French prisoners camp while waiting for a ship from Havana? What would they eat? How could supplies be unloaded without finding a deep inlet with calm mooring waters? How long would it be before an army of Ais warriors arrived and boxed them in against the inlet?

It was just at this point of deliberation that Amaya rafted up to his friend Vélez. "I'll go in search of a good inlet further south that isn't controlled by the Ais," he told his fellow captain.

Diego de Amaya used the north wind to propel his zabra down the coast. By one o'clock in the chilly afternoon Amaya had gone fifteen miles down the coast and knew that he must turn back soon if he were to arrive back at the soldier's camp with a glimmer of light left. He also knew his failure to sight an inlet would produce despair and more talk of desertion and death at the hands of the advancing Ais.

On the sixteenth mile of his probe Amaya reached a broad opening that flowed to the sea. The first soundings indicated a shallow bar he could not cross, but then he took heart when one of his sailors shouted out "A village. People. Canoes." Amaya's crew had erected a crude wooden platform about fifteen feet up the single mast that functioned as a makeshift crow's nest, and from his perch the sailor began to cry out as he maneuvered his spyglass: "I see a big bay or wide river with many Indian houses. To port I see people on a beach inside this bar. I see many canoes drawn up on the sand. On the starboard side I see a big hill with a thatched roof on top of it and an even bigger one below, like a meeting house."

"Do you see any tributaries to the inlet?" Amaya shouted back. "Perhaps another way to the ocean?"

The sailor scanned the horizon silently with his spyglass. "I think maybe," he said at last. "On the port side, where all the canoes are beached I see a river or a creek where water is flowing into the big bay."

The tide was coming in—a good sign, thought Amaya. After a dozen trips among Florida and the Indies, he had a good instinct for how wind and shifting currents formed inlets and barrier islands. "One more mile," he shouted to the helmsman.

"Trust in the Father, Son and Holy Ghost," murmured the captain to himself as he stroked a small rosary that hung from his belt. And then in a half-mile: "Saints be praised, there it is!" His six sailors all let out a whoop at once. Just to their starboard was the bluest water he had seen this side of the Caribbean. Again relying on his instincts, he ran the ship beyond the mouth of the inlet, then swung her back to starboard and tacked in directly. "Lower sail," he ordered. Then "Oars," and six men began heaving the ship inside through calm waters. As Amaya bent over the port gunwale, he saw no bar, just blue water so clear that he could see conch and orange starfish eight feet below the hull. He had hardly noticed the bounding fins of two dolphins following astern. They veered back into the ocean as the little ship left behind the last foamy vestiges of incoming surf.

"Far enough," he shouted to the oarsmen when the ship was a hundred feet inside the inlet. He ordered it turned about so that they could make a quick escape if called upon. It was also standard procedure to stack loaded arquebuses unseen in case of sudden hostility. But again, Amaya's experience told him that Indians typically were usually curious and cordial on first contact. It was only later misunderstandings that produced hostility and flying arrows.

Still, Amaya had the crew drop anchor in the middle of the inlet until he could get his bearings. He had been so intent on avoiding shoals that this was the first time he had a chance to survey the scene around him. Along the sheltered back side of the barrier island a large fish trap stood in the water like a picket fence. On the high ground overlooking the beach on the other side were a row of thatched huts. On the shore were piles of oyster shells. A few feet further were oval bones which he judged to be the results of past whale hunts—another good sign of plenty. Further toward the inlet entrance were tall pines—and for the first time he could see faces of young men staring at him from concealed lookout stations in their lofty crowns. He examined the open thatched huts again and realized that the curious faces looking out on the ship were probably those of warriors, no doubt primed to let loose a hailstorm of arrows upon command.

Amaya tensed and almost called for the arquebuses, but he relaxd when he saw naked children descending from the ridge line to the shore, their curiosity overcoming their temerity.

No one would want to kill their child with a stray arrow.

Then, rounding a bend in the mangrove-lined inlet came three canoes headed directly for him. He sized up the occupants. *No sign of arms. Mostly older men. No warriors among them, except perhaps for a muscular youth paddling in the rear.* They circled the ship once, came to a halt in the water and stared up impassively at the Spaniards leaning on a gunwale above them.

Language was Amaya's number one problem.

"Jeaga? Jeaga?" he asked.

"Yes, Jeaga," answered the young muscular one from the back of a canoe.

A wave of relief swept over Diego de Amaya. They were out of the Ais sphere of power and in the presence of a person who might make them understood.

"You speak Spanish?" he said to the lad.

"*Solamente un poco.*" Only a little, said the youth. "Speak not fast."

A labored conversation ensued, Amaya making up his story as he went along. "I came to your land with these and other men. We have stayed as guests of the chief of the Ais. We then departed the Ais in ships to go to our home in Cuba. One of our ships like this sunk in the ocean. We lost our food and supplies. I must go to Cuba to get a ship to bring my men food and take my men back to Cuba."

Amaya spent ten minutes re-stating his sentences, waiting for the youth to translate his words to the older men, and pausing while they questioned him. The captain was beginning to worry that at this pace he would not return by nightfall and that the Spanish camp would dissolve in the gray haze that enveloped the shoreline at sunset. Finally he interrupted: "Who is your cacique?" he asked the lad.

He pointed to Deerstalker, the man in front of him.

"Please ask the cacique, will he allow my men to stay here in this inlet until I can go to Cuba and bring them food and another ship?"

The youth consulted again with his elders. "How many days here in Jeaga Town?" he asked.

"Fourteen," guessed Amaya. He could see this produced confusion, so he sent a sailor to his cabin to fetch a paper and quill. He drew a sun with rays and a crescent moon and put a circle around them. He stroked fourteen short lines on the paper and handed it down for the youth and his cacique to peruse.

"Ah," nodded the cacique without waiting for his interpreter.

"When I come back I will give you many things from Cuba," Amaya quickly added. But for now he realized that he had none of the usual beads, tools and trinkets that seemed to entice Indians, so he began improvising. "We will bring you good tobacco." He motioned to a sailor, who reluctantly produced a pouch from his pocket. "Throw it to him," muttered Amaya.

"We bring you many other things," he said again. With a flourish he undid the large silver-buckled leather belt holding his waistcoat up and handed it down to the chief. "We will give you fine cooking pots," he said, jerking his head toward the astonished cook, who darted inside to find one. "And fine metal knives like this," he said, slipping a scabbard from a startled sailor's waistband and handing it down to the young interpreter.

Finally, Amaya took off the broad straw hat that had been protecting him against the sun and sailed it down to another elder in the second canoe. "We will bring these and many jewels besides."

Then he asked the all-important question. "Will you trade us fish and fruits and venison for things like these?"

The men in the canoes conferred again. "Yes, we will," said the interpreter. "You stay this many days," he said pointing to the paper in his hand with the fourteen scratches.

"Tomorrow we come back here," said Amaya with a formal bow over the railing. They pulled up anchor and began rowing out, all with one eye on the arquebuses that stood loaded in the hatchway. With luck they would return sixteen miles northward with light to spare—and good news that might help mend the tatters of the Spanish expedition to the Ais.

"Let us note that the day is December 13, 1565," said Amaya to the men around him after they had reached the Gulf Stream and relaxd in its surging power. "It is the feast day of Santa Lucia. When we build a fort at the inlet of the Jeaga, we will name it Santa Lucia as our adelantado would no doubt wish."

From the age of ten, Coral Snake had learned to distrust and detest Deerstalker, the interloper from Lake Mayaimi who had been made cacique of the Jeaga by the distant King Calus. Coral Snake was the chief of the Gray Panther clan. His father, Eagle Feather, had been cacique of all the Jeaga until one night sixteen years beforehand, when Calusa warriors had stormed into his father's thatched hut and caught him with sacks of Spanish gold. Two warriors had pinned Coral Snake in a corner and forced him to watch as the others carved out Eagle Feather's eyes and hacked his head off until it rolled in the sand floor with its open, disbelieving mouth still twitching.

No one had ever implicated Deerstalker himself in the killings. And although Coral Snake lived with the ember of that horror still burning in his head, and even though the chief from Lake Mayaimi lived with a Mako Shark wife among their people, the Gray Panthers had tolerated the interloper cacique only because Deerstalker had the power to summon the Calusa again if threatened.

But now Coral Snake was so incensed that he had sent a runner to the Mako Shark compound to demand that Deerstalker come immediately to the inlet. On the previous day, Coral Snake had been in one of the three canoes as Deerstalker and his strange nephew attempted to decipher what the Spanish ship captain was up to. He never had understood much of it, only that Deerstalker had agreed to let a few Spaniards remain near the inlet for fourteen days until another ship could bring them supplies. During that time the Gray Panthers might benefit most from any trading because they lived along the ocean and inlet nearest to where the visitors would stay. The Mako Sharks lived largely along the River of Turtles at the north end of the inlet. The other clans of any consequence lived farther upriver or five miles south on Great Long Lake.

A few Spaniards? But what was *this?* Two ships had pulled into the inlet around nine that morning, disgorging more than a hundred soldiers with metal hats, spears, and the long ball shooters that the Calusa general had described in their War Council two months before. Without so much as greeting or asking anyone, the men had deposited their bulky baggage atop the ridge on the sandy platform that had been made firm and level over many months as the site of the new council house. Soldiers were already standing guard over the place. Inside the perimeter, Coral Snake had seen a shaman of some sort unpacking what looked like a contraption for worship. On a long shelf he put some silver metal cups and a painted mask of, no doubt, the man who had come back from the dead. Beside it the shaman had placed a good luck cross of shiny gold, just as the Calusa priest had foretold.

Coral Snake decided to clamber down from the ridge top to the inlet and wait for Deerstalker's canoe to appear around the bend. Behind him were the two Spanish ships, tethered to trees along the waterfront, where men were unloading supplies down a wooden walkway. A crowd of Jeaga onlookers had formed, but guards with loaded arquebuses kept them at a distance.

Coral Snake saw the same ship captain from the day before, but the man was too busy shouting at his men to even notice him. Soon there was a great hubbub and the Gray Panther chief could see why. As the captain yelled and waved his arms, several men emerged from one of the ships pulling the longest, thickest ropes he had ever seen.

Following them were other soldiers pushing a black tube so heavy that it bowed the wooden gangplank. Once they wrestled it on shore the men stopped and cheered. In a minute they began pushing and pulling the black tube up the steep hill and into their camping place.

The chief from Matacumbe had told them all about the big cannons that fired metal balls so big they could crush a ship. So loud you had to hold your ears. But why here?

In the next instant Coral Snake heard the unmistakable crunch of a large tree falling. The Ten Pines, the local landmark in which the Jeaga kept two of their lookout perches, were now the eight pines, and two men were pushing back and forth across another trunk with the biggest metal cutter he had ever seen.

Before long two canoes appeared from around the bend where the inlet met the Loxahatchee River. Deerstalker and his nephew Lujo paddled one. In the other were the Mako Shark elder Red Hawk and Coral Snake's young messenger.

Coral Snake wasted no time on formalities. "You said there would be a few Spaniards staying fourteen days," he sneered in his most disrespectful tone. "These boats have brought over a hundred so far and they say they are going back for more. They are taking over our homeland! They just cut down two of the Ten Pines."

Deerstalker frowned at Lujo. Then he looked at the first boat. The captain they had spoken to on Santa Lucia Day was leaning on a bow railing, lighting his pipe.

The Jeagas approached him on the beach below and clapped for his attention. "Yesterday your ship had six men on it," he said through Lujo. "Now you bring many, many more on two ships...."

Diego de Amaya held up his hand with a polite smile and cocked his head as if not understanding.

"Please tell the cacique that I am just captain of this one ship. I will bring the captain of all the men."

Amaya left and soon returned with a stern, bearded officer, telling Lujo "I must leave in my ship now." He turned his back and began shouting to his crewmen.

The Jeaga were left facing the impassive stare of Captain Juan Vélez de Medrano. He had been abandoned—well, left temporarily—by his adelantado in a strange land, had been chased down the coast by hostile Ais Indians, and had been dishonored by mutiny of his own men. And now he was in no mood to nurse another tribe of Indians of suspect loyalty.

Deerstalker (speaking through Lujo): "How come you bring two ships? The other captain say you had two and one sink in the ocean."

Vélez: "I know nothing of what another captain may have said. I was not there with you. We have two ships, which you see here."

"How many more men will come?"

"Just one more trip, as soon as I can leave to get them."

"Why have you come to occupy the top of the ridge? You could go down the beach past the inlet."

"We have to be up high to be able to see the supply ship when it returns from Cuba."

"Why did you bring the big loud cannon?"

"If there is rain or clouds when the supply ship comes, we fire the cannon so they can hear us and find the inlet. We also need it in case our enemies, the *Francois*, come in ships to attack us. They are bad people and will kill us all if we don't protect you."

"Why are you cutting down these trees?"

"We need their trunks to make strong walls in case the *Francois* bring men here and try to shoot us with guns." (Vélez pointed to the arquebuses held by the Spanish guards who looked down on them from his ship.)

"Where are the things you are going to trade with us?"

"The other captain said this? Ah, well, they will be on the next ships that come. And we will bring some more when the other ship comes back from Cuba."

Vélez stood in silence for about ten seconds, awaiting another question. Concluding that there were none, he said simply "I leave you now" and bounded up the gangplank to his ship. In a few minutes both zabras were on their way out of Jeaga inlet and riding the Gulf Stream, hoping to fetch their remaining men from their precarious camp sixteen miles to the north before the Ais discovered them.

Coral Snake still wasn't sure what he had heard and kept asking Lujo to repeat his answers as if the lad were part of a Spanish plot against the Gray Panthers.

"Stop!" Deerstalker shouted at last. "The fact is that they are here. Let us just try to make their stay short and prepare to drive them out if it is not. Do you not remember the advice of Escampaba, the Calusa, at our meeting? Don't mingle with them. Don't show them where you have hidden food supplies for the winter. Don't show them how to dig for roots or pick fruits. Don't show them the oyster beds or what to do with them. And don't let your women near them!"

Coral Snake was still fuming on the shore when they left in their canoes. "Don't *mingle?*" he shouted. "How can you not mingle when they are sitting on top of us?"

It was mid-afternoon when the three paddled back to the river-front. Deerstalker had kept silent for the fifteen minutes, but just as they nosed into the sandy shore he could contain himself no longer.

"How could you not hear that they had so many soldiers?" he fumed at his nephew. "You said it was just a dozen. How could you forget something so important?"

Enough of his carping and his crap, thought Lujo.

"I never said a dozen men. I never asked how many," he said his neck muscles straining as he glared at his uncle from six inches away and hissed through clenched teeth: "I didn't say it because *you* never asked. I am just your interpreter. I am not the cacique and never will be. I've heard *that* a thousand times from you. I never asked to be an interpreter, either, so if you want someone who can talk to the Spanish better than I can, go find him!"

With that Lujo jumped in the canoe and paddled off furiously. "Wait!" shouted Deerstalker, but the lad didn't look back. He was headed upriver to his secret canoe camp where he already had built a temporary log-and-hide lean-to atop his new watertight raft. Soon the sun would go down on an already chilly day and he had forgotten in his haste to fetch warm clothing. But the fire inside him would keep him warm for quite a while.

By the time the moon rose over the new Spanish camp in Jeaga Town, 236 men had been landed, including fifty French prisoners under the sworn protection of the absent adelantado. Two more of the Ten Pines had been felled and the new fort now had crude barricades for the length of its perimeter. Men had also begun to rip up sea grape, buttonwood and mangrove from the inlet shores in order to cut and whittle sharp stakes to be hammered into the ground as pickets in front of the barricades.

Indians milled and mingled throughout, not paying much attention to the guards and their arquebuses because they were oblivious to the power of the long guns. Older Gray Panthers stood with folded arms and expressions of disapproval, but the younger the age the more curiosity and less restraint. As the afternoon wore on, the scene began to resemble a festival. Young women pranced and preened in their best jewelry. A Spanish sailor and a young widow were seen strolling arm in arm. Hunters and warriors pestered Spanish soldiers to trade—some even producing gold coins and jewelry that had long been stashed away and unveiled now despite knowing how the Calusa treated those who brandished Shipwreck booty. A gasp of astonishment went up when the artillery master, Diego López, fired the cannon, explaining that he needed a practice shot to be sure the great gun was calibrated. In truth, López had prevailed on Captain Vélez only by arguing that the gun's power would send a message to the Jeaga in case they should think of turning unfriendly.

The cannon firing may have been the highlight of the day, but the most entertaining was the parade of a dozen or so hogs that were herded from one of the ships into a pen at one end of the fort-in-the-making. No Jeaga had ever seen a pig, and it seemed that every child had a turn at peeking through the barricades to see the pigs sleeping, nursing and rooting about.

Pigs also provided the first tense encounter between Jeaga and Spaniard. One of the young male boars wriggled loose through a gap in the balustrade of logs and scampered down the main pathway, with children laughing and chasing behind. When the young boar suddenly wheeled about and faced the startled children as if to charge, a Gray Panther warrior standing nearby whipped an arrow from his quiver and shot it through the pig's heart. The warrior held his hands high in triumph, thinking he'd be hailed a hero, but he was quickly grabbed by two Spanish soldiers and dragged before Captain Vélez.

The commanding officer, having chronically faced starvation for weeks until Amaya's supply boat caught up with him, was accustomed to flog or hang anyone caught tampering with precious food stores. But on this night he was enjoying some wine while the supply lasted and was content enough to have transplanted 236 men without an incident. He asked for the cook.

"What are we having for dinner tonight?" he inquired when the man arrived, wiping his hands on a towel.

"Roast pork," said the cook.

"Have you slaughtered a hog yet?"

"Not yet, Capitan."

"Good. This Indian has taken the trouble to do it for you." He pointed to the carcass with an arrow sticking from it. Then he nodded towards the young bowman cowering before him. "This is Barabbas," he announced theatrically to all within earshot. "I am Pontius Pilate. This pig has died for your sins. I order you to release the murderer."

When Diego de Amaya appeared before Pedro de Menéndez on a January morning in Havana, he had good and bad news, but felt great reluctance in reporting the latter. The adelantado, the man who had led a fifty mile march from Cape Canaveral while scarcely breaking stride, the man who sailed fifty desperate men to Cuba without a compass, looked tired and pale hunched behind a desk piled with scrolls and charts. He sniffled and blew his nose a lot, but assured his old comrade in arms from Asturia that he'd be fine "if only the weather improved and my ships stopped sinking so much."

Amaya thought of his own supply ship breaking up on the bar at San Mateo, but decided to bring a ray of sunshine first. "I'm happy to report that our troops from the land of the Ais have been removed to a much more friendly inlet sixteen miles south," he said. "The men have what I judge to be two weeks supply and the food stocks around the fort seem to be abundant. The inlet is deep and full of fish. I see many oyster and conch shells piled up everywhere. The French prisoners seem well integrated with our soldiers and believe they will see France again as free men once they arrive in your hands. But I do believe we need more glass beads and hand tools to trade with the Indians."

"Thank you," said Menéndez with a thin smile. "But before I

begin dancing with joy you must also tell me about St. Augustine and San Mateo."

So Amaya overcame his reluctance and did so, addressing the issue of starvation, but not burdening the adelantado with the images of sunken cheeks and swollen bellies that still burned in his conscience. "Alas," he concluded, "I am obliged by your own regulations to deliver to you these letters from various settlers at these two settlements." At his side was a black leather case with fifty or more letters, some stained by the salt air and faded by the Florida humidity.

Amaya upended the case and spread them before the adelantado so that he had no choice but to sift through several. They wrote of hardship, despair, sickness, hunger, Indian cruelty, lazy neighbors and corrupt overlords. Some were addressed to Menéndez, some to friends and family in Spain. The latter warned against ever coming to this land of bugs, poor soil, hostile natives and shattered dreams.

Suddenly Menéndez was his old self again. "We cannot allow these letters to reach Spain," he exclaimed, pounding his fist on the desk. "They would discourage all immigration and ruin the Enterprise of Florida. Don't these people realize they signed an oath of loyalty? If only they knew the facts!

"Their delusion is but temporary," he declared as if Amaya were one of them. "After you departed for the Florida settlements, I received a letter from King Philip announcing that 1,800 men are sailing from Spain to reinforce the forts of Florida. I have written him back urging that these troops be sent directly to St. Augustine and San Mateo rather then converging on Havana and its governor, the devil incarnate. In a few weeks these same complainers will be petitioning me for lands and titles as rewards for their bravery and loyalty!"

Amaya left the room laughing as Menéndez walked him to the doorway and sent him off with a clap on the back.

Days later the adelantado received another letter from a royal *adviso*. King Philip had now been informed of the fall of Fort Caroline and congratulated Menéndez for his gallant deeds. However, since 1,800 combat troops would no longer be needed, he had pared the number of arriving troops to 300 for what would no doubt be a postwar security force. And since the adelantado was sure to reap the financial benefits of a secure and peaceful Florida, Philip served notice that he expected Menéndez to pay and supply the 300 men at his own expense.

Once again, the adelantado had no money for men or supplies. Perhaps a loan from the viceroy of Mexico? Perhaps another advance from Castillo in Cadiz? His financial burdens in the coming weeks would be greater than ever, but the least of them would be the newly-relocated troops at Jeaga Inlet. Hopefully, they could remain comfortable enough until March. Then he would sail away himself and take them all back to St. Augustine, San Mateo and another fort he hoped to build further up the coast.

No ship came for the Spanish within fourteen days, or for fourteen afterwards. By late January it was clear to the Jeaga that the rations the strangers had brought in their ships that first day were now all but exhausted. They could see it in the gaunt faces and sullen demeanor of the soldiers. They could see how hunger was breaking down the discipline the commanders had over the men in the fort.

The Jeaga sensed a major change when the strangers all but stopped trading. At first they were eager for the few gold coins and silver bars the Gray Panthers produced. Next they wanted hides and pelts. But these interests quickly gave way to food—meat first, then fish of any kind, then fruits and then even the bitter palmetto berries that made men grimace when they chewed them. But even then the strangers had little to trade beyond their own items of clothing and their own tools for cutting or stirring or sewing.

So wide was the gap between promises and reality that the Jeaga even considered "church" a form of trading. At first the man who called himself a "priest" invited a few dozen of the Gray Panthers and Mako Sharks to the council house and told them about Jesus, the man who came back from the dead. If they learned a song and a certain chant, the priest gave them pieces of a brittle, bland cracker and necklaces with little wooden crosses hanging from them. But they weren't enough to make people sit there for so long. After two of these meetings no one came any more.

By the turn of February Indian forbearance and Spanish discipline were like two dry twigs being rubbed together. The fort and its occupants' need for fires on crisp mornings and cold nights consumed pines and oaks along the inlet at a devastating rate. The large fish trap that Little Heron had helped build had been emptied by hungry soldiers and most of its picket stakes pulled up for use in the fort barricade. Spaniards commandeered canoes on Jeaga Town beaches and left them in the inlet below the fort. But the Jeaga could not retrieve them because they were banished from the inlet after two boys climbed into the anchored ship at night and stole the captain's compass.

And yet the Spanish were anything but banned from associating with women in the Gray Panther neighborhood around the fort. At first living outside the fort was strictly banned, but in time Captain Vélez rationalized that those who chose to live with Indians might consume less of the fort's stores and might also pick up valuable intelligence as to Indian intentions and the whereabouts of any hidden caches of food. The scuttlebutt that filtered back to him suggested that Jeaga women found the Spaniards "softer" and not so demanding and demeaning as the home-grown male.

As for caches of food, they learned nothing. Several weeks before, Deerstalker and the Council had a secret rendezvous upstream in their canoes. The cacique repeated the Calusa instructions about not showing the Spanish how to find food or how to prepare it. "That's easy for you to say because you're not living by the fort," Coral Snake had argued. "Some of them who live with our women have learned how to make coontie flour better than the women!"

At the secret meeting all had agreed that each clan would store up a cache of nuts, dried berries, coontie and whale strips to last through the winter in a place known only to its elders. The shaman passed the black drink and all swore that if any of them divulged its location, the penalty would be death.

Indeed, no one did. Meanwhile, the Spaniards' search for food expanded ever wider, but with disappointing results. One day two Spanish soldiers appeared at Deerstalker's doorway and read from a piece of paper in broken Jeaga to say that the Captain would like to meet with him and his elders in the Council House. When they assembled, he spoke through a cook who had learned a smattering of Ais words from his servants and assumed that was good enough for the Jeaga.

Vélez repeated his assurance that the supply ship would arrive "in a few days" to take them away. Meanwhile, the shortage of provisions had made it necessary for him to issue an *ecomienda*.

The cook now faced a daunting translation task. With heads cocked and ears straining to understand him, Jeaga elders learned that The Great King of Spain had told the captain to command the Indians to work by day for them at any task he wished. This would be good for both peoples. In this case the "work" would consist of sending out four groups a day—to the north, south, the east (ocean) and west. Each hunting party would consist of two skilled Jeaga hunters or fishermen, "assisted" by four soldiers. At the end of the day, Spaniards and Indians would divide their yield equally.

After an hour of watching Vélez' hand and facial gestures as they tried to decipher the bumbling translator, the Jeaga elders had understood the gist of it. What they hadn't grasped at all was a final clause in the *ecomienda*. If the day's total catch or gathering were not enough to feed the fort on any day, the Jeaga would contribute from their portion until it was sufficient. To make it official, as demanded by an edict of King Charles V some twenty years before, the terms of the "agreement" were produced on a parchment in writing and nailed to a timber in the Council House for all to read.

None could, of course.

Chapter Eleven

Menéndez and King Calus

February-March 1566

On February 10, 1566 Pedro Menéndez de Avilés finally undertook a diversion he had long anticipated. After leasing a warehouse in Havana and sending some ships to Mexico to provision his garrisons in east Florida, he set sail to see for himself what was on the other side of the peninsula.

That it would be no idle sightseeing expedition was evidenced by the fact that it involved five ships and 500 men. First among the adelantado's objectives was finding the mouth of an interior waterway that might enable ships to reach the east coast and thereby cut several days of dangerous sailing for the treasure fleets that traveled from Spain to Mexico. Indians had told his men of a large inland lake that might connect rivers running east and west. Ponce de León had indicated as much in his explorations some fifty years before. In any case, Menéndez was determined to find a deep water channel from Cuba to western Florida through the labyrinth of small islands off the southern coast.

The second objective—and the reason for taking so many soldiers—was to meet and convert the legendary Great Cacique who held sway over virtually all Indians in South Florida. Somewhere on the southwestern peninsula the adelantado knew he would encounter the headquarters of Calus and he expected to find several Spanish shipwreck captives being held there. Perhaps even one of them would be his missing son, Juan.

The latter strategy called for Menéndez and his long-time sailing companion Diego de Amaya to probe among the islands in two shallow-draft zabras while the larger ships followed in the deeper Gulf of Mexico.

Eight days into the voyage, after successfully negotiating the maze of small islands that dotted the Florida Straits, the two zabras had emerged into a wide estuary and were startled to see a canoe appear from behind a small island and approach Amaya's boat.

The lone occupant, a young man with sun-bleached hair, called out in Spanish: "Welcome Spaniards and Christian brothers!"

As he drew nearer, Amaya could see he was indeed as Spanish as any of them. "God and Mary have told us that you were coming," he said joyously. "And the Christian men and women who are still alive here have directed me to wait for you here with this canoe to give you a letter."

As the equally joyful sailors quickly helped him into Amaya's boat they found him to be a handsome man of thirty years, clad only in a small deerskin loin cloth and painted like an Indian. When Amaya asked about the letter he bore, the man dug into his loin cloth and produced a cross. "This," he proclaimed, "is the letter that the captive Christians send you, beseeching you, by the death suffered by our Lord for our salvation, not to pass by, but to enter yonder harbor, rescue us from the cacique and take us to a Christian land."

By this time Menéndez' boat had pulled aside as the captive explained that he was among the last of some 200 survivors who storms had cast into Calus' kingdom over the past twenty years. All but twelve had been sacrificed to his idols since then. Led by the adelantado, all knelt on the deck to thank God for their good fortune on this day.

As their new guide led them north to the town of Calus, they would learn that he was Hernando Escalante Fontaneda, son of noble Spanish parents who had become leading citizens of Cartagena, a leading port city of New Spain. He and his older brother were being sent on a returning treasure ship to be educated in Salamanca, Spain when a hurricane drove the ship across the Keys and into the southwest coast of Florida. Forty two had survived the wreck and all—including Fontaneda's brother—had been sacrificed to Calusa gods except the dozen who remained.

Since they were now navigating in the shallow waters between the mainland and barrier islands, Menéndez and Amaya had lost sight of their well-armed barcs at sea, but suddenly to their port side they passed a wide inlet to the Gulf and Menéndez could see his three ships standing guard just outside. If he encountered hostilities, two cannon shots would send up to three hundred armed men in longboats.

Thus far, they had encountered only scattered huts along the coast, hardly a sign of a mighty empire. But Fontaneda explained: "Mound Key lies at the southern end of a long chain of Calusa islands and towns. At one time the caciques lived on Pine Island in the middle of them, but Mound Key is more protected from raids by the Tocobaga and Spanish. It is near the entrance to the Calusahatchee River, which leads to the Lake of Mayaimi and the eastern vassal tribes, but Mound Key is a fortress unto itself."

Soon they would see why. As they passed the wide entrance to Calus Pass to the west and crept north, the landscape of mangrove islands was broken by one with hills of forty and more feet serving as platforms for large structures. "On the left is the great meeting house," said Fontaneda. "On the right hill is the house of Calus. In the middle is the harbor with a canal in the center. This leads to the houses of their shaman and royal families. Every house has a lookout and from these they can see well out into the Gulf. You can be very sure that they have already seen *us*. But I think we will be well received. Calus seems to like me because I know his language better than the others. And I know how to make him laugh."

As they drew within two hundred yards, Menéndez asked about a smaller, nearby island with several huts on stilts. "They call that the Island of Outsiders," explained the guide. Its origin goes back to the arrival of Ponce de León. When he was met by Senquene, the father of Calus, he said he was seeking the 'Fountain of Youth.' Sometimes they called it the 'River Jordan.' Ponce had heard that anyone who bathed in it would be cured of his ills or be restored to the body of his youth.

"Well, the Calusa thought this was hilarious indeed—and I can tell you that I have swum in just about every river in their kingdom and agree with them. But somehow the legend took hold and people started coming here in search of it. Indians from all over Florida and lately people from Cuba, too.

"Over time there got to be so many that Senquene made them all go and live in one place, which you see over there. But it may serve a purpose because lately there have been a lot of Indians who have come down with diseases that their shamans can't cure. That's where Calus makes them live."

Rather than land, Menéndez sent Fontaneda by himself in a dinghy. The captive announced to the guards on the beach that The King of Spain had sent an embassy, bearing gifts for the Great Cacique and his family, to secure his friendship.

Obviously the news had stirred a commotion atop one of the mounds, but Menéndez waited patiently, his arquebusmen standing at attention with matches ready for lighting. Within a half hour, the tallest Indian any of them had ever seen descended the hill, accompanied by a phalanx of naked bowmen that numbered two hundred or more.

Menéndez, startled at the size of the entourage, pulled his anchors and let his two zabras drift away on the outgoing tide until they were turned with his artillery facing the island. Then he took two longboats with thirty of his arquebusmen and a large rolled-up carpet. Once on land, he had the carpet spread and bid the cacique sit at the other end. But Calus instead knelt down and extended his arms with the palms of his hands upward—the highest mark of reverence that a Calusa could pay a superior.

Menéndez placed his own hands atop the cacique's. Then he began distributing presents—a shirt, a hat and a pair of silk breeches for Calus and various smaller gifts for his family. This was followed by bread, wine and honey, which the Indians enjoyed even more.

Calus then presented Menéndez with a bar of silver and some gold and silver jewelry. This caused a stir among the arquebusmen because the silver bar confirmed rumors they'd heard even when in St. Augustine. The cacique of the Calusa was supposed to have hoarded as much as a 100,000 ducats worth of gold and silver from sunken Spanish ships. If Menéndez' intent was to leave a garrison on Mound Key, they wanted to be a part of it.

Calus was clearly enjoying his wine and asked for more. The

adelantado replied that he had not brought enough for so many people. But if the Great Cacique and a few of his principal men would join them aboard one of his larger ships beyond the bay, he would serve them an even more savory repast.

Fontaneda's translation caused an immediate hubbub among Calus' advisors. The king was also wary, but his curiosity won the struggle. With twenty of his men in the longboats, the king was rowed out to the waiting zabras. As soon as the Indians were seated—side by side with Spanish soldiers—Menéndez drew up his anchors and headed away from Mound Key. The Calusa sprang to their feet in terror but were forcibly restrained by the soldiers beside them. Menéndez explained that he was only moving away slightly so that more Indians would not be tempted to swim or canoe out to the feast he was about to serve them. With that more food and gifts were distributed.

When the Indians were mellow with wine, Menéndez stood and announced that King of Spain wished very much to be friends with Calus. In fact, he would be honored if the Great Cacique would accept the name of Carlos, who was the Spanish king's father and the greatest monarch on earth.

Calus beamed and said he would.

Menéndez then said that to consecrate the friendship, the King of Spain would appreciate the return of all Christian captives being held by the Calusa. Refusal, alas, would reluctantly mean the death of all aboard ship. But agreement would bring the fruits of a beautiful alliance, including assistance against enemies of the Calusa.

When King Carlos nodded his assent, the adelantado was not about to give him time to change his mind. The longboats were put out again and within an hour five women and three men were delivered up and clad in European clothes that Menéndez had brought along for such an occasion. The king even offered to fetch two more Spaniards who were living somewhere around the Lake of Mayaimi.

The next morning the men aboard the Spanish zabras were beginning to stir when one of them spotted several canoes making their way from Mound Key. The canoes were full of unarmed men and women, waving palm branches and singing joyfully. Among them was King Carlos, who said he had come to fetch the Spaniards and bear them on the backs of Calusa in a triumphant march to their main village. This tradition, he said, was a mark of honor that had been shown to other Christians who had visited their country. "For we are all God's creatures," the cacique proclaimed with a sweep of the hand.

But the previous evening Menéndez had been listening to the stories of the former slaves and had been told that the real "tradition" was to slaughter the Spaniards as they walked through a grove of saw palmettos. The adelantado thanked the Calusa for their courtesy, but said that those who accepted such treatment in the past were "false Christians." He could never consent to such a tradition.

Later that day, Carlos, blinded by his desire for more gifts, paddled out that afternoon with a half dozen companions. Aboard the zabra he offered Menéndez his sister in marriage. He asked that his sister be taken back to a Christian land and then returned so that he and all his people might become of the same faith. The Adelantado said he would consider it. He walked to the bridge with Amaya and watched the king's entourage paddle away.

"It's clear that we're both trying to outwit the other," said Menéndez, gazing toward the island and the king's lofty house.

Surprisingly, Amaya was all for the marriage idea. "The men have gotten gold fever," he said. "Yes, they came to Florida on the promise of land and crops, but in their hearts they crave the gold of Mexico and Peru. They have suffered many hardships and have nothing to show for it. Do not hold what I'm about to say against them, but yesterday while we were having our happy little feast on this ship some of the Indians offered to trade. It seems that some of the arquebusers found their offers irresistible."

"Like what?" Menéndez asked with a frown.

"Well, I heard that one who shall remain nameless traded an ace of diamonds for a piece of gold worth about seventy ducats. Another said he traded a pair of scissors for some silver worth a hundred ducats. That's quite a transaction when your pay is three ducats a month and you haven't seen it in a year."

"Yes, and that same short-sighted fellow will no doubt be petitioning me in a few months for hectares of land worth 20,000 ducats," said the adelantado ruefully. "In any case, my friend, you and I as Christians cannot convey to these people that our purpose here is to trade for trinkets. We have a higher purpose."

Amaya gazed at the Mound Key hills in a few moments of respectful silence. Then he resumed his gentle plea on a different tack. "I do think that higher purpose would be well served if we did pay Carlos the visit he wants," he said. "I also think we should bring his sister back to Havana and then return her with a group of religious as an example of Christian conversion. It would go better for the friars."

"But *marry* her? He surely thinks all of us have several wives."

"Well, maybe we can navigate around that issue," said Amaya.

"What about our security?"

"They've seen our artillery. But as an extra measure, let me leave now with my zabra and contact the larger ships waiting outside. I think it will be safe to bring one of them at least within sight of our anchorage and we can make it a point to tell them that there are two more like it waiting to blow up their kingdom if necessary."

Menéndez sent word to Carlos that he would pay a visit the next day.

Shortly after noon on another balmy March day, the adelantado, twenty of his officers and 200 arquebusiers assembled on the small beach and began to march. Striving for all the pomp and circumstances he could muster, Menéndez had insisted on full dress for his men. Together they marched with unfurled banners through the mangroves and saw palmetto. Preceded by two pipers, two drummers, three trumpeters, a harp, violin and a Psalter, they sang from the 95th Psalm:

Oh come let us sing praise to the Lord.
Let us make a joyful noise to the rock of our salvation.
Let us come before his presence with thanksgiving
And make a joyful noise to him with psalms.

After reaching the great hall of Carlos, Menéndez stationed his men around the perimeter looking in, the wicks of their arquebuses lit for an instant response should it be required. Carlos, determined to match the Spanish splendor, sat alone on a raised seat, his muscular torso painted in black and red and his height augmented by a headpiece that made him seem twice as tall as the Spanish king's envoy. Yet, as Menéndez entered, the Great Cacique stepped down from his throne and with a theatric sweep of the hand, offered it to the adelantado.

Menéndez declined with equal emoting, and so the two sat side by side. Near them was the king's sister, tall, plain, impassive and surrounded by a court of squatting Calusa women. Before they could converse, a chorus of a few hundred youths appeared outside the main entrance and began singing. Soon men and women joined in, and then the family of Carlos, all dancing and pirouetting.

When the dance abated and Menéndez could see serving people gathering with trays of food, he asked for a short delay so that he could address Carlos and his sister. He also asked that the king's wife be brought in. As an observer recorded it,

> *She proved to be a handsome young woman of twenty, with fine eyes and eyebrows, shapely hands, and graceful figure, naked as Eve before the fall except for a covering which she wore in front, a rich necklace of pearls and precious stones, and some golden trinkets about her throat.*

The adelantado, who could employ charm as effectively as a battle ax, took her by the hand and seated her between himself and the sister. She looked at her husband for approval and Carlos appeared resentful of having his wife subjected to the eyes of so many covetous Spaniards. But the adelantado assumed his most fatherly demeanor and begged the king that she be allowed to stay.

Menéndez then began to speak, haltingly, but in the Calusa language. The day before he had sat with Fontaneda and some Spanish captives jotting down various words of the Calusa. Thus, when he spoke the Indians were astounded, some even thinking that the paper Menéndez was reading from had spoken to them as if by magic.

The adelantado's words of peace and friendship were followed by a succulent repast featuring grilled fish, roasted and raw oysters. The Spaniards contributed honey, biscuits, sugar, and wine and quince. The officers sang a chorus of Spanish songs. When the feast was over and Menéndez rose to leave, Carlos held his arm, and motioned for Fontaneda to translate. The Calusa, he said, were expecting him to wed his sister. And if it didn't happen they might be insulted enough to rise up against the Spanish.

Menéndez could see his arquebusiers were still positioned around the building, but for the moment he was completely surrounded by Carlos and his Calusa warriors. He chose to discuss theology.

"Christian men are allowed only to marry Christian women," he said through Fontaneda.

"Ah," said Carlos, "I am a Christian because I have already taken you as a brother."

"But you worship many deities," said the adelantado with a patient smile. "There is but one God and all creatures here on earth must worship and obey him alone, so that when a Christian dies we see our wives, children and friends, and are ever joyful, singing and laughing. But they who in their ignorance do not serve or worship God instead serve a chief called the Devil. And when they die they go to him and are forever weeping because they are either very cold or very hot and never have anything to satisfy them."

While Carlos was still digesting these words, Menéndez was already consulting with the officers around him as to what course he should take. All concluded that the only way to convert this intractable chief and his people would be to marry the woman. So that same night the cacique's sister was baptized as Doña Antonia, followed by a wedding ceremony. With that a new round of singing and dancing broke out among the Indians, and it was continuing as Menéndez and his tired contingent walked down the hillside and pushed off in their tenders.

Several days after the adelantado's fleet departed, a single ship arrived at Mound Key from Cuba. Leading a contingent of some thirty soldiers—including six noblemen and six soldier-farmers—was Francisco de Reinoso. Newly promoted to captain, Reinoso had been among several officers to lend Menéndez money during the expedition, and the opportunity to sniff around the legendary riches of King Carlos was rumored to be an implied reward for his financial faith in the adelantado. Officially, however, Reinoso's orders were to explore for the fabled waterway across Florida, begin agriculture on the island, and cultivate the friendship of Carlos as well. While his men began work on a garrison, Reinoso himself was given a house in the town. In front of its entrance a large wooden cross was erected, and the Calusa were urged to kneel before it in worship whenever they passed.

The fact that thirty Spaniards could expect to survive intact on an island of some 2,000 Calusa was secured by the departure of Doña Antonia and six of the cacique's elders on the ship returning to Havana.

CHAPTER TWELVE

Fort Santa Lucia

February-March 1566

February 1566 descended on Jeaga Inlet with cold clear skies and calm seas. By now relations between the Jeaga and the ill-clad denizens of Fort Santa Lucia were as brittle as a pine twig and any of many reasons could make it snap.

For Deerstalker, chief of the Jeaga, two causes were sufficient. The first was that foraging expeditions didn't work. Deerstalker knew they wouldn't because the elders had agreed to make a sham of leading the intruders to productive food sources. But when they did not, or even when the Spanish kept an entire day's catch for themselves, they would patrol the pathways along the village huts in search of a pot of elderberries, a bowl of coontie flour left by a fire pit or perhaps a strip of venison hanging out to dry that might be confiscated as their just due.

The cacique's second reason was personal. Jeaga women had also taken to foraging greater distances in search of enough nuts and roots to survive the winter. Ordinarily, Bright Moon could count on Lujo to do her gathering, but he had not re-appeared for two weeks after his quarrel with her brother. Anhinga, the wife of Red Hawk, had accompanied her as they walked some two miles westward. Most berries and acorns were produced in spring or fall, so the women were determined at the very least to bring back what the Jeaga often called "famine foods" of winter. One was the sabal palm heart, which required a certain expertise to extract the white, crisp hearts, which could be eaten raw or boiled. Another of Bright Moon's objectives was the greenbriar root, which could be chopped up and pulverized in a mortar. It would then be boiled into a powder which could be mixed with water to make a pudding or dropped in a pot to thicken a stew.

Bright Moon and Anhinga were on their knees chopping at a large greenbriar root when they heard the sound of footsteps and plants being crushed. Then suddenly into their clearing emerged two young Spaniards with pikes, breastplates and brass helmets. They were as startled as the women, and the first thing they observed when they took a step back was the large basket of greenbriar roots beside the women.

What also caught their eye was the long gold chain and locket that Bright Moon wore whenever she went outside her hut. Instinctively she covered her breasts and the gold chain. Neither woman had seen a Spanish soldier up close except for the time when two of them came to the doorway of Deerstalker a few weeks before. They were no taller than her and heavily bearded. She would have found their puffy round breeches comical if she weren't trembling with fear.

She caught them looking at each other, wondering what to do. It was then she realized that they were also eyeing the knife she held for cutting greenbriar. It was Spanish, handed down to Lujo by one of Amaya's men when they had first seen the Spanish ship in the inlet. He had thought to use the knife for hunting, but then gave it to his mother for chopping food and cutting twine. It was sharper than any Jeaga shell knife, and the soldiers were wondering why she had it.

"Where did you get the knife?" the first one asked.

Bright Moon understood nothing. "Keep your distance," she said in Jeaga.

The Spaniards understood nothing. "Where did you get that fine gold chain?"

Their words were gibberish. She scooted back on her haunches and pointed a finger. "I am the wife of Calus the King. Calus. *Calus!* He gave this to me and will kill anyone who takes it."

He tried moving her left forearm from her chest and found it rigid. She raised the knife with her right arm.

"You must have spread your legs for a viceroy," he sneered. "Or maybe a bishop. What's in that locket?" He pointed to the small gold heart on the chain and reached out his hand.

Bright Moon flailed clumsily with her knife and the soldier jumped back. "Maybe she stole it after he fell asleep," said the other one. "I think we need to see that locket."

The second soldier eased around behind her so that she now faced one man in front and one to her rear. As she wheeled around to face him the first one grabbed the arm with the knife and pinned it to the ground. She shook her head vigorously and shrieked, but the second soldier managed to wrestle the long, loose chain from around her neck.

"Look here," he said to his companion as he opened the locket. "The Virgin Mary. Defiled by some Indian whore! You disgrace the mother of Christ! Our Lady of Fatima, let me put you in a safe place."

As he turned to put the necklace in a leather pouch on his belt, Bright Moon summoned a burst of strength and broke free. In one motion she grabbed the Spanish knife and thrust. It clanged against the man's breastplate. She slashed higher and saw a crimson streak erupt from the soldier's nose to the length of his chin. As he reached for his sword hanging from his waist belt, Anhinga, who had been cowering in the background, summoned her courage and jumped on the man's back with both arms locked around his neck.

"Enough! Let's get out of here," the second soldier yelled. "You're bleeding. We have avenged the Virgin Mary. We have found some very nice gold." He pried away the shrieking, clinging Anhinga and they stomped off. Seconds later the second soldier returned, grabbed the basket of greenbriar roots, and was off again.

As Bright Moon, bruised and sullen, told her brother what happened, everything suddenly came into focus for Deerstalker. The Spanish had lied from the beginning. They were not about to leave. Things would only get worse.

Two days later, as dawn broke, twenty elders of the five largest Jeaga clans assembled on top of the Place of the Sun and Moon. The Spaniards would not bother them here because it was across the river and too far removed from their guarded oceanfront garrison. But so as not to tempt fate, there would be no fire, so the men were huddled in bear and deerskins that folded around them like so many cocoons in a circle. They smoked their pipes for warmth.

"As I have told you separately," Deerstalker began, "These evil little men are not about to leave any time soon. They destroy our fish traps. They pollute our women. They roam through our fields taking our game. They rob food from our homes. We have welcomed them and waited as the Calusa general said. We have traded until there is no more to trade. We have seen them exhaust their own food supplies and grow thin and weak. The time has come to attack them and kill every one."

There were nods and murmurs, but not with enough passion to spark a war. Deerstalker could see that the clan chiefs from Long Lake, five miles to the south, had not felt the oppression of the Spanish as intensely as the Mako Sharks and Gray Panthers. And yet the Panthers were not sharing his ardor either.

Coral Snake rose. His father's legacy, a splendid black bear coat, reached below his knees. "Our cacique demands war but does not realize the death and damage that will happen to those who live closest to this fort," he said. "Besides, I know that they *do* believe their ships will come soon to take them away. They post lookouts every daylight hour. I say we wait. They can only get weaker and hungrier."

Deerstalker had remained standing, his lower face painted red and the three cormorant feathers in his hair giving him a defiant look. His buckskin cloak was accented with red geometric designs.

He now confronted Coral Snake. "How do you know they will grow *weaker*"? he said slowly and deliberately. "Have you considered the whales? They did not come in January. They should arrive very soon. And when the Spanish see the first ones in the inlet they will order us to slaughter and carve them. Then they will take all the meat and grow stronger. We will lose our main winter food. Then it will be we who will grow weaker."

"You know that the whales don't *always* come each year," Coral Snake groused.

"Yes, but nearly so," said the elder Gray Shark. He had ridden more whales than anyone and his word carried respect.

"We should worry, too, about the food we have stored up," added Deerstalker. "If we bring some in from the woods each day and they just take it from our homes, what good is storing it up? No, we must drive these people back into the sea and back across to where they came from. And we must teach them a lesson so that they don't send other ships full of invaders like the Calusa warned us about!"

"We may not have enough men," said an elder from Long Lake. "If the Calusa are so concerned, let us ask them to send warriors."

Deerstalker was prepared for such a thought. "That is what we do *not* want to do," he shouted. "The more the Calusa help, the more they will expect of us in return. The first thing they will do is ask us to send them soldiers to fight their endless blood feud against the Tocobaga. We should be *trading* with the Tocobaga, not fighting them."

"I don't know if my people will rise up," said Coral Snake with a frown. "Their homes will probably be destroyed and many people killed."

But mention of the whales had struck a chord and the cacique could feel that his words were carrying the day. "You and the Gray Panthers will fight, and bravely," he declared. "If they do not, I will see that the Calusa *do* know about this war and inflict the proper punishment on those who did not do their part." He had been prepared to say "just like they danced with the head of your father," but decided that Coral Snake had been humbled enough.

In the end Deerstalker offered a compromise of sorts. The Jeaga would muster around 500 warriors against the 200 or so hungry, emaciated Spanish soldiers. If they failed, he was confident they could persuade the Ais to arrive with 200 reinforcements. If that still weren't enough, they would appeal to the Calusa.

They would attack at dawn three days hence. Meanwhile, the cacique would distribute the entire supply of chert stored up in the council house and everyone would make arrows—thousands of them.

"Where is your nephew, the arrow maker?" one of the elders asked Deerstalker as they were walking back to their canoes.

"He went off in his canoe several days ago," said the cacique obliquely. "I suppose he's hunting, but I don't know what he does out there to occupy himself."

In truth, Deerstalker had much regretted the tongue lashing that had made Lujo snap. He was needed for arrow making. He would be needed to translate the cacique's taunts when they captured the

Spanish captain and were about to put his eyes out.

Most of all, Lujo's mother needed him. Bright Moon sat inside her hut with her black and blue arms wrapped around her legs, her loom strung with the same twine that had been on it when she went into the woods. Deerstalker knew that she suffered the loss of her son, who had so abruptly declared his independence of his mother and uncle. But worse, the gold chain with the blond lady's painting had been her gift from Calus, her husband, the King of the Calusa, who had given it to her as a sign that he would come for his queen one day. She had been, at least in her own eyes, someone special. Now she was just another middle-aged Mayaimi woman living amidst a tribe of indifferent strangers. She was "The Weaver Widow" again, only much older.

At dawn in the second week of February 1566 a crescent moon tugged a blanket of stars around the skies and began to dissolve in a yellowish haze. A light breeze from the north blew a gentle cascade of waves on a beach of white shells and horseshoe crab husks. At Fort Santa Lucia sentinels stood at each of the four rectangular corners, their heads bobbing up every few minutes as they tried to fight off sleep. A soldier wearing a stained apron left the fort and disappeared into the small compound that had been staked as a latrine. Below it, two guards looked after the tethered zabra in the inlet, one propped by his pike on the stern and the other clearly dozing in a sitting position on the bow. In a half hour, the blare of a brass *degüello* would pierce the quietude and shake the men awake. Father Mendoza would offer mass and 220 men—sixteen had died of syphilis or fever—would resume the same monotonous struggle for subsistence that had consumed their every hour for over two months.

But this day would be different.

With drums and gourd rattles, whoops and animal shrieks on every side of the fort, Jeaga men attacked with a flurry of arrows. The four sentries at the fort, the cook running back from the latrine, the two men on the boat and two soldiers who had come out of the front entrance to stretch and watch the sunrise were all cut down instantly and lay like large porcupines, moaning and twitching with arrows protruding.

From the crowns of the nearest pine trees, warriors with atlatls flung spears the into the fort compound as half-dressed soldiers scurried and staggered to the summons of blaring trumpets.

The plan adopted at the Place of the Sun and Moon was to surround, surprise, contain, starve and destroy. The first few minutes of surprise had taken off nine Spaniards. During that time the surrounding Gray Panthers were to lay low, waiting for the Spaniards who lived among them to rush out for the fort in answer to the trumpet calls. When they did the Gray Panthers grabbed their bows and killed six more as they ran.

For the next four hours five hundred Jeaga warriors rained down more than 5,000 arrows and spears into the barricades and into the compound. The steady *pop* and wisps of smoke from arquebuses firing also filled the morning air. But as the sun approached its apex, the guns repeated less often. Ammunition was low and the Indians were now positioned too far away to hit anyone except by chance.

The Jeaga wounded no more that day either, except by luck. But they had signaled a new era of desperation and despair for the Spanish and their French prisoners. From now on the intruders could expect to be surrounded around the clock by warriors with bows half drawn and arrows in place. A man could not venture out to the latrine without rolling the dice on instant death. Hunting and foraging were no longer an option. If the besieged realized their quandary and agreed to leave at once, their ship was left intact to take them away. If not, the Jeaga would burn it and then kill everyone left in the fort.

In the first week of March Lujo returned. His uncle, the cacique, was away directing the siege of the fort most of the time and made no demands on the lad except to tell him: "Be with your mother. And while you are, make arrows." He was content to do that for a few days and happy at last be in his warm clothing. But eventually he grew curious about the fort and decided to canoe into the inlet and have a look.

Approaching the crude rectangular structure on this morning he saw his old mates from the work gang and "rebirthing" ritual. Bobcat and Screech Owl had been among the many bowmen who had been posted about a hundred feet away to keep up the siege. But even at that distance Lujo gagged at the stench of human waste and rotting flesh.

"Oh yeah," said Bobcat watching him adjust. "We're not warriors, we're the shit patrol. I don't know how they stand it in there. The only way we deal with it is we have a contest."

"A contest?"

The two laughed. "That's right! Every morning they come out and fling buckets of shit and whatever else over the barricade right over there. So we play this game. We wait for a hand to show over the wall there and we wait for it to heave what's in the shit bucket. We've had our bows ready, so as soon as the hand shows we shoot. So far I'm ahead. I've hit one hand and two buckets. The rules are that you have to hit the hand or the shit bucket before the shit hits the ground."

"I'm gaining on him," said Screech Owl. "Today's going to be my day."

Lujo laughed along with them and made his way down to the beach, hoping the morning sea breeze could rid his nostrils and stomach of this sad, acrid death trap. In the hollow of sand, wind-swept turkey oaks, prickly pears and sea grapes that separated the high ridge from the beach he saw her for the first time in the daylight. The same girl from the night. The one he had thought about so often while in his lonely canoe making camp far upriver.

She was on her knees sitting back on her heels, the long black hair he remembered so well flowing over her shoulders. Her hand was held out, and he saw why. It held a sea grape or nut and very quickly a scrub jay landed on her hand and took it. The bird cocked his head for a second and flew away. Lujo was quiet as another did the same.

"They trust you," he said, breaking the stillness.

She turned her head, recognizing him and his voice without a start.

"So now I know why your name is Scrub Jay," he said.

"Yes, I learned to do this when I was five years old," she said softy. "I don't know why, but they seem to like me."

As he approached, Lujo thought she seemed heavier, sadder. Her voice had a tone of resignation. Maybe it was because he had only seen her at night a long summer ago. But then she straightened her posture and he realized that she was quite pregnant.

"Oh," was all he could manage. "From that night last summer?"

"Yes."

"Oh."

She stared ahead and held out another sea grape. "My father and brothers made me leave. I lived with an aunt at first. Then this Spanish soldier said he would make me a hut. I cooked for him. At first we couldn't understand each other, but we learned. He was an officer over many men." She dropped her head and Lujo saw tears glisten in the corners of her eyes."

"And then?"

"He treated me well. But on that first day of attack when it was so terrible, my officer tried to run back to the fort. They killed him with arrows."

Her sadness was heavy, like his own mother's. "Who killed him?" he asked.

"The warriors of Coral Snake. My people."

"But they needed to attack the fort and drive the invaders out."

"I suppose," said Scrub Jay as another bird fluttered into her outstretched hand. "But he was so kind and I was becoming at peace with myself again. It might have lasted if it weren't for the Mako Shark cacique wanting war."

Lujo gave a silent start, realizing that she had no idea who he was. He had no red paint like most Makos used and no blue that the Panthers preferred. He had no tattoos of war. He might well have drifted down from the moon on that dark night when they had first met.

Something urged him on. "The soldiers in the fort don't want to fight," she told him. "They want only to leave. My officer told me that. The Mako Sharks want to kill them before their ships can come to take them away. But our elders want to help them."

"Help the Spanish?"

"Yes, so they can go back to their land across the sea."

The Gray Panther elders want to help them? Just how?

"The men who got you this way, were they not Gray Panthers? And then the clan rejected you? And then your own clan killed your Spaniard?"

"I know," she answered. And now the tears were streaking down her cheeks. "I'm confused. I only know that this man loved me, would have cared for my baby, and now he is no more. I only know that the Mako

Sharks forced my people into it. And now I hear that our chief may try to help the Spaniards escape."

Help the Spanish escape? Coral Snake?

Lujo wanted more, but knew that he had probed enough without raising alarm. He asked the girl he had dreamed about—now about to bear a child made as quickly as a turtle lays an egg—if he could have a turn at feeding Scrub Jays. After leaving her with a gentle kiss on the cheek, he walked slowly back to the inlet. Then he raced his canoe back to the Mako Shark compound to tell his uncle what he had learned.

By early March, conditions inside Fort Santa Lucia were far worse than anyone on the outside could have imagined. Vélez and his chief lieutenant had been seriously wounded in the rain of arrows on the first day. For a while, the soldiers had kept their vaunted Spanish discipline, rationing one pound of corn between ten men,

But eventually they succumbed to the macabre. There was no wood for fires in the chilly winter. Near naked men wrapped themselves in filthy rags that had once been splendid uniforms when they had departed Cadiz not even a year before. Unbeknownst to the Indians outside, disease and starvation had chopped the number of troops to a mere seventy-five. The human waste that hadn't been heaved outside the wooden barricades was now piled up at the south end of the outdoor compound. It was overwhelmed by the pile of rotting corpses, their limbs and heads gnawed at by an army of plump rats.

When the corn had run out, any gold or currency that remained among the survivors was eagerly swapped for anything to stay alive. A dwarf palmetto sold for a ducat, a snake for four ducats and a rat for eight reales. The men dug up and ate the bones of fish and animals that had been dead for years. Then they gnawed on leather boots and shoes.

It did not take much longer for the minds of desperate men to deduce that human flesh might be more savory than leather belts. It began when the first French prisoner succumbed to hunger. Inside a starving Spanish soldier's one-track mind, logic ran something like this: *They are, after all, the enemy. We kill them on the battlefield. In order for us to prevail, there must be more of us alive at the end of it all than of them. If their death keeps us alive, it achieves much the same objective as death by arquebus or arrow.*

Once the habit was established, devouring a fallen countryman took only a slightly further reach of the same logic. *My newly departed comrade and I would want each other to survive. The king would want me to survive to serve him again. So, just as my spirit would make my flesh available to a survivor, I accept my comrade's generous offer and will light votaries to him and help look after his family for the rest of my days on earth.*

By March 14 only thirty of the original 236 men were deemed to be fit enough to defend the fort.

It was also the day of final desperation. Emerging from the entrance door to the fort, from which protruded the shafts of some twenty arrows, was a tattered white flag, which no Jeaga would recognize, and a red painted pole, which all Florida Indians *would*. Under these flags of truce, a single emaciated soldier limped until intercepted by three Mako Shark warriors. It was the same cook who had gamely tried to translate for Captain Vélez in the Council House weeks before. He asked to see "the cacique."

"Deerstalker?' a warrior asked.

"No," answered the walking corpse. "Coral Snake."

When this intelligence was reported to Deerstalker that same morning, he met with Red Hawk and two other elders to digest it. Lujo had reported that the Gray Panthers accused the Makos of starting a ruinous war. Now the Spanish had asked to talk to Coral Snake alone. And they seemed willing to put up with an inept translator rather than the better one the Makos could have offered. What did it add up to?

The Spanish were making some sort of deal with the Gray Panthers.

What would they want? Food from the Panthers and safe passage to escape in the ship tethered by the inlet.

And what would the Panthers want in return? All of the speculation led to only one answer. Their chief had hated Deerstalker and the Makos ever since the Calusa had killed his father and installed the outsider from Lake Mayaimi as cacique of the Jeaga. The Spanish would agree to return with a full force, liberate the rest of their men from their fetid tomb, kill Deerstalker and install Coral Snake as cacique of the Jeaga.

"We will go at once and be sure the ship is guarded by men other than Gray Panthers," said Deerstalker. Then he looked at Lujo. "Meanwhile, I want you to do two very important things. First, you are to take your mother and my wife Morning Dove to the safety of their people at Lake Mayaimi. Then from there you are to hasten to the Calusa and inform the Great Cacique that Coral Snake has betrayed him and the Jeaga people us just like his father. Do it this very day."

Deerstalker's assessment proved only partially correct. When the Spanish cook was led to Coral Snake, it was indeed to plea that three of the ablest men be allowed to take their boat to Cuba on the promise that they would return only to remove all survivors from the fort. The three sneaked out of the inlet that night. But none knew how to navigate and lacked a compass besides. After a few hours of fighting the Gulf Stream's reverse pull, they managed to make their way back through the inlet by daybreak.

Death and despondency resumed their reign over Fort Santa Lucia. But a week later the Spaniards had another spark of hope. Sails were spotted on the horizon. A ship was tacking to and fro like a cat sizing up its quarry. Indians and Spaniards alike spotted the familiar flag of Aragon and Castile. The Spaniards alone recognized a signal flag flying below: a yellow square flag meant it was requesting permission to land. More likely, the ship's captain was seeking to know whether the Spanish were still masters of their fort and the inlet. If so, it must be a supply ship.

Again, the so-called interpreter went out from the fort with a red pole of truce to seek out Coral Snake. Would he let the ship into the inlet? The Gray Panther chief knew that if he consulted Deerstalker and the Makos the answer would be no. The siege, stench, and sapping of Jeaga food supplies would go on until every last wretch of them perished. So without too much further thought Coral Snake sent the Spanish cook back with orders that the ship could enter if it brought "many gifts" and if every last Spaniard was gone by nightfall.

Back inside the fort, the survivors capable of animation argued over how to communicate with the ship. They had no signal flags. At last they agreed to stoke the brass cannon that had thus far sat idle, able to fire only pointlessly at the sea. Perhaps a single shot to sea would assure the ship's crew that the Spanish were still in command of their arms. Perhaps it would be seen as an "All's Well" sign. After all, what could they lose? Lopez the artilleryman, began to swab the cylinder, thinking that he had almost forgotten how to do the job that ordinarily would pay him five times what a soldier made.

At around three in the afternoon on a clear, cloudless day the tropical tranquility was shattered by a *boom* that scattered birds within a two-mile radius.

Deerstalker, collecting oysters a half mile up the Loxahatchee, stood with hands on hips wondering what to make of it. He decided to round up a few Mako Shark elders and investigate.

The captain of the caravel *Ascension,* a mile at sea, had never been to Jeaga Inlet and was indeed seeking a sign. He had come from the Yucatán with a load of corn, sent by Menéndez in what the adelantado thought would be a welcome supplement to their diet and a gesture of more to come. More importantly, the pilot of the *Ascension* knew they would welcome a message that the adelantado had every intention of transporting them to one of the more established Spanish forts within a few months.

Inside the fort itself, determination battled despair and desperation. Vélez de Medrano lay stretched on the floor, propped up on one arm, barely braving the gangrene that advanced up the arm from his arrow wound on the first day of attack. The ship would bring food and ammunition and enable them to hold the fort until Menéndez came, he insisted sourly.

The more their wounded captain talked about defying the siege, the more deranged he seemed to most of the ragged survivors. Some began circling him like jackals, each one growing bolder with his jibes and taunts.

"So you're ordering us to fight *on?*" laughed one with a vicious sneer.

"I don't care if the ship brings us roast beef and stuffed goose," said a skeletal soldier. "We're getting out of this stink hole."

"I'm not waiting around to get an arrow through me and have you eat me a week from now."

The last of the taunts had come from a sergeant who had once led Menéndez into Fort Caroline. He grabbed an arquebus that had been leaning against a wall and pointed it at Vélez. "When that ship pulls in, it's not staying, and I'll be on it," he said looking down the shaft. "I'll carry you aboard if you ask, but I'll be on that ship."

Vélez muttered a curse, hung his head and retreated into a sullen daze.

As the captain and his crew from Mexico eased the sixty-foot-long, shallow-draft caravel up the inlet, they had begun to seek out a landing spot when they were confused by a commotion on shore. As they drew nearer they could see a gaggle of walking skeletons motioning to them wildly. Staggering downhill from the fort were more walking cadavers, some wearing only matted nightshirts, some attempting to carry tattered seamen's canvas bags on their shoulders. All about them Indians were gathering in a gauntlet of punching, pushing and jeering. *Oh, merciful God, these are my fellow Spaniards,* the captain realized.

The first of them broke through, lunging at the boat with glazed eyes before the crew could even put down a gangplank. "Where is your commander?" the ship captain asked as one man clung to a ship's rail.

"Back there," the cadaver said with a jerk of the thumb. He could now see some of the men carrying and pulling litters with arms and legs protruding from them. As the soldier struggled for a footing to scramble aboard the ship, the captain instinctively embraced him under the ribcage and found himself lifting a body so light it felt more like a turkey in a poultry shop.

Now the gangplank was down and the wretched survivors nearly pushed each other overboard in the clamor. "Where is Vélez? Is this a mutiny?" he asked no one in particular. None answered, but it was clear that if it was not a mutiny, it was as wild and unmilitary as a watching a herd of panicked horses stampede in Andalusia. Vélez lay slumped in a corner, his lips moving silently. The crew of the *Ascension* was in no position to protest whoever was asserting authority

Now there was an added hubbub among the Indians on shore. In the middle were two older men and they were waving their arms and shouting at each other. Some Indians continued to jab and poke the last of the Spanish soldiers, but others had turned their attention to the two men.

"You can't do something like this without consulting the Council," said Deerstalker, his neck straining.

"Just let them go," Coral Snake kept repeating. "Let them go."

"The Calusa want us to kill every last one of them!" the cacique argued. "Now they'll just come back full of revenge."

"No they won't," said the Gray Panther leader. "You don't know what's like to live near that filth and stench every day. We can't breathe. We want it gone!"

Coral Snake's voice was rising and Deerstalker realized that he and his two elders were surrounded by Gray Panthers. This was not the time or place to challenge his adversary. In fact, he wondered if his rule as cacique of the Jeaga had already come to an end.

When the corn ship *Ascension* unfurled its sails on leaving Jeaga Inlet, it immediately became clear who was in charge when the hapless captain was ordered to sail south towards the Yucatán. The mutineers from Fort Santa Lucia had eagerly traded certain death by siege and starvation for the *possibility* of death by hanging.

On March 19, 1566 the *Ascension* was about forty five miles north of Cuba when the billowing sails of two larger ships were spotted on the horizon. The two ships raised more sail and made straight for the lone vessel. Their captain was none other than Pedro Menéndez de Avilés, recently returned from Mound Key. After re-provisioning in Havana he was on his way at last to deliver long-overdue supplies to the forts at St. Augustine and San Mateo, except that he was now in hot pursuit of what from afar had appeared `to be a French corsair ripe for the plucking. How surprising and perplexing it was to discover he was about to intercept his own corn ship from the Yucatán. But where was his captain and who were all the ragged scarecrows his telescope spotted on deck?

Menéndez boarded and held court. The rail-thin supplicants begged him to let them proceed to the Yucatán or even Havana. They no longer cared so much about food. But, please, for the love of God and mercy of Jesus Christ, let them go anywhere but Florida.

They would swear never to tell anyone in Spain about their experience in Florida!

All this was pleaded tearfully by battle-hardened men on their bony knees, groveling before the adelantado like condemned slaves before an oriental potentate.

Pedro Menéndez de Avilés listened and summed up his options. He could turn back to Cuba and hang the mutineers, thereby delaying provisions for the other forts. Or he could sail on, ignore the mutiny and turn these bony whiners into productive, grateful members of the Enterprise of Florida.

In the end, he reminded them of the loyalty oaths they had signed in Seville. And the three ships sailed on. The ringleaders of the mutiny would face trial and Menéndez, convinced that the sad plight of Fort Santa Lucia was caused by lax discipline, vowed to decree new regulations imposing tougher penalties for misbehavior.

CHAPTER THIRTEEN

Lujo at Lake Mayaimi

March 1566

As soon as Deerstalker and his elders rushed to investigate the *boom* from the cannon at Fort Santa Lucia, Lujo quietly began planning an escape from Jeaga Town. First, taking his mother, he called at the hut of Deerstalker's wife, Morning Dove, and their ten--year-old son Osprey. When he told them the cacique's orders, Bright Moon and Morning Dove began to choke back tears—his mother because she would be going back to her Mayaimi people stripped of her status as the Great Cacique's wife, Morning Dove because she would be leaving her husband in a precarious status and going to an unfamiliar land.

"Don't think of it being forever," assured Lujo. "Deerstalker just wants you in a safe place until the Makos settle their differences with the Spaniards and the Gray Panthers. "In fact, if anyone asks where you are going, just say that you've been invited to a wedding feast at the Lake of Mayaimi."

"Whose?" asked Bright Moon?

"I don't know. Make it up between you." As he spoke, Lujo realized that he was beginning to sound more like the parent, and she like the child. He now began to dismantle his mother's loom and fold it into a bundle. "You see those two canoes on the riverfront? I will pack one with the loom and as many threads as I can, plus clothing for Osprey and myself. The other I want you to pack with enough clothes and food for two days. I'll come back for the rest later," he lied, knowing that he might never return if the Spaniards and Gray Panthers overthrew Deerstalker.

It was early afternoon when the two canoes shoved off in the River of Turtles, Lujo and the boy in one and the two women in the other. Lujo looked east over his shoulder to see if there were any signs of commotion at the fort, but all was as still as the water they paddled upstream.

In two miles they had left the last Jeaga huts behind. Soon the river began to narrow into a curving sheet of golden brown glass so clear that they could see mullet, tarpon and snook scurrying over the sandy bottom. In another five miles they came to the entrance of a large creek on their right that emptied into the River of Turtles. Lujo motioned for them to turn inside, and after several yards of passing ancient cypress trees they saw a strange log-hewn floating platform tethered to some cypress knees.

"Spaniards!" hissed Bright Moon. "Turn around!"

"No, mother," laughed Lujo. "This is what is going to take us safely to Lake Mayaimi. You always wondered what I was doing during my long absences. I was building a large canoe—a barge—for hauling people and their goods on rivers. You see, it's large enough for people to sleep on at night without alligators taking their toes off. I was planning to present it to King Calus, but now we have a better use for it ourselves."

As Lujo helped the women from their canoe, they looked beyond the rim of cypress trees on the waterfront and saw the large workspace Lujo had created over many weeks. In the center was a fire pit strewn with large chunks of charcoal and several fish bones. Hammers and awls were piled up nearby. Strands of twine hung from low tree branches. At the far end was a thatched lean-to with deerskins piled on a crude bed. All about were stumps of pine trees felled by fire. .

Osprey jumped on the platform boat with glee as the women examined it from the shore with furrowed brows. Below the waterline it rested on two sturdy logs that ran the twenty-five-foot length of the boat and came together in a vee at the bow. Over these Lujo had strapped thinner pine logs starting with short ones in the front and gradually extending their length toward the stern. Atop the short logs, all made watertight with pine tar between them, was a ten-foot long, roof-less enclosure made from more thin pine logs. Behind it were seats for paddling.

"You can actually paddle this thing?" Morning Dove asked, suppressing a giggle. "It doesn't look very fast."

"I didn't say it would be fast," said Lujo. "We don't care how long we take to get to the lake as long as we get there safely. With this you can tie it up out in the water at night. If some bad person wants to put an arrow in you, you can hide in your little fort until you drift away from him."

"What about running aground?" Bright Moon wondered aloud.

"Well, even canoes run aground," said Lujo. "See those long poles in the rear? You use them to push away from whatever you've run into.

"I think I could make it faster by doing what the Spaniards do." He added. "Those boats they bring into the inlet are rowed with long poles that have paddles on the end, but I haven't figured out how to hold the poles in place when you're pushing on them. I was going to do that next, but I ran out of time."

Lujo piled everything he could find at the site that would fit into the new boat. When all the goods were transferred, all four maneuvered the "Lujo boat," as the women called it, into the River of Turtles and they again headed upstream, two persons paddling at a time.

In another six miles they were into the marshy headwaters of the river and dark was closing in. It was dry season and the danger of running aground was too great at night, so they pulled deerskins over the top of the enclosure and slept inside. But for a long time Lujo lay outside on the stern, checking his mooring lines and staring up at the full moon and blazing stars above. When he peered over the sides, he congratulated himself for having built his little floating fort. All around him were the glittering pink eyes of alligators and yellow glint from the eyes of raccoons and other woodland creatures. Overhead the still, cold air was a hubbub of hooting owls and screeching night birds. All seemed to have turned out that night to inspect the strange "Lujo boat."

The next morning the four refugees from Jeaga Town began following the ancient westward trail of creeks and man-made canals that wound past the River of Turtles headwaters and through the swampy slough of saw grass that separated the river system from the Lake of Mayaimi. The trails, some dug out over more than a thousand years, had always been marked with red twine every forty paddling paces. Just as the red pole was respected as an emblem of truce, water trail markers were inviolate to all tribes and never obliterated or moved, even in time of war. When one was missing or too faded to recognize, the first passer-by was obligated to replace it. And twine aplenty Bright Moon had.

At the end of the second day, they knew they had left the western edge of the saw grass slough because they now entered a single winding canal through a thicket of custard apple trees. Strung with garlands of moon vines, the squat custard apple trees grew so gnarly and intertwined that no man could ever hope to penetrate them save those who, longer ago than anyone's memory, waded in deep muck to cut the canal through them.

At the end of the five-mile canal they found themselves at the eastern edge of the great lake and decided to spend the night tethered to a pond apple tree that hung over the shore. Lujo felt fear when he looked across it for the first time and saw only an expanse of water, wind and waves. However, his mother assured them all that Guacata did indeed lie on the other side and that they could reach it by taking a canal that ran inside the southern rim.

Until then they had seen absolutely no person or house from the creek of Lujo to Lake Mayaimi. But now they began to pass occasional huts along the canal, then clusters of them, then full villages with large fish nets hanging from tree branches. The first difference Lujo noticed were the houses themselves.

"Why are they all built up on logs?" he asked his mother. "The land is dry beneath them."

"Ah, but it is not always dry," she answered. "Only in the winter months. The great lake, as my father explained to me, is like a giant shallow saucer with hard rock on the bottom. It is fed mostly by a big river at its northern shore. And in the rainy months when the river brings much water into the lake, it can't sink into the rock bottom, so it has to spill over the edge of the saucer. It flows from north to south, so the people here on the southern rim have to build their houses up high."

"Well, I guess it's good for fishing right from your house," laughed Lujo.

"Yes, but not so good if you have children playing and a big alligator comes crawling in front of your house."

Despite her earlier anxieties, Lujo noticed his mother becoming more relaxd as they glided among the homes where she grew up. He could feel it, too: a serene, changeless air about the place, people secure in the comfort of doing their daily chores. No clans clashing or Spaniards to surprise and unnerve them with cruel demands. No cruel Calusa either. Maybe Calus didn't care as much about this place as he did about the gold and whale meat of the Jeaga. Maybe his mother would also leave behind the memory of Calus and her fantasies about living regally on Mound Key.

Added to this was the warm, joyous welcome Bright Moon and her entourage received as soon as they poled the Lujo boat onto the shore of Guacata in front of her father's house. Before they had a chance to walk the few feet to the old cacique's hut, fishermen and children were pawing at the Lujo boat asking where it came from. In moments the curious cluster was parted by Alligator Teeth and his wife Night Heron, their arms outstretched for warm hugs.

That night, a feast of grilled bream and bass was scarcely finished before Night Heron was clucking over Lujo and comparing the charms of young women who would make him fine wives. He listened in silence, mostly worrying about the security of the Lujo boat. "Perhaps I'll just marry them all," he called out with a wave as he returned to the boat to spend his first night among the Mayaimi.

Guacata was the largest village on the Lake of Mayaimi, though still smaller than Jeaga Town. Nearly all of the twenty or so villages lining the big round lake's shoreline were but clusters of a several stilted houses, some belonging to a single extended family. Some said that many more years than anyone could remember the Mayaimi were a much more numerous and powerful a people. Those who said so talked of big mounds and a canal complex on some place called Fisheating Creek, which apparently existed no more.

Guacata got its sense of pride from being the gateway town to the Calusahatchee River. In fact, a stranger would usually require a local Mayaimi guide because the Calusahatchee was reachable only after a series of ponds and canoe trails that twisted for some five miles to its headwaters.

By decree of King Calus, no traders from the north were allowed to proceed from Lake Mayaimi and down the Calusahatchee without first being subject to an inspection by the cacique of Guacata.

Outside of that, Guacata was boring. Men went to fish or hunt deer each day. Since Lujo had no family to fish for, he had little to do. No one else, including the chief, knew *what* to do with this stranger from Jeaga Town who looked like a Calusa.

So Lujo told himself he had better get on with the task of going to Mound Key and telling Calus about the treachery of the Gray Panthers. He would rest and go tomorrow. But then two, three days passed and Lujo had to face a fact: he was frozen with fear that the Calusa would discover his lineage. Rather than being hailed as the king's eldest son, he would be scorned as an embarrassing surprise, a usurper of the son whom the twenty year old wife had borne the king. And if there were factions against Calus, as was rumored in Jeaga Town, Lujo feared that one of them might thrust him forward as the rightful heir.

This he weighed against reporting the plight of Deerstalker and the Mako Sharks.

One day a caravan of canoes appeared from the northwest rim of the lake and landed in front of the home of Alligator Teeth, just short of where the lake began flowing into the Calusahatchee for its sixty five mile westward run to the Bay of the Calusa. Lujo was among the gaggle of warriors, women, children and barking dogs who gathered on shore to greet them.

Lujo counted seven canoes of about twenty feet, each paddled by two men wearing handsome furs—all part of a trader's attempt to convey their commercial success. A man in the lead canoe displayed the red pole of peace, but he needn't have. All knew the delegation as Potano of northern Florida, who came once a year on a mission to the Calusa. The Potano were especially welcome because they served as middlemen, trading with tribes in the lower Appalachian Mountains for metals, furs and precious stones, and then bringing them all the way to southernmost Florida.

"What news?" asked Alligator Teeth as the leaders sat smoking with him in a circle outside his hut. In this way the Mayaimi learned of the unrest at St. Augustine and San Mateo, as well as new attempts by the Spanish to establish yet another outpost much further up the coast. They told of seeing more Calusa captives in the camp of the Tocobaga, through which they had also passed. In turn, Lujo, who had already caught the traders' attention with his unique boat, was called on to tell them about the uprising at Jeaga Town and the precarious state of Fort Santa Lucia.

After the pipes and a meal, Alligator Teeth and the caravan leader walked down to the shore to conduct a business ritual. As demanded by the Calusa, the Potano traders were required to swear upon death that they were not spies for the Tocobaga. And as they had come to expect, they were ordered to open the deerskins covering their goods to show that they were of variety and quality worthy of being sent to Mound Key. A load of acorns, for example, was examined to show that they were the delicious meat of the white oak of northern Florida and not the red oak or water oak of the south, which contained bitter-tasting tannic acid. When the inspection was concluded, the cacique of the Mayaimi was entitled to a gratuity of goods for his efforts and hospitality—more if he conducted a friendly, casual inspection, less if he proved difficult.

When the traders prepared to shove off, Lujo stood by the lead canoe and addressed the leader. "I propose a trade I think you would like," he said to the much older, heavy-set Potano. "I spent many, many weeks building the wooden boat that you have discussed so favorably. Indeed, it is protected by hard pine tar from leakage. It can carry as much as three or four of your canoes. You will be able to return with many times more goods from the Calusa."

"Yes?" The trader's eyebrows were up. "And what do you propose?"

"I propose that you give me one of your smaller canoes, a small sack of those quartz crystals, a bag of acorns…."

The man looked incredulous.

"And a beaver coat."

Beaver coats were usually worn only by Calusa royalty, but that would not be the trader's problem. "Is that *all?*" the older man asked with a smile, still pleased with his one-sided bargain.

"One thing more. Very important. I want you to swear by the eyes of Taku that you will deliver a message directly to the Great Cacique, King Calus. I want you to tell him all about the Spanish soldiers building a fort at Jeaga Inlet. Tell him that Deerstalker, the cacique of the Jeaga, has led a valiant fight to destroy the invaders. Tell him that Deerstalker has been betrayed by Coral Snake and the Gray Panther clan, who have conspired with the Spanish to let them escape. Tell him this Coral Snake is the son of the cacique who stole the king's gold several years ago, and who caused Calusa warriors to remove his head."

When a second Potano walked up at the end of their encounter, Lujo repeated the message just to be sure at least one of them would deliver it.

"Give him any beaver coat he wants," the lead trader said to his second.

As goods were transferred from the canoes, Lujo felt a great heaviness lift from his chest. His uncle would not be left at the mercies of Coral Snake and his clan. The arrival of the Potanos had been a gift from Taku. He had not gone to the Calusa personally, Lujo told himself, because he had realized that his barge was too large to be paddled by one person in a swift current like the Calusahatchee.

Two days later Lujo was inspecting his new Potano canoe on the waterfront when he was surprised to see a lean Spaniard with long sunbleached hair walking up the shore. Although his feet were bare, he wore a soldier's breeches with a wide waistband and flowing cotton shirt. With a smile and a wave toward Lujo he disappeared into the hut of Alligator Teeth and Night Heron as if he were one of the family. Later he emerged, strolling down the shore waving to several Mayaimi friends who waved back with smiles.

"Who was the Spaniard?" Lujo asked the cacique as soon as he could.

"We know him as Fontaneda," said the old man. "He was captured by the Calusa after a shipwreck and has lived among them for more years than I can count. I think he knows more of our languages than any one of us. Every now and then he comes up to the lake to visit some other Spaniards who married our women and live on the lake. But I really think he comes up here to mount as many of our women as he can. He is very clever, which is, I suppose, why Calus has spared him from the sacrifice."

"He also brought news," said Night Heron, who was grinding some corn garnered from the Potano traders. "It seems the Spanish have come to Mound Key with several ships. They made a peace with Calus and the Great Cacique agreed to return all of his Spanish slaves, however many may be left. Fontaneda said he had come here to tell his fellows that they must leave now to go on the ships."

"Do you think they will?" asked her husband lighting his pipe.

"Some won't, I think," mused Night Heron. "Rodriquez bears the marks of the hunt. He wears more paint than a warrior. He loves his wife and children. The other one down the shore, I don't know. He seems to like any woman who will lie with him. Who can tell where his urges will lead him?"

Later, Lujo was beginning to build a fish trap in two feet of water when he again saw the Spaniard Fontaneda approaching.

"You don't look like the folks from around here," he shouted good-naturedly. Where are you from?"

"Jeaga Town.....Jeaga tribe," offered Lujo, suspicious of anyone from Mound Key.

"I've never been to Jeaga Town or the Land of the Ais," said the smiling Spaniard. "They're only two places I haven't visited around here. Have you any Spanish captives over there? The adelantado would reward you handsomely for any information about Spanish captives."

"The adelantado?"

Fontaneda suddenly straddled the rear of the canoe and proceeded to tell Lujo more than he had ever known about the Enterprise of Florida and the legendary Pedro de Menéndez de Avilés. He retold the news about the adelantado visiting Mound Key, imposing a treaty of peace on the Calusa and leaving a garrison behind.

"I don't understand," said Lujo. "The Jeaga made war on the Spanish because Calus the king ordered us to. Now you say Calus has become their friend and wants to hand over all of his captives? Why would he do that?"

"Maybe because he knows this Menéndez can show your people the correct ways of living. He also wants to free captives like me so we can go back to their own land. I know he especially hopes that the Calusa can help him find his son Juan, who was commander of the Spanish treasure fleet. He was known to have wrecked in a storm somewhere off the coast of the Ais about three or four years ago. Do you know anything about the Ais?"

"Only a little."

"Did you see any Spaniards in the Land of Ais?"

Lujo groped for an answer. He felt the heaviness of fear in his chest again.

"Well, I saw a couple of them once when they came to a festival. What did he look like?"

"I don't know. I've never been there," said Fontaneda. "Menéndez the father is kind of thick-set with a black beard. They say his son would have been around twenty four years old when his ship went down."

Lujo felt his chest and throat tighten again. His mind raced back to a man squirming with eyes agape in the fire pit of the Temple of the Sun and Moon.

No, this Marinero seemed much older than twenty four. But could many months of foraging for survival in blistering sunlight shrivel a young man into old age? Marinero said he came off the wreck the year I was born. But he could have been lying just as when he talked of palaces in Spain. But would an adelantado's son live in such places?

Lujo's mind was a jumble of flickering images. "Well, I wouldn't know," he answered with his own lie. "I was just a young boy at the time."

Fontaneda rose from the canoe, his gaze fixed on Lujo. He waved to another Mayaimi approaching on shore and walked off without saying another word.

Later that afternoon Lujo was again standing in the water measuring the stakes he was placing in the sand for his fish weir. Suddenly he straightened up as the end of a sharp object poked him between the shoulder blades. A voice said in Spanish:

"Raise your hands over your head or I will cut your head off!"

Instinctively Lujo raised his arms and looked around. It was Fontaneda, armed only with a short stick.

"I thought so," he smirked. "You speak Spanish. You know more than you're telling. Perhaps the adelantado would like to meet you."

Now the fear clawed at Lujo's throat and chest. "I...I only speak it a little," he stammered.

"How did you learn?" The stick dug into his back.

"We had an old Spaniard who swept up and cooked at our council house. When I was a little boy I hung around him because he would give me treats. He liked teaching me words. He was very old and he...."

"What was his name?"

"Um. I think they called him López. He died a couple of years ago."

I am amazed how good I am becoming at lying.

"Why didn't you tell me about him in the beginning?" Fontaneda was enjoying the refreshing role of interrogating a terrified Indian.

"I...I guess I was afraid that you and this great general might take me off to Spain," Lujo said forcing a smile.

Fontaneda walked away as if to leave. Then he turned abruptly and shouted, "Do you realize you were talking to me in Spanish the whole time? You know something."

It was in the idleness of chatter over grilled fish that Lujo asked his maternal grandfather, the cacique Alligator Teeth, "Do you have a Place of the Dead here?"

"Well, yes."

"Where is it?"

The chief motioned with his thumb. "It's over there. Up Fisheating Creek."

Lujo noticed the same reluctance to talk about dying that his mother showed in Jeaga Town. "Fisheating Creek? Isn't that the name you gave to the place where the Mayaimi were once a mighty nation?"

"Yes," said the chief, "but now the Place of the Dead is near where the old city used to be. The main dock for the city is now a charnel house."

"Are there any people there?"

"Yes...*people.*"

"Do they take care of the dead there...or what?"

"Yes," said the chief, beginning to show irritation. "We do not discuss this subject much because the shaman says it can invite spirits of the dead to inhabit our homes. And they can make much trouble. So we speak little of it."

Lujo pressed on. "Well, what do you do when a person dies? Do these people come and pick them up?"

"Not quite. We go part way up Fisheating Creek to where there are poles in the water and a platform for the dead. We put the body there and blow on a conch shell that sits there. Then we leave a nice gift and go away. The people pick the body up. Then we go home and burn all our clothing. And that's all I am going to say about it."

It was enough to kindle Lujo's desire to explore. Or maybe he just yearned to be alone again:

To elude his uncle and the curse that would befall him if the Jeaga cacique were to learn that his nephew had not personally gone to Calus.

To slip the shadow of Calus and the curse of having this cruel despot for an accidental father.

To escape the suspicions of the Spaniard Fontaneda should he return to Guacata.

To avoid any meeting with the great Menéndez and the questions he would ask about his son.

To disappear from his mother, who already seemed to spend all her waking hours weaving in a small hut, her lips moving silently but saying nothing.

The next morning Lujo felt himself driven by some inexplicable urgency to get away. He told Night Heron he would be gone "briefly" to explore some creeks, but already in his large Potano canoe were some provisions and tools that reflected his soul's yen for a longer stay.

He'd been told that the mouth of Fisheating Creek was just five or so miles up the shore from Guacata, but exactly where was it? Lujo had expected to discover a wide stream, flowing into Lake Mayaimi. Instead he found himself half paddling, half dragging his canoe through knee-deep patches of saw grass, mud, snails and snakes. For nearly a mile he struggled westward, grumbling aloud how he had wasted his time nosing into one dead-end after another.

Lujo was still lamenting his bad fortune when he suddenly realized he had entered an altogether different world. The marsh had deepened into a clear, wide stream with a sandy bottom.

How could it have changed so abruptly? The answer had to be that he was in a man-made waterway. The shore was straight and deep on both sides.

But if someone wanted to build a canal, wouldn't it naturally flow deep into the big lake? Lujo thought again and concluded that it must have been dug at a time when the lake was larger and reached another mile wider to the edge of the canal. And if so, the canal would have had to been made a long, long time before the lake shrunk to its present size.

If so many men worked so hard to dig the canal, must it not lead to something or some place very important?

Lujo lost his train of thought in the quiet, brooding splendor that spread out before him. The oldest, largest cypress trees he'd even seen spread their feathery limbs to embrace one another, drapes of maiden's hair reaching down to touch the water. Between the cypresses were large green ferns and pond apple trees full of new fruit. As he passed the high banks, Lujo took in immense flocks of cranes and roseate spoonbills, wild turkeys idling about and herons of all shades.

In a mile or two he understood more fully why the canal was built. Now on either side of him were large mounds rising twenty and thirty feet about the water level. Other canals diverted this way and that, suggesting that the mounds were actually islands—probably with temples and homes of the mighty.

When he rounded one bend, perhaps six miles upstream, he saw the "platform place" Alligator Teeth had described so reluctantly. Two large upright logs were tethered to a tall pine and they supported a layer of cypress planks big enough for a body and perhaps the "gift" the cacique had mentioned. All that lay upon it on this afternoon was a conch shell, an oddity so far from the ocean. .

Lujo's curiosity propelled him on. Soon the canal widened to a large, circular man-made pond. On one shore was a flat wooden platform stretching—he measured with his eye—seven or eight times the length of his canoe. Standing upright along the rectangular platform were majestic, tall woodcarvings. He stared at them open-mouthed. At either end a panther sitting on his haunches. In between the huge cats, seven tall birds with wings spread. Eagles, hawks, owls. All as if transformed from real life to wood with the magic of a shaman's scepter.

The animals and birds seemed to be guarding the platform, on which lay large oval bundles tied with a heavy twine. As Lujo put his paddle in his lap and sat idle before the sight, he looked down and saw more of these strange bundles six or more feet below on the sandy floor of the pond.

So gape-jawed was Lujo that he had scarcely begun to take in the scene behind the platform. Back on the canal bank was a large open thatched house, but smaller than the council house in Jeaga Town. Arranged unevenly around it were five huts with various tools hung and strewn around them. He picked out four, five, six people sitting in various positions with their heads down, all working separately on something too intently to notice him. Should he have announced himself on the conch shell?

His question was answered by a white-haired man who approached him from the large house. "Welcome. Did you blow the conch shell? If so we didn't hear you," he said. "Did you bring someone for us?"

"No," said Lujo. He hadn't prepared anything to say that seemed plausible. "My name is Lujo. I came from Guacata just to see your beautiful Fisheating Creek," he said. Then absent-mindedly: "Would you like some crushed acorns? Some traders from the north came two days ago and I got some white oak acorns."

"Then come," said the old man in the friendliest manner.

As Lujo walked behind him, and as he drew closer to the people at their chores, he blinked in disbelief. One man who he thought was sitting at a table full of clay jars was in fact standing—a dwarf with grotesque features. A man who seemed to be cleaning fish appeared at first to be very short. Instead, he had the upper torso of a powerful warrior, but his legs were so shriveled and bony they would not support him. When the white-haired man pointed out his wife, she was leading a beautiful girl about Lujo's age by the hand. "Her name is White Sparrow," said the man. "She is blind."

"This is Lujo," announced the old man. Those who looked up from their work waved to Lujo with smiles.

A household of castoffs! Why do I feel like one of them? Why is it I feel at home in this brooding, majestic Place of the Dead?

CHAPTER FOURTEEN

Rogel and Carlos
January-May 1567

During his years serving Charles V, Pedro Menéndez de Avilés had befriended a young nobleman who had since renounced his worldly life to join the Society of Jesus as a priest. As the ship captain had become an adelantado, his friend, Francisco de Borja, had risen rapidly to become Father General of the Jesuit order in Spain. Now, in Havana and at the height of his frustration with Florida, Menéndez penned a strong appeal to this Borja. He had long felt that the missing link to his success in Florida was a strong, committed clergy to convert Indians and inspire his own soldiers to walk the straight and narrow path of Christian service rather than confiscating food and women.

It might have been expedient to recruit among the Franciscans or Dominicans who were well settled in Spanish Mexico and Peru, but Menéndez would have been going to the problem for his solution. The second-generation clerics who had followed the original explorers tended to be priestly bureaucrats who were comfortable in their routine of conducting mass and teaching the Catechism to local youth.

The Enterprise of Florida called for a different kind of man—the same toughness that one could find in the lancers who charged in the first row of the cavalry in the battlefields of Flanders and France. Hoping to make his friend Borja understand his angst, Menéndez described the challenge in confronting the Indians of Florida:

Their ceremonies consist for the most part in the worship of the sun and moon, and idols of dead game and other animals. And every year they celebrate three or four festivals in their honor,

251

in which they worship the sun and go three days without food,
drink or sleep. And he who is weak and cannot endure it they
consider a bad Indian and the noble sort become enraged. And
he who can best endure these trials is held most worthy and is
treated with much courtesy.

"I have already given [Indians] crosses, which they worship,"
Menéndez added, "and I have given them soldiers to instruct them in
the Christian doctrine. But it is a waste of time to attempt to plant the
Holy Gospel in a country by means of soldiers."

Menéndez had appealed to the right man and his letter struck at
the heart of the mission the Father General envisioned for his fast-
expanding corps of clerics.

The Jesuits had been founded only thirty two years before by
Ignatius of Loyola, Francis Xavier and four others as an unfettered order willing to travel like crusaders to India, Japan and other far corners
of paganism to spread the Gospel of Christ. The Jesuits had secured
their first foothold in Spain as recently as 1547. When Ignatius died in
1552, some three hundred young, idealistic Spaniards enrolled as novitiates the next year in hopes of emulating his heroic sacrifices. Thus far,
the Jesuit zeal had been focused on accompanying Spanish armies in
their wars against Islam and the Protestant Heresy; but, after winning
King Philip's blessing, Borja agreed to send three men to Florida in the
name of the Jesuit province in Spain.

All had already been toughened by many tests. Father Pedro
Martínez, thirty three years old, had once been a rich man's son who
had once squandered his study hours at the University of Valencia
drinking, fencing and swaggering through alleyways in search of duels.
But he had undergone a religious epiphany, joined the Jesuits and survived battles against the African Moors at the side of Borja.

Father Juan Rogel, raised in Pamplona, had earned degrees in lit-
erature and medicine from the University of Valencia.

The third traveler was Francisco de Villareal, a lay brother on his
way to becoming a full-fledged priest.

On July 28, 1566 the three Jesuits departed Spain on a Flemish
supply ship that was part of the fleet to New Spain. Orders called for it
to leave the convoy once it reached northern Florida and provision the

fort San Mateo near St. Augustine before going on to Havana.

But the storm season had begun again and the Bahamas Channel soon became a cauldron of whitecaps engulfing all on board in violent seasickness. Moreover, the Flemish captain confessed that he hadn't sailed to Florida before and couldn't find the inlet that led to the harbor at St. Augustine. On September 14, after tacking back and forth in the angry surf, Father Martínez and four Flemish sailors volunteered to take a rowboat closer to shore to see if they could spot the inlet.

The breakers were so high and relentless that the rowboat was quickly heaved up on the beach like a piece of driftwood. The riptide swept the mother ship out to sea, and for ten starving days Martínez and the four Flemish sailors waited on the beach for it to return, afraid to search for food inland for fear of meeting hostile Indians.

It wasn't long before the ship's crew turned on their Flemish captain and forced him to head for the Indies.

Eventually the castaways righted the rowboat and headed south in the choppy breakers. On September 28 they came upon four Indians fishing in the surf. The Indians quickly ran off and soon reappeared with forty more. A dozen or so charged into the surf and tried to take control of the boat. As the four sailors were being clubbed senseless, Father Martínez leapt from the boat and staggered onto the beach. There he knelt in the sand, palms up to the heavens. In the next instant a dozen conch hammers were striking his head and Father Martínez met the martyrdom that all Jesuits vow to accept if necessary.

After being blown by storms all the way to Santo Domingo, it wasn't until December 15 that the beleaguered Flemish supply ship finally worked its way back to Havana. By that time, Rogel and Villareal were wracked with malaria and were being bled and purged to ready them for the trip to Florida with Menéndez. Meanwhile, the adelantado wrote to the bishop of the Yucatán begging for a monk to replace the martyred Martínez, but none could be found with enough zeal to serve in such a forbidding land.

On March 1, 1567 Menéndez, his nephew Pero Menéndez, seven ships, 150 soldiers and the two surviving Jesuit missionaries left Havana for the kingdom of Carlos. Rogel and Villareal had barely recovered from their ills and their grieving for Martínez. Had they reached Havana the previous September as planned, they would have had time to learn the Calusa language and hone their skills among the small community of Indian transplants just outside Havana, but the adelantado's needs were simply too pressing. His three-year contract with King Philip would expire in 1568. He wanted to return to Spain triumphantly to report that five garrisons were flourishing in Florida and that he had discovered the fabled inland waterway between its east and west coasts. All this meant planting soldiers in the lands of the Tequesta and Tocobaga, strengthening his ties with the Calusa on Mound Key and bolstering morale on the chronically undersupplied outposts at St. Augustine and San Mateo. Indeed, Menéndez had already instructed a contingent of soldiers from San Mateo to head south down the St. Johns River to the land of the Mayaca, where they could expect to meet another Spanish cohort from the west.

But so far there was no expedition to wait *for*. When he was fretting over the whereabouts of his Jesuits, Menéndez was receiving alarming letters from Reinoso on Mound Key that King Carlos had again returned to his truculent ways and had even been caught plotting to kill the Spanish captain.

The Adelantado had encountered a similar obstinacy in Havana from the Great Cacique's sister. Antonia had taken to Spanish dress well enough. She had even sat through catechism lessons at the small Indian chapel of San Juan that served the Indian community, but she would complain to anyone within earshot that her much celebrated marriage was a sham. Menéndez had totally ignored his nuptial obligations and she demanded to go home. Since she had already been in Havana longer than the six months he had promised Carlos, Antonia and her half-dozen Calusa hostages had wrangled their way on the small convoy, ready to blurt out news that would enflame her brother even more.

Upon arrival at Mound Key, it was clear to Father Juan Rogel that religious conversion was not uppermost in the minds of Menéndez or Carlos. To be sure, the adelantado had ordered his men to erect a small chapel in which Rogel would perform his duties; but having done so, Menéndez was off again, probing the coast in hopes of learning which of the rivers that emptied into the Gulf of Mexico would lead an expedition of Spaniards to the other side of Florida.

Meanwhile, Father Rogel, a man in his thirties whose dark brown hassock made his spare figure seem fuller, was left to ply his mission in a little open thatched hut with a wooden cross in front that looked up at the hilltop Calusa temple adjoining the king's residential complex. Inside, on a dirt floor, Rogel had placed a crucifix of the bleeding Christ, an altar table of pine logs and slabs, corporal linen brought from Spain, a pewter plate for bread, a silver Communion chalice and an assortment of crude log benches. On the altar he had placed the Bible that his fallen companion Martínez had left aboard the Flemish ship—a constant reminder to Juan Rogel that God would now expect him to do the work of two priests.

At first he felt overwhelmed and gratified. Soldiers filled the little hut for daily Communion, and for a few days they seemed to enjoy the novelty and the whiff of Spanish civilization on alien soil.

Several Calusa were lured at first by trinkets and little packets of corn, but Rogel felt stifled by the language barrier. "I taught them to chant in Spanish," he would write to his superior in Spain. "I was afraid to trust an Indian interpreter to repeat the Holy Word in their language." Nor would he baptize Indians at first for fear that they would not understand the concept.

But eventually, when the corn and trinkets gave out, the Calusa stayed out. The priest knew that King Carlos could change the minds of his subjects overnight, and on two occasions Rogel had climbed the hill to the Great House with his religious implements, waited like a supplicant, and tried to preach the Gospel while his potential convert glowered down with arms folded. When Carlos appeared to listen to the story of Jesus Christ and the salvation of souls, the coterie of courtiers around him seemed attentive as well. When Carlos yawned or suddenly rose and walked away, the others yawned or fell into conversation as if Rogel didn't exist.

It was a relief when Menéndez returned. He announced that the inland waterway was probably reached via a river that opened into Tampa Bay a hundred or so miles to the north. It meant going to the heartland of Chief Tocobaga, Carlos' arch-foe.

A year before, Menéndez had won the Calusa king's allegiance in part by promising to "assist" him against his enemies. But that was before the matter of the inland waterway. Now it became imperative that the Enterprise of Florida achieve the supplication and support of the Tocobaga so that Spanish soldiers could explore upriver. And this presented the tricky challenge of convincing Carlos to make peace with the Tocobaga.

Would he? Carlos weighed the "suggestion" with grim countenance. Spanish usurpers had already built a fort on his main island, dishonored his sister and sent men to tear down the religion that he was sworn to uphold. In fact, the cacique had become so openly hostile that Menéndez reasoned that it was better to have Carlos and his leading elders aboard his ships than be left to conspire on Mound Key. To lure them aboard he offered food and wine and waved off any discussion of war for the moment.

But Carlos thought the Spaniards were sailing north to destroy the Tocobaga.

As the smaller of the Menéndez' ships followed the coastline to Tampa Bay, Father John Rogel stood like a sentinel at the ship's rail absorbing everything he passed. Thus far his view of Florida had been a storm at sea, a sick bed in Havana and an Indian shantytown across the harbor. Now he was seeing why some said the empire of Carlos the Calusa was as grand as that of Mexico's legendary Montezuma. With scarcely a gap between them, busy Calusa villages straddled the shoreline, with thatched houses and large fish nets hung out to dry. Many of the houses were built high upon what seemed like layer upon layer of large shells. Rogel thought of the gothic Cathedral of Valencia, finally finished in 1238 after decades of placing stone upon stone. But the Spanish builders could call on ladders, scaffolds and pulleys. The foundations of these buildings, raised from the sand, were made by hand and probably took centuries as well.

He also felt the enormity of his challenge for the first time. How could he have the love and devotion necessary to bring God's word to so many who had never known it?

Fontaneda, the first man they had met when approaching Carlos a year before, had promised that the voyage would take two days. And as dawn broke on the third, four of the six Spanish ships had glided so silently into the harbor of the main Tocobaga town that nary a man or dog stirred inside the row of huts that rung the shore. Menéndez, after standing on the bow working his spyglass, had gone back to his quarters to retrieve a chart when inside stood the dour Calusa cacique, his head slightly bent to avoid bumping the ceiling timbers. The King was fully clad for war, with feathers atop his long black hair signaling that he would fight alongside his soldiers in combat. His eyes were blackened to accent his sinister look. Entwined several times around his neck was the longest, heaviest Spanish gold chain Menéndez had ever seen. A display of wealth that might be lavished on helpful Spanish soldiers? Or simply a way to show arrogance and power?

"Kino cantabara ibo Tocobaga?" Carlos said with both of his thick red-streaked arms gesturing. "Cantabara ibo Tocobaga!"

Menéndez raised a hand and sent for Fontaneda, who had been brought along as guide and interpreter.

"He asks when we will burn the town down," said the ex-slave, looking sleepy-eyed and perhaps hung over. "He says 'We must burn the town down!'"

Menéndez smiled weakly and spread his arms in a gesture of calm before the man who towered above him. "Try to persuade him," he said to Fontaneda, "that it is better for all that we come in peace, that our king and our God require that all men live as brothers."

"No brothers!" Carlos snorted with no interpretation.

"There is only one God and we are all his children," said the adelantado in his most soothing tone.

When Carlos simply sneered with his most menacing glare, Menéndez as usual had another card up his sleeve. "I am told that the Tocobaga hold nine Calusa prisoners," he said through Fontaneda. "One of them is the sister of you and Antonia. Did you know that?"

The cacique nodded sternly. "Yes, he knows it," said Fontaneda. "He says burn the village anyway."

But events overtook them. As Carlos spoke they could hear the commotion of confusion. The lead ship had cruised to within a hundred yards of the village and suddenly Tocobaga men, women and children were scurrying out of their huts and running into the woods to the east. No one stayed to contest the invaders.

Later that morning, as Menéndez and his crew strode through the village, under orders to leave everything intact, a Christian captive came to offer thanks for not burning down the village of the chief. He turned out to be a shipwrecked Portuguese trader who had spent several years in Menéndez' own town of Avilés. Now he drew water and cooked for the chief.

Later the cacique and six elders appeared. Chief Tocobaga readily agreed to a turn over all of his captives and become a vassal of the King of Spain. He explained that his people had run away because they had heard of what had happened many years ago when some people came from a Spanish ship and demanded corn. When none was forthcoming, they had killed the chief's grandfather.

Menéndez expressed his shock and outrage. "These were false Christians," he assured the chief and his elders. "They did not share the true spirit of love and mercy." What followed was a conciliatory speech Menéndez had nearly memorized after so many similar landings.

All agreed that the Tocobaga would pay tribute to the Spanish king at a ceremony two days hence. At the same time, the Spanish would produce Carlos, who had been left to fume aboard ship, to consecrate a peace treaty between the two tribes. Meanwhile, since no one knew what to do during the interval, Father Rogel was thrust forward to explain the Holy Writ to Chief Tocobaga and his elders.

It would be his first real dialogue with a chief, and he would find that Christian logic clanged against Indian tradition like arrows bouncing off a metal helmet. Later, he would describe it in a letter to his provincial general:

> *On the feast of St. John the Baptist I said mass there and I made the king* [Tocobaga] *and his leading men attend until the offertory, and through an interpreter I preached to them about the oneness of God and about how He is the Creator and*

universal Lord of all the world to whom all men must owe vassalage and reverence. And I preached about the immortality of the soul and the resurrection of the dead and about the reward and punishment that God has in the next life for those who are good and those who are evil, and of their self-deception in their adorations of their idols....

What I learned about that king was that he was so attached to his idols that, when his subjects told him falsely that we going to destroy his idols, he wrapped himself in a shroud and was determined and prepared so that if we should burn them, he would throw himself into the fire together with his wife and children so that they might be burned along with them.

Overcoming old rituals was no less daunting. When Rogel asked about how the Tocobaga dealt with death, the chief said that when he died his body would be divided into small pieces and cooked for two days until the skin fell from the bones. Then the skeleton would be reconstructed. After four days of fasting, the people would bring the skeleton to their temple, deposit the bones therein, and hold a lavish feast.

All this took place with King Carlos and his sister Antonia still sulking aboard ship. On the final day they were prevailed upon to join Menéndez in a tribal peace ceremony that saw the return of the long-lost sister and eight other captives. The Tocobaga also consented to let the adelantado leave behind a garrison of thirty men. Yet, any success, in the eyes of Menéndez, was offset by the chief's disclosure that he was engaged in a bitter war with the Mayaca to the east. There was no way he could guarantee protection to the small detachment that was ready to search for the elusive inland route to the Atlantic. The adelantado called off the mission and headed his convoy back to Mound Key.

Father Rogel had hoped that once back at Mound Key, Menéndez might persuade Carlos to lead his people to the little church, but other pressures again vied for the adelantado's attention. A supply tender brought news that one of the officers at the thirty-man garrison he had left to guard his interests in Havana had run off with several of his men to join the gold rush in Mexico—aided by no less than the prickly governor Osorio.

Such a treasonous act called for rapid action and a public hanging, yet Menéndez was already beginning to witness the rancor that had boiled within Carlos during the return trip from Tocobaga. To help offload their ship supplies onto the garrison at Mound Key, Menéndez had asked the king to lend him a dozen manned canoes. Before the canoes arrived, one of the Calusa women who had taken up with a soldier whispered that Carlos had ordered his men to roll the supplies overboard and drown any Spaniards who happened to be aboard. Moreover, the alarming report was verified by a source who would change the tide of Calusa history.

The confirmation came from none other than Carlos' cousin and military chief. Only then did the Spanish begin to pay serious attention to rumors that the Great Cacique faced serious dissent from within the Calusa—from the Mound Key royalty to the many villages from Pine Island to the Tequesta tribe living far southeast on the Mayaimi River. The division had little to do with the Spanish. It had been simmering ever since the chief shaman had agreed to rule as regent until the rightful heir, Escampaba, was old enough to assume his kingly duties. But when Escampaba became of age, the shaman instead installed his own young son Calus (the same Carlos). Immediately a pre-emptive strike was launched against all possible opponents—the same one that brought the beheadings in Jeaga Town that made the Mayaimi Deerstalker chief of the vassal tribe. Escampaba was made chief military officer, married a sister of the new king, and for all these years had chosen to co-exist at his side. But now he saw his chance for revenge, and the Spanish would be his spearhead. All he had to do was be a quiet informant.

Menéndez and Reinoso were eager to help him. At one point, the adelantado had been ready to pull out of Mound Key. Now he ordered that another fifty men be attached to the fort, bringing the total to seventy. Then he had the garrison, now named Fort Antonio de Carlos, enlarged and strengthened on its hilltop across from the king's Great House. In between the two hilltop camps was a gulley and canal along which lived the Calusa of lesser rank. On a path between the village and the garrison was Father Rogel's tiny church.

That done, Menéndez could tarry no longer, especially because he had an errand to perform on the way. Taking with him Brother Francisco Villareal and thirty soldiers, he would stop for four days at the southeast tip of the Florida mainland and establish still another garrison in the land of the Tequesta on the Mayaimi River. Its chief had already signaled that he was ready to subject his tribe to the Spanish King Philip on the promise that Menéndez would protect him from the clutches of the closer and crueler king of the Calusa.

Back on Mound Key, the departure of the seven Spanish ships left the old soldier Reinoso in a constant state of military anxiety. Ironically, Father Rogel became bolder. Arrival of the supply ship that had brought Menéndez his bad news had been good for the Jesuit in the form of corn, fishhooks and glass beads that would lure the everyday Calusa to sit on the dirt floor of his little chapel and listen to his halting dialect. This time he swept the catechism aside and preached ardently against their false idols and pagan rituals.

Rogel and Reinoso began to argue daily almost every time they faced one another at night chewing their shrinking supply of corn, dried beef and Cuban black beans. "You are going to get us all killed," the stern captain would say heavily.

"You see only men with bows and arrows and atlatls," the priest would answer with a patient smile. "I see men with souls ready to find salvation."

"I see your Father Martínez lying dead on a beach," the soldier would retort.

"I see his spirit helping us win souls for Christ," Rogel would counter.

And so it went. But before long, Juan Rogel found he could no longer walk down the hill from the fort to his church. Word had come through Escampaba that Carlos had ordered him to position warriors on the path from the fort to the chapel, ready to jump the priest and haul him off to the temple for a sacrifice. The report was all the more believable because the three day spring solstice festival would begin soon.

A few nights later the men of San Antonio had finished their evening meal of wine and beef stew when they saw swirls like turbulent water in the tangle of sea grapes and saw palmettos below them. It seemed that insects were unusually noisy as well that night. When they strained over the ramparts to see better they soon realized that the path upward to the fort was a moving collage of hideous masks and that the insect buzz was an orchestra of gourd rattles shaking in rhythm. Then came the chants. They could make out a few words: Taku. Jesus. España. Muerte.

The power of Taku kills your god Jesus. The Calusa push the Spanish into the sea.

Over and over. As the parade of bobbing masks drew nearer, Rogel could count fifty or so without knowing how many others were snaking up the trail. It was now getting dark and dangerous.

The path led to the fort's flimsy iron-railed gate. Father Rogel rushed outside, bravely brandished a crucifix and shouted for the marchers to go back to their homes. In a language they couldn't understand.

More frenzied than ever, the men in the masks of shark, barracuda, wolf and human skulls began to shake the gate's hinges loose to a rhythm dictated by a dozen rattles and drums. Suddenly Reinoso appeared out of the blackness, shoved the priest aside and smashed the butt end of a lance at the nearest mask. The lance handle went through the mask's open mouth like an arrow through a bull's eye and knocked the wearer so far backwards he somersaulted downhill.

The crowd let out an angry roar, which quickly dissolved into an eerie *hiss* when they saw standing behind the captain four soldiers with their arquebuses cocked and aimed. Reinoso raised his right arm in a universal signal that one more outburst would trigger an order to fire and leave at least four masked men dead.

It finished the Calusa for the night, but it also had drained Reinoso's last ounce of compromise. He had begged Menéndez to take his men off this tyrant's island and now he wasn't going to wait for instructions from Havana. The next day the seventy Spaniards would dismantle the fort and re-locate what they could salvage on one of the small islands that lay not far offshore from the Calusa capital.

Reinoso's judgment was vindicated when in the melee someone noticed that Antonia was gone. The king's sister had upheld her hostage role by living at the fort. Now she had slipped away to the royal residence and her brother, according to word from Escampaba. The captain-general also reported that Carlos had begun to move his gold and silver treasure to a secret location on the mainland. Why? The Spaniards could only conclude that he was planning all-out war and wanted to leave nothing on hand in the event that Spanish retaliation turned to plunder.

On a clear calm morning not long after the "march of the masks," Spanish sentries on the new island fortress blinked in disbelief as a single catamaran canoe approached. It contained four unarmed paddlers and, seated on his familiar wide platform, King Carlos himself. Looming a good seven feet above the water on his regal perch, he smiled down on the guards and held out a large cloth sack. They flinched as he reached inside, but just then a Spanish voice spoke up. It was the interpreter Fontaneda, one of the four paddlers, who of late was always at the king's side.

"The king wants to bring the captain some fresh fish and oysters," said Fontaneda. "Very tasty. May we come calling on him?"

Seeing the king nearly alone and unarmed prompted a low buzz among Reinoso and his men. Carlos had never been seen on land except in his well-guarded great house, and never on water without a large convoy of war canoes. Why now? Was he not supposed to be planning war? If so, was he acting as his own reconnaissance officer? Reinoso ordered his men to make a lot of noise in the woods behind the fort to exaggerate their numbers.

Seated at the opposite end of Reinoso's crude mess hall table, the king was the soul of simpatico. He forced a paternal smile. He regretted the "situation" that caused the Spaniards to abandon their mainland fort. He hoped the captain and his "nobles" would enjoy the fresh catch. And, by the way, some of his people wanted to paddle over to the island in a few days and show their friendship by trading with the soldiers for gold and silver. Would that be permissible?

Reinoso smiled back. The Spaniards might be happy to entertain the Calusa traders, but he would let the king know exactly when.

After a few more pleasantries and questions about when Menéndez, his esteemed brother-in-law, would return, the king rose, re-boarded his regal catamaran and glided back across the bay like a tourist on holiday.

Within a few hours, Reinoso had the correct interpretation from Escampaba. Carlos' so-called traders would all be warriors bent on killing both the captain and priest. Then a second wave of warriors would arrive to besiege a leaderless fort. When a contingent of "traders" arrived in eight war canoes, Reinoso frightened them off with a cannon shot and a beach lined with arquebusiers.

All pretense of peace had now evaporated like ocean fog on a crisp morning. Escampaba sent word that Carlos had ordered all villages up and down the coast to "make arrows," the Calusa euphemism for war preparations. The most populous village was commanded to send enough warriors to encircle the little island for an early morning raid. But after Escampaba warned the Spaniards, the invaders again lost their nerve when they heard the cannons roar and saw the fire-sticks aimed at them.

The next morning found Captain Reinoso and Father Rogel sitting alone before a skimpy breakfast of wormy potatoes and dried beef. "If all the villages are going to follow them," Reinoso said wearily, "then the time will come when their sheer numbers will embolden them. When a king is so ferocious that the punishment for not going to war is worse than the threat of having a lead ball fly through your stomach, then you know that wave after wave will keep coming. Your Father Martínez would agree to that because he saw the Moors fight in North Africa."

"He was there for Christ," said Rogel, "not to kill Moors."

Their discussions had always led up the same blind alley. They had also become predictable, lapsing into a few limp retorts that served as language markers like two dogs raising their legs on a signpost to signify that each still deemed his position paramount.

Then something happened that gave Reinoso the last mark. In the first week of May a supply ship from Havana arrived and the captain again confronted the priest. "You haven't exactly been able to spread the Gospel to Indians on this island. Correct?"

The priest nodded cautiously.

"Well then, why don't you pack your things and board this ship back to Havana? The adelantado has spoken often of the great need for priests to help the Indians at the Church of St. John. My dispatch says that the Tequesta have sent four of their nobles there to be converted and baptized. That's more than you've got here."

"But my orders from the Father General are to work among the Calusa."

Reinoso rose and stood gazing seaward from the room's narrow window. He wore black leather boots that were scarred from the scrapes of too many prickly pears and faded to a chalky gray by too many days in sun and sand. Also worn away was his dream of finding Calusa gold or a waterway across Florida or even of retrieving the money he had lent the silver tongued adelantado. Now he just wanted to live to see his wife and children again.

This priest was admirably earnest but also annoying. "Look," Reinoso said at last, about-facing and peering deeply into Rogel's eyes. "You may be responsible for thousands of souls, but I am responsible for the flesh and blood of seventy men."

He spoke slowly and sadly. "I am going to kill Carlos very soon. It would not be a good thing for you to see how it will be done."

Rogel thought of the seventh commandment, but no words came out. When the supply ship departed for Havana, he was on it, his communion cup and plate wrapped inside his corporal linen.

Later, in Havana, Rogel learned that three days after his departure, the captain had invited Carlos and three his chief advisors to the island for "peace" negotiations. All were instantly shot and then beheaded with a battle ax.

Escampaba was proclaimed king of the Calusa. The new Great Cacique had even promised to become a Christian.

Chapter Fifteen
Lujo at Fisheating Creek
April 1567

When Lujo had bedded down in his canoe on his first night at Fisheating Creek, he expected to depart the next morning. But he lingered another day—then another. And after a week his thoughts were of where to find the supplest of saplings so that he could build a hut of his own.

Before he knew it, a year had passed. He was eighteen and twice the man who had been called that in name when he emerged from "re-birthing ceremony" at the Temple of the Sun and Moon in Jeaga Town.

It was the tranquility that had drawn him here and made him stay. The constant ocean winds and blistering sun of Jeaga Town had surrendered to the shaded canopy of ancient cypress trees. Drooping thatches of maiden's hair filtered out the wind to leave an eerie calm which, he supposed, was why some ancients chose it for the Place of the Dead.

The rhythm of life at Fisheating Creek was reflected in the people there, always working alone at one craft or another, but always smiling or humming to themselves. And how strange: except for the elderly leader and his wife, all were deformed or lame or blind.

It had taken him a year to understand.

On that first day, when Lujo was invited to join in the evening meal, he took from his canoe the small sack of corn he had traded for in Guacata and offered it to the leader, whose name was Spirit Helper.

"Oh no, I cannot accept this," the old man said handing it back.

"Why?"

"Because we might come to like it too much and want more," said Spirit Helper. "Then we would have to plant and fertilize it. But there are only six of us and we can't spend the time to guard it from all the animals and insects that would come at night to eat it. Then we couldn't do our work at day."

Lujo showed his puzzlement. "But what is this work you do all day? I mean, don't you just wait for a body to arrive? You seem so busy."

The others had been listening because they all looked up from their plates and laughed in a good natured way.

"So many questions," said Spirit Helper. "But I would like to ask you one first. You seem big and strong. Can you track and hunt? As you can see, all of us here are unable to do so."

"Yes, yes," answered Lujo, eager to repay a kindness and assuming that they might want a couple of turkeys shot for the next meal.

"Good," said the old man. "Now I will answer your questions. It is true that the name given to me by the chiefs of the Mayaimi is Spirit Helper, but all of us here are spirit helpers."

They were seated in a communal cook house at the top of a thirty-foot mound. "Let me begin down there," said Spirit Helper pointing to an adjoining mound. At its base there was an earthen platform with a small dug-out pool in front of it. A few feet beyond that lay an oval pond about a hundred feet across. Standing out in the water was the expansive wooden deck whose carved animal and bird images had captivated Lujo on his arrival. Heaped on the deck helter-skelter were several large bundles wrapped in cloth.

"We perform the sacred funereal rites," said Spirit Helper. "When a body arrives, my woman and I must cleanse it, wrap it properly and place it on the charnel platform. We then wait for the sun and time to decompose the flesh. Much later when the time is right, the body is unwrapped and taken to the earth platform. The flesh comes off easily and the bones are cleaned in the small pool you see in front of the platform. Then the bones are put in a special clay jar and the family returns here for the sacred rites. After that the clay jar is placed on the bottom of the pond."

"Why is all this done over the water or in the water?" asked Lujo. Spirit Helper frowned. So, you are not a Mayaimi? Where from?"

"Um, I was raised a Jeaga."

"Ah," said the old man. "I thought you might be one of the Calusa. If you were Mayaimi you would know that a spirit can come back and cause great mischief throughout a village. Or it can take revenge on old enemies. The wrapping confines the spirit and water weakens its power and ability to travel. Eventually, the spirit accepts the need to rest and wait until it can be born again as a lesser being."

Lujo's eyes were darting to the deformed, disfigured people seated around him. The blind girl seemed to read his mind.

"I am White Sparrow," she volunteered. "I sing the sacred chants and comfort the bereaved."

Next to her sat a silent, impassive man of thirty or so. His chest and biceps were massive, but his legs sprawled from his log seat like gnarled twigs. "This is Running Deer," said Spirit Helper. "He makes the sacred pottery, which must be fired extra thick to last centuries. He also uses the ashes to make lime, which we use to make incense for the sacred rites and preserve the departed."

Throughout the discussion a dwarf no more than three feet tall waddled amicably among them dispensing plates of food and collecting the remains. Spirit Helper extended an arm and stopped him so abruptly that he spun around comically. "This is Little Mouse, who does everything to feed and keep us alive while we go about serving the dead. He keeps the garden, makes the best gopher tortoise stew and even makes potions to keep the mosquitoes away."

Lujo's eyes darted to the last of the seven, a squat portly man as old as Spirit Helper. He sat cross legged on the ground, perhaps deep in thought or oblivious to the conversation for a good reason. *Perhaps an imbecile?*

"Ah yes, this is Chief Tonsobe, for whom is named a Mayaimi village. It is famous because it is on the north part of the big lake where the Kissimmee River flows in with its traders from the northern tribes. The Chief came to us after his village decided that a younger man should take his place. They said he was, er, becoming forgetful, but this was clearly mistaken. There is no matter of importance on which I would not seek his advice and wisdom."

If the chief had heard them, he remained silent.

"By now you see that all those here except my wife and I have something in common," said the old man. They have been selected as special spirit helpers. It wasn't always this way. This sacred burial site has been here for hundreds of years—over fifty lifetimes of our people. Many years ago, before the Calusa overwhelmed us and killed so many, the Mayaimi had many great towns around the lake. The Society of Spirit Helpers had many people living and working here to take care of all their needs. Today our numbers have dwindled greatly, but we have adapted."

Lujo was straining to follow him, but Spirit Helper continued. "In your land of the Jeaga when a baby is born with strange features or a child becomes too ill to take care of, you set them in shallow water and pray that the tide will bear them away. Correct?"

"Yes, it is that way," said Lujo.

"Well, it was the same way here. But now such people can be redeemed through service as a spirit helper.

"Redeemed?" Lujo was becoming even more confused.

"Redeemed or reborn if you will. When White Sparrow here was born sightless, her village shaman learned that it was because Taku had seen her mother in the act of adultery. Running Deer was a strong boy, but his legs began to wither away because his father had been seen running from a battle like a frightened deer. No one is sure about Little Mouse, but some say a shaman put a curse on his mother. She had been promised to him, but she married another man.

"A few years ago the chiefs and shamans of the Mayaimi met and decided that if such people were able to serve as spirit helpers they could hope to be redeemed and restored to health."

As Lujo sat silently trying to absorb this new information, Spirit Helper changed the subject. "And now that I have acquainted you with the Place of the Dead, I will tell you why I asked if you could track and hunt." He said. "I have seen you staring at the wooden carvings of birds and animals on the charnel platform. For many lifetimes they have been there to mark the sacred nature of this place. But they also serve a practical purpose. They frighten away vultures and various animals that would tear open the bundles and prey on the flesh of the deceased. But lately we have had two predators who seem to pay no attention to the carvings."

"Raccoons?" said Lujo. "They are fearless thieves."

"No," said Spirit Helper. "When the raccoons get too aggressive, Little Mouse scares them off by blowing in a conch shell. I'm afraid I'm talking of panthers. Two large ones."

Lujo felt his heart pound. Of all the bragging he had heard among the boys in Jeaga Town, none had ever mentioned facing a panther.

"And you have no hunters among you?"

"Look around you," said the old man with a sweep of the hand as if taking inventory of a blind girl, a dwarf, a cripple and an old "chief" whose only sign of life was to light a pipe. "My son had been our hunter, but he and his family have gone away for a long visit. Two nights ago the panthers damaged one bundle and dragged off another. They will be back soon, I'm sure."

Night had fallen, the fire pit was reduced to an orange glow and the buzz of mosquitoes meant it was time to seek the safety of the individual huts that dotted the mound below the cookhouse.

"I will think hard about the best course to take," Lujo told Spirit Helper.

That night, as he lay in his canoe covered by his beaver coat, Lujo pondered two courses. The first was to shove off quietly before the sun rose and leave these perplexing people. But what could be more daunting than returning to face his addled mother, an angry Deerstalker, and the suspicious Spaniard from the land of Carlos?

The second course was to try killing two panthers—and without them turning on the helpless people in the camp. For what seemed like hours, he churned various scenes over in his mind, always coming back to the scene where his careless friend Bobcat had tried to trap an alligator, only to be nearly killed by the surprise appearance of another one.

The next morning Lujo encountered Spirit Helper finishing a plate of broiled fish and coontie bread. "I have a plan," he announced. Everyone seemed to stop chewing at once and turned toward Lujo. "Because there are two large cougars, I cannot try tracking them because they could easily pounce on me from two sides," he said. "This means they will have to come to us and be killed here."

Lujo pointed to the wooden charnel platform in the pond with its thirty or so bundles. "Do you see where the path from here ends at the entrance to the platform?" he asked. "Right there I propose erecting two tall pine logs with another one lying across them at the top. From that crossbar I will hang some tasty bait up high so that the cougars will have to stretch or jump to get at it. If I can have your dwarf and the man with the strong arms to help me prepare, I will ask nothing more of you but one thing. All of you must bring your sleeping mats to the cookhouse tonight until this is over and we are eating cougar stew."

Lujo was now a man with a purpose, the first time in his eighteen years that he was directing a project with two assistants and others who were anxious for him to succeed. For the first part of the day he felled a sand pine tall and straight enough to make two twelve-foot poles and a six-foot crossbeam. Since burning didn't need to be as precise as when creating a canoe, Running Deer was able to hatchet and burn the tree into three pieces by noon. Meanwhile, Lujo was felling smaller trees and cutting the slim trunks into six-foot pieces just as the Spaniards had made pickets for the perimeter of Fort Santa Lucia in Jeaga Town.

Back at the entrance to the charnel platform, Little Mouse was using a conch dipper to dig two post holes. Then, about thirty feet up the walkway he would dig a rectangular trench for the log stakes that would house the hunter while waiting for his prey.

That afternoon Lujo used the remaining chert in his canoe to make a dozen arrows. He thought of how lustily the alligator on the River of Turtles had jumped up snatch the turkey his friend Bobcat had used for bait. But venturing out in the woods alone to hunt turkey was too dangerous. Instead, Lujo untied his canoe and let it float up the creek, his bow string taut as he searched for a wading bird or perhaps even a turkey that might be perched on one of the branches that overhung Fisheating Creek.

Through the clear amber water he could see eels as fat as a man's thigh. *Would cougars eat eels?*

He passed two alligators sunning themselves on a bank. *Too large and too risky.* Around one bend, an eight-foot rattlesnake was stretched out atop a ridge taking in the sun. *Arrows didn't work well with snakes.*

He passed a cluster of black vultures pecking at a dead possum. *Would anyone eat a vulture?*

Lujo was so transfixed on the thought of game that with a jolt he realized that the landscape had suddenly changed. Both sides of Fisheating Creek now had steep embankments more than ten feet high.

Off to his left was a man-made canal, and above it terraces overgrown with palmettos and pines. There was no sign of houses or habitation. This canal was obviously made by the same people who dug out the entrance to the creek from Lake Mayaimi.

Around, always veering to the right, the great canal wound itself in a semi-circle until it re-connected with Fisheating Creek a mile upstream from where Lujo had entered it. Along this loop he had passed entrances to other canals that probably crisscrossed the great circle.

This must be even older than the Place of the Dead. Eerie. Quiet. Terraced mounds, all made by digging out sand and muck and hauling it upward. Why? For protection from rain and floods? For growing something? For some temple or great chief's house?

Now Lujo was headed downstream again and still empty-handed. A large blue heron stood in the shallow water deep in concentration. Only a desperate man would eat a bony, bitter heron, but he let fly an arrow into its chest, hoping the cougars would feel otherwise.

He passed the vultures again, still huddled around their possum, and shot one of them dead. As the others scattered, Lujo reached over, grabbed both the vulture and the bloody possum and flung them in the front of the canoe. By the time he stepped onto the shore behind the cookhouse he had added a large raccoon that had been washing its paws in the creek.

That night after dinner the six spirit helpers peered out from the cook house as Lujo walked down to his newly made "fort." It was six feet long, four feet high and topped with a roof of glued-together logs. Lying on the ground just outside was Lujo's bow, which was too big to fit inside.

Running Deer had made a front "door" of logs that could be pulled shut from inside by a rope. As pitch black darkness began to envelop the little compound, Lujo now lay inside his fort with nine arrows at his side, ready to snatch. Also within easy reach was the steel knife the Spanish ship captain had dropped in his lap that day in Jeaga Inlet.

Outside, hanging from the crossbar over the entrance to the charnel platform were a raccoon, heron, a vulture and what remained of its possum feast. Looking more appetizing than any of these was a huge catfish that Little Mouse had urged on him at the last minute. It had been intended for the night's meal, but the cook was so concerned that the cougars would shun the scrawny, ugly bait that he had insisted on hanging up the fish as a "sacrifice." Peering out from his log sanctuary, Lujo thought: *If cougars like lots of blood dripping from their prey, I'm in luck.*

The night was still and a new moon made it nearly black. Lujo was asleep, the side of his face flat on the earthen floor. Suddenly a low growl and a loud snarl snapped him awake. He lowered the rope that held his front door closed to see two large cats on their hind legs pawing up at the meat hanging above them. The bloody pieces were swinging, meaning that the cougars had already been swiping at them.

Lujo's hands were shaking, but he managed to lower the door slowly. He had already decided that he would rather kill one animal for certain and let the other go free than put all these helpless people in jeopardy. Both animals were fully extended from toe to tip and would soon snatch away their prey. Lujo grabbed his bow from the ground, placed an arrow between his trembling fingers and forced himself to wait. Both animals had their backs to him. When one of them swung around to swat the dangling bait, Lujo let fly with a *thunk* into its midriff. The cougar seemed to be frozen in the extended position. The second one was still swiping at the bait. Lujo quickly bent down, placed a second arrow, and fired again into the cat's soft underbelly.

This time it collapsed. The other cougar sniffed at its slumping companion, turned around, saw Lujo and let out a blood curdling scream that set off every bird on Fisheating Creek as if all had been watching the drama paralyzed in fear. Lujo had loaded a third time and, now with the second cat facing him, he put his arrow between its front haunches. As the cat reared back to charge, the arrow protruding from its chest, Lujo scooted backwards inside his little fort and drew back the log door most of the way before it stuck only partly closed. Now the big cat was in a state of frenzy, prowling and swatting the length of the little enclosure. Suddenly part of a paw thrust through the front opening, all four huge claws extended. Lujo could smell its foul breath. He grabbed the Spanish knife and sliced at the claws until blood spurted. The claws withdrew and Lujo could hear the cat's breathing become loud and quick.

Then it was gone.

Soon the spirit helpers in the cook house were frantically calling "Lujo! Lujo!" He lowered the door enough to wave an arm and shout that he was unharmed. But no voice came out. His heart was racing and his breath was as labored as the cat's.

The Battle of the Cougars had taken barely a minute. Now it would take Lujo many minutes to track down the second cougar—*if* he was lucky. But if he had failed in his mission, his new friends didn't know it. They hailed him with words like "great warrior" and compared his courage to that of great Mayaimi chieftains with names he knew not. Lujo had never experienced appreciation or adulation in his eighteen years, had never before felt the warm inner glow that came with so much love and respect.

Even luck now came his way. When daybreak came, Lujo took his Spanish knife, bow, six remaining arrows and began following the trail of blood spots and paw prints that led away from the mound and into the forest. He knew the confrontation would come soon because the blood spots were joined by a trail of oily scat. No healthy cat would do that. The wound had made the animal lose control of its bowels.

Not a hundred feet into the woods he found the wounded cougar draped across the base of a large old cypress tree as though leaning in that position helped it to breathe. The arrow was still in its chest. This time there was no growling or snarling as Lujo calmly stood a few feet away and fired another arrow into its heart.

Soon afterwards, he would wear the head of a cougar as every hunter's ultimate headdress, just as had the Jeaga Panther Warrior when a band of boys would have given their souls to have one like it.

"Will you stay and become one of us?" Spirit Helper asked often during the next few days.

"I will let you know sometime soon," Lujo would answer. "Right now I would like to be left alone. I will hunt for you and build a fish trap, as I did in my homeland. I will build a hut up on the mound. I would also like to explore the ancient city that lies up the creek. What can you tell me about it?"

Alas, Spirit Helper could tell him little except that people did in fact build the canals. "It was so long ago that I am not even sure they were Mayaimi people. They probably planted crops on the terraces."

"Corn?"

"I would imagine so."

"Well, I would like to try that, too," said Lujo. "The traders from up north bring corn from *their* fields. What's so different about them? Besides, Running Deer burns shells to make lime. The people up there soak their corn in lime to make it easier to chew. If we could do that, we could raise corn and trade it in the villages of Lake Mayaimi and even take it downriver to the Calusa. They wouldn't have to wait for traders to bring it a couple of times a year."

"Yes, my boy, except that we are the Society of Spirit Helpers and this is The Place of the Dead."

"With all due respect, sir, I am not a member of the Society—at least not yet. So I think I will have a try at growing corn—unless the ancient spirits put a curse on me."

Spirit Helper chuckled indulgently. "Maybe, but it might be rabbits and worms who put the curse on you."

So after building a hut of bent branches and thatching over them, Lujo would take off most mornings in his canoe and head to the ancient mounds. His routine was so busy it scarcely left time for everything. First, he would explore a new canal, then climb to the top of the highest mound and plant or tend to his corn. He had to admit that the old man might be right about doubting the success of the corn idea, but the solitude of being atop the ancient mound gave Lujo the same piece of mind as when he had built a secret camp on the River of Turtles for making his log canoe.

On the way back in the afternoon, Lujo would hunt—turkey, deer, geese, rabbit—usually enough to win praise from Little Mouse, the cook. But he could always stop at his fish trap by the canoe put-in and count on bringing back some a bass or snook instead.

Once back at the camp, Lujo could expect to find White Sparrow, the blind girl, waiting by his hut with a rainstorm of questions. "Ah, I can smell fish for dinner," she would exclaim. " Or, "Your steps are heavier. You're swinging something from your belt." Or "I can tell you're happy. You must have had a good day." Or. "I sense heaviness in your heart. What happened?"

And he would answer with a feigned annoyance, such as "My heaviness is bearing up under the burden of your questions." At first he found her somewhat child-like despite being only two years younger, perhaps because her features were delicate and her breasts small like still trying to become a woman. But he also came to bask in her attention and concern. No one had ever shown such an interest in him or what he did.

One day White Sparrow leaned into Lujo's hut in the early morning and blurted out, "The only time I was ever in a canoe on this river was when I was brought here at the age of six. Will you take me with you in the canoe?"

Lujo was still rubbing the sleep from his eyes—too early to form arguments against the scheme —so after a brief breakfast she was seated facing him in the canoe as he paddled slowly upstream. At first, he attempted to narrate a sort of guided tour as he passed this bird or that animal, but she was a torrent of excitement and curiosity. "Oh an alligator? Where? How big? Are his teeth showing? What color is he? Little Mouse says they look like big logs. Will he attack? They have nests? They lay eggs? Can we eat the eggs?"

But beneath the outpouring of pent-up curiosity Lujo sensed the essence of a superior intelligence. And as she faced him across the canoe, he studied her features again, feeling guilty because she could not sense or reject his stare. She wore no paint or jewelry, which accounted for the childish plainness, but it also revealed a simple beauty.

Instead of continuing his unsatisfying tour of animal life on the creek, Lujo tried to learn more about the spirit helpers and White Sparrow eagerly complied.

Lujo: "Where has Spirit Helper's son the hunter gone and who was he visiting?"

White Sparrow: "His young wife quarreled with him constantly about remaining among the Place of the Dead. She threatened to run off with their two infants, so they all went to re-settle with a cousin on Lake Mayaimi."

Lujo: "On many days, old Chief Tomsobe gets in his canoe and heads downstream. Where does he go?"

White Sparrow: "I don't quite understand that either. Spirit Helper told me he has a secret place where he studies ants. All I know about ants is that they bite my feet when I am not careful."

Lujo: "I don't think the story about Chief Tomsobe being of weak mind is true. What is the real story?"

White Sparrow: "Only Spirit Helper knows. And what is the real story about Lujo? Where does he get the courage to fight giant cougars?"

And here she broke into a lilt:

The handsome stranger arrives
And brightens all our lives.
He saves us all from strife
Then claims himself a wife.

"How do you know I am handsome?" he laughed. "Didn't they tell you I have a face like a porcupine?"

They were interrupted when Lujo paddled an abrupt left turn and into the canal that was flanked by two steep terraced mounds.

"I will show you my corn patch," he said. Taking her by the hand, he led White Sparrow up the steep path he had made to the top. In the other hand he had two rolled-up deerskins and his beaver coat. Spreading them on the ground, he guided her to her knees and then a sitting position.

Lujo had planted five thirty-foot rows of corn—all the seeds he had from the traders at Guacata—and another three of squash for good measure. "Nothing has come up yet," he said, "but I can see the green tops peeking out and soon I will be the biggest corn trader in Florida, I think!"

She laughed. "There's a cool breeze up here."

Several seconds passed, just being together and enjoying the breeze that filtered through from Lake Mayaimi.

"Do you remember in the canoe?" she said softly. "I asked 'Who is Lujo?'" She was still on her knees, but now cupping his chin in her hands. "Let me feel this porcupine face. Aha! I don't feel bristles. They say you have big muscles like Running Deer."

She reached out and groped at his chest, then ran her fingers along his biceps and forearms. No one had ever done that. His skin tingled.

"Lujo," she said, "I don't know what I look like. Am...am I pretty?" It was the most important question she had ever asked.

"Yes," he stammered. "But you wear no paint or jewelry, so it's hard to tell. No. I mean..."

"I asked Wolf Mother to paint me, but she said that if she left this world there would be no one to do it and that I would only make a mess of myself."

"I will do it," he answered. "At least I will try. And I can make you jewelry...maybe a nice necklace."

She said nothing. And then he could see she was trembling and crying softly.

"Will you hold me?" she asked, her chin raised so that it almost touched his. Lujo's mind filled with images of the rape he had seen on the beach beside Jeaga Town. At least that girl had eyes to see! This one was...

She sensed his hesitation. "You won't hold me because I can't see? You think seeing with eyes is all there is to life?"

There were no more words. Lujo kissed her neck, then her forehead, then her lips. She thrust her small breasts in his chest and as they lay on the beaver coat all he could say was "gently...gently....gently" lest she overpower him in her embrace.

Almost every morning, Lujo and White Sparrow would head upriver in his canoe to "plant" or "inspect" or "weed" his tender corn crop. Lujo would adhere to his rigid timetable of responsibilities, except that they now included a blissful interlude in the arms of White Sparrow.

As summer approached, the heat and rains brought a profusion of tasseled corn stalks. As summer waned, the stalks were ravished as armies of leaf miters, earworms, aphids, fly larvae, flea beetles and chinch bugs battled against an onslaught of rabbits, deer, raccoons and grackles. One evening at dinner, Lujo confessed to Spirit Helper that he had been wrong about planting corn.

"Oh is that what you've been doing?" said the old man between chews of broiled catfish. "When I was young we used to call it 'planting seeds.' Why don't you and White Sparrow just spend your nights here in one hut? You could save a lot of paddling upriver and back each day."

Since there were no conditions mentioned about joining the Society of Spirit Helpers, Lujo complied willingly. And he also found himself with more time. One day he made sure his hunting took him south not long after he had seen old Chief Tonsobe depart the same way in his canoe.

As summer cooled and dried into the mild fall of South Florida, White Sparrow and Lujo had developed a morning ritual as regular as lovemaking. "Make me pretty!" she would exclaim, and Lujo would put aside his thoughts of hunting or fishing and reach into what she called his "magic box." One some days she would emerge painted, as with matching wisps of red streaks across her cheeks and soft white egret down in her hair. Or he might proclaim "jewelry day" and bedeck her with carved bone hairpins and perhaps a small white bay scallop held on her delicate forehead by a thin leather band. Her anticipation would make her quiver until she would ask, "Am I pretty now?" He would always say "Yes, my queen," and when he saw the joy in her sightless eyes, he would know it had been worth his small sacrifice.

Lujo still stayed clear of the charnel scene down by the pond, but now that he had stayed, the others opened up to him—even old Chief Tonsobe. One night at the cook house as the chief walked slowly back to his hut, Lujo found Spirit Helper smoking his pipe in a corner. "What does the Chief do?" he asked simply.

"He waits for his wife."

"What? Where?"

"Down there," said Spirit Helper, pointing to the charnel platform.

"You mean she's in one of those bundles?"

"Yes."

"Which one?"

"I don't know, but *he* does. He will tell me when the time is right for a ceremony. Then maybe when he feels assured that she has come to rest, he may decide to join her."

Lujo gave the subject some respectful silence. "Yes, but what does he do all day while he's alive? I see him go downstream…"

"He is a wise man," said Spirit Helper. "Why don't you ask him?"

"I don't think he wants to talk to me."

"You may be wrong," said the old man. "Beforehand, he may have suspected you of being a Calusa spy. Or maybe he saw you as a youth who would leave soon. But now he has seen you become a man and a friend to us."

So the next night before Chief Tomsobe reached for his pipe, Lujo crouched before him with his palms extended up, a sign of paying respect to an elder. He began with awkward small talk. "I have always wondered…how does one get to be a chief?"

"My father was a chief," Tomsobe answered slowly without looking up.

"Yes," said Lujo assuming a place beside him, "but I am young and trying to understand. Why in the first of days did a village or tribe decide that it needed to have a cacique? They know how to hunt for themselves or raise their children. Why do they need a cacique to tell them what to do?"

The old chief sucked on his white clay pipe and took a long time blowing out smoke. "When you were growing up in Jeaga land," he said finally, "did you know of anyone who enjoyed spreading sand over the latrines?"

"No, I guess not."

"Well, someone had to order that it be done.

"When you hunted whales, did everyone just jump in their canoes and float around the ocean, or did someone order that so many canoes go out and tell them how to surround a whale?"

"Again, the cacique," Lujo answered.

"Once in my village," Tomsobe said slowly, "a man was too lazy to go out in the forest and cut wood for his fire pit. So he went to the land around the hut next to his and cut down some pines he found growing there. Now those trees, you see, had provided shade for the family in the other hut. The father of that family was very angry and wanted to punish the wrongdoer, but he was a smaller man and had only one son. The offender was bigger and had three sons. The only way to get justice was to go to the village cacique."

With that Chief Tomsobe looked up for the first time, expecting that the lad had grasped his meaning. Lujo had his head cocked waiting for more.

"Well, the cacique ordered the two families to trade houses, so that the one who had been wronged would now have shade. But now the offender himself became resentful. When he thought the chief had forgotten about the matter, he forced the people out and reclaimed his old home.

"This time the chief had the shaman put a curse on the offender and his family. But the man only laughed at the shaman. So this time the chief sent several of his warriors out to hold the man down and put out one of his eyes with a hot stave."

He looked up again to make sure the lad had gotten the point. "So you see, the justice of Taku would not have been delivered had not a man been entrusted with the sacred power to make it happen."

Lujo pressed on. "Yes, I now understand in the case of a village, but why should there be a cacique in charge of a whole tribe of many thousands?"

The Chief relit his pipe, perhaps trying to decide whether to retire for the night or try again to penetrate the lad's ignorance. "Why don't the Ais attack the Jeaga tomorrow?" he said between puffs. "Or why don't the Tocobaga attack the Mayaimi tomorrow? The answer is because there is a Great Cacique of the Calusa who so powerful that he can punish anyone who disrupts the order of things."

"But the Jeaga think the Great Cacique disrupts the order of things by making them pay tribute or making them trade only with them," said Lujo.

The chief smiled and raised a finger. "Ah, but if someone should invade them or capture some of their warriors, what do they do? They go to the Great Cacique and ask him to deliver justice," he said. "And how can he do that? Only by being strong, and he stays strong by controlling trade and having villages bring him tribute.

"He also does great works that keep his tribe strong. Let us imagine it is many centuries ago and you are the first Calusa arriving on Mound Key. Do you think that each family, going its separate way, would have decided to build those great mounds and then a great house on top that could contain a thousand people? No, of course not. It took a Great Cacique to make it happen, and today the successors of all those kings can point with pride to the mounds and buildings that prove the power of the Calusa."

Lujo turned to a question that he had never dared ask his mother or uncle. "Why can't a village or a tribe just vote for the best man to be cacique?" he asked. "Why does it have to be passed down from father to son?"

"A vote does not guarantee a just and fair cacique," said Chief

Tomsobe. "A majority can always harm or even kill the minority if it wants to. Besides, successions aren't always as simple as a vote. Tribes have sometimes wound up having wars to decide a succession. And what good is it to be a cacique if no one else is left standing? No. Father to son is better."

"But what if the cacique is cruel and unjust?" asked Lujo.

"Sometimes they are—or they may have a higher purpose for doing something that the common people don't understand. Remember that there is a strong incentive to be a just and wise ruler. If a cacique becomes insane or cruel for too long the people rise up and kill him and all his family. Who wants to be killed with his whole family?"

"What if a king has more than one son?" It was the question Lujo wanted to ask the most.

"It is better to have just one son," said the chief. "Calus has too many. It creates an opportunity for enemies of the king to rally around one of the younger sons."

"Is it right for a king to kill off his other sons?"

"Sometimes," said Chief Tomsobe with a yawn. His pipe had gone out and the mosquitoes were taking their cue.

This is a wise teacher. I have never had one.

As the old man wrapped himself in a deerskin shawl and began hobbling downhill, Lujo shouted after him. "May I go with you sometime when you visit the ants?"

No one had ever asked him that question. Chief Tomsobe pretended he hadn't heard. He would think about it.

The next day it rained and Chief Tomsobe stayed in his hut where he could be seen stitching and cutting some garments. The next night it was still drizzling. The spirit helpers were preoccupied with enjoying catfish fried in coontie flour and Lujo was again speculating on the ancient terraces upriver and why they had been abandoned. He was surprised when Chief Tomsobe said without missing a chew, "The ants could tell you a lot about the old mounds up there."

"Ants?"

"Yes. The gods put man on earth to hunt and fish for their food. Otherwise, why would they have made so many animals and fish?" said the chief reaching into a bowl of persimmons. "But they didn't make an endless supply. When people make too many babies and they grow into hungry men and women, they have to go further and further in search of food until there is no more within a great distance of their home. So then they have to get their food by planting crops. But after a few years the soil loses its power to produce enough crops for all the people to eat. Then they starve to death or someone stronger comes in and kills them."

"And you learn all this from *ants?*" said Lujo.

"Yes." The chief finished one persimmon and bit into another.

"How long have you visited ants?"

"About as long as you have been alive."

Lujo was dumfounded. In all the years he had studied the habits of animals and learned to follow their tracks, the only times he had even thought about ants is when one of them stung him. "Where do you do this?" he asked.

"Only about a mile down the creek. Behind the shore there are whole worlds of ants."

Lujo hardly knew what to ask—only that he yearned to learn more. He knew enough not to appear to be making light of the chief, so he concentrated on showing reverent respect. "May I ask, sir, why you study ants?"

By now all six other spirit helpers were just as eager to hear his words. The pit-pat of the rain outside drew them closer together to hear.

"For one thing, you can see a whole world in one space," the chief said, seeming to enjoy the attention. "Think how much smaller ants are than people. I can stand in one place and when I look around I see the Tocobaga tribe, the Mayaimi, the Jeaga, the Tequesta, the Calusa all around—only they are ants in their own towns. The length of an ant's life is in proportion to its size compared to us. In a few years I can see a whole cycle of birth, growth, wars, death. I can learn why some survive and others don't. So far I have seen many of these cycles happen."

"But are ants smart like people?"

"In their own way," said the chief. "I am certain that ants live mostly by smell. I think one tribe may have a different smell than another. When you see them in long lines and they seem to stop and bump each other, I think they give off different smells to tell the other one that they have found food or something else. Each one may even have its own special smell, like Lujo here," he deadpanned.

"Lujo smells *sweet*," White Sparrow giggled. She was listening as intently as the others. She'd never heard the chief speak so much about his "work."

"But people don't live all by smell," said Lujo. "How are ants like people?"

"Many ways," said the chief. "They share food. When they are done eating, they take what's left and put it in a midden like we do. They have queen, just like you do, Lujo."

More laughter.

"You could have a nest of ten thousand ants and they would all exist to work for the queen and bring her food. When she lays eggs, she seems to have ability to decide that some will be soldiers and some of them food hunters. You can easily see that the soldiers are larger and have big jaws sort of like tiny alligators. And when they go to war the soldiers puff themselves up in order to look bigger and scare away their opponent. It's no different than us wearing masks or Lujo's new panther headdress. And when they attack, several of them will pin one of the enemy to the ground and try to bite its head off with their alligator jaws."

"Do they marry and have children?" squeaked Little Mouse from his perch on a log.

"No," my friend, "only the queen makes babies. The man ant helps her but then he dies."

"Ooooh, but not Lujo!" exclaimed White Sparrow.

Chief Tomsobe continued. "Right now I think another major war is about to start between two nests. I call them the Crickets and the Lizards to tell them apart. Each has many thousand ants—so many that each nest looks like a mound, but only as high as your knee."

"How can you tell there will be a war?" asked Lujo.

"I can't be sure, but something big has happened. I think the queen of the Crickets has died. You can't tell for certain because the queen lives maybe three or four feet underground. But in the past several days I have noticed that fewer and fewer worker ants of the Cricket nest are coming out each day to look for food. When they have done so, they seem very slow like people do when they are weak from starvation.

"Now the second reason I suspect," said the chief, "is that soldiers from the Lizard nest have come over in a sort of parade to show their strength. They get all puffed up, as I explained, and march around the nest in a circle. Today, the soldiers from the Cricket nest came out of their opening in big numbers and now they are marching around in the opposite direction, all puffed up. You can see some of them climb up on a stone or stick and wave their feelers around as if to challenge the other soldiers. I know some people who do that, too!"

Chief Tomsobe reached for his pipe and settled into a long diversion of stuffing it with tobacco and reaching into the fire pit for a piece of hot kindling to light it. He seemed to signal his dissertation was at an end. Lujo realized only then that he had been listening the whole time with his mouth agape. Tiny creatures like humans! A war between thousands a mile away! He was as transfixed and eager to visit this place as if Taku had invited him on a journey to the moon. But he knew it would be a breach of trust simply to show up in Chief Tomsobe's private preserve.

The next night when Lujo asked about "the war," he was told that "the soldiers are still puffing themselves up and parading" around the Cricket nest." For two, three nights, the answer was gruffly the same: "still parading."

"Don't they ever rest?" Lujo finally blurted out in frustration.

"Ah, I forgot to explain," said the chief. "Ant soldiers are also like our warriors in that when the sun starts going down, they march back to their nest to rest. Then the next day they march back and start the parade again."

After nearly a week, the chief volunteered some new information at the cook house. "Things are getting worse for the Crickets," he told Lujo in almost somber tones. "The Cricket workers seem to be starving. The queen is definitely dead because her workers are eating her eggs and hatchlings. This is their last source of food inside the nest. When they try to go out and forage, the Lizard soldiers attack them immediately. If you want to see the war, you should come with me tomorrow morning."

Yes! Yes! Lujo felt a tingling of excitement that compared only to the night when he faced two big cougars with his bow.

Early the next morning Lujo was surprised to see Chief Tomsobe walking towards his hut, carrying what looked like a rolled-up deerskin in his left arm. "I think the war will start today," he announced. "Maybe even before we get there."

As they paddled his canoe down Fisheating Creek, the Chief spoke in anxious tones with a quickened pace. "There are many things I have forgotten to tell you," he said. "You will see a pile of lime on the shore. Step your feet into it so that you'll have protection against bites. Be careful where you do step. Remember how small ants are. A stone to you is like a hill to them. A clump of grass is like a small mountain. The Lizard nest is only thirty feet from the Cricket nest, but to the Lizard soldiers it's like marching five miles before they start demonstrating."

When they had eased the canoe onto the bank and approached the site, Lujo realized that the battlefield his mentor had described was but a knee-high mound, no more than six feet across, located between two sand pines. But when he looked more closely he could see thousands of moving, wiggling, gyrating ants circling one another in two directions.

"There has been a change since yesterday," Chief Tomsobe announced. "The Crickets are no longer defending their whole perimeter—just the half that has the entrance to their nest in the middle of their formation. And the Lizards have tightened the space in which the Crickets can parade. This does not necessarily mean defeat for the Crickets. The Lizards have cleared all of the Cricket foraging area of food, so they may just decide to accept the greater hunting ground that they've established for themselves. It's what the Calusa did to the Mayaimi when they invaded many years ago."

The chief returned to the beached canoe and produced the bundle Lujo had seen him with earlier. "If you want to learn about this and pass on your knowledge," he said, "you need to observe everything from close range just as I did when I began this study. See the two trees that mark the Cricket nest? When I was younger I strung a hammock between the two so that it was just a few feet above the nest. I can't do it anymore because it hurts my back. But I brought this for you."

With that he unfurled his bundle, which was two deerskins sewn together with a rope at each end. "See the hole at one end?" said the chief. "You can look through it and see everything that goes on."

It was clear that Chief Tomsobe, after so many years of solitary study, was offering his pupil a place of honor in which to observe an event as historic as the Jeaga attack on the Spanish at Fort Santa Lucia.

The two fastened a rope at each end. Lujo swung into it and found himself curled in a hammock like Taku gazing down as 10,000 of his creatures struggled for survival.

Within a few minutes the old man was saying "Look, look! The soldier ants are now bumping one another as they pass by. Soon something will happen. One person—ant—will do something hostile that will set off the whole war."

Yes, exactly," said Lujo. "I see one ant attacking another like two soldiers with spears."

"That should set off the signal," said the chief.

As soon as he had uttered the words, the Lizards seemed to receive an instant message to attack en masse. No sooner had Lujo reported this to his mentor when the Crickets quickly dove into the entrance. As the Lizards massed to rush the hole, the Cricket soldiers suddenly re-appeared, pushing pebbles and dirt into the entrance hole. "They're sealing it up," shouted Lujo excitedly. "Now what?"

"What we have here is the reason why I think ants go by smell," said the chief. "If I'm correct, you will see the Lizards continue to circle around the covered entrance in a confused way because they can no longer smell what's inside. So now we have a siege where they will try to starve out the Crickets."

For two more days the Lizard soldiers continued their patrol outside the entrance, further clearing the entire twenty feet surrounding the Cricket nest of anything that might be dragged back and eaten. Lujo's concentration was waning and his back was hurting from his hammock observation post. But just then he yelled to the chief, "The hole is being pushed back. A few of the Crickets are coming out. They look weak."

Chief Tomsobe had been seated, leaning against a tree. Now he snapped to his feet. "The Lizard patrols will kill them instantly. This is the beginning of the end because the Lizards will now smell where the hole is."

The chief was remarkably accurate. "Yes, I see the Lizards swarming over the workers," Lujo shouted. "Now I see lots of Crickets at the entrance of their hole."

"The Lizards are massing, calling in all their forces," reported the chief.

"The Crickets are forming a line at the entrance. Could they be linking arms?

"Yes, yes," said the pleased Tomsobe. "They are forming a chain in front of the hole. I don't think they will hold."

The chief was right again. The Cricket picket line was not numerous enough. Soon the Lizards were tearing open breaches in their ant chain and beginning to pour into veins and capillaries that ran three and four feet deep. Whatever smells the Crickets had relied on for their commands now collapsed in chaos and within a minute it was every Cricket for itself. Those that weren't torn apart in the tunnels made a run for it outside and were killed by Lizard patrols or the crowd of beetles, birds and other predators that had been attracted by the commotion.

Within a half hour the whole pent-up drama of parade and pomp, preen and parry, patrol and prey, had come to an end. The labyrinth of tunnels that had housed ten thousand Crickets for a dozen generations of invincible queens, had been left devoid of all life. The Lizards, content to have widened their foraging range, never ventured back inside.

That night at the cook house, the spirit helpers were enthralled by the story Chief Tomsobe allowed Lujo to tell. When the excitement and questions had waned, Lujo asked his mentor: "Now that the Lizards are victorious, what will they do?"

"Their numbers will grow greatly and they will prosper," he said somberly. "Then they will die."

"*Die?*" all exclaimed together.

"Die and disappear," answered the chief shaking his head sadly. "I have seen this five, six times."

"But how?" So many questions came at once that the chief held up his hand for silence and again lit his pipe as if to clear the air with his smoke. "In a year or so there will be not thousands, but millions of the Lizard tribe with many, many tunnels spreading out hundreds of feet. Before long they will eat everything on the ground—every grub, worm, and spider—then they will start climbing up trees to eat whatever they can find up there. Pretty soon all the squirrels, mice, birds and bigger animals will be gone because the ants have eaten all *their* food as well.

Now the ant tribe will have no enemies at all. So when their scouts find another ant nest on their path, their soldiers have no need to puff themselves up and parade around. They just invade and destroy it as soon as they can."

The cook house was silent as the chief re-lit his pipe. Down on the charnel pond a large osprey fluttered down and perched atop the tallest wooden bird sculpture.

"But the ant tribe has already begun to destroy itself without knowing it," he continued. "The biggest change is that it will start to have many hundreds of queens. I'm not sure, but it may be that workers and soldiers lose their sense of smell, or at least their ability to recognize the original queen. So they begin mating with many females and the result is many smaller queens. Pretty soon there are smaller workers and soldiers as well.

"But the main cause is that the ant tribe starts to starve from within. The workers on the outer edge of the tribe's territory may find new food, but the distance is now too great to take it back to the main nest. The workers inside the original nest become weak and start eating their eggs and hatchlings to survive. In time the whole vast network dies off."

"How can you tell when such a big tribe is beginning to die?" Lujo asked.

"One way you tell is that plants begin to die," said Tomsobe. "Bees and butterflies don't come to pollinate, so plants don't flower and start to turn brown. But I also watch certain insects. Normally a spider preys on an ant. But if you see several soldier ants tracking down a spider, you know the ant tribe has overwhelmed the area."

"I can't believe all the ants just die," reflected Lujo.

"Ah, but I didn't say *all* ants die," said Chief Tomsobe, raising a stubby finger for emphasis. "Today as you watched the battle from your hammock, there was another ant nest on the other side of the tree that has been there just as long the Cricket nest. I call them the Moles. They are small in number and stay very quiet, never challenging the bigger nests. In a few days we may see the Moles take over the destroyed Cricket nest. And later, when the Lizards have destroyed themselves with their success, the Moles may become bigger and spread out in the same way."

"And this is the way of people as well?" asked Lujo.

"Yes, just as you wanted to plant corn on the ancient mound that had been abandoned. You were the Moles seeking to live in a destroyed nest."

"Will you go back tomorrow?" Lujo asked as the old man rose and wrapped his shawl tightly around him.

"Oh yes," he answered over his shoulder. "I will be looking in on the Moles."

For several minutes, the others sat in silence, listening to two owls exchanging mating calls and a noisy mockingbird that seemed determined to ignore nightfall. Soon only Spirit Helper, Lujo and White Sparrow remained.

Spirit Helper cleared his throat. "Perhaps it is time you knew more about my friend the chief, he said quietly. "When Calus became king of the Calusa, probably before you can remember, there was great consternation among his own people and the surrounding tribes. Many thought his cousin should have been made king. There was talk among the villages here of rising up against the Calusa or backing the cousin against Calus. On the northern shore of Lake Mayaimi are four villages that were approached by agents of the Tocobaga to become part of their nation. The Tocobaga promised them that they could control the trade that came down from the Kissimmee River and cease paying tribute to the Calusa.

"Well, three of the village chiefs had just about decided in favor of joining the Tocobaga. Tomsobe was not in favor. I think he just wanted to lay low and let time pass—perhaps like the Mole ants he described tonight. But as the other chiefs were still debating, the Calusa sent warriors to each of the three villages and killed their chiefs. They didn't touch Tomsobe. He says he doesn't know why and that he had nothing to do with it. But the people in the villages didn't believe him. When he heard that they were going to kill him, too, he and his wife escaped up Fisheating Creek. Here he has been ever since."

It was now mid-April 1567. Lujo had been at the Place of the Dead for just over a year. On this bright morning he decided to canoe downstream in search of a bend in the creek that was supposed to contain a pool of large snook that liked to lie in its cool deeper waters. But since it had also been a few weeks since the Great Ant Massacre, he knew he couldn't resist stopping off to find the Mole nest and see if Tomsobe was right that they would begin to occupy the dead zone of the Crickets.

The chief was not in sight when he pulled up—perhaps off tracking the Lizards in their next conquest. Again, Tomsobe had guessed correctly. A few Mole worker ants were going in and out of the entry hole to the Cricket nest and as they did they traveled in a straight line back to the Mole nest, stopping to bump or feel each fellow worker that they passed.

Still scouting. No mass movement yet. I will come back later to check.

When Lujo turned about, he was startled to see another figure standing on the shore—one foot in Lujo's canoe and another in the one that had brought him there, his arms folded across his chest. From the hundred feet that separated them, he knew the man was not Mayaimi or Calusa. After a few cautious steps, one hand on the handle of the Spanish knife that hung from his waist belt, Lujo felt himself shiver as when he had watched the two big cats from his small enclosure.

The Spaniard. The Calusa slave I met on the shore at Lake Mayaimi. I didn't like him then. I don't now.

"Hello there," he said in Spanish without moving. "I thought I would find you at the Place of the Dead. So much better to meet you *here.*" You remember me? Hernando de Escalante Fontaneda? Do you still understand Spanish?"

"Not so well anymore," lied Lujo.

"Well, you know enough to understand what I just said, because I am here to bring you a message from the Great Cacique of the Calusa."

Calus. Carlos. He finally found me!

"Calus has a message for *me?*"

"No, not him. Carlos, your f-a-t-h-e-r," he said dragging out the words, "is dead." Fontaneda didn't express any sympathy. He simply delivered the news evenly to test Lujo's reaction.

"Who says he is my father?" said Lujo, probing in turn.

"Your m-o-t-h-e-r. I have met her in Guacata. A nice woman. She is very proud of it."

"How was he killed?"

"The Spanish captain Reinoso was forced to do it." said Fontaneda, his eyes on Lujo's hand resting on the knife handle at his hip. "Carlos was getting ready to kill him first. Later the Calusa had to kill his three-year-old son. I guess that would be your brother. If they knew about you, you would be next in line to succeed Carlos."

Lujo's skin had become cold and clammy. "I thought they *did* know about me."

"Ah, no. Only *I* know about you," said the Spaniard with an icy smile. "And right now I have locked your secret in my heart. But I require your assistance in an important task. I have remained alive these seventeen years by being a very good translator to King Carlos. And lately I have been just as valuable to the Spanish captain. I am *too* valuable. I want very much to go back to my homeland to see my aged mother and my family before I die of some disease or at the hand of a dagger like the one you are clutching so dearly. If I can train another interpreter, they say I can go back on the next ship to Havana. It is as simple as that."

"But why not train a Spaniard?"

"The Spanish captives have all gone back with Pedro Menéndez. The soldiers have no knack for it, and the new king doesn't trust them anyway. He wants only an Indian—Calusa—to be his translator if it is not to be me."

With that Fontaneda relaxd and sat on the edge of his canoe. He had cowed his quarry.

"New king," muttered Lujo. "Who?"

"That would be Escampaba, son of the man who had been king of the Calusa before your father took the throne. Carlos was son of the king's brother, who would be your uncle. But now we call the new king Escampaba *Don Felipe* because Felipe is the name of our king in Spain. We offered him that name to show our respect—and he accepted it."

"Why does he need a translator so badly?"

"I will try to explain," said Fontaneda, searching for words that could be understood by a backwoods boy unskilled in political relations. "We Spaniards want to live in peace with the Calusa. The new king also wants to, especially because King Carlos did not. Don Felipe says he will become baptized"—he dipped his hand in the creek and sprinkled water over his head—"and become a Christian. You know... Jesus of the cross?"

Lujo nodded weakly.

"The Spanish priest won't baptize anyone unless he has studied and understood the sayings of Jesus and the sacred chants—just as you have sacred chants. So they need someone who can help him understand. Don't worry," he added, "I will be at your side, working with you until I leave," (which, Madre de Dios, I pray will be the next day, he thought to himself).

"If they don't think I am Calusa, the new king won't want me," Lujo protested.

"Yes, but you are the closest I can come to what he wants."

"I don't want to go to Mound Key," Lujo said in an almost desperate whine.

Fontaneda let Lujo's feeling of entrapment harden, then became grim and steely. "I said your secret was locked in my heart, but I did not throw away the key. Come with me until I can leave on the first ship and your secret will be forever safe across the ocean in a distant land."

The Spaniard was like the Lizards, pressing in on the Crickets until they scurried down their hole. "I will think about it," he said, "but I can't leave just now. I have a woman here. I hunt and fish for these people. I have a nice beaver coat and some things I would need."

This man is smaller and older. I can kill him now and drag his body where some giant ant tribe will gnaw it away. I've killed a Spaniard before....

"You must leave now," said Fontaneda forcefully as if reading Lujo's mind. "Everyone leaves a woman at some time or other. Your beaver coat is best left back there or you *will* start to look like a son of Carlos. But more importantly, the fact is that Don Felipe—King Escampaba— told me that if I didn't return in five days he would send men to kill us both. This is the second day."

Just after dusk the two canoes of Lujo and Fontaneda emerged from the gray marshes that ended Fisheating Creek and plunged into Lake Mayaimi. They quickly sought deep water, sighting only flickering fires among the trees as they skirted around the town of Guacata. That night they navigated the narrow waterways that led west into the Calusahatchee River and camped on a high bank safe from the many alligators that lurked below.

"How long will I be gone?" Lujo asked the first of many times as they were underway again the next morning.

"Oh just a few days," Fontaneda would answer lightheartedly. Or he might say: "A week or two," or "The supply ships come regularly, so it won't be too long."

The westward current on the Calusahatchee was so strong on its way to the Gulf of Mexico that the two men could often just lean on their paddles and glide. Fontaneda would pass the time by telling Lujo of his seventeen years with Carlos.

"You know, I saved many lives of captives," Fontaneda was fond of saying. "Before I arrived, Carlos would have this or that Spaniard brought before him ask him to dance or something else to amuse his court. But the Spaniards would just stare at him. The king thought it was because they were being defiant, so he would have them killed.

"But after I had managed to learn the language, the king—your father—summoned me often. One time he said 'Escalante, tell us the truth, for you know well that I like you much. When we tell your compatriots to dance and sing, why are they so mean and rebellious that they will not? Or is it that they do not fear death and will not yield to a people of another religion?' And I, answered, 'My lord and master, as I understand it, they are not contrary, but it is because they do not understand you, which they earnestly strive to do.'

"He said it was not true, that sometimes they would obey and sometimes not. But I said 'No, lord. They simply do not understand. Bring some of them before us.' And when come captives were brought up, the cacique said in your language 'Run to the lookout and see if anyone is coming!' And they just stood there looking at me for instruction. When I translated for them, they ran off to the lookout and returned to the king with happy faces because they had pleased him. This made him happy as well, and he ordered that no one should tell captives what to do unless I was there to interpret for them. So you see, that king and the present king all believe greatly in translating languages—and it has allowed me to save many lives."

After a few paddle strokes, Fontaneda paused again and added, "Maybe you as an Indian can find where your father has hidden his gold and silver. I never have come close to knowing after all these years, nor has Captain Reinoso. But I can tell you that I have seen over a million ducats of plunder from shipwrecks on both coasts of Florida brought to the Great House on Mound Key. Another thing I have never discovered is the Fountain of Youth, and I have swum almost every river and lake in the Calusa kingdom."

Lujo nodded and paddled on. He had no idea of what a million ducats of gold and silver represented, but concluded that finding the treasure must be many times more valuable than the tattered sack of Spanish coins and silver bars he had once found in a gopher tortoise lair. As for the Fountain of Youth, he knew only that it wasn't in Jeaga Town or on the charnel platform at Fisheating Creek.

As the sun dropped to the west and they approached where the river emptied into the Bay of Calusa, the more the wiry, wily Spaniard's mood brightened with thoughts of his escape from the clutches of captivity. His spirits were also leavened because here he was delivering to the new Calusa king the son of the man who had killed his brother and so many other captives.

How delicious! And to make it even better, he wouldn't give the new king Escampaba the satisfaction of knowing who his interpreter was unless Lujo himself forced him to "unlock" the secret. Maybe Lujo would even decide to kill this king to avenge his father.

Hernando de Escalante Fontaneda didn't care a gnat's pimple as long as he got aboard that ship.

CHAPTER SIXTEEN

Cross and Mask on Mound Key

May—Dec. 1567

Pedro Menéndez de Avilés had now been away from Spain and the king's ear for a year and eight months, a midway point in his three-year contract as adelantado of Florida. On May 18, 1567 he sailed for home in a very light twenty-ton ship carrying just thirty-eight men. Among them were the brother of the Tequesta chief and two of his elders—all to be displayed as splendid models of the Indians who would be pacified and proselytized under his rule if properly instructed by another delegation of priests.

Also onboard—and the most pressing reason for the crossing—was a captain of the king's soldiers who was being brought back in chains. Pedro Redroban, one of the 300 troops King Philip had sent to fortify Havana and the Florida outposts, had been put in charge of the Spanish garrison in the Cuban capital. During Menéndez' absence on Mound Key that March, the conniving governor Osorio had persuaded Captain Redroban that he—not the adelantado—should command all troops in Cuba. Since the garrison controlled the adjoining warehouses and ships that supplied Florida, and since the governor had no interest in supporting what he saw as a wasteful dalliance by a greedy buccaneer, the mutiny posed the adelantado's most serious challenge to date. But when Menéndez landed in Havana harbor, his commanding presence quickly wilted the mutineers' resolve and sent Redroban into hiding.

It didn't take Menéndez long to track down the ringleader, and on April 12 Redroban was sentenced to be beheaded in the town square. But an officer was entitled to an appeal; and when Redroban asked to be tried in Spain, Menéndez, the man who was already pilloried about in Europe for having lopped off the heads of 150 French captives behind a beach, no doubt felt obligated to bring the accused before the Council of the Indies for a proper hearing.

The timing was just as well. It was time to visit his wife in Avilés and confess that the search to locate their shipwrecked son Juan had grown cold. And even though his contract with the king was only at its mid-point, it was time to begin a campaign for soldiers, settlers, clerics and cash.

In the eyes of the adelantado, another three-year contract was proper recompense for his efforts. His progress had been both swift and faithful to the king's agenda. The French Fort Caroline was extinguished and the Protestant Heresy washed out on the shores of Florida. Six garrisons had been strung out along the coast to police French marauders and help rescue treasure fleet crews wrecked in storms. More potentially important, the outposts would become anchors of Spanish exploration and agriculture that would rival New Spain to the south. Menéndez had commissioned a brief expedition to the foot of the Appalachian Mountains, which were said to contain gold. He had sent men part way to the interior in search of the waterway line between the two coasts. Soon he would settle the Chesapeake Bay and go on to rule the fisheries off Newfoundland and Nova Scotia if only given sufficient support. Rome was not built in a day, he would tell the king, but at least its builders were provided with funds to buy hammers and chisels.

To be sure, he could expect to meet a small shockwave of enmity on shore. He knew the king would have been excoriated by his wife in France for the so-called "massacre" at Fort Caroline. The adelantado expected to be accosted in his native northern Spain by bankers still waiting to be shown something for their investment. And he would have to contend with the relatives who would show him letters from loved ones decrying their hunger and misery in godforsaken Florida.

The few disappointments and shortcomings could almost all be traced to absence of discipline among soldiers, the shortsightedness of bureaucrats and others jealous of his authority.

Had he not been generous to Indian chiefs and displayed saintly patience in the face of their superstitious obstinacy?

Was it his fault if the pace of religious conversion had been slowed by the foolhardy priest Martínez getting himself killed on the beach because his clot of a ship captain couldn't find the inlet to St. Augustine?

Had he not maintained his calm as the mischievous governor Osorio refused him money for his starving outposts, jailed his men, cultivated mutineers and refused him ships? Now the king would hear all about Osorio personally.

But as the first islands of the Azores drew into sight only seventeen days later, Menéndez still brooded under a haunting cloud of helplessness at Osorio's potential to obstruct the twelve ships and 150 men as they tried to re-supply the Florida forts from Havana.

As Lujo and the Fontaneda paddled their way down the Calusahatchee River in late May, 1567, the Spaniard drilled his protégé with a steady patter of translations—Calusa to Spanish and back again. "Remember that the Calusa don't use as many words to say something as the Spanish," he would say. "So if a Spaniard says something and you don't understand all of it, just eliminate the words you don't know and it will come out about the same length. The important thing is to get the general meaning, Watch their hands and faces and you'll learn just as much as from the words."

"Yes, but I don't want someone to lose his head because I didn't understand him," said Lujo.

"Look at it this way," Fontaneda shouted across to the other canoe as they paddled side by side. "You do more good than harm. Half the time people don't really know *what* they want to say anyway. You determine their mood or their request and you say it in a better way. Translators can unite nations and make treaties."

Or cause wars, Lujo thought to himself.

It was later afternoon on their second day and the sun was shining directly into their eyes. The Spaniard had his head cocked towards the shore and each time they passed a Calusa village it seemed that a woman or two would wade into the water waving to him. "Ah, I'm going to miss you all," he sighed.

Soon they had turned to the south and were into an emerald green estuary. Now they passed a dozen or more men in canoes returning to their villages with catches from the sea. Lujo saw oyster beds and fish traps that for the first time made him lonesome for Jeaga Town. Then ahead, he could tell without an introduction, was Mound Key with the sprawling great house and home of Chief Escampaba on the two highest hills.

A modern version of the mounds on Fish Eating Creek.

As they passed the entrance to the canal that gave the island an inverted U-shape, one of the sentries standing guard on the shoreline raised a spear. Fontaneda simply waved back with a broad smile and the sentry took off uphill at a trot.

"What does that gesture mean to you?" the Spaniard asked.

Lujo just shrugged.

"Well, to me it says that we are important to the king, that he has had his men on the look for us and that he wants to know about our arrival right away. Maybe he wants to call off the warriors who were going to go hunting for our heads if we didn't show."

Lujo felt himself shudder with fear that he would be brought before the king—his uncle—and somehow recognized as the son of his dead rival.

But Fontaneda passed by the canal and went around the sheltered east side of Mound Key. "That reminds me," he said playfully. "Do you want to stay in the fort or in the king's house?"

"The fort," gulped Lujo.

"Good choice!" Fontaneda was enjoying their mutual secret.

As soon as Escampaba had seized power, Captain Reinoso had again felt safe enough with their former "confidant" as king to abandon the makeshift garrison on the spongy mangrove isle nearby and relocate at the original site with its strategic hilltop view.

By the time they had landed at the garrison's sheltered dock, Lujo was already drawing suspicious looks from soldiers he passed on the log-hewn stairs uphill. Silently, he unsheathed his steel knife, handed it to Fontaneda and walked with his palms open so as to make his peaceful intent as plain as possible. He decided then he would also be quiet and dumb. Just a translation machine. No tracking. No talk of killing cougars.

Inside the garrison Fontaneda led Lujo into the windowless, thatched mess room where half-dozen soldiers were lounging on crooked benches. "Ah, Escalante," said one. "Out a'whoring this time or finding the Fountain of Youth?"

"Well, I did find a *youth*," he bantered. "This is Lujo, who happened to learn Spanish back on Lake Mayaimi. He'll be helping me interpret for the new king. Where's the captain?"

The same man walked up to Lujo with a smirk, spouted a stream of Spanish words and cocked his ear for a response. Lujo shrugged and looked at Fontaneda with pleading eyes.

"Ha! Your boy just flunked Spanish," said the soldier to a chorus of guffaws.

"He's just talking crazy," scoffed the Spaniard to Lujo. "He was making jokes about your mother and various soldiers. It's just the way soldiers talk. Now we must meet Reinoso."

They found the captain in his low-ceilinged, clay-walled room furnished only with a canvas covered bed, an officer's trunk and the desk at which he was writing. At hearing the introduction, Reinoso looked over his shoulder, nodded and muttered "Well, he sure is a *big* enough interpreter. Tell him I'll need him for logging detail as well."

"He understands you."

"Oh, correct." Reinoso gave a backhanded wave.

"Captain, has a supply ship come in while I was gone?"

"If it had, you'd see me with a wine bottle at my desk now wouldn't you," said the captain dourly.

"Soon? You think?"

"Soon, I think," muttered Reinoso, his hand already pushing his quill again. "I want to have this letter ready to go when it *does* come."

For the next three days Fontaneda would walk Lujo down to the fort dock each morning after breakfast. There, sitting cross-legged or dangling their feet into the water, Lujo would be schooled without letup until late afternoon. Instead of merely translating phrases, the Spaniard focused on religion with a studious intensity not seen before.

At first it was simply single words: Christian, baptism, heaven, hell, Holy Spirit and so forth. But what each of the words meant couldn't be answered in a word or two. "The most important thing to a priest is baptism," Fontaneda would say as Lujo strained to understand. "The reason is that you cannot be a Christian unless you are dunked below the water by a priest" (and here he grabbed Lujo's head in his hands and pushed it down).

"If you are baptized by a priest, you go to, where?"

"Heaven—the good place. Live forever."

"And if not?"

"Hell—the bad place. Full of fire. Very hot!" Lujo laughed and yanked his hand from the dock plank as if it were a hot stove. "But if I go swimming and sink my head, I no baptized. Still go to hell."

"And who is the cacique of hell?"

"The Devil. Very bad. Put bad curse on you forever."

I wonder if this devil is the same Catalobe whose helper we chased around the Place of the Sun and Moon.

"It is important that you can explain this to your people," said Fontaneda, "because the priest Rogel will not baptize anyone unless he is sure they understand what it means.

"Now we will talk about how to be a good Christian once you are baptized," Fontaneda said solemnly. "Christian means follower of Christ, the son of God, who was born on earth in human form like you and me. His name was Jesus. He taught people to stop their lives of sin and follow his path. And what is *sin*, Lujo?"

"Doing bad things. Steal your friend's fish. Have many wives. Marry your sister."

"And?"

"And bow down to idols." Lujo had learned to use the word *idols* because he could not bring himself to say *Taku* or the names of the sacred masks. He knew that their curses could be worse than being in the Christian hell after death because of the bad things the Indian curses could do to you while still living.

What perplexed Lujo the most were the wooden crosses that the Spaniards wore or displayed on walls. *Jesus was the son of God. He did good things for his people. So they killed him. They fixed two logs together and hung him from the logs. And now you worship a cross of little wood pieces that looks like the big logs where he was killed.*

"Why do you worship the little cross but the Calusa can't worship idols?" Lujo would ask.

Fontaneda put his hand to his chin and thought. "The cross is a *symbol*," he said at last. "A symbol means it *looks like* the real thing."

"But the masks of our gods are just symbols that look like the real gods."

"But they stand for things like bears and barracudas. You can't worship animals. There is only one God."

On it would go, sometimes with Fontaneda throwing up his hands and exclaiming "I do not know everything! I am not a priest—just a boy who got shipwrecked on his way to school seventeen years ago!" More often, he would simply change the subject in frustration.

To the Trinity, for example.

Fontaneda: "It stands for the Father—the big God. Then there is the son, Jesus. Then the Holy Ghost. That's the unseen spirit of God that can be in you, Lujo. They came from one source but all three show themselves in a different form."

Lujo: "But you can't see God. You can't see Jesus and you can't see the Holy Ghost."

F: "Correct."

L: "Can they speak to someone who is baptized?"

F: "I don't think they have voices like we know them. They live in your heart."

L: "Can they put a curse on you?"

F: "No, they don't put curses on people."

L: "Then why must you pray to them?"

F: "Because they can forgive your sins and they let you into heaven when you die."

L: "But if you get baptized with the priest and the water, you already go to heaven. Yes?"

Fontaneda groaned and sat silently with both hands rubbing his thinning, sun-bleached hair.

L: "If I help the people become Christians, can I go back to where you found me?"

Just after dawn on the fourth day after Lujo's arrival a ship's cannon rang out from the Gulf of Mexico. Instantly a whoop went up and sixty men sprung from their hammocks. Within an hour a convoy of canoes from the garrison would begin streaming through Calus Pass to the ship moored at sea. It would take the entire day to unload the provisions and haul them to the fort.

Escalante Fontaneda and Lujo were among the first to climb the netting that had been thrown over the port side of the *Nuestra Senora del Rosario.* The Spaniard quickly spotted the spare Father Juan Rogel in his brown hassock, leaning on the ship's gunwale, and led his protégé before him like a tethered goat. "Father Rogel, the entire island is delighted upon your return," he said beaming. Then he introduced Lujo and nudged him to begin a greeting the two had spent an hour practicing.

"I am very pleased to meet you and look forward to assisting you in teaching my people about Christ."

As Rogel's eyes beamed with approval, Fontaneda's eyes had begun roaming through the large quantities of goods stacked on deck. Often the entire cargo was small enough to stow in the hull. "Looks like you are being very good to us this time," he said to a sailor who was leaning back against the forecastle.

"Oh yeah, you got that right," he answered. "There's over 8,000 pounds of biscuit, a ton of meat, 300 bushels of maize and seventeen barrels of flour. You shouldn't lack for wine either. I counted ten barrels and there are more cases of bottles besides."

"Why do you suppose there's so much?" asked Fontaneda.

"Well, I think you can thank the adelantado for that," said the sailor, shifting to the other foot. "He probably wanted to be sure you poor bastards out here in the cosmos could survive after he left for Spain. But it may also be that this will be the last shipment for quite awhile. The governor and the adelantado don't exactly get along, you know. They tell me the governor has already confiscated two of our ships for not paying merchant bills and port charges."

By sunset the fort's quartermaster had expertly stashed the largess from the canoes in the small warehouse, mess hall and armory. In the mess hall men were enjoying their first wine in weeks. As expected, a jovial King Escampaba had arrived in the same catamaran canoe his predecessor had used in other visits to the fort. This time the Great Cacique expected and received several gifts such as the shirts, hats, and belts that were laid out on an impressive red carpet for his delight. But what he liked most from the Spaniards was their wine. He had long been known for his gregarious disposition—in sharp contrast to the somber Calus—and wine made him want to sing and laugh.

The king saw Father Rogel approach, a young Indian in tow. "Where is my man Fontaneda?" he asked, accepting a goblet of Madeira from a soldier.

"I do not know," said Father Rogel greeting him with palms up and having learned barely enough Calusa to reply. "Are you ready for a Catechism lesson tomorrow?" he asked, nudging Lujo to join him and translate.

Lujo swallowed and fell into what would become his pattern—simply eliminating words he didn't understand. One of them was *catechism*. So what the king heard was "Will you do the instruction tomorrow?"

"Why yes," said the cheerful Escampaba, glowing inside from with his first quaff from the goblet and willing to deal with whatever "instruction" it was on the morrow. "So you are helping my friend Fontaneda? Where is he?"

Lujo simply shrugged and begged the king's leave so that he could search.

But Escalante Fontaneda was not to be found in the fort—or on Mound Key—ever again. He had borrowed one of the many canoes at dockside and slipped out quietly in the still, moonless night. Gliding up to the moored *Nuestra Senora del Rosario,* he held up the four bottles of wine he had promised the sentry on the ship's stern and was quickly hoisted aboard. By dawn he would be sleeping beneath the canvas of a longboat as the *Nuestra Senora* weighed anchor and headed back to Havana.

Because Juan Rogel knew nothing about his interpreter or his competence, he decided not to confront the king initially with his promise to become a Christian. Instead, he would work with the people. Down where the valley separated the hill of the fort from the hill of the great house lived the same villagers who but a few weeks before had tried to overwhelm the combative priest with a parade of their most powerful spirit-masks. There he had the soldiers erect a large wooden cross in the sand and put some benches around it.

Every morning around nine Father Rogel would conduct catechism, requiring all who attended to cross themselves and genuflect before the big wooden cross before they were seated. Because he had no confidence that the people would actually understand a homily, he taught them to memorize the Our Father in Latin and Hail Mary in Castilian. He even made it rather enjoyable because those who chanted correctly received small bags of corn from the *Nuestra Senora's* largess. So enthusiastic did some become that they could be heard in their huts at night reciting their chants.

Lujo proved so reliable and likeable that the Jesuit began explaining various aspects of Christianity to his classes. But the gap between memorizing chants and understanding doctrine was nearly unbridgeable—especially when Rogel would venture to dispel Calusa "superstition." The effort imploded when Rogel, through the halting Lujo, attacked the Calusa concept of three souls—the shadow, the image in a pool of water and the pupil of the eye. "None of these is the work of the one and only God," the Jesuit declared. "It is therefore wrong to believe that upon death two of the souls depart and that the pupils remain in the body."

After much murmuring among the Indians, a woman with an infant in her lap turned to Lujo. "Ask him this," she said: "Why it is the Spaniards can have the Father, Son and Holy Ghost but it is wrong for the Calusa also to have three spirits, or souls?"

"Because your spirits are just lies that were told to you!" Rogel stammered in exasperation.

When Lujo offered his best translation, the people of the Catechism just sat in silence. Finally one of them said "Will we be getting the corn today?"

On the afternoon of the disruption over souls, Rogel asked Lujo into the little room he occupied for sleeping and studying. "I don't think we are getting much beyond chanting," he said. "I need to know what they are thinking and talking about—like all the muttering I hear as soon as I'm done speaking. Could you act as my eyes and ears among the people?"

"I hear them saying they are afraid of the Spaniards," said Lujo, avoiding a yes or no on becoming the priest's eyes and ears. "They have seen what happened to King Carlos and they fear that they will be captured and sent away as slaves. I myself have heard soldiers tell them this will happen if they don't obey."

"Ah, the soldiers," sighed the Jesuit. "Sometimes they act like the devil's disciples. What else do the people say?"

"I also think they are just confused," said Lujo. "They have been believing in these things for many, many lifetimes."

"Yes, my son," but other people were also practicing false beliefs for centuries before Jesus came. That is *why* he did so."

"Please, Father," said Lujo, "maybe it would have been better to say what you just told me than to tell them their beliefs are all lies."

The priest reflected in silence, his head in his hands.

"Please Father," Lujo added, "when I hear them talking to themselves, I know they are also believing these things because their cacique wishes it."

Rogel looked up, smiled for the first time, and said "Thank you, Lujo. I think you are right. We have been trying to make Christians from the bottom up as did the early apostles. But I think in this case it must come from the top down. Tomorrow we will pay a call on King Escampaba."

After sending Lujo off with a wave, Father Rogel kneeled beside his mariner's trunk and withdrew three sheets of expensive parchment. They had been reserved for something special and this was it. Since he was already kneeling, he offered a prayer for guidance. For better or worse he would make a running account of his missionary work on Mound Key and send it on each supply ship to his ultimate superior, Francisco de Borja, Father General of the Jesuit Order in Spain.

The next morning Father Rogel, with Lujo in tow, entered the throne room and found the king and his entourage of advisers happily entranced at the singing of a dozen small girls—a surprising contrast from the stern separation from his subjects that Calus had taken such pains to cultivate. When it was over and Escampaba had reached into a tray-full of fruit, the priest approached his raised dais and simply announced that since the king had promised to become a Christian, he was there to see that the instruction began soon.

A week later he made this entry in his letter-journal to his Reverend Father in Spain:

I believe the Lord has provided us with this king, who now reigns, because he encourages his people and gives very good advice to us as to how we should deal with the Indians in order to keep them and plant the faith in them. And he himself admonishes them and persuades them to it, telling them that he intends to do it also upon the return of the adelantado and that all should follow him.

He said to them also that the best means that they can take to live in their houses with calm and rest and without any fright is to maintain strong friendship with the Spaniards, and that it was for this reason that he had become a vassal of the king of Spain.

Because of his being on such good terms with us, some of his vassals have attempted to kill him—some by treachery and some by witchcraft— but these he has punished. And thus, with the support he has from us, he makes himself feared and is well served by all his vassals. Because of all this, I strive to do everything that I am able so that all of us may cherish him and avoid giving him any offense. If this man were to continue his rule peacefully with our support, it would be a very good incentive for all the neighboring caciques to do the same and to become vassals of the king of Spain and the Lord Jesus Christ.

One of the good signs I see in this cacique is that he truly wishes to become a Christian. He listens and ponders what I have to say, and then tells me clearly when he does not believe something that I tell him about our faith. Thus, when I questioned him one day whether he believed in the immortality of the soul and the resurrection of the dead, he replied that he did not. But when I asked him whether he believed in the oneness of God and his being the creator of the universe, the king said he did. He said this was one of the secrets that his forbearers, as kings, held guarded in their breasts and that they did not communicate it to anyone except to their successors.

The cacique then asked me how I knew what God said to us. I replied that we had it written down many years ago after he spoke it and re- vealed it. After reflecting on this, he said that the things we have written down must have a greater semblance of truth because theirs comes only by tradition and can be changed with the second or third passing of it.

And so, the king has become more inclined to accept this truth about the immortality of the soul and the resurrection of the dead. At the same time, I should think this knowledge would give him more enthusiasm for the desire of his salvation than what he has shown. Nevertheless, I seek almost constantly to instill in him the great value of the soul—that it is of the lineage of God and so precious that it is worth more than all the heavens and the earth and sea.

Even so, some challenge me about the truth that God cannot be seen in this world. They say they have seen god after fasting or running or venerating their idols. To this end I emphasized that God does not have a body, that they saw nothing other than the devil appearing to them in these forms in order to keep them deceived.

The argument by which they are convinced the most is that they and all their forbearers have been enemies of God and have offended God greatly. In asking idols for health, long life and victory in war and then thanking the idols for what has been bestowed by God they do God a great injury. To make them understand this, I compare this to a king being offended if his vassals offered the enemy the respect that they owed to him. God is not in the habit of doing such favors for his enemy, the devil.

The cacique has promised me many times that upon the return of the adelantado he will abandon all of his idolatry and hand over all of his idols to me so that we may burn them. Yet, I find his deeds contrary to his words because I see him very much involved in his idolatries and strongly attached to his witchcrafts and superstitions. And when I tell him of my feelings about it, he repeats that he should be able to live according to his rites until the adelantado comes.

Still, some Christians and Indians have told me of how they have seen the king at night on his knees before a cross in his house. When I questioned him about it, he said that he offers himself to God with all his heart; and he offers the same sacrifice that he is accustomed to offer to his idols.

Accordingly, what I have decided upon is that when—God willing—the adelantado should arrive, I shall ask the king for his word: that he will burn his idols, cut his hair, dress in the Spanish manner, be instructed in all things of the Christian faith and be baptized only when I am assured that he is asking for holy baptism from his heart.

On a hot, still night in July Lujo escaped from his stuffy store-room onto the veranda that ran the length of the fort. Standing together, Captain Reinoso and Father Rogel were talking in low tones as they gazed across the main valley on Mound Key to the Great House. Normally, it would have been dark on the Calusa side of the island, but on this night they could see a red glow with sparks from a large fire flitting among the stars in the sky above. They heard a din of noises and musical rhythms punctuated by chants and animal calls.

'Some of the men told me this afternoon that there were many more canoes in the great canal than usual," Reinoso said to the priest. "I should have listened more carefully."

Seeing Lujo standing at a respectful distance behind them, Reinoso said "What do *you* think they are doing over there?"

"A festival?" Lujo answered cautiously. "Maybe the festival of masks. Maybe even a Great Gathering of all tribes."

"All tribes?" Reinoso stiffened. "To discuss war plans? My charge in defense of these men is to know about such things before they happen."

"I would be just as concerned about sacrifices being performed," said Rogel. "Are we sure there are no Spanish captives left? What about children? Lujo, do you think Escampaba would sacrifice people at a festival?"

"I need to find out what's going on," the Spanish captain interrupted. "If I send soldiers, they might cause a violent response. Lujo, I want you to take your canoe into the great canal. Go up to the Great House and report back to me in two hours what you see and hear. Just be a lizard on the wall."

It was not to be that easy. Any hopes that every Calusa on Mound Key would be in the Great House were dashed when Lujo was confronted at the town canoe landing by the same burly warriors he had seen standing guard before.

"What tribe?" demanded one of them glowering down at Lujo before he could climb out of his canoe.

"Jeaga, I suppose," said Lujo meekly. But the two were buzzing among themselves and didn't hear. "You're from the fort. You're the new Fontaneda, aren't you? What are you? Spanish or Indian?"

"I was captured by the Spaniards," Lujo half lied.

"We'll see," said the sentry. Up the path of shell fragments they went, one guard leading the way and one closely behind Lujo. Soon they were on the highest plateau of Mound Key and Lujo got a closer look at the goings-on than he might have scrambling among the trees. Just inside the entrance, he could see that the noise that had aroused the Spaniards was a celebration of some kind. Men and women were dancing to the rhythm of drums and gourd rattles. The same chorus of young girls that he had seen on his first visit to the throne room was singing and chanting. Sprawled on the throne was Escampaba in un-kingly position. His black hair hung to his painted shoulders and on his forehead was the silver disk that was a Calusa monarch's symbol of authority. Seated at his feet were two young women. Seated beside him and smiling adoringly as he held her hand, was a woman more his age. In his other hand he held a Spanish silver cup and in it, Lujo was sure, was the same red wine that the king had come so fond of in his visits to the fort.

Spotting the two guards in the rear with Lujo, the king beckoned with his wine cup for them to come forward, then for Lujo alone.

"Come close to my ear," he said. Lujo began to bow but Escampaba kept urging him closer. "So, Lujo, our mutual friend, you've decided to come back to us?" he said, his lips practically touching Lujo's ear.

Lujo's brain raced for a safe answer. "I was curious about the sounds and the fire light."

"You mean the Spaniards sent you," smiled Escampaba mischievously. "You can tell them we are sacrificing no Christians. No one at all, for this is a joyous occasion. Tonight I have married my sister, Oripoka."

The sister-bride had left his gaze and was keeping time to the rhythm with her head. "Oripoka, my queen, this is Lujo, a son of Calus who was raised by the Jeaga. Now he serves the Spanish."

Lujo's mouth went dry and his brain empty as the king raised his cup to his lips, his stare never leaving his quarry. "Who...how?" was all he could stammer.

"Fontaneda? No, he ran out on us, didn't he? Let's just say that the Jeaga chief is very loyal. He showed us all how to remove a Spanish fort. So we help each other. He rules in peace now that we have removed that troublesome Gray Panther Clan from Jeaga Inlet."

Escampaba delighted in Lujo's quandary. "Come now, you don't look Jeaga, do you?" he said playfully. "Have you ever looked in one of those Spanish mirrors? There you will see the soul of a Calusa noble. How old are you now?"

"Twenty."

"Twenty and no bride," said the king in a theatrically sad tone. "I will see that you get a fine one." He whispered something to his bride-sister and the two of them gazed about the festive hall.

"Ah, see there?" The king nodded to a girl about his age seated cross-legged with her hands wrapped around her knees. Adorned all in white shell necklaces and earrings, she was as beautiful as she was sad.

"Yes, her," Escampaba whispered. "She was the wife of Calus. A *queen!* He was too old for her anyway. Now I don't know what to do with her. Maybe you can help me?" he said with a wink.

Lujo smiled weakly. "Yes, maybe."

"Well, for now you go back to the fort. Don't mention to the priest about the wedding," the king whispered in a slurred voice. "Just tell him we danced with the heads of ten Spaniards, then he'll have something else to think about!"

As Escampaba roared with gusto at his own joke, Lujo began to back away, but the king's powerful hand reached out around his neck and brought their foreheads so tight together that Lujo could feel the impression of the king's silver emblem pressing on him. "Go back now," he muttered softly but sternly. "Our people need you to tell us of the Spaniard's intentions. Are they in league with the Tocobaga? Do they plan to massacre us? Go back for now, and when this occupation is over we will claim you again and find you a bride."

Lujo left on rubbery legs. The rest of the night he lay in his canoe under the stars in the quiet Bay of Calus. Spanish or Calusa? Time was running out on the need to decide between two choices. Either one gripped him with fear. All he really wanted was to go back to Fisheating Creek.

Dear Reverend Father, the Peace of Christ be with you, etc.

Recently, since the king has told me he wishes to become a Christian, he has done some things that make me very suspicious that he is not proceeding in this matter with as much sincerity as I would like. The first thing was that he has married his sister, not to mention the many other women he has. I have made him aware of how abominable and detestable a thing such as marriage was in the eyes of God. For even the heathens perceive this to be evil and contrary to Natural Law.

He did not reply to this as I desired, saying that he had asked permission from us to live in accord with his own rites and heathenism until the Adelantado should come. He said it was a very ancient custom for the cacique to have his own sister as wife and that it was permitted to him alone. He said his vassals had requested it of him and that he could not fail to do so, but that he was giving his word that before he became a Christian he would leave her.

This seemed like an occasion to bringing up a topic I had long delayed—that Christians do not consent to polygamy. I explained the law of God that no man can have more than one woman and that upon becoming a Christian he would have to resolve to share his life with that one alone who was his legitimate wife.

He did not receive this with good will. He replied to me that it is a very difficult thing to change who have been accustomed from their infancy and undertake another very different one was impossible of achievement. Instead, he asked that I might instruct little children and youths who up to now know nothing about their rites the things of Christians as I saw fit. As for the big ones, he said, I should content myself with burning his idols and doing away with all the witchcraft that he has practiced up to now. He said they would not kill children even when his sons or he himself die. He will cease staining himself black, cut his hair and do the rest I tell him to do. But to prevent him from having more than one wife he would not be able to endure. If we would permit him this, he would do everything else that God commands.

So I appeal to you most Reverend Father, that this one request be granted so that we might enlist the most powerful Indian king in our mission to bring the word of the Lord to all the tribes of Florida. This king even came to me later and said that if this were granted he would not have more than two wives. I solemnly believe that without cooperation of the king and his chief shaman, the rest will not change their ways.

By July 1567 the weather and the Spanish garrison on Mound Key had slid together into a sluggish and monotonous routine. By noon even the calm Gulf waters felt hot to the touch. Every Spanish soldier's shirt was soaked with new sweat covering the stains of other days. Downpours came daily in late afternoon and a steamy mist thereafter. Night brought mosquitoes, the maddening croaks of a million tree toads and finally, exhaustion and sleep.

For the Calusa, who had known nothing else for hundreds of lifetimes, July was enlivened by the sudden "Dance of the Sturgeon." The great Gulf fish, which lived as long as twenty-five years and grew to 200 pounds, would leap or balance themselves upright like totem poles as if to announce their arrival up the rivers of western Florida to spawn for another year. And with the first sightings, Calusa men would set out in teams of canoes with their spears ready to thrust and their conch hammers ready to finish the kill. All along the shores, women and children would be preparing smudge racks of buttonwood and mangrove branches so that the catch could be smoked for meat to last the year. It was the Calusa version of the whale hunt at Jeaga Town.

But at Fort San Antonio, each day with no sighting of a supply ship just thickened the tropical torpor. Father Rogel continued to walk down to the little village in the valley and sit before the large wooden cross, but no one came for catechism because there were no more packets of corn to hand out.

Most afternoons the Jesuit spent in his little room, studying, writing and praying.

Sometimes an individual Indian would call, curious to examine the priest's Christian books and icons. Soon Rogel would turn the topic to Christian beliefs, with Lujo always on hand to translate. Rogel would come to cherish these visits as "my little victories."

Once a week or so Escampaba would appear and the two would have a lively but inconclusive discussion, usually ending when the cacique would wave and say "When the adelantado returns"—his euphemism that he would undergo a metamorphosis on that magic day.

Never in his visits did Escampaba ever give any hint that Lujo was more than a totem that translated. On one odd occasion, however, the cacique arrived with three young women squeezed into his catamaran and announced that he was there to show them the fort.

When the brief tour was over, Father Rogel said to Lujo, "I thought that was strange. The young ladies seemed to spend more time looking *you* over than seeing the fort. Did you notice?"

"No," said Lujo. But he *had* noticed, quickly realizing that one of the three women was the young widow of Calus that he had glimpsed the night he burst upon Escampaba's wedding feast. Obviously she had requested first-hand reconnaissance before signaling her intentions.

"I would be careful," a voice behind him said. Reinoso, the captain, had overheard them. "They may be trying to lure you over there and kill you. Maybe they have convinced themselves that if they can't understand us they will have an excuse not to obey us."

"And perhaps we are all going a bit mad from nothing to do," said Rogel with annoyance. "No supply ship. No adelantado. No catechism. Captain, I would like your permission to leave with a small contingent and visit the keys to the south. The Matacumbe Indians there are most friendly to us and have said they are ready to burn their idols."

"The adelantado would not want me to risk losing any men or another of his precious priests," said the captain, standing in the same faded high boots he had worn since leaving Cadiz.

"Danger and missionary priests go hand in hand," said Rogel. "If you're worried about losing men, just give me a canoe and one Indian."

"No," said the captain gazing idly over the porch railing.

"Well, then, let me go to the Tequesta and help Brother Francisco. The Indians there are friendly and when I last heard he had already made three baptisms. And I'll be in a fort with thirty men to protect me."

"If I'm going mad, you are as well," said Reinoso with a dismissive wave, his back still turned as he scanned the hill of the Great House to the east.

The Jesuit sighed, resigned to another impasse. The reason he hadn't pursued his yearning to escape the island was that he knew in his heart that his absence would trigger more abuses of the Calusa by bored soldiers with pent-up frustrations. Although he preached Christian kindness to the men at every mass, Rogel had seen increasing instances of bullying and beating. A trading dispute. A tussle at an oyster bed. A girl resisting a soldier's "charms." So far they were individual outbursts; but like kindling wood, throw enough pieces into the fire and you can produce a blaze that runs wild.

On December 8, 1567 Father Juan Rogel made a final addition to a letter that had grown lengthy over months of entries:

> *Today we received the first supply ship since last May. The cargo was very scant for both our fort and the one at Tocobaga. We have learned that there is very great need at Tocobaga because during the season of abundant rains all their provisions became soaked and rotten. The captain of that fort has sent word that I should go to Havana when that boat returns in order to let the suppliers of the adelantado know what was happening so that they could respond as quickly as possible. And so I am writing this at sea on my way.*
>
> *I depart with concern for my mission at Fort San Antonio because I have other reasons to doubt the sincerity of Chief Escampaba. Let me begin by saying that not long after my arrival at Fort San Antonio it happened that a high councilor to the cacique came down ill with a pain in his side. It brought him to such a point that we thought him to be in his final agony. They called me at night so that I might visit him and persuade him to be a Christian and abandon all idol worship. He showed good indications, saying that he believed in God and in Jesus Christ, his son, who became man in order to make men friends of God.*
>
> *The sick man said he regretted the blindness in which he had lived all his life, and that he intended, if God spared him, never to adore idols again and to be a good Christian and vassal of God. With this I waited a bit, and when I saw that the illness was tightening its grip on him and that he would die before dawn, I baptized him.*
>
> *Almost immediately he began to improve. I took him under my charge at once and fed and clothed him from the provisions of the fort, regaling him as much as I was able and giving him other little things to attach him to us. He continued improving so that in a while he was completely well and healthy. I persuaded the cacique to free the man from all the duties he had in the house of the idols, for he was now a Christian.*

Very soon thereafter the shamans were to perform certain sorceries and idolatries. At that time I saw this man, adorned after their fashion, going into the house of idols. I sent word that he should not do so, but he went anyway to perform the idol worship and I have no doubt that the king concurred in it.

Much more recently, one of Escampaba's daughters fell sick, a young girl whom he loves supremely. As she was in danger of dying, I sought to persuade her father that she should be made a Christian through baptism. I said I trusted in God that by virtue of the holy baptism that the child might be cured; but that, should it be God's will to take her, that her soul would go to heaven. And I said that if she were to die without baptism, she would go to hell; and that if he loved his daughter so much he should not do her such great harm as to deprive her of so great a benefit. But as much as I tried to convince him, he played deaf and dumb and never gave me a reply. I learned that instead he had cured her with his witchcrafts and inventions of the devil.

CHAPTER SEVENTEEN
Marquéz and Escampaba
January-April 1568

Pedro Menéndez Marquéz, the adelantado's battle-hardened, seafaring nephew, commanded all Florida during his uncle's hiatus in Spain. In January 1568 he set sail from Havana with three ships for Tocobaga and Mound Key. Since the priest Rogel had returned with his dire warnings of starvation at Tocobaga, it had taken Marquéz a month to scrounge enough supplies from the Yucatán and various Indies ports. God knows, the wretched governor Osorio had sabotaged every effort to extract them from Cuba and had forced Marquéz to beg for cash advances from the adelantado's agents in other Indies ports.

But Marquéz got the job done. He always did. For twenty years he had raided corsairs with his uncle, captained his fleets from Asturia and now directed a dozen ships and 150 men in the intricate business of supplying the struggling garrisons in Florida. He had always been the man who drew crucial special assignments, be they dispatching French prisoners at Matanzas Inlet or taking off the truculent Calusa cacique Carlos. Over and over Marquéz heard his uncle promise that one day he would be governor of all Florida. And that conviction sustained his every risk and hardship.

Marquéz had been planning to quell some Indian threats at St. Augustine, but the priest Rogel had insisted fervently that the situation at Tocobaga was even more precarious. The Jesuit had even tearfully vowed to go to the bishop of the Yucatán and beg for whatever goods he could spare.

Added to all this were the words of the adelantado before leaving for Spain the previous May. "Look after the priests," he said. "I'm going to be asking for more of them, and I don't want the Jesuit Order getting dispatches about Indians dancing with the heads of their brethren."

Father Rogel was aboard the lead ship as they spotted the village at Tocobaga, and here is what he wrote:

I accompanied Pedro Menéndez Marquéz in order to console the Christians who were there by hearing their confessions and saying Mass for them. I was also there to persuade the Chief there to make amends to Escampaba for certain wrongs he had done in raiding some of his towns and breaking the peace established with the adelantado.

When we reached there, no one came out to receive us. And as we saw no Indian at all walking about through the settlement, we suspected there had been some great wrong. And so, Captain Marquéz consulted with his officers as to whether it would be best to land at once or wait until the next morning to see if perchance a Christian might come to the boats with some news about this turn of events.

At dusk we fired some shots so that, if there should be some Christians hidden in the woods, they would learn that we were there and come to us. But no one appeared. On the following day, fifteen soldiers, well armed and ready for war, went ashore and found no one in the settlement except for two dead Christians whom the Indians had killed the day before when they saw us coming. Later we saw another one who had been killed and thrown in the river.

As we learned later, they had kept alive in order to use them as slaves. They had killed all the rest earlier, caught off-guard and unawares, scattered about one area or another.

On seeing this horrible sight, the soldiers set fire to the entire village and to the house of the idols. They returned to the ships with the bodies. We read the service for the dead over them and threw the bodies into the water as we passed over the bar. Then we returned to Fort San Antonio.

Why did they kill these Christians? After we returned we encountered some Indians who had once deserted Carlos for Tocobaga and who had returned to the service of Escampaba. They said that the Spaniards there were very mean spirited—which in their language translates into "of very small heart." They said the Spaniards put their hands on everyone except for Chief Tocobaga and his captain general. In addition, as their food rotted on them, it ran out earlier than the suppliers in Havana expected it to. I believe that with the hunger the Spaniards began to be more of a burden and more bothersome to the Indians.

I learned that Chief Tocobaga himself had been away visiting his own village at the mouth of the bar. The killing was done by his captain general, and it was because the Tocobaga were fearful lest our soldiers do to them what those at Fort San Antonio did to Carlos. And thus he wanted to get the jump on them.

Now that I have returned to San Antonio, I can only say that Escampaba does not seem grieved by the fate of the Spaniards at Tocobaga. The Calusa have always waged war with the Tocobaga, and now he is urging us to increase the number of soldiers at the fort and his own people to make more weapons for war. Pedro Marquéz has in fact left ten more soldiers here and returned to Havana.

Indeed, Marquéz did strengthen the fort, but not to do battle with the Tocobaga.

By April 1568, Fort San Antonio was a drum drawn taught by fear and tension. Soldiers bickered over card games that once brought their greatest amusement. Soldiers began searching Indian kitchen servants before they could enter. Indians scowled and smirked, muttering unfathomable curses that soldiers inflated into outbursts of insurrection. Rumors festered that over in the house of idols, men were parading and chanting with their hideous wooden masks. The priest Rogel was becoming an annoying busybody, clucking over various factions like an old dueña. Reinoso was mostly silent, brooding.

On April 4, Palm Sunday, everyone on Mound Key was surprised to see a lone ship appear just outside the bar at Carlos Pass. A surprise bonanza of meat and biscuits? No, the first canoes that arrived from Fort San Antonio to take off supplies received only grim and embittered men from the fort at Tequesta. A year earlier, the work of pacifying and proselytizing the Indians at the southern tip of the Florida mainland had been deemed so successful that Menéndez had taken three of the Tequesta elders to Spain to be shown off as model Christians. Now the alarmed men of San Antonio heard from their fellows how the Tequesta had arisen without provocation to kill four of their number and torch their fort. Only a lucky stopover by Marquéz on his way north had enabled the rescue of the eighteen survivors from certain death.

Now the air at Fort San Antonio was charged with even more alarm and alert. The eighteen soldiers from Tequesta spat invective at any Calusa within hearing range. Reinoso and Marquéz could be seen pacing the long porch, speaking softly to each other in fervid tones lest even their own men hear of their confusion and anguish. How had both Tocobaga and Tequesta been able to rise up so spontaneously? Was this a coordinated effort? Might the interpreter Lujo be a spy? If so, Escampaba had to be the instigator. Yet, the cacique showed no signs of hostility. He still called often with broad smiles and departed happily with his ration of wine. He still inquired about the adelantado's return. But he also pleaded at each visit for the Spanish to make war on the Tocobaga.

A week following his arrival, after the men had scattered for their morning duties, Marquéz summoned Reinoso, Rogel and five officers to a corner of the loggia outside the mess hall. "Very soon I must return to Havana and resume my trip to St. Augustine," he announced in a hushed voice. "Here at Fort San Antonio we are nearing a solution to the difficulties that have confronted us."

"Yes, a *solution,*" Captain Reinoso interrupted grimly.

"By late afternoon I will be sending the *Nuestra Señora,* our largest ship, back to Havana so that it can be provisioned with all haste for the trip to St. Augustine that I have delayed for too long."

He now faced the priest. "Father Rogel, I want you on that ship so that you can administer to the spiritually needy people of St. Augustine. There are many more of them there than here. We also need a report sent to your order in Spain from St. Augustine as to what their new missionaries might expect in Florida."

Rogel nodded silently. He could not fault the logic of Marquéz.

But his stomach churned because this scenario bore an eerie semblance to the one that had preceded the killing of King Carlos.

"Do you think the cacique could be persuaded to come with me?" Rogel asked meekly.

"Not at this time," said Marquéz brusquely. "Perhaps later on the other ships."

"What about Lujo, my interpreter?" Rogel asked almost as an afterthought.

"Well, hardly," answered Marquéz. "You've said he's trustworthy, so we'll need him more than ever on our expedition into the interior."

"But what of *me?* What of me, my father?" Lujo had later confronted Rogel in his stark room as the Jesuit stuffed some books in his trunk for the trip to Havana. He felt panic in his stomach and his voice came in short gasps.

"Marquéz has assured me that you will be needed," answered the priest, his eyes on his task. "In fact you will be even *more* necessary because I will not be here. There is no one else to translate."

"But, but what about *after* that? What if there is war? If Marquéz kills the Calusa, he will kill me, too. If the Calusa kill the Spaniards, *they* will kill me. Please, my father." He dropped to his knees with tearful pleading eyes.

Rogel stood still in silence for many seconds. Then he knelt beside Lujo and prayed in Latin. "Father, forgive me, for he is right and I am guilty of being influenced by haste. Father, I pray that you will bless what I am about to do."

After crossing himself, he said "Lujo, I will baptize you now if you are ready to accept. By this you will be protected by the power of God's love, by the cross that you will wear and by the brotherhood of your fellow Christians."

"Yes, yes, I am ready."

"But not here. It must be in the presence of witnesses. And I will do it, not in the Latin language I just used, but in Spanish so that you can fully understand. When I ask you a question, simply say yes if that is your wish. Now remain here for a few moments."

The priest took his Bible, a silver bowl and a standing crucifix from his writing table and soon found Marquéz and Reinoso hunched over a chart at the mess table.

"Excuse me," he interrupted brusquely, "but before I depart today, Lujo wishes to be baptized and I am going to do it. *Now.*"

The two heads jerked up, speechless at hearing the mild priest ordering military officers about.

"I need as many men as possible in this room as witnesses."

"How long will it take?"

"A few minutes only."

Reinoso rose without comment and in a few minutes he had dragooned a dozen or so men into the room—one holding a frothy shaving mug and another one barefoot with boots in hand.

"This won't take too long," the captain told the puzzled soldiers. "Father Rogel is going to baptize the interpreter Lujo and needs you as witnesses."

Rogel had placed the cross on the mess table with the Bible and bowl of water on either side. He now brought Lujo forward and bade him kneel at his feet. As he clasped the Indian's hands together in prayer, he could feel them trembling.

"I bring the Indian Lujo into the presence of God and before these Christian witnesses," the priest intoned in his most authoritative voice. "He has learned the catechism from me directly and understands the meaning of baptism. Pedro Menéndez Marquéz, please hold this bowl of holy water while I perform the baptism."

The acting governor of all Florida was so stunned by this "innovation" that he simply stepped forward as told.

As Lujo answered "yes" when questioned, Rogel described the six doors of the church that were opened through baptism: the removal of guilt of the original sin; removal of all punishment owed by way of sin; the infusion of God's grace; becoming part of the church body; becoming a part of Christ; and being eligible to take the sacraments.

In reciting the six doors opened by baptism, Rogel was reminding the surrounding soldiers that their relationship with Lujo had changed. With Marquéz holding the bowl of holy water, he sprinkled it over the head of Lujo as he baptized him "in the name of the Father, Son and Holy Spirit."

Then to underscore what had just happened, Rogel again addressed Marquéz. Looking directly into the governor's eyes, he said "It is an ancient custom that adults are not admitted to baptism without god parents representing the expanded spiritual family. The church plays the role of mother. You, Pedro Menéndez Marquéz, are to become the god parent who will protect this child of faith and help him live up to it."

With that the priest helped Lujo to his feet and pressed his right hand into that of the stunned Marquéz. He then directed each of the surrounding soldiers to shake the hand of Lujo.

Then the priest was gone before he could hear one of the Tequesta survivors muttering to another one as they returned to their duties. "How am I supposed to be his *brother* when his people killed my own cousin without any provocation whatsoever? Never!"

When everyone had left, Lujo went looking for Rogel in his room. It was bare. He rushed to the porch in time to sight a soldier in a canoe paddling the priest and his belongings toward the ship that was moored outside Carlos Pass.

Juan Rogel had conducted his second Indian baptism in Florida, albeit more improvised than he would have liked. By his quick departure there would be no opportunity for anyone to undo it.

The next morning King Escampaba was surprised in his great house when Captain Reinoso appeared at the entrance accompanied only by Lujo. Reinoso advanced to the cacique's high seat and made a flourish of presenting him with three bottles of port—his favorite among the ship's deliveries. "The captain would like to know if it is possible to have a word with you apart from your elders," said Lujo in a confidential tone.

The cacique frowned, but he shrugged and dismissed the others with a wave. "Is Marquéz still at the fort, or did he go back on the ship that left yesterday?" he asked first.

"Ah, you have such vision," answered Reinoso. "That is partly the reason I am here. The admiral had been planning to leave, but he has reconsidered your remarks about the Tocobaga. The time might be advantageous for a joint enterprise to the Tocobaga, this time with weapons to enforce our intentions. We now have several additional soldiers at the fort and all are good fighters. But we must both act quickly because the admiral is already overdue to call at another fort far away on the other side of Florida."

"Yes, this does interest me," said Escampaba leaning forward, struggling to conceal his glee. "Tell me more about this alliance."

"Well, as you know, my king, I am outranked by Marquéz. I am only the captain of one fort, he of many. He would appreciate a visit from you at San Antonio as soon as possible. Tomorrow, perhaps?"

"Alone?"

Reinoso had prepared for that. "Well, did not the two of us just come to you alone and unarmed?" he said spreading his palms. "I know that you and the adelantado have formed a special bond of trust over these years," *Especially in your conspiracy to kill Carlos.*

Reflecting on the invitation, Reinoso broke in via Lujo: "There is one important part of such an alliance that Governor Marquéz would want me to mention. If we must move on the Tocobaga, it must be as an alliance of Christians—Spaniards and Indians—and part of the objective would be to bring them the word of God as the priest Rogel has done to you and the Calusa. Indeed, Lujo here has become a Christian himself."

The king squinted at Lujo with what seemed like a grunt of disgust. If Lujo hadn't already known it, he sensed now that his possibilities of being sheltered or even tolerated by the Calusa had all but disappeared. For better or worse, he had become a Spanish Indian.

"As Lujo and the priest both know, I pray to your God every day at my own cross," said the king. "I have agreed to do all things required to become a Christian except for keeping my wives. I have promised to do this as soon as the adelantado returns."

"Yes, my king, but please consider that it may be quite some time before the adelantado returns. He is meeting now with the great King of Spain and, like your own elders, he serves there until the king releases him. But you do have at this fort the very man whom the adelantado has placed in charge of all Florida. And he may be willing to make some special accommodations in the interest of our alliance."

"But the priest makes no accommodations" said Escampaba, "I have tried many times."

Reinoso replied that the priest had gone back to Havana, but Lujo ignored it. "Instead he said "Marquéz has more powers than one priest. He rules all priests.""

Escampaba cocked his head and smiled. "If I am baptized, may I keep my wives?" he asked.

"If you agree to be baptized in the Christian fashion and live according to God's ways, perhaps only God will have to know how many wives you have," said Reinoso.

"Must I burn all my idols and worship only the cross?" asked the king.

Said Reinoso: "Marquéz believes that the Christian God is so powerful that he will overcome any idols. So it would be of little concern if a good Christian Indian keeps a few idols from his past."

Lujo tried not to think of the withering scorn he would have received from the absent priest Rogel. But he said nothing.

Escampaba smiled. "I will consider all this with my councilors," he said. "If we agree, I will come tomorrow morning. If not, I will send a messenger to tell you."

Usually Lujo awakened to the chirps of morning birds and the crowing of the few cocks that pranced about the fort's perimeter. On this day he awoke to the sounds of men's boots in the corridors and trunks being pulled across rough floorboards. When he lifted the muslin sheet that afforded his only privacy, Lujo saw sailor's trunks being stacked up against walls. Along the walls of the loggia outside the mess hall were stacked dozens of pikes and arquebuses.

"What is happening?" he asked a soldier who was rushing by in the hallway.

"Just following orders. We're to ship out today."

When Lujo asked the captain at breakfast, he was told that either Escampaba would come that day and they would set sail for Tocobaga, or the king would not come and they would sail anyway—only for Havana.

As the sun rose over the east to brood over another hot, humid, rainy July day, sentries at Fort San Antonio scanned the bay for a sign of the royal visitor. At nine Lujo watched as a guard rushed up to Reinoso and reported that the king's catamaran was in sight with three men in it. The captain summoned his master sergeant and the two huddled in hushed tones for few minutes before the soldier scurried off.

Lujo had a sickening premonition that something bad was going to happen that day and that the Spaniards were not telling him what.

In short order the fort's cook appeared in the mess hall with a clay bowl full of water. A soldier slapped a Bible on the mess hall table and left. Another soldier appeared with a crude wooden cross standing in a bucket of sand. Soon thereafter, Escampaba himself then appeared, walking with Marquéz. Following behind with Reinoso were two Calusa.

Escampaba, seeking support for his "conversion," had brought with him his captain-general and leading shaman. All were ready to be baptized under the same terms as described the day before. Then they would plot how they would attack their life-long enemies under the Spanish-Indian banner of Christianity.

"First, we will undertake the ceremony of baptism," said Marquéz after making introductions.

"Where is Father Rogel?" asked Escampaba after surveying the room.

"You may recall my telling you that the priest had to return to Havana on the ship that left yesterday," said Captain Reinoso. "But do not be concerned. Anyone who is a Christian may perform a baptism. Pedro Marquéz himself will conduct the service in your honor."

"Shall we?" said Marquéz? With Lujo at his side, he beckoned the king and his two lieutenants to kneel before him. They did so nervously, noting that a Spanish soldier stood behind each one. But since the soldiers were unarmed, they raised their chins and looked at the cross in the bucket before them.

In the mind of Marquéz, he could not allow the ceremony to proceed to the pronouncement of baptism "in the name of the Father, Son and Holy Spirit," because such blasphemy would lead to his eternal damnation. But if the ritual were interrupted in the course of fulfilling one's fealty to King Philip and the adelantado, it could be annulled at a later time.

"We are gathered here to observe the sacrament of baptism," Marquéz intoned.

As Lujo began translating in front of the three kneeled Calusa, he could see a soldier emerge from the porch with three pikes and hand one to each of the men standing behind the Indians. Before Lujo could finish his sentence, the three soldiers had thrust their spears into the backs of the Calusa king, his shaman and captain-general. All three assailants were survivors of the Tequesta fort and had cast dice for the honor of performing the deed.

Lujo froze. Blood spattered his arms and face. As each of the Calusa lay groaning and doubled over, more soldiers rushed from the corridor and plunged their pikes into their prostrate, bleeding targets. And with combat efficiency, a stout Spaniard followed up with swipes of a heavy battle ax that hacked off all three heads in three blows.

Within another five minutes the carcasses of the reigning Calusa nobles had been carried off and the bloodied floorboards washed off with buckets of water.

Down at the fort dock, Lujo was retching into the water. His equilibrium had been shattered—again.

Within another ten minutes Marquéz had summoned his officers into a now-tidy mess hall to receive their newest orders. "The captain and I have agreed that you will have one day in which to discover the legendary Spanish gold that the caciques are supposed to have hidden around here somewhere. Everything you obtain of value you must bring back to this room to be divided among all men and officers in an equitable manner.

"If you meet resistance, you may put to the torch the house of the cacique, the great house and the house of idols. As for the village huts, spare them when you can, for these people are wretched enough already."

But the Spaniards were fated to be frustrated again in their search for gold in Florida. Down at the fort waterfront, the four paddlers who had awaited the royal party's return took off in frenzy as they saw the bloodied Lujo careening down the hill. The terror in his wild eyes had told them all they needed to know.

And so, when the first squads of soldiers approached the three great hilltop houses, they found all of them empty and ablaze. Down in the valley, no one was left in the village huts. From the great canal that cleaved the island, canoes full of Indians and their household effects poured out the entrance and made their way east to the mainland.

The Spaniards could claim Mound Key as theirs, but they would have no more of it than a hermit crab occupying an old bleached shell.

Lujo still lay on the dock as the sun went down that night. After dark he pulled himself along the tree trunk railing, up the path and into the fort. Inside is was a hubbub. Some soldiers from the looting squads were sprawled on benches, the rest on the floor, their sweaty, sooty faces creased with scowls of disappointment. The corridors were stacked haphazardly with trunks, bundles, pikes and arquebuses leaning at all angles. In the kitchen men were emptying grain from bowls into sacks and packing clayware in large crates. It was obvious that Fort San Antonio would be evacuated very soon.

Although hunger had overcome his nausea, Lujo passed through the kitchen quietly and wove his way through the chaos. When someone seemed to notice him, they would look away as though unsure whether to acknowledge his presence. That night he lay on the floor of his little storeroom, enduring the suffocating heat and the acrid air from the billowy black smoke from the royal buildings on the opposite hill.

Pedro Marquéz had planned everything precisely. Whether or not the hunt for gold been successful, he had determined that all eighty soldiers and their cargo would depart early the next morning. This was because he had taken pains to chart the depths from Carlos Pass to Mound Key. Next, he had determined the high tide to be around 7 a.m. on that day and had decided that the two smaller ships that he had left out in the Gulf could be brought to the fort dock at Mound Key at that time for a much speedier lading than relying on a wobbly chain of canoes and tenders. But an operation taking over one hour might increase the odds of running aground in a hostile land.

As the veteran navigator eased the first ship through Carlos Pass, Captain Reinoso stood with his officers in the mess hall, one eye searching for iron fixtures that might be pulled loose and brought back to Cuba. "This has been my home for over two years," he mused aloud. "I might have gotten to like it if there had been gold."

Reinoso turned and saw Lujo standing in the doorway holding a small bundle. "I go with you, yes?" he said with pleading eyes.

The Spaniards froze in place, their eyes on the captain. "Lujo," he said, "you go back to your quarters while we talk about it."

"I need some opinions quickly," Reinoso said to the officers after Lujo had gone.

"How do you know he wasn't in on the plot to destroy us all?" said the man who had been captain of the Tequesta fort. "He could have been reporting in secret about everything we do at the fort."

"Yes, possibly," said Reinoso, "but has anyone ever seen him talking to any of the people around Escampaba? *I* haven't. He has performed a useful service for us."

"He disappeared right after we took off Escampaba and the others," said a lieutenant. "How do you know he didn't alert the rest of them? How did they manage to get word so quickly and start those fires?"

Alvarez, Reinoso's second in command, said "Our biggest concern should be about him reporting what happened here once we get back to Havana. He's close to the priest. The priest can probably get an audience with anyone he wants."

"Possibly," said the captain, "but he could also be a very credible witness *for* us—that we were forced to act in self-defense. After all, he was right there—a third party, if you will. But the tide and time are running out on us. Wait here while I go and talk to him."

Reinoso found himself standing in the doorway of the little storeroom, propping the privacy sheet over his head while he confronted the nervous, frightened Indian inside.

"Lujo, tell me why you want to go," he said quietly.

"Because I am Christian." Lujo had rehearsed for such a conversation. "Marquéz, a great man, is my godfather."

"Leave that aside for now," said Reinoso in his most fatherly tone. "I want you to think about your safety. What happened to King Escampaba and his men was because we had reports that they were going to try to kill us all and burn the fort—just as they nearly did at Tequesta and Tocobaga. If you go to Havana and tell a different story, I do not think your life would be safe for very long. Do you understand?

Lujo nodded. And he decided that for once his secret might be used for his own benefit. "I am the son of a king," he said. "King Calus was my father. I am the only son of a king to be Christian! I think the adelantado would like to know this!"

Reinoso returned to the men fidgeting in the now-empty mess hall. "He goes back," he announced. "He is the godson of Marquéz and says he is the real son of Carlos. Whatever the case, the godfather Marquéz will have time to sort it out in Havana."

Chapter Eighteen
Lujo, Rogel, Segura in Havana
April 1568-January 1569

Pedro Menéndez de Avilés had been known best as a man who could set a goal, fire the souls of his men and then cling to that vision even when hardship and disappointment had blurred that goal for others. The vision he articulated was a populated and prosperous Florida, but the one he kept to himself was returning on the road to Madrid, people recognizing him in towns with huzzahs, and some even joining his growing entourage until the king greeted them at the palace doors like Caesar Augustus bestowing a laurel wreath on a conquering general.

In truth, on July 20, 1567, as the adelantado entered the king's chamber for morning visitations, summoning his best swagger and nodding at this and that courtier, all he generated were raised eyebrows and delicate bows. The Duke of Alba was whispering something in the ear of Philip II and the king's head jerked up in a startled stare. Then he manufactured a condescending smile.

The reason for no outburst of applause for conquering an area as large as New Spain was that Philip saw Menéndez as just one piece in a long, weary war against the Protestant Heresy to the north and the Moorish menace to the south. He had just sent troops from the south to reinforce the imperial presence in The Netherlands while at the same time decreeing that all Moors in southern Spain adopt Christian dress and abandon their daily rituals. Now he feared that the Turks would invade southern Spain to avenge the insult to Islam—and here was this adelantado asking him to roll the royal dice again and send more of his precious troops and supplies across the ocean!

Worse, the French ambassador had been hounding Philip to release all of the prisoners that Menéndez had captured at Matanzas and Cape Canaveral. During every audience with Philip the ambassador had demanded the conviction of the adelantado for beheading 150 Frenchmen. And now here was Menéndez himself striding into the king's presence to flaunt this effrontery!

Later that day in a private interview the adelantado had beseeched the king to intervene in yet another dispute with the intransient Casa de Contratación. When he had left Havana in May 1567 Menéndez had written Phillip that the Florida forts were down to three months' supply. He had asked for 50,000 ducats to finance more ships, troops and a large contingent of Jesuits. The Casa had authorized only 12,000 ducats and the convoy had yet to depart. Why? When the king inquired, he was advised that Menéndez was being investigated on charges of diverting royal supplies in Havana, selling them at auction and starving his soldiers in the process. It was 1564 all over again!

What to do? The king decided to let the pot simmer. He ordered the adelantado to write a report to the Council of the Indies documenting his achievements and expenses. Menéndez eagerly complied, but mostly because he would need the same information for a multi-layered lawsuit he would file against the royal patrimony. One did not sue a king, who enjoyed divine rights. The mention of crude commerce in the king's court would be like dragging a filthy pig onto the royal dais. No, a private citizen named Menéndez would file suit against the king's treasurer.

As the adelantado and his lawyers piled on their charges—eleven ships lost, the perfidy of the Cuban governor Osorio, Indian attacks and the supplies destroyed during mutinies—King Philip now felt free to bestow some of the titles and emoluments that Menéndez had sought. The easiest one was agreeing that Governor Osorio was a bad apple. Menéndez was made governor and captain general of Cuba. And because no one had ever questioned his seafaring skills, he was named captain general of a new royal armada responsible for defense of the entire Caribbean.

Other royal grants assured that Menéndez would for the first time have a steady though unspectacular income. But the chief benefit of this kingly attention was signaling to everyone in Spain that Menéndez enjoyed royal favor. This in turn would pry open the doors of banks and investors, for Menéndez had even greater visions of massive Spanish settlements in Florida.

However, two factors made this goal elusive and increasingly difficult to reach. The first was that word had already spread through the Spanish countryside that Florida was full of hostile bugs and Indians and all too lacking in arable soil and fresh water. The second factor was the curse of time—the inevitable six-week or more delay between an event happening in Florida and Madrid finding out about it.

Menéndez had no way of knowing that by April 1568 his forts in Tocobaga and Tequesta had been burned out and the one at Mound Key under grave danger. He would also learn that Fort San Mateo, the defense of St. Augustine, would in that same month be imploded by mutiny and then sacked and burned by an alliance of Indians and French corsairs.

The French had gotten their revenge, and when the French ambassador had greeted Menéndez in Madrid with a mischievous smirk, he had already known that the corsairs were on their way to San Mateo. Had King Philip known as well, Menéndez might not have received the trophies of his "triumph."

In Cuba, provisioner to the forts of Florida, the number of Taino, or native inhabitants, had shrunk from about 3 million to around 2,000 during just fifty years of Spanish occupation. One could almost laugh when told that the founding conquisidor, Diego Velázquez de Cuéllar, had received a royal commendation for his "gentle and enlightened" treatment of the native population.

In April 1568 all of Cuba contained only 20,000 or so people and Havana itself around 12,000. In a little settlement across the bay from the docks of Havana Harbor, Father Juan Rogel toiled almost alone— but contentedly—in a melting pot of perhaps a thousand Taino, displaced Indians from Florida and black slaves from Africa and the Caribbean. His base of operations was the little church of San Juan, built a few years before from the stones and rubble left from cathedral building in the heart of Spanish Havana.

The Jesuit's days began before dawn and scarcely offered time for his two meals until he retired well after dark after studying the Guale and Calusa languages by candlelight. He was cheerful because his "people" were grateful for his attention and not steeped in the culture of rejection imposed by royal Indian chiefs in Florida. Rogel had read of a priest in Mexico City who won the hearts of the Aztecs with songs and games. When the priest gathered the poor people of Havana to clap and sing simple songs of Jesus, he found smiling faces for the first time since leaving Spain.

Still, bursts of joy were brief because nearly everyone in this bowl of mixed races woke up each day with something tormenting their bodies. Most commonly it was diarrhea, skin pustules, chronic fever, or a hacking cough and hurting stomach. These maladies already had names like cholera, smallpox, typhus and influenza, but there was no one to diagnose or treat them in the little settlement known only to Spanish Havana as "Across the Bay." All the impoverished people there knew was that they had no such diseases when they had lived with their own kind before the Spanish came.

Rogel had been told that he would be wasting his time on the black slaves, but he found them the most receptive of all to his message of salvation and redemption. In one letter that month to Father Jerónimo Ruíz del Portillo, Vice Provincial of the Jesuit Company of New Spain, he wrote:

> *I taught the catechism each day to the children of the church of San Juan, first gathering them together and going through the streets singing. In addition, as there is great neglect in this village in looking to the salvation of the dark-skinned people, I did what I could to persuade their masters so that they would look out for the Christianization of their family. And I also reprimanded other public vices that exist here. The majority were of the blacks were living in concubinage. Some were trying to marry their lovers and some were trying to separate from them.*
>
> *In addition to teaching children the catechism in the afternoons, I would each day at sunset go to the harbor fortress being built in this town to greet the workers when they abandoned their work. More than one hundred black slaves belonging to the king are engaged in this*

project, and I had them all assembled and taught them the catechism.

It is a great pity, Father, to see the great ignorance that they all have in all matters pertaining to the Christian faith. I am writing all this to your Reverence so that if it should seem suitable to you in the Lord to write to Spain about it, you could strive to see that the king and his council would be made aware of this so that they could provide some remedy for such a great multitude of souls going to hell because of the lack of concern and negligence of those who have charge of them.

The matters of the Indians have shown well what talent we shall require for them, because we all too easily come to be disgusted with them and even loathe them. But I have learned that they are rational animals well prepared for saving themselves. In fact, they are a harvest so ripe that one can swing a sickle on whatever side one chooses as long as they see in their minister one who preaches life and truth to them.

The ministers of God who deal with them must not grow weary or angry as does the mother with the child she rears. She may clean that child a thousand times a day and does not become disgusted by it. So if the minister of God truly loves them, they will respond. If true understanding is lacking in them, the love and zeal for our Lord, whose ministers we are and whose doctrine we preach, must not be found wanting in us, for our Lord suffers more for us than we are capable of suffering for them and the many failings that they have.

Rogel wrote the above in part because he had just received word from Spain that more Jesuits were on the way. Menéndez' tales of success in Florida had so bedazzled his friend Francis Borgia, the Provincial General, that a ship was already sailing with a contingent of Jesuits that included no less than three priests, three brothers and eight young catechists.

The morning Rogel had received the dispatch he had read it once and jammed it into his hassock. His immediate reason was that he had to finish preparing to teach catechism to his children. However, he was simply too overwhelmed by the message to comprehend its meaning in one glance.

In the late afternoon, as he sat on a crude bench in a quiet church lit only by a single votary candle, Rogel pulled the letter out again and squinted in the flickering light. He half expected to find himself mistaken about what he'd read so fleetingly that morning. Could it be? But there it was: *fourteen* Jesuits coming to Havana? Where would they stay amidst all this disease? If only he'd had the opportunity to swap a couple of them for just one physician. The adelantado must be thinking all these men would be parceled out to the Florida forts. But most of the garrisons were now but smoldering memories.

He re-read the letter and saw something he missed: a "college" would be founded in Havana for the sons and daughters of Indian chiefs to make them Christians from the ground up. Maybe all these men were to be the faculty. If so, the grandiosity of an adelantado's foresight was beyond the grasp of a simple priest who had baptized but one Indian boy and one sick Calusa elder in two years.

He traced the Jesuit names with his forefinger. The three brothers he knew not. Probably straight from seminary. He focused on the brief biography of the mission's leader, Juan Baptista de Segura, who was arriving with the new title of Father Vice-Provincial for Cuba and Florida. Obviously, the man had no experience in Florida, but perhaps in China, or among the savages of Africa? No, the new Vice-Provincial was a native of Toledo who had studied four years of theology and two of Holy Scripture at the University of Alcalá in Madrid. The same university had produced St. Ignatius of Loyola, the revered co-founder of the Jesuit Company. Segura received holy orders in 1557 but didn't become a Jesuit until 1566. His mission experience? A couple of years in rural Spain. Then named rector of the college of Valladolid.

A rector? That probably meant approving student admissions, mediating faculty disputes and such. Juan Rogel, his bony bottom sore from too many minutes on a bench made of coral rock, contemplated the softness of a university rector's life, smothered a noisy mosquito in his hassock sleeve, and then said a prayer to God for more humility. He would not pre-judge a man he didn't know.

Any lingering thoughts the priest might have dwelled on were crowded out the next morning by an event that had occupied much more speculation in his mind. On a bright morning in mid-May an

Indian boy came running to the Church of San Juan shouting that "two *urcas*" were coming into the bay. Father Rogel strode outside and down a rough stone path and instantly recognized the two supply ships that had been left behind at Mound Key. Both were already lowering sails. A pair of dolphins was jumping in their wake. Gulls and frigate birds were riding the air stream from the masts. And in the harbor, Rogel could see the usual cluster of black dots on the water: pelicans lining up for handouts, no doubt eager to forego diving for their day's sustenance.

The priest told the boy to get his father to row him across the bay so that a hundred questions could be answered at last. Had Escampaba remained faithful to his promises? Was he still king? Had he made peace with Reinoso and Pedro Menéndez de Marquéz? What about Lujo? Still a Christian? Would Marquéz remember his responsibilities as the young man's godfather?

The dingy approached the other side just as the two urcas were docking and tossing lines to harbor hands. He looked for clues, and as his rower pulled their little boat around the bow of the first ship, he saw the first one. Far more people were streaming down the gangplank than would have been the case on a returning supply boat with a crew of eight or so. Soldiers with full packs. Kissing the ground. Reaching out to a swarm of women, all probably prostitutes and concubines. Soldiers trying to steady themselves on wobbly feet. Not drunk, just getting their land legs back after three days of swaying.

The priest had now climbed a ladder to the dock level and tried to inventory the disembarking passengers. Two scruffy soldiers knelt at his feet, one of them crying "Bless me, father, and pray for me that I will never go back to Mound Key." By the time he dismissed them, the line of passengers on the gangplank was thinning. Then he did a double-take. The last man off was a large, muscular Spanish sailor he hadn't seen before. No, a Calusa Indian wearing canvas breeches and a sailor's cotton shirt. With his wide leather belt and boots he looked more like a Barbary pirate.

"Lujo!"

"Father!" Before Rogel knew what to say he was in the lad's embrace. "I am so happy to see you," said Lujo like a small child greeting a parent. "I thought they might just forget about me and I go wandering."

They sat on a bench near the boats as the unloading continued and the passengers thinned out. The priest listened quietly as Lujo told the turbulent story of Escampaba's last days and the fate of Fort Antonio. And for the first time, the priest learned of Lujo's claim to be the son of Carlos.

At the end of it, all Rogel could say was "Well, I am happy you survived. This is not as our Jesus Christ would wish it but we can talk about that at another time."

"Can I come and stay with you like at Mound Key?" the Indian asked.

"I have thought and prayed about that even though I didn't know if you would be on the ship," said the priest. "But the fact is that you can't stay in the place where I am. My duties have called me to a place"—he pointed across the bay—"which is a settlement of slaves, Cubans and people from many of the Indian tribes in Florida. First, there is a problem with disease. We call it an epidemic because it can spread from one person to another."

"*What* disease?'

"Many diseases. We don't know what causes each one. I think it comes from too many people living too close together. Of course your people—Indians—say it's caused by angry gods and their curses, but only God can bring a plague or cause a cure. I just don't know and that is why you would be at great risk. He left unsaid the fact that he had also prevented Antonia, the displaced sister of Carlos and official wife of Menéndez, from living across the bay.

Did she know she was Lujo's aunt? Would she care?

Lujo began with another question, but Rogel held up his hand. "There's the matter of your royalty. If you swear upon the cross that you are the son of Carlos I will believe you, but there are Indians living in Across the Bay who will not be pleased about it," said the priest. "The Tequesta blame your father for making them pay tribute against their will."

Lujo shrugged and said nothing. Revealing his royal lineage had helped him on Mound Key, but that might have been the end of it.

"No. I think we should go visit Pero Marquéz and decide what to do," concluded the priest.

At the end of the long wooden wharf stood the main warehouse of the absent adelantado's supply fleet, and adjoining it the arched building of stone and coquina rock that served as the headquarters of the his acting governor. As the priest and Lujo approached, they could see that most of the crowd that had left the ships had transplanted themselves in or outside Marquéz' building. Some were waiting to retrieve mail, some asking about shipping schedules to Spain, some seeking back pay or some with grievances. Inside they could see Marquéz behind the large tabletop desk of Menéndez keeping time with his head like a metronome as a petitioner orated with both hands in motion.

"What will they do with me?" Lujo asked as they leaned against a wall, waiting their turn.

"First, remember that God is always with you," was all Rogel could offer. But the Indian soon forgot his plight and became like a boy again, gawking at sights he had never seen in Jeaga Town, Lake Mayaimi or even Mound Key. His head bobbed up and down at sizing up three-story buildings with elaborate wrought iron balconies. He was transfixed by the spires of the cathedral towering behind them. He was jarred from his gaze when a farmer drove past with a team of bullocks hauling a wagon of large wine casks. When two boys on horseback raced down the dusty street and then tied up in front of the two men, Lujo walked twice around them. "So this is the horse I hear about." he exclaimed. "No horse in Calusa land. But when I meet Fontaneda, he tell me all about horses!"

At last, after the line of waiters had dissipated, Marquéz spotted the two figures in the window and crooked his finger as a signal to enter. All that remained in the large room were a secretary with his head down scribbling and the captain general, who was rubbing his head with both hands.

"I apologize for making the distinguished Jesuit father wait until last," he said wearily, "but with your meek demeanor I know you will not mind because the Bible says you shall inherit the earth." Then getting to the point: "May I assume you have heard all about events on Mound Key and the, ah, fate of Escampaba?"

"Yes," said the priest, "and a most unfortunate situation. Your godson here seems to have been a witness to it."

Marquéz peered above his reading glasses. Reinoso had been first in the captain general's door and had explained all about the Calusa lad. "Ah, Lujo. I hardly recognized you" he said in a fatherly tone. "Welcome to Havana. However, I would ask that you leave us alone for a moment to discuss several issues in private."

"I go to see the great cathedral for myself," Lujo said with a wave to the two Spaniards.

Rogel began by describing Lujo as the son of Carlos, but the weary Marquéz interrupted. "I have no doubt that he is. He looks more or less like Carlos and I'm not going to waste our time disproving it," he said. "Indian chiefs take wives from many villages and this was no doubt the result of what happened when he took a wife over at Jeaga Inlet."

"All right, said the priest, "but now we are responsible for where he stays here and what becomes of him from now on."

"We?"

"Actually, *you,* said Rogel. "You are his godfather and that information is entered in the rolls of the church"

"But I'm a soldier, not a dueña. And I do think you duped me that day of the so-called baptism. So let's say it's *we* who are responsible."

"Very well, *we,*" said Rogel. He explained all of the reasons why it would be too risky for Lujo to live in the rag-tag settlement across the bay. "Could we put him up in the cathedral? Perhaps it would reinforce his Christianity."

"I doubt it," said Marquéz. "I've already put that Antonia woman there. She's a strange duck and she might not enjoy finding out that this Lujo who she knew as a translator was actually her nephew all that time. Besides, we'll need all the space we can find in the guest quarters for this contingent of Jesuits who will be arriving soon."

Marquéz walked around from his desk and began pacing, chin in hand. "I think I may have something," he said at last. "Tell the young man he can stay for two or three days in a storehouse in this building. That's where he was at the fort on Mound Key, I believe. After that I think we can move him to a place that will be most pleasing."

"I suppose that will work," said Rogel. "Right now he probably expects to be turned out among the farm workers."

"Between you and me," said the captain general, "what I have in mind would have him living in a place that would make you and I look serfs by comparison."

340

What had clicked in the mind of Marquéz was the name of Diego Gomez de Valezquez, largest cattle raiser in Cuba and chief supplier of meat to the ships that served the Menéndez contingent in Havana and his Florida forts. If the Spaniards hadn't paid him a twenty per cent premium price for his butchered meat, Valezquez no doubt would have succumbed to governor Osorio's strong-arm tactics against trading with the distained adelantado, but so far the cattleman had kept to his contract.

Now it was time to ask a big supplier for a big favor. Would Valezquez accept the Indian prince *Lujo de Carlos* as his houseguest for an undetermined period? After all, the handsome Indian would add a dash of élan to an estate of 5,000 acres some fifteen miles from Havana. There Valezquez presided benignly over a rural fiefdom that included a village of 300 farm hands, a sprawling hacienda, a chapel and a Dominican priest who educated his two daughters. There Lujo could learn to read, write and act like a Spanish nobleman. Perhaps he could even be presented at court as an Indian Christian example of why King Philip should finance the next settlement mission to Florida.

At three in the afternoon, on what could have been any sticky day in July 1568, Juan Rogel found himself praying for an early thunder shower, not that it would stop the sweat from rolling down his loose hassock sleeve and into his already-wet lap. The heat was paralyzing in the dining room of the monastery where the newly-arrived Jesuits were quartered, yet The Father Vice-Provincial continued to drone on as if oblivious to the same elements. Tall and expressive with long swept eyebrows, he often repeated himself and would stop in-mid sentence to pray for God's guidance for the next thought he was about to articulate. Then he would forget the thought.

All around him sat the new arrivals, slumped in their seats or leaning on elbows with hands in chins, enduring this, the second day of a "conference" called by Jean Baptista de Segura to decide upon the thrust of their renewed mission in Florida. Among them, only Rogel lived Across the Bay and had to be rowed back and forth, which gave another reason to pray for an end to the dreary affair. The only religious with any actual experience among the Indians in Florida were Rogel at Tocobaga and Mound Key, and Father Antonio Sedeño, who had served in Guale and Fort San Mateo. And yet the new Father Vice-Provincial seemed hardly to notice or seek advice from either of them. Instead he constantly invoked the spirit of Father Martínez, who had died a martyr upon first touching the beach near St. Augustine.

Now Segura was "summing up" the day's discussion for the fourth or fifth time. "We have been granted a rare opportunity to glorify the Lord in Florida," he intoned professorially. "We have unprecedented authority to found a college for the education for the youth of Indian nobles. We cannot fill it with students until we go to Florida and win the hearts and souls of Indians in their homeland. And yet I am being told that all of the places we have gone are no longer, uh, available."

For the first time that day he looked at Father Rogel. "You say that the people of Mound Key are no longer receptive. Why is that?"

"Because their main town was burned down, Reverend Father."

"Who burned down their town?"

"The men of Fort San Antonio, Reverend Father."

"And what of Fort San Antonio?"

"I cannot say for chert because I was not there at the time, but Captain Reinoso says it was being burned by the Indians as his ship departed."

"And why do you suppose that was?"

"I suppose because our men burned down their town, Reverend Father."

"How long were you there?"

"The better part of two years."

"And how many Indian souls did you win for Christ?"

"Two on Mound Key, and just last week an old woman over at Across the Bay. I presume that also counts," he added in his first public hint of the irritation that simmered inside.

Segura ignored it. "Well, what about the Indians south of Mound Key—the ones in the Florida Keys? Some have heard they are friendly and disposed toward the Gospel."

"That may be," said Rogel. "People have told me so, but I have not been there."

"And we have no soldiers there?"

"Not that I know of, Reverend Father."

"Well now, doesn't all this tell us something?" said Segura spreading his arms like Christ delivering the Beatitudes. "Where you have soldiers you have trouble and cruelty. Spain gets evicted, and with it the soldiers of God. But when we first encounter these Indians in friendship, they are friendly in return. I see a pattern here."

As Segura began grilling Father Sedeño as to promising posts on the other side of Florida, Rogel leaned back and closed his eyes long enough to pray that God would guide the new Father Vice-Provincial along the paths of reality. Then he carefully began opening a letter he had received that noon while it was still concealed inside the long sleeve of his hassock. Gradually he worked the unsealed letter free from his sleeve and placed it atop some conference papers.

Dear Father, it read,

I am write to you my first letter. I learn to read Spanish from my tutor and now I write, too. Father Rodríquez is a good teacher. He and I read Bible. I try to learn Guale, too.

I wear good clothes and even like boots. I have a big room. I love horses and go riding a lot. I am having a good time. Maybe you can come visit.

Yours in Christ,
Lujo de Carlos

The much-prayed-for thunderstorm seemed omen enough to suspend the conference for the day. As the rain invaded from open windows and men snatched up their papers, Segura called across the table.

"Father Rogel, I noticed you reading something and smiling a lot. I don't recall anything on the agenda being humorous."

Rogel forced a sheepish smile. "I am sorry, Reverend Father. I had received a letter from someone this morning and couldn't resist the chance to take a peek. It was very short. As a matter of fact, it came from the Indian who became a Christian at Fort San Antonio. He is now staying with some friends of Menéndez de Marquéz outside of town. He was our translator in Calusa and now he's studying Guale. He is also the son of the great chief Carlos."

Oh, Jesus, forgive me for trying to impress this man. And forgive me for using this "son of Carlos" information for my own convenience.

"Son of the chief Carlos a Christian?" Segura's luxuriant eyebrows were undulating up and down. "Studying Guale? Maybe this translator could be a shining beacon for Christ in our new Florida mission! Tell me more!"

Rogel promised to arrange an interview and the Father Vice-Provincial soon departed with his Bible and satchel of papers. As Rogel turned away he saw that the only other person in the room was Father Sedeño, who seemed to be waiting for him.

"Some day when convenient to you, I would like to go across the bay and help you in your work," said the priest, a thickly-built Andalusian with curly black hair.

"As humble as it is, you may find it more interesting than meetings like this," replied Rogel.

"It seems that we already have something else in common to begin with," said Sedeño with a sardonic smile. "We're the only ones here with experience among the Florida Indians."

"We're the only ones who seem to notice. It doesn't count for much, does it. That's because our new Father Vice-Provincial sees us as part of the failure of Menéndez. Do you know that he has actually talked of petitioning the king to bar Menéndez from returning to Florida? He thinks that priests alone can win hearts for Jesus."

"I would give anything if it were true," said Rogel. "But you know from Guale and San Mateo that it isn't, just as I learned at San Antonio and from Father Villarreal at Tequesta."

The two stood in silence beside the open window, watching the rain now fall straight and splash into rivulets in the cobblestone street outside. "I must say," offered Rogel at last, "he is not at all what I expected. I thought even with his lack of experience, his days as a university rector would have made him skilled at eliciting ideas from many and consolidating them into a realistic strategy. This man, may God forgive me, seems only interested in going out and kneeling on the beach unarmed like Father Martínez. And these young catechists all nod their heads eagerly. If I am to become a martyr, I would pray it could be *after* I've done some useful work and not before."

"Would you like some insight on why he behaves like this?"

"Oh yes, it would even answer a prayer," said Rogel.

"Well," said Sedeño, "when I was at Guale I served with an officer who had known him in Valladolid. And because I now live here with the new men, I also pick up things they say. I think I can say with confidence that when Segura first joined the Company he wanted only to be a soldier for Christ in some alien land, like our St. Ignatius. At first that's what he was when he spent a couple of years in the poorest part of Spain. But because he came from a good family and had very good grades, he was made a university rector and put into a position where he had to settle bureaucratic and jurisdictional disputes that seldom made both parties happy.

"What probably made the kettle boil over was when the leading Jesuit professor at the university allowed himself to be the beneficiary of a wealthy woman's estate. The Jesuit did this without permission from the Provincial or from Rome and the woman's family protested to Segura as university rector. He tried his best to come down the middle with a decision, but it pleased no one and made him so miserable that he told the Provincial he would either be made a missionary again or quit the order.

"When he did get the assignment to Florida, it was only as the head of the mission—another rector-like position— but he took it anyway," continued Sedeño. "Then, as he was preparing to sail from Seville, his parents visited him and asked that he forfeit his part of a family inheritance. Why? Because his two brothers had already squandered their share and were living in poverty. He did so, and I think it could be that it was like cutting his bond to Spain forever. He would go to Florida and stay there or die a heroic martyr for Christ."

Rogel again watched the rain in silence for awhile. "I suppose, then, that this is why he so willing to lead these novices onto strange and hostile shores," he said.

"And it is why you and I must ask the Lord for guidance so that their trust and zeal is not misplaced."

September 1568

The setting: A weekend at Ranchero de Extramadura, the 5,000-acre hacienda of Enrique de Valezquez. After a day of riding horses and shooting wild boar, the guests have gathered after a late afternoon nap just as a conveniently cooling rain shower has subsided. They are seated at the table in the main dining hall. Behind them stand female servers and large men with fans of woven palm fronds to churn the steamy tropical air into tolerable breezes.

The hosts: Don Enrique de Valezquez, his wife Martina and their daughter Veronica.

The guests in order of rank:

Pedro Menéndez Marquéz, acting governor of Florida and Cuba in the absence of his uncle, the adelantado.

Juan Baptista de Segura, Father Vice-Provincial of the Society of Jesus for Cuba and Florida.

Father Juan Rogel, a Jesuit priest.

Father Manuel Rodríquez, a Dominican friar and now tutor to the household.

Alvarez de Ramirez, a neighboring rancher, and his wife Isabel.

Lujo de Carlos, an Indian prince of Florida.

The feast:

Oysters from Havana harbor, baked in the shell rather than raw, as preferred by natives.

Candied yams, glazed black with the sugar of the hacienda's fields.

Thick beef steaks, grilled freshly from the livestock of Cuba's foremost hacienda.

Roast pork, from the morning's hunt.

Corn, shucked from the hacienda's own garden.

Bread from the hacienda's growing wheat field.

Yellow rice from the fields of Mexico.

Madeira wine from the private stock of the adelantado.

Flan, frothy custard prepared from eggs freshly laid in the hacienda's own henhouse.

When everyone was seated, Valezquez began with a toast to his guests and to the success of the day's hunt.

"But I really must chide you, Don Enrique," said Marquéz to his host mischievously. "Here we are being served the adelantado's favorite Madeira, and yet I cannot find any in stock in our own warehouse. How does this magically appear?"

"You are correct—by magic," said a smiling Valezquez with a bow of the head. "One trades a bale of hay for a bushel of corn and then later perhaps a few leather hides for some barrel staves and—*poof!*—at the other end of all these transactions appears a cask of wine. I simply cannot explain it. An act of God!

"But your comment reminds me of another magic—and one that only you can perform," Valezquez quickly added. "I would like the help of Pedro Menéndez de Avilés in obtaining a license to import slaves."

"How many?"

"Perhaps up to 300. Please let me explain why. As your main provisioner of fresh meat, I have much to lose since you have reduced the number of forts in Florida that need my services. Besides, with Osorio out of the picture, you'll be able to obtain meat from many other sources. I think it is in the best interests of Spain and my family that I diversify the activities on his hacienda, and to that end I am thinking of producing sugar cane. It comes up every year, doesn't depend on the appetites of Spanish troops in Florida, but does find a stable, steady market in Europe. In fact, we can take the casks of wine that arrive here and use the empties for sugar molasses."

"How wonderfully efficient," Marquéz mumbled through a mouthful of roast pork.

"Ah, but to harvest this crop I need manpower."

Marquéz took a deep breath and a swill of his Madeira. "Yes, but so *many* slaves, Don Enrique? Your lands are formidable, but would they require that much labor?"

"Well, part of my request has to do with establishing a sugar mill on my property," said Valezquez. So much of this operation depends on manpower to crush the cane and grind it into molasses. And this is where I also would like to involve *you,*" he said to his neighbor, Alvarez de Ramirez, who he had conveniently seated on his left.

"Me?"

"Yes, you, my good friend," said Valezquez. "With the help of the adelantado I will erect a mill on my property. All you and the other land owners around here have to do is cut down your cane once or twice a year and haul it to my mill. I will pay you cash on the spot for it. You won't have to sell it on the market or do anything else except go back home and plant your next crop of sugar."

Ramirez looked at his wife, who offered a noncommittal shrug. "Don Enrique, I'm a rancher, not a farmer."

"Nonsense," said Valezquez. "You raise vegetables for your kitchen.

Just think of this as a bigger garden. And when the cane is cut, your cattle can graze on the stubble. It's actually getting twice the amount of use for your land. All you do is have your people cut it and haul it to your friend Valezquez, who gives you instant cash. Better than going to a bank. Oh yes, and one thing more. When the cane is growing it makes for a wonderful thicket full of quail, grouse, rabbits and wild pigs. In fact one of the boars we roasted tonight came running out from that one acre of sugar we have just down the main road. Isn't that right, Lujo?"

All eyes turned to the "cacique," as some in the household had begun calling him for short. But Lujo hadn't heard because he was peering over his wine goblet and rolling his eyes at one of the Valezquez daughters, who was fluttering her delicate fan in turn.

"Lujo!" he called, pretending to ignore the obvious. "We were talking about how you killed the boar that ran out from the sugar patch. We've all killed pigs around here with arquebuses, but I've never seen it done with a bow and arrow."

Lujo was flushed with wine and the sudden attention. "Thank you, Don Enrique," he said with a head bow, "but I only did what I was brought up to do. Your big guns scare me. I would probably shoot myself and not the boar. In my land I was trained to be a tracker of animals, but in this case the boar came out tracking me. Actually, he wasn't tracking, he was chasing. So I am just glad I could get off my horse and load my bow."

Father Rogel was stunned. He had never heard Lujo say more than a few sentences at a time—and usually just to translate someone else's words. Now here he was, in a silken shirt with puffed sleeves, drinking wine and making convivial conversation with the leading citizens of Cuba. Rogel glanced sideways at Segura, who had a dreamy smile on his face.

"And he actually *made* his own bow and arrows," Valezquez added. "Tell us how you did it."

"Oh, every Indian in Florida knows how," Lujo said modestly. "I find a young tree about six feet long and this big around" (he held up rounded fingers to indicate a three-inch diameter). "Then you take knife and split it down the middle."

"Father, he made one for me, too," exclaimed Valezquez' daughter, Veronica.

"Well, when you split the young tree down the middle, then you have the makings of two bows," interjected Lujo. He explained how the saplings are bent by soaking them in hot water, and then the making of arrows. From that point on Lujo was at the center of the dinner conversation and object of unrelenting fascination.

"What does the name Lujo mean?" the wife of Valezquez asked.

"My uncle gave that to me when I think he was angry with me because I didn't do very well at riding a whale. In Calusa it means something like "strange" or "hard to understand.""

"How interesting," said Señora Valezquez. "In Spanish *Lujo* means something else. *Lujo* can mean a special guest, or fine raiment or unlimited wealth. So you have gone from being strange to being very special—like a good luck charm."

Lujo blushed again as a server poured his third glass of wine. "No, I am just lucky to be in this house with such a generous hostess," he said.

"I want to hear about riding a whale," piped up Veronica. And so the evening went, with Lujo entertaining the guests with stories of tracking alligators, finding Spanish gold, attending a wedding in the great house on Mound Key, of his conversion by Father Rogel and so forth. All the while, Rogel himself sat in silence, his mind filtering how deftly the so-called prince wove his story to make it seem—without actually saying so— that he had been raised on Mound Key in the royal household. Clever, thought the priest, he is becoming before my eyes the eldest son of the most powerful cacique in Florida.

It was the Father Vice-Provincial who veered the conversation onto a bumpier road. "So you were there at Fort San Antonio with Don Pedro Marquéz here when the Spanish presence came to an end, correct?"

Lujo's face froze. He took a sip of wine to recover.

"Yes, I was there." His glance darted between Rogel and Marquéz.

"Well, what I want to know is whether the work of the Lord and his priests was enhanced—helped—by the presence of soldiers."

Lujo struggled with a hundred thoughts. "Well, Father, the priests helped the soldiers in their lives. They held services and…."

"That's not quite what I meant," interrupted Segura. "Did you see evidence of cruelty to the natives—your people—that would turn them against Spain and the Holy Gospel? Or did the soldiers help advance the Gospel?"

"It's very ah, complicated," stammered Lujo.

"He was our interpreter and he played a very neutral role," broke in Marquéz. The governor could see where Segura was headed and it could only lead to the killing of Escampaba—a destination neither of them wanted to reach. "It's very late for such weighty conversation," he said instead. "Besides, if my gracious host would offer me a small brandy out in the loggia, we could watch the moon rise and talk more about growing sugar cane."

With that the diners began to separate, with Segura steadying himself on the arm of Father Rogel as they made their way to their rooms. The Father Vice-Provincial was in his cups and about to have one of his visions. "This Lujo is indeed special, just like his name suggests," said Segura. "I see myself as the St. Ignatius of Florida, and this young man as Timothy was to Paul. Or it could be like St. Francis Xavier in Japan, with Paul of the Holy Faith as his trusted assistant. With this Lujo's knowledge of Indians and my zeal for Christ, we could overcome all obstacles that stand in the way of the Holy Gospel! Why even his name means 'good luck!'"

In Across the Bay, the little Church of San Juan, which some called simply the "Slave Church," had begun to take on a more lived-in ambience then when Juan Rogel had first opened it. Upon entering to the left was a large table of votary candles. On the wall behind the altar, with its Bible and small silver cross, hung a large wooden cross with a crudely carved six-foot figure of a brown Jesus in his dying throes. Hanging from either end of the cross were necklace-like strands of fisherman's rope that reached to the ground. Rogel had accepted the cross from the African slave who carved it, but had never asking the meaning of the rope for fear of appearing ungrateful.

In a small alcove to the right of the altar stood another statue—this one carved by a Mexican Indian—a bent-over figure of Jesus, the red crisscrosses on his bare back showing his scourging by Pilate's soldiers.

It was late afternoon in January 1569, and as Rogel entered, expecting an empty sanctuary, he nearly tripped over a large sail-cloth duffle bag with what looked like a note of some kind pinned to it. Wary, he walked softly towards the altar. In the alcove to the right he saw the back of a man kneeling in prayer before Christ the Scourged.

"Lujo," he said softly. The Calusa "prince" turned slowly towards him. He was clad in the same cotton shirt and sailcloth breeches he'd worn when walking down the gangplank in his first day in Cuba. "What happened? Why are you here?"

"You are my priest," came the answer. "Will you hear me in confession?"

The question carried special import to a priest in the new world. Many of the Indians who were baptized had not been offered confession or the sacraments until they could be observed for a while and judged to be true believers. Lujo had never confessed to him.

"Perhaps," Rogel answered after a pause. "But first I think I had better read the note that is pinned to your baggage. May I?"

Lujo gave a subtle shrug and the priest walked back to the bag. The note read:

> *To the church:*
> *I give you back Lujo. Make him disappear or I will.*
> *Enrique de Valezquez.*

"All right," Rogel said at last. He sat on a stone bench and motioned for Lujo to sit on the one in front of him, his face pointing away from the priest. "We are now before God. Tell me your confession. Begin with why you are here."

"Because the people of the hacienda think I have become too Spanish for an Indian."

"That does not have the ring of truth," answered Rogel. "Remember that you are before God, who already knows the truth. You are telling it for *your* benefit."

"This is confidential, Father? You no tell anyone?"

"That is what confession is all about. It is my sacred duty to keep a confidence."

The Indian's shoulders seemed to sag, as if already unburdened. "I and the girl Veronica," he stammered. "We go horseback riding. We look for a place where I can show her how to shoot the bow and arrow. After a bit of time she say she is hungry. She pulls this sack of food from her saddlebag."

"Just a sack of food?"

"Some wine, too."

"And this girl is how many years old?"

"Fifteen, I think. Maybe fourteen. I don't know. We go sit under a tree. Then pretty soon she is kissing me and making me do, you know, do *it*."

"She must be very large and strong to overpower the son of Carlos."

"You make fun of me."

"No, Lujo, you make fun of *yourself* in God's presence," said the priest. "This was the only such time?"

Pause. "Well…..not the only time together. The only time doing *it*."

"How did Don Enrique find out?"

"Don't know." Lujo had begun mumbling in his agony. "I think maybe Veronica go back and tell her mother. Maybe get scared to have Indian baby."

Suddenly he whirled around and faced the priest in an angry tone. "This is not right. Anywhere in Calusa land girls are with husband and becoming mothers at this age. It is something we greet with joy, not punish. I tell you Father, I had the same thing happen when one of the kitchen girls came to me for the same purpose. She told the cook about it and nobody got angry or anything. They say even Don Enrique helps himself to a little 'snack in the kitchen,' as they call it, and nobody says anything. So you see, they have one rule for Indians, one rule for Spaniards, just like on Mound Key."

"I remind you again that this is a confession, not an argument," replied Rogel. He motioned for Lujo to turn around again.

Now the Indian hung his head in his hands. "I ask God and the Lord Jesus," he said through tears. "Who am I? Am I Calusa? Am I now a Spaniard? Where do I go? Why can't I live somewhere where I can just be *me?*"

"Where would you wish to spend the rest of your life?" the priest asked softly.

"I think I just like to go back to Lake Mayaimi and a little creek near it where there is a little village. There I found peace and beauty.

And there I found a girl who loved me without even knowing what anyone else said about me. Can you send me back there?"

"Lujo, I am sure the adelantado is not going to send any more men or ships back to that part of Florida," said Rogel. "God is very sad for you, but he understands your heart."

The Indian whirled around again, his face wet with tears. "Then I ask you again. Who *am* I now? Where do I go?"

"Alas, it would be difficult for you to stay here in Cuba," said the priest. "Valezquez says he will make you disappear if you do. It might be convenient for Marquéz as well if you did not remain in Cuba. And it would be as well for the Tequesta who live here Across the Bay.

"But part of your question I can answer. You have become a Christian and the love of the Lord will sustain you in your life's journey. Your road seems to point toward continuing as an interpreter and missionary in spreading His word. While you think about that, I believe I can arrange for you stay with the Father Vice-Provincial in the annex to the Cathedral in Havana. He has the power to keep you safe until he decides where our mission will go next."

"This Provincial—Segura—you like him? You trust him?"

"Lujo, this is not *my* confession. He is my superior and my brother in Christ. It is my duty to love and obey him. Now I am going to give you some prayers to say to atone for your sins."

CHAPTER NINETEEN

The Segura Mission
1569-1572

As the few cool days of 1569 melted into a sultry summer, Juan Baptista de Segura continued to flagellate his flock of Jesuit monks with meeting after meeting to divine God's will for their mission in Florida. Nipping at the heels of their decision making was the fact that a special ship—the first ever built solely for a religious expedition in Florida—was nearing completion in Havana harbor. The adelantado himself was expected back in Cuba at any time and would be flabbergasted to learn that the vessel had not sailed for *somewhere.*

By mid-July Segura had completed a laborious "review" of the abandoned outposts in Tocobaga, Mound Key, Tequesta, Santa Lucia, Cape Canaveral and San Mateo. He reluctantly concluded that any attempts to re-settle them would be undone by hostile Indians. Why? Because ground that once was fertile for the cultivation of Christians had been despoiled by the overbearing Menéndez and his undisciplined men. The Vice-Provincial was soon vowing before his underlings that he would do everything in his power to prevent the adelantado from playing any role in the conversion of native peoples.

In November 1569 the now-chronic epidemic claimed the life of Brother Augustin Vaez, a skilled Jesuit linguist who had been counted on to master Indian dialects quickly. Segura's stomach had begun rejecting food and his bowels ejecting anything that slipped the blockade. But he complained not, telling himself that it was no worse than the "thorn in my flesh" that God had given his beloved St. Paul to remind him that his physical weakness made him spiritually strong.

In the next month Antonia, the sometimes Christianized, often rueful sister of King Carlos, succumbed to the same scourge. Lujo had been staying in the same wing of the cathedral where Antonia had a room but had been prevented from seeing her for fear of contagion. But he saw Father Rogel coming and going each day, had stood in the hall to hear him pronounce last rites, and had seen the tears in the eyes of this loving, patient priest who had cared so much for the sister of a man who had plotted so often to kill him. And in Rogel he thought he could see a glimpse of Jesus.

Then, there was the omnipresent Father Segura, constantly appearing at Lujo's side or reaching an arm around his shoulders and crooning words like "You are my Timothy. Soon we will win souls together for Christ." Once at a dinner table full of monks he raised a wine goblet in Lujo's face and loudly predicted that "after our success in Florida, my Timothy and I will sail to Spain and tell the king and the pope about it. We will produce a written testament and—who knows?—the man sitting before you here might one day become the first Indian Bishop of Florida!"

Ever since the forts of lower Florida were discarded, Segura had trained his sights much further up the American coast to the region of Guale, with its fort of San Felipe and nearby settlement of Santa Elena. After all, the Indians had been judged by Rogel himself to be of "mild" disposition and all of the surrounding villages spoke dialects similar to the Ais and Jeaga. Besides, the soil reportedly was not sandy and sterile like that of South Florida. The few Spanish farmers who had already landed there had shown promise in producing wheat, grapes, pumpkins, beans and chick peas.

But as the summer of 1570 approached, a more sobering assessment had again slapped Segura in the face. Eyewitnesses reported that there were only twenty or so farming families left in Guale, all of whom had been drawn there by Menéndez' promise that the fertility was "as good as the plain of Carmona" (in Andalusia). In fact, the low-lying island was subject to ocean floods at high tide and winter frosts could cripple whatever survived the summer. Rats and moles worked year-around. So did wandering cattle, pigs and sheep which Menéndez had provided the farmers. Whatever crops the roaming animals didn't eat, foraging Indians did. Soon the farmers were reduced to hunting the shores for oysters, seafood and herbs, which put them in conflict with the Indians, who invariably knew how to do it better.

It was the same story in St. Augustine, except that there were only a dozen farmers left.

In June 1570 construction of the long-awaited Jesuit ship was completed, signaling to Father Segura that the time of deliberating and dithering must cease. Havana was headed into another summer miasma and it was sure to tighten the grip of epidemic. So the Vice-Provincial announced that a "final meeting" would be held in the dining hall behind the cathedral. All surviving arrivals from Spain were ordered to attend, plus old hands Rogel and Sedeño. Inviting Lujo was never considered.

As the others straggled into their rigid oaken seats, Rogel noticed that Segura had arrived with a Bible, from which was protruding several white sheets resembling bookmarks. Odd, he thought.

After prayer, the Vice-Provincial announced simply: "The ship is ready and we must begin our mission. After much thought and study, I believe our Lord is directing us to sail to the Chesapeake Bay. This is a land unsullied by the hands of soldiers, and there we will begin anew among the Indians we find there."

"How many soldiers will go, your Reverence?" asked Sedeño in his usual direct manner.

"Soldiers? None."

Sedeño was too stunned to speak. Rogel came to his rescue. "Have you considered the fate of Father Cáncer in 1549 as he knelt alone on the beach at Tocobaga?" he asked. "Even more recent is the memory of our courageous friend and compatriot, Father Martínez, who was killed on the beach while trying to find St. Augustine."

"I believe that no good can come of trying to frighten or erode the resolve of these determined men here," said Segura with a face full of scorn.

"Reverend Father," said Sedeño, "Father Juan and I concede that our soldiers have often treated Indians cruelly, have taken their women and so forth, but an Indian who does not know Christ can be equally cruel, and as eager to put an arrow in a strange man as easily as a deer."

Segura let go a long sigh of waning tolerance. After a pause to make sure that all eyes were upon him, he said "Let me tell you a parable. As the others here know, before arriving in Cuba our ship stopped for water at a Caribbean island where there were no people. When I went ashore I found birds—scrub jays—that would eat nuts out of my hand. They had no fear because they had no predators. Rather than act with hostility, they trusted. And I have faith that if we as men of God arrive in a land untainted by our own violence and cruelty, the same result will ensue."

Rogel observed heads nodding among the brothers and catechists. "You see," continued Segura, "faith and courage are at the heart of our mission. Did Paul know what awaited him when he struck out alone on the road back from Damascus? Did St. Francis Xavier, not knowing the language or the disposition of the Japanese, come armed with anything more than faith?"

And here he opened his Bible to one of the bookmarks. "Paul tells us in Ephesians to… [and he began reading]

> *…put on the whole armor of God that you may be able to stand against the wiles of the devil. For we are not contending against flesh and blood, but against the principalities, against the powers, against the world rulers of this present darkness, against the spiritual hosts of wickedness in the heavenly places.*

"But I was not speaking of principalities and world rulers," answered Sedeño, "only of a few Indians who might be frightened by strange-looking men and want to shoot first…."

But Segura had already flipped his Bible to another of the bookmarks. "And from Paul's letter to the Romans," he said with rising voice and flourish of the hand,

> *We know that in everything God works for good with those who love him, who are called according to his purpose. For those whom he foreknew he also predestined to be conformed in the image of his Son in order that he might be the first-born among many brethren. And those whom he predestined he also called; and those whom he called he also justified; and those whom he justified he also glorified.*

The Vice-Provincial now peered over the Bible he held with both hands and his eyes swept those of the seated brothers and catechists at the table. "And Paul says to you,

If God is for us, who is against us? If he who did not spare his own Son but gave him up for us all, will he also not give us all things with him?

"And Paul goes on to write something all of us learned by heart in seminary:

For I am sure that neither death, nor life, nor angels, nor principalities, nor things present, nor things to come, nor powers, nor height, nor depth, nor anything else in all creation, will be able to separate us from the love of God in Christ Jesus our Lord.

"Amen, Amen," echoed the young voices around the table as if Segura's words of Paul were ringing in their ears like the campanile at Valencia. The Jesuit leader, flushed with his oratory, drew a cotton cloth from his hassock folds and wiped his brow.

Next he looked at Sedeño and Rogel. "Did you think these were just words to be learned in seminary?" he asked with an air of a schoolmaster addressing two miscreants. "Or were they not the Holy Scripture? Were they not meant to be applied to those who followed Paul—Xavier, Ignatius and ourselves? Of *course* there will be trials and hardships!"

Rogel raised a hand to reply, but Segura had already flipped to another of his bookmarks. "From Corinthians II, I read you more familiar words of Paul:

Five times I have received at the hands of the Jews the forty lashes less one. Three times I have been beaten with rods; once I was stoned. Three times I have been shipwrecked; a night and a day I have been adrift at sea; on frequent journeys, in danger from rivers, danger from robbers, danger from my own people, danger from Gentiles, danger in the city, danger in the wilderness, danger at sea, danger from false brethren; in toil and hardship, through many a sleepless night, in hunger and thirst, often without food, in cold and exposure.

"And Paul concludes," Segura said glaring at the two senior priests, "by saying that he even feels danger from within his own church."

As Rogel absorbed the withering rhetoric and saw the rapturous beams on the faces of the apprentices surrounding him, he struggled inside with the ingrained custom of yielding to a superior versus the urge to stop this man from dragging these innocents into his personal fantasy.

"With all due respect, Reverend Father," he said, trying to mask his impatience, "Father Sedeño had pointed out the very real possibility of death without military protection."

"Yes, yes," said Segura wearily, a teacher exasperated by the dullness of his schoolboys. "And I have been giving you my answer all along. Danger and death will be lurking all around us, but I speak only of danger of the flesh." He flipped the Bible pages again. "I personally am like Paul writing in Philippians."

My desire is to depart and be with Christ, for that is far better. But to remain in the flesh is necessary on your account.

"But should death come to me or any one of us, we know that it is only death of the flesh," said Segura with a serene glow. "For as Paul assures us in Corinthians I,

O death, where is thy victory?
O death, where is thy sting?
The sting of death is sin, and the power of sin is the law. But thanks be to God, who gives us the victory through our Lord Jesus Christ.

The lanky Vice-Provincial now had both hands raised—one holding the Bible—as if in a benediction. It seemed clear that this final of countless meetings was about to be adjourned, but now it was Sedeño who spoke up. "Reverend Father," he said quietly, "I would greatly appreciate it if Father Juan and I could have a word with you in private."

"The peace of Christ be with you all," Segura said dismissing the others. Soon the newly-arrived Vice-Provincial in charge of all Florida sat alone at one end of the long table with the two Jesuits who had survived three years of tumult among the Spanish outposts.

Gone was any trace of deference in Sedeño's demeanor. "Juan Baptista de Segura," the priest said coldly, "you are about to send a ship full of inexperienced men to a place 900 miles away that you have never seen. You have no military escort and you do not know how many Indians you will face. You don't even know what language you will have to speak. I beg you not to bring all these men into your personal quest for reckless martyrdom."

"*Reckless martyrdom?*" The last two words stung Segura's ears. All the other insults he had heard before. But *reckless martyrdom?*

Segura rose and paced, turning sharply to the two seated men to emphasize a point. "The two of you embody the failure of these military forts over three years" he said sharply. "How many did you baptize? Two? Four? In three *years?* Was it because you hid under the shields of the soldiers and were afraid to go into the villages without an armed escort? And when the soldiers misbehaved, you were all too willing to excuse or condone the hurts they caused the people you had come to save."

Segura was spitting out pent-up anger as he paced. "Perhaps when you were sitting in your secure rooms inside the forts you might have at least read more of St. Paul and our Jesuit pioneers. If you had you might have also realized that this expedition can bring more glory to God than St. Ignatius' mission to Japan!"

Silence sank in as the two priests fought back the urge to retaliate. "If your mind is made up," Sedeño said at last, "I would ask that you assign me elsewhere,"

"I would respectfully request the same," said Rogel.

Segura's mouth dropped in mock surprise. "Who ever said you were going to Chesapeake Bay? Oh no, I would not want the aura of failure to follow my men around Florida. No, no. Stay here in your little safe village across the bay and tend to your safe little church among the leftover people from Cuba and Florida."

"Who then are you taking to the Chesapeake?" Rogel asked as a heavy dread crept over him.

"They have already been chosen," said the Vice-Provincial stiffly. "Perhaps each of you suffered in your efforts because you were largely alone. This mission will have *ten* workers for Christ including myself." He then named the inexperienced Father Luis de Quirós, three equally untested brothers, three young catechists, the altar boy, Alonso de Almos, and Lujo.

The two priests sat as if stunned by a bludgeon. "The altar boy?" stammered Sedeño. "But he is only ten or eleven."

"He is very helpful in serving mass," said Segura.

"And *Lujo?*" interrupted Rogel. "He thinks he's going to Guale. He doesn't know the languages north of that…"

"Lujo is bright and will learn," Segura said as he stood up and collected his papers. "You do God's work as you deem necessary and we will do ours," he said with a pained smile. "And if we die it will be for the glory of God and Jesus Christ."

In the starkly simple cell that Father Juan Rogel occupied behind the cathedral, a slender beam of light carried the late afternoon sun through a small portal on the wall above. It projected directly onto the Jesuit's folded hands as he sat on the edge of the cot praying in the quiet that preceded the evening meal. Or was he simply musing to himself?

Should I confront Segura again? He would be irritated…but if it might save only a life or two? Should I do it at the crowded mealtime or perhaps alone after vespers? Should I try to persuade individual members of the expedition? If I did, would I be censured by my superior and perhaps exiled from the Company? Was Segura correct? Was I too timid on Mound Key and in fear of my own safety? Lord Jesus, answer me.

A soft knock came at the thick rustic door.

"Yes?" Rogel had barely emerged from his cave of contemplation.

The door swung slowly open to reveal Lujo.

"Father, I hear about this new voyage."

"Yes?"

"To Chesapeake?"

"Yes."

"But I don't know anything about *Chesapeake*." He spat the word with contempt.

Rogel searched for a soothing answer. "Father Segura says you are very smart and will learn the local language quickly. You might even find it's a lot like Guale or Calusa."

"But…."

Again, Rogel resorted to habit. "Father Segura is our superior—our *cacique*. He believes that God's love and the gospel of Jesus Christ are more important to winning the hearts of native peoples than knowing a language."

Lujo contemplated all this in long silence. "Well," he said at last, "I follow you on Mound Key. I suppose I can follow you again."

It was all Rogel could do to make his eyes meet Lujo's. "Lujo, I'm not going," he said softly.

"What?" The Indian stiffened and his back slammed into the door as if he'd been pushed.

"Father Segura believes I should stay here and continue my work in Across the Bay."

Now Rogel could see fear and anger in Lujo's eyes. "Then I stay, too," he declared. "I help you like before."

"Maybe you're forgetting," said Rogel. "Don Valezquez and his daughter? Don Valezquez will hunt you down if you stay here. But remember, too, that you are now a Christian. The past is forgiven. You are now called to 'put on the armor' of faith, hope and charity and go out among your people."

Lujo's knees seemed to buckle and he knelt before the priest. "Father, I want the Confession," he said.

"Right here?"

"Yes. But nothing I say gets out. Yes? "

Rogel nodded and Lujo began whispering in a low voice. "I no like some of these *religiones,* as you call them. Two days ago I was in the kitchen. The cook said for me to get him a sack of potatoes from the storeroom. I open the door and, and I see this Brother Gómez. He... he has his lips on the lips of the young altar boy. And his hand was...."

He didn't finish because Rogel cringed painfully and held up a hand as if begging to hear no more. And Lujo knew then that it wasn't the first time his father confessor had heard such things.

But Lujo bored in again. "This Father Segura is the superior—yes? But there is something about him, too. He makes me pray with him and he holds my hand. He is always putting his arm on me. I do not like it. In Florida the Jeaga, the Calusa deal with such people by"—and here he made a swift knife-like motion as if to slice off his male member.

Juan Rogel felt the hot sting of a truth that he hadn't allowed himself to think about. He'd heard whispers about *it* but had never witnessed it.

Yet Lujo will be going on the mission. Rather than feed his doubts, I must inspire in him a glorious vision.

"Lujo, this mission is about far more than what you have just spoken of," the priest said. "It is not about physical life with all its deformities, but about eternal, spiritual life. All of us—you and I—are sinners in one way or another. Maybe you have killed a man. I did so once on a battlefield, may God forgive me. But in our roles today we represent the link between ignorant people and Jesus with his message of love and eternal life. We must look beyond our own weaknesses, as did the apostle Paul. There are thousands of your people worshiping false idols and believing that these pieces of wood or stone are gods with the power to rule over their lives. These people need *you,* Lujo."

Lujo stood silent, stony.

Rogel fixed his eyes on the Indian's. "Lujo, tell me that you are a Christian."

Silence. Then, almost surly: "I am a Christian."

It wasn't enough. "Lujo," said the priest, "tell me again in this Confession that you are a Christian."

Lujo, with irritation: "I *am* a Christian."

"Lujo, look at me," said Rogel slowly. "The pupils of your eyes are gone....disappeared."

Both of the Indian's hands went to his eye sockets. "No! Aiyeeee."

As Lujo clutched his head in terror, Juan Rogel slumped to the ground beside him. On his knees, he exclaimed: "Christ Jesus, my master, forgive me! I have resorted to a despicable trick when I should have had faith in the power of your love." He covered his face in his hands and for the first time Lujo could see the wetness of tears trickling between his fingers. And now it was the young Indian who reached out and helped his father confessor to his feet.

After a long silence the priest spoke again. "Lujo," he said softly, "go with the missionaries to the Chesapeake. Do your best to preach the gospel of Christ's love and salvation to the people who live there. But if for some reason you cannot, go back to the place that you hold dearest in your heart. Remember all the lessons you learned before you came to Mound Key. I know you were a tracker and a maker of arrows and a builder of canoes. All of these skills will get you where you want to go if you ask God's blessing. Now as your Father confessor, I bless you wherever you may go and will say prayers for you every day."

In the first week of September, 1570 the ship of missionaries finally entered the Chesapeake Bay, land of the Ajacan Indians. It had been a stormy month-long journey marked by many probes into uncharted inlets that yielded no bay as majestic as Pedro Menéndez had described the Chesapeake. The trip had taken twice the time anticipated and the ships' occupants had already consumed all of their flour. Only two of four barrels of biscuits remained on board. The ship's captain was now concerned only with finding a calm riverside on which to disgorge his burdensome cargo and return with enough provisions to avoid starvation.

On September 10 the captain nosed his ship northwest up a broad river and then glided into a small tributary. There his crew unloaded the eight Jesuits, the altar boy Alonso, their Indian "guide" Lujo and what supplies the ship could do without. Father Segura beseeched the captain to remain moored until the Jesuits could secure a camp, meet some natives and find some local sources of sustenance. But the captain was adamant, fearing that waiting days would give any hostile Indians time to mobilize and destroy them all. No, he would remain for the night, but the next morning he would depart.

During the day Lujo did establish contact with a few curious Ajacans, but learned that the area was sparsely settled due to a drought and famine that had lasted nearly six years. The summer's scanty yield of corn had already been devoured and local tribes had already left the area, leaving only a few elders who were resigned to dying in the place of their fathers. Despite their own meager provisions, the Jesuits shared a generous meal that night with their new Indian friends. In turn, they got permission to settle near an Indian village about six miles further up the broad creek.

The next morning the ship's captain was given a precious letter that the Vice-Provincial had assigned Father Luis de Quirós to write. Quirós, the product of a noble family who just three years before had been rector of an elite college in Granada, now urgently pleaded to

Havana for supplies. And they must arrive within four months and include corn seeds that could be planted by early spring. He ended by pleading that survival of the ten Jesuits represented the last hope for revival of the Menéndez mission to win the soul of Florida.

As a further inducement, Quirós added a tidbit sure to gain the attention of Menéndez and his nephew Pedro Marquéz. He wrote that Indians had reported that "three or four days yonder" was a mountain range, and on the other side of it a "sea" that was doubtless the fabled, elusive Northwest Passage to China.

Father Segura and his pilgrims then canoed up the creek where they built a crude log group house and small chapel. Then they waited, praying fervidly when not scavenging every herb, fruit and root within a day's walk in all directions.

When no ship appeared by January, Lujo offered to seek out another Indian village where they might relocate in order to scrounge in another circumference of forest for subsistence.

On February 2, 1571, with no sign of either Lujo or the ship, Father Segura concluded that the wretched little band would surely waste away anonymously in this frozen land if their Indian guide could not be found. Moreover, not quite two weeks before, the two dozen Indians who lived in the nearby village had suddenly packed up their teepees and silently stolen away. So Segura decided to send out the group's three most senior members—Father Quirós, Brother Gabriel de Solís and Brother Juan Bautista Mendez—on a six mile journey to the village where Lujo had supposedly headed.

When the three were finally directed to the chief's hut after several hours of crunching through soft snow in torn, wet boots, they were escorted to a clearing along the creek a few hundred yards from the village. There they saw several fallen logs that were being strapped together to make a floor of a raft or barge of some kind. Over the platform an Indian was bent, and when he turned to them they were stunned. It was Lujo all right, but gone were his Spanish boots and woolen winter tunic. Instead he was dressed in Ajacan buckskin from his heavy beaded shirt to his breeches and moccasins.

He stood with arms wide open with a large grin. "How wonderful to see you!" he bellowed in the first Spanish he had used for a month. He explained that he was constructing a vessel that would haul cargo down the creek once the Spanish rescue ship arrived. He was just about to return to them and tell them of a new site they could occupy that was not far from some old cornfields that might still have some old cobs for boiling.

As Lujo escorted them back to the small cluster of teepees, a pretty young woman rushed up to him and grabbed onto his hand as if to defy anyone who might have thoughts of taking him away.

"They think I have appeared as if by magic," he said sheepishly. "They make me a kind of special cacique—like an elder. You see, the cacique is old and cannot see well. He thinks I am the son of his who was taken away when the Spanish first came here many years ago."

By late afternoon the three weary Jesuits were retracing their footsteps in the light snow, relieved that Lujo, their lifeline to survival, had promised to return to the missionary hut the next day with some other villagers bringing roots and herbs. The Indians would also help fell some trees and chop wood for the weakened missionaries.

"I guess the young woman accounts for some of the delay," said one, "but I suppose it's understandable."

They were walking in silence when suddenly they heard the snow crunch behind them and were surprised to see Lujo falling in step behind them. "I track you just like deer," he laughed.

Then he shouted, "Please turn around, everyone!"

The three startled friars wheeled about and were instantly hit with a hail of arrows.

Six Indians emerged from the forest and stood silently over the three inert bodies in the snow. When one of the brothers groaned loudly and tried to rise, two of the attackers flailed at his skull with stone clubs until the body moved no more. And with hardly a letup, the Indians began rifling through the pockets of the dead men and removing their clothing.

Two days had now passed inside the missionaries' smoky, fetid hut as Segura, Brother Cevallos, three young catechists and the altar boy Alonso waited for their three emissaries and prayed for deliverance.

On the second afternoon the fire was getting low and Segura sent

Cevallos into the woods with a hatchet to chop up whatever deadwood he could find. Lujo and his war party of six were already scrutinizing the hut from behind a large toppled pine when the friar trudged by them, fingering a rosary absentmindedly as his dark brown hassock skimmed over the icy wet ground. As soon as Cevallos got beyond sight of the hut, he, too, died in a flurry of arrows. This time it was Lujo who bent over the body, removing the heavy hassock.

This left only Segura, the three catechists and altar boy. Although all were wasted and weak, Lujo knew there were a few hatchets and knives inside the hut that might be used against them, for the final step in his plan would require close contact.

Later that afternoon two Ajacans greeted Segura just outside the hut and said by grunts and sign language that Lujo would be along soon with a gift of food. Meanwhile, they had agreed to help Brother Cevallos cut more wood if only they could borrow a couple of hatchets.

Several minutes after the Indians disappeared into the woods, Brother Cevallos appeared before the entrance, followed by the same two who had borrowed the hatchets. All held bundles of firewood in their arms—piled so high that their faces were nearly covered.

"Brother Sancho!" Segura exclaimed as he swung open the rough-hewn front door. With that the man in the hassock thrust his load of wood into the Vice-Provincial's face with all his force. As the priest groggily slipped to the ground the logs spilled around him and he could see the face of his assailant before a hatchet blow to the neck sent him to the martyrdom to which he had so long aspired.

It was Lujo.

Now there remained only the three catechists and the altar boy. As the Indians burst into the hut, all four were on their knees with their trembling hands clasped in prayer.

In a few seconds the Ajacans dispatched them like butchers slaughtering lambs for market.

All but one. As the altar boy Alonso swayed, rubbery with shock and fear, one of the Indians grabbed him from behind and snatched his head upward by the hair to expose his neck. But as he did so he glanced toward Lujo for an instant before striking.

Lujo held up his hand. "No," he said. "Let him live. We will decide later."

The letter that Father Quirós had sent to Cuba in September had been passed around governmental offices like a hot branding iron until it finally landed in the lap of Father Juan Rogel. The man who had so fervently warned Segura of impending doom had now become his sole hope of survival. However, the four-month time frame Quirós had sought had already shriveled to three when the ship returned and no one wanted to captain another boat to the uncharted Chesapeake Bay and treacherous Ajacan Indians. But at last Rogel commandeered a small corn ship from Compeche on the flimsy promise that the whole trip could be completed "in a couple of weeks or so." With him went one Jesuit brother, Juan de Salcedo, and the crew of six.

According to the letter's directions to the settlement, the Jesuits on shore would light a bonfire upon seeing the approaching rescue ship as a signal that it was safe to anchor in the creek. But the rescuers saw no sign of smoke or fire from the ship. Instead, they saw three figures on the thin shoreline gesturing towards them. When the Spaniards pulled as close as the receding depth allowed, they could see that all three men were wearing the familiar brown Jesuit hassock. But when they shouted out "Come! Here are the fathers you seek" in a garbled guttural Spanish, Rogel knew it was an Indian trap.

The crew turned about and made straightaway for Havana with heavy hearts, for they knew that their brethren were either dead or suffering in captivity. Ironically, if Segura were alive and hoping for rescue, it would require ships and soldiers—not just the love of Christ.

Ever since he had returned to Spain in May 1568, Pedro Menéndez de Avilés had been expected back momentarily. Not a month passed that everyone from provisioners to priests to Indian chiefs looked to his arrival to settle a dispute, pay a bill or bestow a promotion. The adelantado yearned to return as well, but always something stood in the way: lawsuits, the treasure fleet, and, lately, the king's need for a swashbuckling seaman who could clear out an annoying covey of corsairs that menaced the waters around Flanders. But the longest delays centered on convincing the king to finance a second wave of settlers in Florida—and then getting the exasperating Casa de Contratación to pry loose the cash to outfit the ships. All this was slowed as rumors spread about the demise of the forts in Florida.

But as luck would have it for Father Rogel, just a few days after his return to Havana the adelantado sailed into the harbor with seven galleons. Aboard were 250 soldiers and 400 farmers and tradesmen. Moreover, the king had added 230,000 crowns to finance a serious expedition to discover the Northwest Passage to China via the Chesapeake Bay. The Florida settlements may have been in disarray, but Pedro Menéndez de Avilés had come to set things right by the power of his will and the king's purse!

First, the adelantado would make a quick trip to drop off some reinforcements at the emaciated fort at Santa Elena. Then he would continue on to the Chesapeake, either to rescue the captured Jesuits or exact revenge for their murders.

With Father Rogel aboard as a guide, two Spanish barcs and a tender eased into the same anchorage on the creek where the priest had seen Indians parading ashore in hassocks two months before. Upon landing, a company of soldiers marched swiftly upon the same two Ajacan villages Segura had known and captured eight Indians. Luckily, the Spanish altar boy Alonso was among them. The overjoyed lad told them that all of the other Ajacans in the area had gone to the mountains to find game and escape the August heat. But among the eight captives, he said, were some of those who had killed Father Juan Baptista Segura and his young catechists before his eyes.

Alas, the ringleader, the treacherous turncoat Indian named Lujo, was not among them.

Asked by Rogel about Lujo, the boy said that a month or so before the villagers had waved goodbye as he departed down the inland waterway in the box-like barge he had been building all winter.

No Spaniard would ever see him again.

Menéndez was not about to wage war in the mountains. He dragged the captured eight Ajacans aboard his barc and tried to question them with the limited language skills of an eleven-year-old altar boy. When no further information could be beaten out of the sullen captives with ropes of hemp, Alonso's own "testimony" was deemed sufficient to convict them. A Spanish chronicle reports: "They were first converted and baptized by Father Rogel. Then all were hung from the yard-arms of the ship."

However, Pedro Menéndez was not on the lead ship that reached Havana. The tenders—one carrying the adelantado and Father Rogel—had stopped in St. Augustine to assess the situation there and offer what supplies they could spare. Alas, the grand vision of a vibrant St. Augustine that had sustained Menéndez for so many years had been punctured by the reality of encountering a St. Augustine with scarcely more than a dozen struggling farm families and a ragged band of sentries in a fort that seemed to exist only as a refuge for sailors lost on trips of the treasure fleet. Surrounding it were Indians who seemed more friendly to the French than the Spanish.

The *dignitas* of the adelantado and governor of Cuba was further insulted on the way back to Havana in January when the two tenders were scattered by a winter gale from the northeast. One of the tenders broke up and washed shore south of Cape Canaveral. All the weapons and ammunition aboard were ruined with seawater. When the Ais Indians realized it, they quickly burned the ship and killed all survivors.

The ship carrying Rogel and Menéndez ran aground just north of Cape Canaveral, not far from the inlet where Jean Ribault and his men had met their grisly fate only seven years before. Thankfully, most of their arquebuses remained dry, for they were needed to stave off an Indian attack that arrived within a few hours. With some rescued provisions and the beached ship's wood, the thirty survivors threw up a makeshift fort. After a few days' rest they began a treacherous, sunburned trek up the coast toward St. Augustine, goaded on by their fifty-year-old leader's unmatched fortitude. Finally they reached St. Augustine—all thirty intact—just in time to help the tattered fort repel an attack by three English ships.

Meanwhile, word had spread back in Havana among the ships crisscrossing New Spain and the Indies that the adelantado had been lost. And in many respects he had been. Although a search ship eventually found him in St. Augustine, the troops aboard the seven galleons had been deployed to the treasure fleet or scattered among various outposts in Cuba and Mexico. When Menéndez finally returned to Cuba, he stayed two weeks and then boarded a ship returning to Spain.

There was no more he could do.

Florida would remain a fabled treasure trove of fertile fields, friendly natives and eternal springs for another adelantado and another king to conquer.

Epilogue

The events and dates involving the Spanish and Florida Indians in this book are as actually happened.

The Society of Jesus (Jesuits) formally abandoned Florida in 1572, perhaps partly due to the death of Father General Francisco de Borja, who had backed the Menéndez enterprise so willingly. Fathers Rogel, Sedeño and the other surviving Jesuits in Havana were transferred to Mexico, where they rendered long and productive service.

Juan Rogel went on to serve in The Philippines and lived well into his seventies. He left a wealth of writings about his experiences in Florida and Cuba, some of which were quoted or paraphrased here.

Capt. Francisco Reinoso, Hernando de Escalante Fontaneda and others who served under Pedro Menéndez de Avilés returned to Spain and joined a long line of petitioners and plaintiffs who had claims against the adelantado and/or King Philip II. Reinoso, for example, sued his former superior for not repaying a loan and for unpaid wages during the dangerous years he served on Mound Key.

Fontaneda, the freed Calusa captive and interpreter, drifted back to Spain and squandered his remaining years griping that he had nothing to show for his long ordeal in Florida. He was especially embittered when a supposedly undeserving friend—another liberated captive of Calus—landed a lifetime patronage job as keeper of the king's swans.

But Fontaneda, a minor player in the Menéndez enterprise, also dictated a twelve-page memoir back in Spain describing Calusa customs and pinpointing all of the towns under their dominion. And so, his name is well-known among scholars today for supplying the bedrock of their research.

Various members of the "Asturian brotherhood" of Menéndez continued to render valuable service to the Philip II as ship captains and colonial officials. They truly changed the balance of economic power between the south and north of Spain.

Alas, the adelantado himself was not so fortunate. After his return to Spain in 1573 he scarcely had time to scheme about another expedition to Florida. The king was absorbed with combating the menace of English corsairs off the coast of Flanders and quickly made Menéndez captain-general in charge of outfitting an armada of more than 150 ships and 20,000 men. While he dutifully resumed the dreary task of mustering provisions and jousting with government paymasters, he again demonstrated his fertile imagination by obtaining a patent on a new instrument for measuring longitude.

But as the months of mounting invoices, receipts and muster lists wore him down, Menéndez' mind turned again to visions of Florida. On Sept. 8, 1574, in a letter to his faithful nephew, Pedro Marquéz, he wrote of his "discontent at finding myself separated from Florida." He reported that the king had promised to let him return "as often as possible" once the Flanders campaign was over. Then, Menéndez added, "I shall be free to go at once to Florida and not to leave it the rest of my life; for that is the sum of my longings and happiness. May our Lord permit it, if possible."

But he would not sail again. Nine days after writing the letter, this paragon of self-confidence who had led withering marches, melted mutineers, stared-down Indian chiefs and surmounted shipwrecks, suffered an attack of "indigestion" at dinner and died the same night. The vision of a viceroy's wealth ended in a snarl of pending lawsuits and creditor claims that left his estate with few liquid assets—and perhaps altogether empty once the lawyers and the Casa de Contratación finished picking at the corpus.

Today the remains of Pedro Menéndez repose in a niche beside the altar of the Church of St. Nicholas in his native Avilés. The inscription reads:

Here lies interred the very illustrious cavalier Pedro Menéndez de Avilés, native of this town, Adelantado of the Provinces of Florida, Commander of the Holy Cross of La Çarça of the Order of Santiago, and Captain General of the Ocean Sea and of the Catholic Armada which the Lord Philip II assembled against England in the year 1574, at Santander, where he died on the 17ᵗʰ of September of the said year, being fifty-five years of age.

The Calusa chiefs—in all their haughty grandeur and base cruelty—are well-documented by the Jesuit Father Rogel and other eyewitnesses. But this represents only the Spanish perspective. In an attempt to sketch the customs and persona of sixteenth century Native Americans across the Florida peninsula—from the Calusa to the Mayaimi, Jeaga, Ais and Tequesta—I created Lujo (a.k.a. Little Heron) and the people in his life.

But please know that Lujo himself is not entirely synthetic. He is based on the true story of the son of an Ajacan chief on the Chesapeake Bay (which the Spaniards called the Bay of Santa Maria). Shortly before Menéndez arrived to explore Florida, a Spanish ship had been blown into the Bay by storms. While putting in for water and a brief rest, the crew had kidnapped the chief's ten-year-old son. He wound up in Mexico, was educated and "Christianized" in a Dominican monastery, then sent off to Madrid. There he lived in the palace of King Phillip II and was paraded about in silk finery as an example of how savages could be civilized. He was also shared by several ladies of the court, who found him an exotic and erotic dalliance.

Now in his early twenties and known affectionately as Don Luis, he was sent back to Havana and groomed to serve as guide to the very real Jesuit expedition to the Chesapeake Bay led by Father Segura. But when this Christian convert arrived back in his native land, he quickly abandoned the ill-prepared Jesuits and then assassinated them ruthlessly, just as described in this book.

Because his people welcomed him back as a miracle who materialized from the dead, I presume the authentic Don Luis remained there living happily ever after.

As for the fictitious Lujo, I prefer to think that he and his box-like canoe-barge eventually found their way back to the hauntingly beautiful Fisheating Creek and into the loving arms of White Sparrow.

Since Florida now has some twenty million residents, the story just told is obviously merely the first chapter in a history now exceeding 500 years.

After an interregnum of some forty years, the Spanish came again. This time the lesson learned was that one can't create settlements along sandy coastal scrubland and then depend wholly on supply ships that can be sunk by storms or enemies. As for defense, the lesson was that military outposts either can be overrun by swarms of natives or the natives can decide to abandon their own villages and leave the settlers with neither farm labor nor Christian converts.

Instead, a new system began to evolve at the turn of the seventeenth century. As in California, the Spaniards began creating a linkage of mission-based towns inland and no more than a day's journey from each other. Farmers and tradesmen from Spain would form the core of each town. Only then would they reach out to neighboring Indians—first as farm laborers and then as Christian converts.

Most Floridians today are amazed when told that more than 150 of these mission towns were created in their state over the next century and a half. They formed a rough "T" shape that stretched west-to-east from Apalachicola to St. Augustine on top and then in a line that ran south down the middle. The system worked reasonably well until colonial America to the north developed an aneurysm that burst into Spanish Florida. As hordes of immigrant farm families elbowed their way into England's southern colonies, Native Americans were forced off ancestral lands and came pouring into Spanish Florida. With them came as many diseases as the Spanish had brought in the previous century. By the early 1700s only ten percent remained of the native Florida population that had existed at the time of Columbus. Disease rampaged south from mission to mission until there weren't enough Indians to till the soil or friars to say Mass. In short, the ants had outrun their nests.

And to all this the English shrugged. If Spanish Florida collapsed, so much the better.

Because Fontaneda said so himself, many have compared the "Calusa Empire" to that of the Aztecs in Mexico. But to paint kings Calus and Escampaba (the Spanish called them Carlos and Don Felipe) on the same canvas as Montezuma requires an intoxicating dram of romantic whimsy. Suffice it to say that adjectives like handsome, strong, proud, arrogant, fearsome and fearless would best explain their durability.

That the Calusa could stave off the "northern invasion" longer than the Spanish missions and retain their identity longer than any Florida tribe was more due to their location at the southernmost end of the peninsula, well beyond the "mission mainline" and with no deep water port to disgorge invading troops. But it also stemmed from their stubborn dependence on hunter-gathering and their aversion to the "woman's work" of farming. In the mid-1700s when some Franciscans brought a crate of hoes to the Calusa in hopes of showing them how to farm, the chief scratched his head and asked, "But where are the blacks to use them?" It hadn't entered his head that his own people should perform such menial work.

And so, whereas other Florida tribes tended to regroup, adapt and merge in the wake of epidemics, the Calusa remained aloof, haughty and suspicious of strangers.

But this, too, broke down in time because the Calusa were eventually battered at both their front door and the back. The "front door" was the Gulf of Mexico where Cuban fishermen began netting great quantities of fish. When the Calusa complained, the Cubans worked them a deal: their fishing boats would deliver fresh catches to various Calusa towns. The Indians would dry the fish and stack them in barrels. On their next trip the Cubans would pick up the barrels and deliver more fresh fish for drying. Increasingly, they paid the Calusa with rum, which proved convenient because the Indians had begun demanding it.

The breakdown at the back door began with the onslaught of slavery in the American south. As the eighteenth century approached, English colonists began to arm border tribes such as the Yamasee and Uchise and send them into Florida on a rampage of kidnapping and killing. Whatever the cost, the yield in new Indian Calusa slaves was far more profitable than rounding up blacks in Africa and bringing them across the sea in chains.

When the Spanish mission towns had been decimated or destroyed, the marauding Indian slavers kept heading south and into Calusa land. Spanish officials shipped their "loyal" Indians crates of firearms and tried training the Calusa in self-defense, but most of them quickly traded their guns for rum. At this point, a Franciscan friar from Havana wrote:

> *"When the men become drunk they take on an extraordinary brutality. There is no longer a son for a father, nor a wife for the husband, and flight into the woods is the family's only security. If they continue in their barbarous style, they will have disappeared within a few years either because of the rum they drink until they burst, because of the children whom they kill, because those of whom the smallpox carries off or because of those who perish at the hands of the Uchises."*

In 1711 the slave raiders from the north had exacted such a devastating toll that Spanish officials in Havana sent a small flotilla to southwest Florida to transport all surviving Calusa to Cuba for permanent relocation (and a short life of grueling work in the sugar fields). Some 270 men, women, children shuffled aboard, representing all the Calusa that could be located in the stretch from Pine Island to the lower Keys.

But not all of them actually departed. A few surveyed the filthy, crowded conditions aboard ship and decided to flee into the Everglades south of Marco Island. It was a wise choice, for within a few months of the ships' departure, nearly two hundred of the Calusa in Cuba succumbed to smallpox and other European epidemics.

Did any Calusa survive? Perhaps one day the Bureau of Indian Affairs in Washington will receive a claim from a group of Everglades Indians alleging to be direct descendants of the Calusa. If verified by DNA tests, the Calusa could rightfully claim to be in existence for at least five times longer than the United States has been a nation.

Glossary of Names and Terms

Adelantado. A Spanish official appointed to represent the king in exploring-settling frontier areas in return for grants of authority, land, and favored tax treatment on goods produced.

Adelantamiento. The contract with the crown spelling out the adelantado's rights and responsibilities (see above).

Ais. Indian tribe generally situated along the barrier islands from Cape Canaveral to St. Lucie Inlet.

Ajacans. Indian tribes situated around today's Chesapeake Bay, known then to the Spanish as the Bay of Santa Maria.

Alcaide. The military governor of a Spanish fort or garrison.

Armada. A general Spanish term for any organized fleet or flotilla.

Arquebus. The primary firearm of the Spanish soldier. A long-barreled, smooth bored matchlock gun, loaded from the muzzle end.

Asiento. Any contract or agreement notarized by a government official.

Atarazanas. Generally, a marine warehouse. In Seville it often referred to the whole dockyard complex.

Atlatl. A wooden shaft, usually two or three feet in length, used by Indians in hunting and battle. When attached to a spear or dart, the atlatl had the effect of extending the thrower's arm and adding both speed and power to the flight of the spear.

Audiencia. The highest regional appeals court in the Spanish colonial system.

Aviso. A term applied both to official correspondence and to the ship that conveyed it.

Barc, or **barco.** Often used to refer to any vessel, as "ship" in English. But also applied to small coastal runners and boats used in harbors to transfer people from moored ships.

Bay of Santa Maria. The sixteenth century Spanish term for today's Chesapeake Bay.

Bergantín. A small two-masted sailing vessel with lateen sails. Lateens, usually triangular in shape, could turn with the wind and enable a ship to tack.

Caballero. A Spanish nobleman, derived from a knight or horseman.

Calusahatchee. Actually a nineteenth century Seminole Indian name for the river that leads west from today's Lake Okeechobee to Charlotte Harbor. Since it contains an obvious reference to the Calusa, I have used the name in this book despite no evidence as to what the Calusa called it.

Capitana. The flagship of a Spanish fleet whose signals were obeyed by all others.

Cacique. A term imported from the West Indies meaning *chief,* be it of a village or tribe.

Casa de Contratación. A body in Seville, appointed by the king, that regulated ship licenses, cargo lading, fitness of passengers to travel, and navigation, Also empowered to levy fines for infractions.

Catechist. A person in training to learn the catechism—a handbook of Roman Catholic precepts.

Cédula. A decree by the Spanish king, having the force of law.

Charnel house. A place where funereal preparations and/or religious rites were conducted.

Cob. Spanish term for a roughly forged precious metal (usually silver) that emerged resembling a thick broom handle. The metal was then sliced off to produce coins.

Cochineal. A much-prized red dye produced from the dried bodies of an insect that feeds on cacti. One of the leading exports from colonial Mexico.

Corporal linen. Primarily a white linen altar cloth on which elements of the Eucharist are placed. Can also refer to any cloth used in liturgical rites.

Corsair. Any ship that preyed on commercial shippers, usually under the official sanction of a monarch. In such cases, the king would be entitled to a percentage of any captured loot.

Council of the Indies. The supreme governing body of the Spanish colonies in the Americas. Composed of from six to ten councilors, all appointed by the king. The Council issued decrees, approved major expenses and served as a final appeals court in colonial civil suits.

Degüello. A Spanish bugle call. Also slang for putting a defeated people to the sword by slitting their throats.

Ducat. A gold coin of .1107 troy ounces. The primary monetary unit of Spanish Castile, but used widely throughout Europe during the reigns of Charles V and Philip II in the sixteenth century.

Dueña. In the Spanish world, an older woman, perhaps a maiden aunt, who acted as chaperone and mentor to a young eligible woman during her courtship phase.

Ecomienda. The right given to the commander of a Spanish settlement in the New World to impose work obligations on native populations. Spaniards explained it as a fair exchange for "protecting" Indians and bringing them into Christianity.

Escampaba. The cousin of the Calusa King Calus. As a young man he was denied by the father of Calus from assuming his rightful place as heir to the Calusa throne. He accepted the role of the king's military commander for several years, then saw in the arrival of Menéndez on Mound Key a chance to overthrow Calus. The Spanish also called Escampaba *Don Felipe* in a flattering comparison to King Philip.

Fisheating Creek. Still known by the name today, this enchanting tannin-colored river empties into Lake Okeechobee between Lakeport and Moore Haven, FL. The lower part of Fisheating Creek can be accessed by boaters and campers. Upstream, on private property, is the site of the ancient charnel house and its sunken wooden carvings, known today as Fort Center for having been used as a temporary U.S. army camp during the Seminole Indian Wars. Some of the ancient carvings from the charnel house are displayed today in the Florida Museum of Natural History in Gainesville.

Fort San Antonio. Name given by the Spanish to the garrison they built on Mound Key in today's Estero Bay, Florida.

Fort Caroline. Fort built by the French in 1564 and a year later destroyed by Pedro Menéndez. The site is now Fort Caroline National Memorial, located on the St. Johns River a few miles from downtown Jacksonville.

Fort San Felipe. Located on Parris Island, South Carolina. Built in 1566 on the ruins of an abandoned French fort, San Felipe guarded Santa Elena, which was the northernmost settlement of Pedro Menéndez along the coast of what was then called Florida.

Galeass. An enlarged, taller version of the three-masted merchant galley. Equipped with thirty two oars, each worked by five men. A gun deck was usually located over the rowers.

Galleon. A three or four-masted ship of 500 to 1,000 tons and carrying 50 or more guns when outfitted for war. However, many galleons also transported goods as a mainstay of the Spanish treasure fleet.

Guale. A term embracing the coastal region from lower South Carolina to Georgia and its Sea Islands. Also applies to the culturally-similar Indians who inhabited the area. Note: the sixteenth century Spanish deemed this and everything up to Newfoundland as "Florida."

Hidalgo. One certified to be of noble blood.

Lake Mayaimi. The Calusa name for today's Lake Okeechobee because it was home to the Mayaimi tribe. The name should not be confused with that of the modern Miami, Florida.

Long Lake. The author's invented name for how the Native Americans might have described Lake Worth, the 22-mile-long estuary that runs nearly the length of today's Palm Beach County, Florida. Lake Worth was named for an army officer in the Seminole wars of the nineteenth century.

Maiden's hair. An invented term for what the Indians might have called the air plant that hangs like long gray grass from the branches of cypress, live oak and other trees. Today it's known as Spanish moss.

Maestre de campo. The Spanish commander of a military fortification, usually of twelve to fifteen companies.

Mayaca. An Indian tribe that dominated the lower St. Johns River south of Lake George to the center of Florida.

Mayaimi River. A natural drainage channel flowing southeast from Lake Okeechobee to what is now Miami, FL. The Tequesta tribe, reluctant vassals of the Calusa, were headquartered where the river flowed into Biscayne Bay.

Matacumbe. Indian name for an island in the middle Florida Keys inhabited by a tribe of the same name.

Patache. A light, speedy two-masted ship used mainly for exploring coasts and inspecting ports. Sometimes used as a tender.

Peso. A term subject to much confusion because several types of currency went by the name *peso*. Most common was the Mexican silver peso

Poder. Spanish term akin to the power of attorney, but somewhat broader. A merchant on one side of the Atlantic would give *poder* to a personal representative on the other side to negotiate loans and trading on his behalf.

Real. A smaller Spanish coin introduced in the thirteenth century. In the sixteenth century eight reales made up one silver peso, prompting the term "piece of eight."

River of Turtles. An invented name for today's Loxahatchee River, which flows towards the Atlantic between today's Jupiter and Tequesta, Florida. Actually, Loxahatchee is a Seminole Indian name meaning "river of turtles."

St. Lucie Inlet, also known then as the inlet of the Santaluces, a little-known tribe that may have been vassals of the Ais or Jeaga. It flows through Stuart, Florida.

Santa Elena. The northernmost outpost settled by Pedro Menéndez. Located on Parris Island, South Carolina in the region of Guale.

San Felipe. The Spanish fort erected to protect the settlement at Santa Elena (see above).

San Mateo. The name the Spanish gave to the fort they built on the site of the destroyed French Fort Caroline in 1565. It became the garrison that protected St. Augustine.

San Pelayo. The name of the 900-ton galeass personally owned by Pedro Menéndez. Used as the main supply ship on his first crossing to Florida in 1565. Later captured on its way to Havana and eventually sunk off the coast of Flanders.

Santa Maria. The sixteenth century Spanish name used most often for today's Chesapeake Bay.

Shallop. A small, open boat propelled by oars and/or sails. Used mainly for exploring in shallow waters.

Tocobaga. The name of the chief and tribe inhabiting today's Tampa Bay and surrounding area. Chief rivals of the Calusa.

Urca. A large ship with a flat bottom, capable of carrying cargo over shallow bars.

Zabra. A small vessel, similar to a bergantín.

Maps

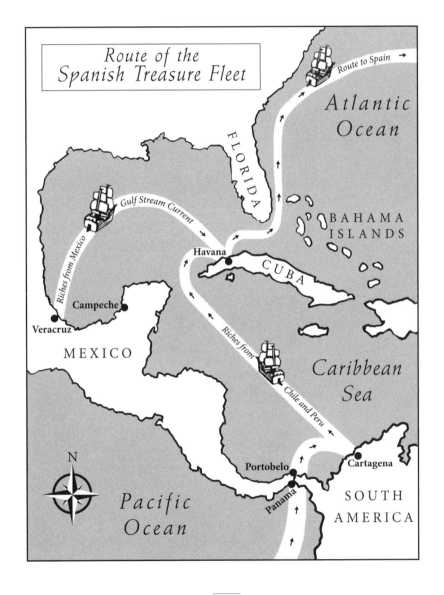

Route of the
Spanish Treasure Fleet

Route to Spain →

Atlantic
Ocean

FLORIDA

Gulf Stream Current

BAHAMA
ISLANDS

Riches from Mexico

Havana

CUBA

Campeche

Veracruz

MEXICO

Riches from

Caribbean
Sea

Chile and Peru

N

Portobelo

Cartagena

Pacific
Ocean

Panama

SOUTH
AMERICA

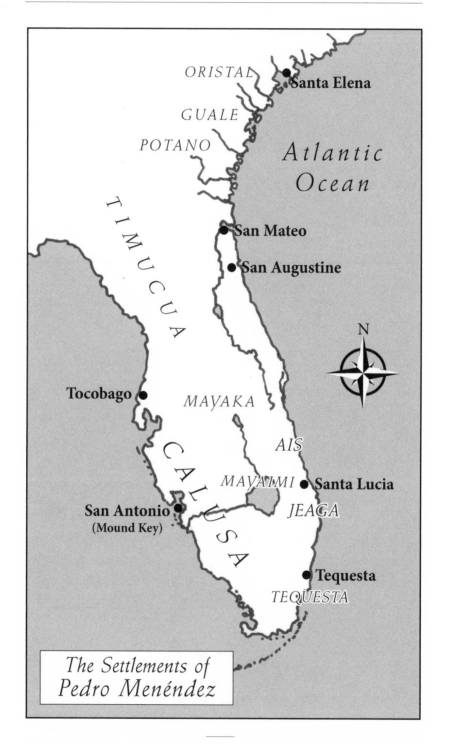

ORISTAL

Santa Elena

GUALE

POTANO

*Atlantic
Ocean*

TIMUCUA

San Mateo

San Augustine

N

Tocobago

MAYAKA

AIS

MAYAIMI Santa Lucia

CALUSA

JEAGA

San Antonio
(Mound Key)

Tequesta

TEQUESTA

*The Settlements of
Pedro Menéndez*

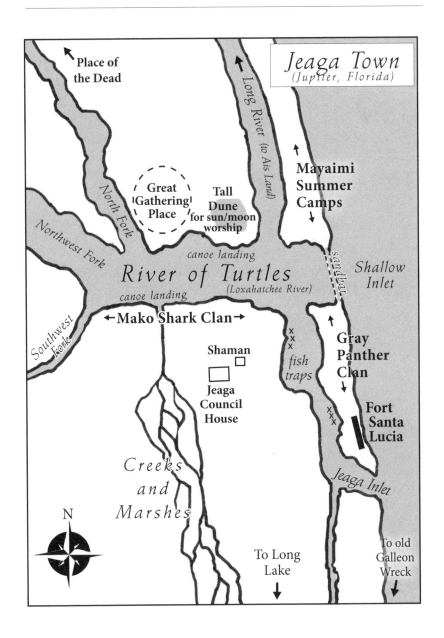

Jeaga Town
(Jupiter, Florida)

Place of
the Dead

Long River (to Ais Land)

Mayaimi
Summer
Camps

Great
Gathering
Place

Tall
Dune
for sun/moon
worship

North Fork

Northwest Fork

canoe landing

River of Turtles
(Loxahatchee River)

sandbar

Shallow
Inlet

canoe landing

←Mako Shark Clan→

Southwest Fork

Shaman

☐

Jeaga
Council
House

fish
traps

Gray
Panther
Clan

Fort
Santa
Lucia

Jeaga Inlet

Creeks
and
Marshes

N

To Long
Lake

To old
Galleon
Wreck

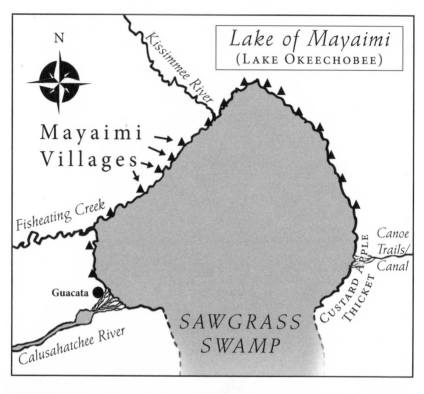

N

Lake of Mayaimi
(Lake Okeechobee)

Kissimmee River

Mayaimi
Villages

Fisheating Creek

Canoe
Trails/
Canal

Guacata

Calusahatchee River

SAWGRASS
SWAMP

CUSTARD APPLE THICKET

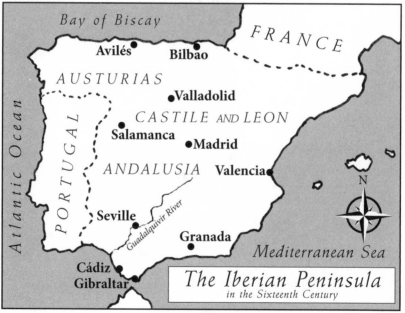

Bay of Biscay

FRANCE

Avilés

Bilbao

AUSTURIAS

Atlantic Ocean

Valladolid

PORTUGAL

CASTILE AND LEON

Salamanca

Madrid

ANDALUSIA

Valencia

Seville

Guadalquivir River

N

Granada

Cádiz

Gibraltar

Mediterranean Sea

The Iberian Peninsula
in the Sixteenth Century

Resources for Readers

For those interested in digging deeper into the story of the Spanish and Native Americans in sixteenth century Florida, the author suggests these resources:

Brown, Robin C. *Florida's First People,* a painstaking compilation of how things were made and used by Florida's Native Americans – all experienced by the author in the discipline known as replication archeology. Sarasota: Pineapple Press, 1994.

Carr, Robert S. *Digging Miami,* an archeological history of the greater Miami area, including the Tequesta tribe. Gainesville, FL: University Press of Florida, 2012.

Hann, John H. *Missions to the Calusa,* probably the most complete compilation of original Spanish observations of Florida in the sixteenth through eighteenth centuries. Gainesville: University of Florida Press, 1991.

Lowery, Woodbury. *The Spanish Settlements, 1562-1574.* Excellent narrative relying on Spanish archival material. New York: G. P. Putnam's Sons, 1905.

Lyon, Eugene. *The Enterprise of Florida: Pedro Menéndez and the Spanish Conquest of 1565-1568.* A helpful, readable chronicle of the years covered by this book. Gainesville: University Press of Florida, 1976.

MacMahon, Darcie A., and William H. Marquardt. *The Calusa and Their Legacy: South Florida People and Their Environments.* Descriptions of the natural setting and daily lives of Calusa peoples. Gainesville, FL: University Press of Florida, 2004.

Milanich, Jerald T., *Florida Indians and the Invasion from Europe.* An overview of the impact of the Spanish incursion throughout Florida. Gainesville, University Press of Florida, 1995.

Morris, Theodore, *Florida's Lost Tribes,* a collection of exquisite interpretative paintings of Florida Indians, which inspired many of the descriptions in this book. Gainesville, FL: University Press of Florida, 2004.

Sears, William H. *Fort Center: An Archeological Site in the Lake Okeechobee Basin.* A scholarly report, but containing the best available descriptions of the ancient sites along Fisheating Creek. Gainesville: University Press of Florida, 1994.

Places to visit:

Collier County Museums. One, featuring several Calusa artifacts, is at 3331 Tamiami Trail East, Naples, FL 34112, 239-252-8476, www.collier-museums.com. An affiliate, the Marco Island Historical Museum, contains many findings from a major nineteenth century excavation on the island. Address: 180 South Heathwood Drive, Marco Island, FL 34145, 239-642-1440.

Fisheating Creek Outpost. This private concessionaire is the gateway to the jungle-like waterway with its ancient trails and mounds. Address: 7555 U.S. 27 N., Palmdale, FL 33944, 863-675-5999., www.fisheatingccreekout-post.com.

Florida Museum of Natural History. A section on South Florida history examines everything from nature to Indian life, including valuable wood carvings from the ancient funereal platform on Fisheating Creek. Address: Powell Hall, 3215 Hull Road, P.O. Box 112710, University of Florida, Gainesville, FL 32611-2710, 352-846-2000, www.flmnh,ufl.edu.

Fort Caroline National Memorial. Site of the fort built by the French Jean Ribault, now part of the Timucuan Preserve. Address: 12713 Fort Caroline Road, Jacksonville, FL 32225, 904-641-7155, www.nps.gov/timu.

Jupiter Inlet Lighthouse and Museum, operated by the Loxahatchee River Historical Society. Museum and grounds cover many Jeaga/Calusa sites and artifacts, as does Palm Beach County's Dubois Park across the river. Address: 500 Captain Armour's Way, Jupiter, FL 33469, 561-747-8380, www.jupiterinletlighthouse.org.

Mound Key Archeological State Park. With its steep shell mounds, the one-time home to Calusa royals and the Spanish fort of San Antonio is accessible today only by boat and offers no amenities. Park staff address: 3800 Corkscrew Road, Estero, FL 33928, 239-992-0311, www.stateparks.com/mound_key_archeological.

Randell Research Center. On Pine Island, the epicenter of Calusa life through the centuries. An arm of the U. of Florida Museum of Natural History. Address: P.O. Box 608, Pineland, FL 33945-0608, 239-283-2080, www.flmnh.ufl.edu/RRC.

Southwest Florida Museum of History. Calusa Exhibits of the Fort Myers and Caloosahatchee River areas. Address: 2031 Jackson Street, Fort Myers, FL 33901, 239-321-7430, www.swflmuseumofhistory.com.

About the Author

Among Jim Snyder's books are five on Florida's rich, colorful history (see below). Raised in Evanston, IL and a graduate of Northwestern University, he spent many years in Washington, D.C. as a magazine editor and publisher before moving to South Florida in 1979. Today Snyder lives in Tequesta, FL on the Loxahatchee River and is active in several organizations devoted to preserving its history and environment.

OTHER BOOKS BY JAMES D. SNYDER

All God's Children: How the First Christians Challenged the Roman World and Shaped the Next 2000 Years. (2000, 680 pp., ISBN 09675200-02.)

A Light in the Wilderness: The Story of Jupiter Inlet Lighthouse & the Southeast Florida Frontier. (2006, 288 pp. ISBN 09675200-1-0.)

Black Gold and Silver Sands: a Pictorial History of Agriculture in Palm Beach County. (2004, 224 pp. ISBN 09675200-5-3.)

The Faith and the Power. A chronological history of the early Christians in the turbulent forty years after the crucifixion and how they confronted the Roman Empire in the darkest days of its debauchery. Winner of the Benjamin Franklin Silver Award for the best book on religion. (2002, 416 pp., ISBN 09675200-2-9.)

Five Thousand Years on the Loxahatchee, a Pictorial History of Jupiter-Tequesta, FL. Over 200 photos and maps. (2003, 217 pp., ISBN 09675200-4-5.)

Life and Death on the Loxahatchee. The story of Trapper Nelson, a real-life Tarzan who fascinated a generation in South Florida. Runner-up for the best book on Florida history, Florida Publishers Association, 2002. (2002, 160 pp. ISBN 09675200-6-1.